Published in 2019 by Amazon KDP Publishing.

ISBN - 978-1-9161038-0-1

Acknowledgements

I would very much like to thank my amazing mum, Karen – she was the first person to whom I read any of this story, and she is undoubtedly my biggest fan. I would also like to thank Camilla – My G. She has been my writer's mate – listening and advising, always with an incomparably radiant smile. Dan Giardina and George Marshall – my guinea pigs, the boys from which the book's preliminary feedback came. I have to, and want to, give a huge thank-you to Eluned Murphy and Naomi Munts – my talented clean-up team. These ladies edited, proofread and formatted this book to perfection – yes, perfection. Louis Durrant, thank you for the cover art; it is wonderfully stylish and simply faultless. Billy and Savvas, and my dad, Chris – your opinions and support mean a lot to me.

Cheers everyone!

For my grandad Doug

#1. Tokyo Burning

Goof Troop

Devil Child – that's what they used to call me.

That was, unfortunately, just my parents' label for my 'hell-raising' attitude towards infant life. Others addressed me by far worse, considering I was just a toddler in the front seat of a supermarket trolley – though I did used to growl at them as they neared. My name is Raynor, but everyone calls me Burt. I'm not sure how or why it started exactly, but that soon became my name.

I never knew my grandfather; he died years before my father's sperm were even stretching out for the big race, and therefore I never had a male role model or father figure in my life… I mean, I did have my father, but he was an absolute bastard of a man. So maybe that's why I turned out to be such a bad egg, or maybe it was due to my mother booming all 36 chambers of the Wu-Tang Clan as she attempted the housework, while I sat in my highchair inhaling R-rated hip-hop…

Life moved slowly through the most of my childhood years, subjected to my mother's resentment and rarely seeing my father for his everlasting work commitments – God only knows what unholy truths that phrase covered up. My dad was an elusive and shady fella. His suppressed ethics nudged him towards family life and providing a loving home for his wife and children, but his many demons shoved him towards the competitively priced girls lit up in red above Madd's Sandwich Bar off the Strawberry Way Roundabout. He had his problems, his addictions, but he kept them hidden from us, a choice I've never really understood for such an openly corrupt individual. We knew what he was and what he did, but my mother, brother and I seemed contented with his absence and privatised hobbies – for we never discovered the bad he could have inflicted had he been a more consistent part of our family. Bradford-on-Avon was where we lived. It's a twee little town, about half an hour outside of Bath in the West Country. It's a quiet place, mostly.

My brother, Jack, was three years older than me, and he was my Superman. We were close – whether it was down to our shared experience of a mucky upbringing or just the fact that we were so alike – but either way or both, we were dependent on each other. We weren't always troublemakers, there were times when we tried to be good and provoke an affectionate welcome from Mum and Dad, but we were persistently shot down. So, we tended to act up, sometimes a little too much. Anything we could conjure up to upset them was seen as a great triumph. Mum got the brunt, though she wasn't one to roll over and take it; she'd give as good as she got. This infinity ring of stubbornness perpetuated by both sides was what caused, or heavily contributed to, the maniacal aura shrouding our crazy cottage in one of England's most beautiful neighbourhoods.

Contrary to the classy decorations inside our home, my mother was a woman of simple pleasures. Enjoying a glass of anything strong enough to submerge the pain she felt about her family's disappointments, she would meander around the house killing time and all consciousness, slowly eroding her once-treasured happiness. Oh how she meandered. Never changing pace nor pattern but always glaring at my brother and I with a look of woe, and above all else: fear.

I first noticed my mother's fear when I was ten years old. Jack and I would play outside from the moment we woke to the moment we were called in for yesterday's tea. We would explore and adventure whenever and wherever our imagination took us, which was usually just past the second farmer's field adjacent to our neatly kept garden. We would make camp, hunt for treasure, toss rotten fruit at the farm animals, whatever we wanted really. As long as we had each other, we could accomplish almost anything. We never did, but it was comforting to know that we could.

One day, the two of us had just reached the third farmer's field after a particularly successful morning. We had managed to trap Mum in the cupboard under the stairs, because Harry Potter had just burst on the scene and she had taped over our VHS copy of *The Philosopher's Stone* with the Emmerdale Christmas omnibus. So, we went full-on Uncle Vernon.

In truth, Jack and I should've been at school, but with Christmas being less than two weeks away, we just decided not to go. It was as good an excuse to skip school as any, and besides, Mum was becoming unaware of the days and Dad wasn't even home. It could've been the weekend. It might even have been Christmas for all they knew or cared to know! But this was it, my Christmas day: a Friday with Jack with nothing to do but explore. We were rearranging the entrance to a camp we had taken the day before from the albino-looking kid and his little brother that lived two roads down, when Jack suggested we go one step further –

into the fourth farmer's field. After the morning's victory, he had a strong desire to go further than we had ever been. And who was I to say no? At first I was hesitant, uneasy about what awaited us in that field, but as we leapt the gate and scrambled through the surrounding hedges, I remembered the overwhelming sense of discovery I had felt when taking the third field. Without a second to gather my thoughts, my brother's hand emerged from the heavenly-lit break in the hedge and I was pulled through doubt, through clarity and through fresh cowpat, into the daunting fourth farmer's field.

Back at the house, my mother had shaken herself free. And she was fucking livid. With a belly full of hatred and Swiss-toasted muesli, she tied on her boots and headed out the back door to track us on our pointless quest. The little consideration we had for her well-being had blinded us to the animosity she must have been fuelled by, and we hadn't shed a thought on the consequences we would face when we arrived back home. But she had chosen to come looking for us. She couldn't wait for us to return home before she set about the corporal punishment. She wanted revenge sooner than that. Too bad Mum was about to witness the exact kind of evil she intended to administer.

After entering the fourth farmer's field, nothing seemed very different from the previous three – although it was deathly quiet and eerily lit from the covering trees. Jack led as I followed behind, unaware of which path or direction he was taking and focusing only on the grip I had on his baggy grey sweatshirt. We wandered for a while before we stopped to rest in this cavern-like pit thing, which was raised slightly above the rest of the field below and on the edge of the woods. Somewhat taken aback by the normality and, in all honesty, disappointment of the fourth field, we cracked open the provisions we had stolen from Dad's secret drawer back at the house. It was a light lunch of expensive whiskey, Manchego cheese cubes and some funny-tasting chocolate brownies. Afterwards, Jack lit up my first cigarette. He had been stealing cigarettes from Dad's drawer for almost a year, but I (being only ten after all) fell innocently to the wayside as he snogged his way through the old man's tobacco.

Today, however, I felt ready. I was bright-tailed and bushy-eyed, so I took the glowing stick from him and proceeded to suckle on it like some government-rated teat. It was rough – I couldn't take more than two puffs before I dashed the remains away into the bushes. Jack smoked all of his down, then we packed up and headed back across the deserted farmland for home. We left behind the whiskey and cigarettes. We assumed it was better that the entire bottle and the whole packet were declared missing, rather than just a few glasses and a couple of fags; that way it seemed less likely that we had taken them and more likely that either Mum had, or that Dad had forgotten he even had them.

Little more than five minutes had passed on our return leg across field four when we were unexpectedly ambushed by a tidal wave of conkers, launched by hand from the west. Open to all the elements of attack, Jack fell down, pulling me down to join him as he kissed the dirt. Grounded, we had no time to collect our scattered thoughts. We only had time to devise a half-witted plan to escape the sudden chaos. I suggested making a run for the fifth farmer's field, but I was soon halted by my anxieties, especially as field four had just turned sour enough for it to be our last. Jack reassured me of my safety when he sheltered me from the constant fire with himself. Then he murmured softly and heroically in my ear:

"Stay 'ere, Burt. Be low n' quiet yeah. I'm gonna run, out into the woods, they might folla me. Go 'ome when they stop lobbin' conkers. Go straight 'ome. Don't tell Mum, all right Burt?!"

With that he rose like the superhero he was in my eyes and was gone. His spindly adolescent legs hurdled the long grass and guided him towards the woods. It's pretty tough for a ten-year-old to comprehend his best friend's absence in the midst of such madness. I wasn't sure whether to do as he said or follow him, as I had done so all my life. So, I did what made the most sense to me at the time, which was neither. I quickly collected as many stray conkers as I could find on the floor around me, shoved them into my rucksack and headed stealthily back the way I came. Across the way I realised that it was far past conker season. Whoever was throwing these conkers had clearly saved them up, perhaps for this very moment.

As the conker fire slowly calmed, I knew that I had to move swiftly in order to keep up with my brother and the unidentified firing squad. My Wu-Tang rucksack was now overflowing with recycled conkers and the strain of carrying the weight forced me to stop. I slowed long enough to see I was back at the small pit in which we had paused for elevenses no more than ten minutes before the attack. I realised my sudden exhaustion and slumped to the floor, confused by my surroundings and what I came back to do. I had only the energy to tilt my head up to face the wasteland that was the empty field, to spy what seemed to be my mother's silhouette scaling the entrance gate and nearing the surrounding hedgerow. My cheeks tightened. And if breathing was a struggle before, I was now sure I had stopped completely.

Because of the incline of the ground and the vantage point my location had across the woods and the field, I was able to see everything – an advantage to my security but a huge blow to my confidence. I could now see six or seven figures gaining valuable ground on Jack, hurtling towards the edge of the woods. As well as that, I could now see, clearly, my mother nearing the field, still yet to tackle the nearby hedge but instead choosing to mooch around the outer ground, between the fourth farmer's field and the shooting ground behind.

My brain felt like it was lifting from my head – this was chaotic even for a little shit like me. I was feeling things I had not yet experienced and I wondered if I was in fact facing my imminent doom. Little did I know, the true nature of the substances taken from Dad's secret drawer had begun working their charms on my undeveloped structure. I felt hungry, thirsty, sleepy and sick; an array of senses and emotions hit like a wave of conkers within my fragile head. I scanned the cave for anything we had left behind before the ambush and saw the near-full bottle of Scotch and muddy box of cigarettes, and so I clambered over to them. Thirstily, seeing the whiskey only as a drink, I tilted the cold bottle-top up to my lips, ready to satisfy my unbearable thirst, when from the corner of my eye, I saw Mum edging closer to me via the dirt path leading through the hedgerow and around the woods. I may or may not have crapped my pants at this point (that bit is still hazy to me)... And like a sitcom flashback I immediately remembered a scene from one of the Spaghetti Western movies my dad loved so much. You know, the ones where the cool-handed gunner would douse the bar in booze and set it alight to make his escape. I remembered seeing the flame shoot the length of the bar, creating a blazing orange barrier around him. So as my heart pounded with fear and excitement I ran as far as I could along the hedges guarding me from my mother, spilling my father's pricey obsession carelessly in the hope that it would keep me safe.

The bottle was empty. I rushed back to the pit where I fumbled for the matches I knew were hidden away at the bottom of the cigarette box. I had them. I knew I had to do it now or my mother would surely do far worse to me. I had also hoped that the sudden blaze would distract the mob from my brother's trail long enough for him to peel away.

The match was lit. I felt the hot spark pinch my fingers. Scared, hopeful and unsure, I dropped the flame.

The whole world froze for a short second. I watched as the nearly burnt-out matchstick bruised the ground and the world suddenly sped back up: full speed, double time. The fire sprung up, lighting the hedge like a mighty domino chain. The trail shot further and further along the hedgerow, concealing me in a fiery cage and shutting my unloving mother out of the sanctuary. I was immobile for a minute, enough to reflect on the craziness of it all.

The fire moved quickly, quicker than I ever could have imagined it to. My anxieties hit me like a firebolt. The now-hazy shadows in the trees had changed course and were headed my way, though my mother was completely incapable of reaching me now – all she could do was watch in terror and gawk at my roguish tricks. As the posse of shadows drew closer I seemed to regain a clearer head, and I readied myself for action. With my mother's eyes piercing through the back of my head from across the burning hedge, I took one last deep breath in. I steadied myself for my onslaught on these bastards that had dampened mine and my brother's morning. My plan was unclear; up until this point I still had no idea who these fresh-faced foes actually were. But as they emerged from the wooded hideaway and into the smoky arena, I instantly recognised them as the home-schooled Tamura kids of the sizeable Japanese family at number forty-five.

Not such a long time ago, when the Tamura family had just moved in and become our little cul-de-sac's first foreign residents, my mother and father's racial slurs had hit an all-time high. Nothing pleasured their tactless minds more than an afternoon of peeping across the crescent and firing off dim-witted remarks from behind the window netting. Seeing how much this insensitive hobby pleased the two of them, Jack and I took it upon ourselves to break into the Tamura house and steal the seven bikes belonging to the seven Tamura children. What we'd hoped for was that by doing so, we could present them as some kind of warped peace-offering to Mum and Dad. We thought that a miraculous bond would then materialise between the four of us. It didn't. All it achieved was a neighbourly feud and six top-spec custom-made Japanese pushbikes for Dad to flog down at the second-hand bike shop. The seventh one he let us keep. One bike between the two of us. I think we would've preferred none.

The kids of the Tamura family had clearly followed us out for revenge. They must have noticed that we skipped school and then used their weird home-schooled agenda to their advantage. So far they had got their timing spot on. And they'd got what they were out to get – except their bikes, of course – but I wasn't about to let them continue with their feeble attack. Like my mother, I wasn't one to take a blow without jabbing back. As the fire spread further and further out of control along the hedgerow and into the parallel fields, the Tamura kids were drawn haplessly into my trap. I could've been nervous – I mean, I *was* nervous; but I could've been more nervous – if it wasn't for the trick I had been keeping up my sleeve, well, in the front zippy compartment of my Wu-Tang rucksack. In there, amongst the gel pens and Pokemon cards, was my dead grandad's trusty old fishing slingshot. I watched and waited. It wasn't long before the seven Tamura kids were finally within range – they were positioned from tallest to shortest in a formation line across the bottom of the slope. Luckily enough, my pit was at the top of the field. I pulled the slingshot from the front pocket of my bag, unfastened the conker-filled central compartment and opened fire. And if the height of the pit wasn't advantage enough for me, I had near-perfect aim with a slingshot. One by one I picked off the Tamura kids like flies to a swatter, and one by one they began to scatter, but between the burning exit and the merciless conker fire they had nowhere to run.

My attack was relentless, my aim perfect. I showered the Tamuras with constant shots through their cries of ache and distress, and all the while my mother looked on with greater and greater terror as I laughed off the horror I was causing. It took Jack too long to come and find me. Only he could have persuaded me to stop my heartless retaliation, but by the time he appeared through the trees, I had pretty much finished the blitz I had started. My conker bag was now empty, the Wu had been Tanged and the last of the Tamura kids had dashed into the distance. My pulse was rampant, I had a huge rush of adrenaline surging through my body and was nigh on shaking with excitement. My mother had now vanished and my brother stood staring at me in exhaustion and shock. He fell, tired, onto the dusty floor. He took a minute to catch his breath before he rose back up to his feet, half expecting me to strike him back down again. We stared, quietly, at one another.

"Burt...?" he said.

Then he latched onto my quaking arm and pulled me out of my trance, out of the pit and through the field. The fire had grown so very big, it had reached the other farm in the fifth field and we could hear the faint calls of the fire brigade's terrifying tune drawing closer and closer to us. We knew we had to get away, far away, and quickly.

#2. Road Trip

Wasteman

Hank scrambled frantically for the case. When he finally had a grip on its dusty handles, that's when she screamed. Leyla, Hank's lady wife, had just come in from the back garden to see a team of burly, shotgun-wielding blokes leant cockily against the bonnet of her father's 1956 forest-green Ford Thunderbird. Hank, now free from his grubby attic and with suitcase in hand, stepped tentatively to console his inconsolable missus.

Hank was in all sorts of bother. That gambling system, the one he'd so willingly bought into, had come back for a second time, as expected, to chomp at his button-making arsehole. Leyla, of course, knew nothing of this misdemeanour, until Trev, Trev 'n' Trevor had greeted her flustered and un-makeupped morning face as she drew her very expensive Moroccan curtains on that frightful Friday morning. Hank, all in a bother, briefly explained to Leyla the unflattering position he and she were now in. His poorly articulated explanation prompted a salty look and a well-executed slap from his already fiery wife, but as he continued his story it became clear to Leyla what she was now so unjustly involved in.

The two packed desperately as the doorbell screeched and the letterbox box twanged with a resounding... well, twang. The jittery sounds were doing nothing good for the progress of the not-so-happy couple's escape, but as the frenzy stopped momentarily Hank was able to peek through his classy, lead-lined double-glazed windows... The tactless trio were now manoeuvring their way around the property to test the compliancy of the back door. However, as Hank and Leyla's cosy terraced cottage was centrally positioned in the crescent of houses, they had to navigate past the other cottages and along the rear pathway at the back of the gardens. This being the case, Hank and Leyla had just enough time to bundle out of the front door and into the car.

Miraculously, Hank and Leyla made it off their driveway and out of the cul-de-sac without so much as a glance back from their harassers, but it was to be only a matter of time before the two of them were cruising down the Kenny Loggins highway* once more. Hank was headed for the coast – it wasn't too far from their West Country home and on a less traumatic day it was an incredibly satisfying drive. Hank's level-headed parents lived in a beach house in Jersey, so naturally Hank's escape route was to trample scattily cross-country in his father-in-law's rust-free vintage car, all the way to the nearest port. Hank's passenger, Leyla, sat in the shotgun seat at a perfect 180° angle so that she could snarl menacingly at her husband while glancing back to catch the inevitable return of the bad guys.

Hank was bobbing and weaving in and out of every little turn and country track he could drive down to escape the slight traffic on the skinny roads. There was a plume of smoke thundering across most of the surrounding fields. A convoy of fire trucks bullying their way through the lanes seemed to be the main offenders in creating the gridlock. Leyla's expression changed as they waded through the

---

* **Danger Zone** – *watch Top Gun for full effect.*

smog. Hank didn't notice, but something was on her mind... well, something besides the men with the shotguns and the sudden evacuation... and the car chase.

Hank came clean to Leyla when they stopped to refuel somewhere near Castle Cary, as he hurriedly and regrettably poured the cheapest and nastiest petrol into his most treasured heirloom and winced. In the wake of the news and the view of the other forecourt attendees, Leyla went spare. The two of them went at it hammer and tong. Hank had no defence, so he uncharacteristically accepted the brash onslaught. As Leyla paused for breath, though, he pinned her against the bonnet of the Thunderbird like a desperate Heel at a post-WrestleMania Monday Night Raw. A crowd was now well formed around them, and the clock was tick-tocking hauntingly quickly. Whilst pinning his wife to the shiny front of their shiny car, Hank funnelled some bittersweet sense into Leyla. She reluctantly returned to her seat so that Hank could wade through the concerned onlookers to pay the vendor. Hank wiped his sweaty brow, sighed and then stretched his arms behind his back. He was trying to keep calm, but as he reached the serving hatch and dipped into his back pocket, his heart sank to his stomach, and his stomach dropped to the floor.

Leyla had driven off. Hank had, fucking stupidly, left the keys in the ignition, and his deviously brilliant wife took full advantage of the situation. She even slipped him the finger as she sped off past him. Hank was waist deep in Shit Creek and Leyla had stolen his paddle. With saddened and disbelieving eyes, Hank tracked his one true love as she rolled away from the garage and back onto the A303... being driven by his wife. Turning back to face the unimpressed shop assistant, he gazed woefully into the glass barrier.

"My wife just stole the car," Hank said in a beaten monotone.

"And to think, she stole it with a full tank of petrol…" replied the man sarcastically.

Hank stared back with gritted teeth at the self-satisfied shop assistant. He was in more than enough trouble as things stood, so he calmly pulled his wallet from his pocket and settled the bill.

As Hank took his change from the drawer beneath the countertop, the phone in his pocket began to ring. The unbearably irritating petrol pusher pointed pathetically at the 'No Phones' sign and raised an eyebrow. In retaliation Hank answered the call where he stood and looked proudly at the guy as he 'helloed', but when Leyla replied, he turned to walk away. A lot of foul language ensued, all muttered fairly softly for the sake of not making another scene, but the volume did not mask the profanities. Hank's impressive rant stopped when Leyla cackled arrogantly down the line; he was all out of words, but she was just beginning…

Leyla had put two and two together and found a simple way out of their sticky situation. Hank was a fraud, a bad man and an even worse judge of character. The two of them were playground sweethearts with a couple of wedding rings and a nice little country house. Hank had just assumed their love and trust was eternal and unconditional – at least that's what the marriage certificate read – but this time he had really pissed her off. He had been caught once before by the same three men when he had turned their arbitrage betting system into his own little game on the side. Hank had been employed by the three men as a pawn to place bets between different bookmakers, manipulating the margins by spread betting between fixed outcomes on sports games. Hank, however, had broken away to hire people of his own to copycat their syndicate and discreetly muscle in on their cash. He had gotten good at playing the system and his stats proved it.

The first time Hank slipped up, the bookies sniffed him out, but they were not the ones who came down hardest on him – that was the doing of Trev, Trev 'n' Trevor. It wasn't Hank who cocked it up, it was his man on the ground who lost his nerve and gave the game away. Hank managed to escape with a beating only, though a pretty nasty one at that. He was kicked off the team for treason and blacklisted from a string of bookmakers indefinitely. Hank told Leyla that he'd got in a scrap down the pub and she, half not listening and half not caring, chose to believe the lie. This time, though, he'd used her money and her account. So to the bad guys, she looked as guilty as he did.

All Hank had needed was some quick cash to quash some debts with another bad man he was rubbing nuts with. That was all he needed. Except for what he really needed: another plan. He bumped into a lazy lady at the Frog and Fan pub in Bath, an old flame of his from the lesser years, and it turned out she needed a quick fix as much as Hank did. She also needed some quick company, but that's a dirty story for a dirtier time. They partnered up to take down the bookies together, but she crashed and burned on her maiden flight. Maybe it was the burden of guilt – the pressure of imitating Hank's wife and squandering her money – or maybe she was just really shit at quick maths. Whatever it was, she flopped and got found out. There was once again a huge, steaming pile of dog shite laid fresh for Hank to step into, barefooted and on a hot day. The kind of shite that stinks for days and scars not only your sole, but your very soul.

Leyla, now knowing how much trouble Hank had put them in, assumed the three dodgy blokes from the morning's ransack would eventually catch up to them and level the conniving little bastard. Her own fate was the one that she was unsure of. Her assumptions were just assumptions of course, and she wasn't about to make an ass of herself, so Leyla called her and Hank's home number on the off chance those dirty dudes would still be there, and they bloody well were. They didn't answer – they were far too busy gutting the place to take phone calls, especially ones that weren't even theirs – but they could listen to answerphone messages. Leyla revealed all and sold her husband down the river via the talky end of her Nokia 3310, and left him for dead at the small-town garage. She bartered well with the bad guys, giving away Hank's location to save herself from eternal desolation.

It was the final push, the straw that broke the camel's back. Leyla had been looking for a way out of her tired life for a while, her escape inaudibly brooding in her squalid mind. This was it, all she needed for change. The past was already forming faded black shapes as she drove off into the sunset in Daddy's snazzy car. Family was behind her; she had given it a go and it had stung her. Conventionality was no longer an option, neither was tolerance; Leyla was gone – solid gone. She could sell the car for a pretty penny if she needed to – it wouldn't net her a lot, but probably just enough to head to the Med and pick a nice spot to rent for a while. Just until she got her feet back on the ground. She was Huck without Tom. She was Thelma without

Louise. She was Shirley Valentine, happy at last.

So as Hank sat in disarray at the roadside, naively wishing and waiting for the return of his wife and the Ford Thunderbird, it seemed all too fitting that his three best buds pulled into the garage behind him in the most clichéd blacked-out Beemer imaginable. Hank, the vagabond, peeked solemnly over his shoulder. As the window rolled down slowly, there sat Mr. Mann, beckoning him like Death himself.

#3. The Siege of Raymundo J. Oldman's Second-Hand Bike Exchange Part One: The Escape Artist

Sing first. Read later

On a small winding street in the centre of Frome,
Old Mr. Oldman had a work-away home.
A 'Second-Hand Bike Shop' read the sign on the face,
A two-tyred haven of mechanical grace.

The shop was a solid and firm institution
That somehow survived the corporate intrusion.
It stood proud and stood true in the middle of town,
And for the locals it seemed Ray was always around.

A dependable fella, an affable chap,
A grey bearded man with a cheese-cutter cap.
A sole-trader invader, and Frome was his prize;
Arise Sir Raymundo, arise Sir, arise!

But Ray came from London as a much younger man;
He drove down from the city in a beaten-up van.
He came with a vision and a personal dream,
A lost city banker with a soul to redeem.

As a kid Mr. Oldman was a buccaneer biker;
As a teen, a racer, all smothered in Lycra.
As a young adult rider, he slowed in competing,
For his love for the tyres was slowly depleting...

He took a job in an office in the heart of the city,
The people were rude and the prospects were shitty.
Ray swapped in his smile, his time and his joy.
The man had arrived. Gone was the boy.

Ray's bike gathered dust, stowed away in his garage,
Torn apart from its partner; a failure in marriage.
Raymundo J. Oldman: a conformist and fraud,
And for twelve human years he sat dormant and bored.

By his thirties Raymundo was ashamedly dull,
Like a vegan-themed restaurant or a weekend in Hull...
A lost little worker in an ill-fitting suit,
With a rod for his back and a life down the chute.

Ray's boss was a boss in each sense of the word:
Hardnosed and angry, mean and absurd!
But on the 12th of December 1977,
Ray confronted his boss: Mr. Kevin McNeven.

Ray stepped in the boardroom at half-past eleven
And with little discretion began his confession:
"Mr McNeven," he said with aggression,
"You've been the cause of my steady depression!"

A sudden release of his twelve years of sulking
Was like Gamma to Banner and Brucey was hulking!
Inside he was quaking, but his face wasn't showing...
Then the steam in Ray's ears started blowing and blowing!

In a moment of frenzy, a frenzying moment,
Crazy Raymundo stared down his opponent.
The board members fled as things got unstable,
Then maniacal Ray flipped the boardroom's big table!

The wait was now over, and the weight was now lifted,
And the mood Ray was in had just suddenly shifted.
Down with the humdrum, his suit days were over...
Long live the days of Raymundo the rover!

Young Mr. Oldman was as happy as Larry
As he skipped his way home with no care left to carry.
He left without notice, no TTFN,
Excited and ready to be happy again.

Ray headed for home on an unbroken track,
Two steps at a time and not looking back!
So when he got home, he went out to his garage,
Forgetting the world that for now will disparage.

Ray stood at the door in a new state of zen,
He took a deep breath and he counted to ten,
He hoisted the rope that peeled back the shutter,
Then Raymundo was faced with a mountain of clutter!

But Ray stood there smiling, his eyes turned to jelly,
A tear glossed his cheek and a knot pinched his belly.
After twelve lonely years on a purposeless strike,
Ray saw through the rubbish his precious old bike.

The rest, as they say, was a small piece of history,
Ray's sudden departure was a North London mystery.
Fast-forward a couple of decades or more,
And you'll find yourself stood in Ray's second-hand store.

It was small, it was modest, it was humble and lovely,
Raymundo had claimed it his greatest discovery.
It was thatched, it was slanted, looking somewhat enchanted,
"Granted…" Ray chanted, "It's a visual advantage."

The street that it lived on was crooked and cobbled,
An old part of town that had not been remodelled.
The shops on the street stuck in and stuck out,
And Raymundo's wee bike shop stuck out like a snout.

A small six-foot doorway that gated the shop
Was surrounded by bikes for sale and for swap:
There were road bikes and mountain bikes, cruisers and fixies,
City bikes, track bikes, BMXs for tricksies!

The inside was coated with chains, brakes and tyres,
Reflectors and headgear, all things he'd acquired.
There were spare parts and more parts, kickstands and dust caps,
Half bikes and whole bikes, the requisite must-haves!

Ray's escape was complete, his heart was contented,
Long gone were the days of a life he resented.
He was settled out West, he had found his new home;
The only catch was that he'd found it alone.

But the love that he needed was not far away;
Without looking for it, it appeared on one day,
And with this new love Ray was no longer lonely,
'Cos his heart now belonged to a lady called Joanie.

The Oldmans were a charming and contented old pair,
They had met in the summer at Westbury Fayre.
They courted a while, and the romance did linger,
So Ray dropped a knee and put a ring on her finger.

Dear Joanie was sweet. Dear Joanie was loyal.
Old Ray was just glad he had someone to spoil.
A wonderful woman, she was pretty and clever,
And she and Raymundo were happy together.

So happy in fact, without a but or a maybe,
The two of them chose to make a wee baby.
A bundle of joy, a girl they named Tanya,
That when she grew up made a wicked lasagne...

(You can let me off here, because nought rhymes with Tanya...
'cept España, Britannia, or Bacary Sagna.)
But Joanie and Ray's little girl was a winner,
She would work with her dad after school, before dinner.

She was friendly, hardworking and in tune like a Looney,
And in the late nineteen-nineties she went off to uni.
So Ray resumed working, alone in the shop,
Undeterred by his age and refusing to stop.

Time had rolled on, and Tanya was now twenty-four,
Ray was double that number... plus fifteen years more.
As the two of them grew they had drifted apart,
For Tanya's adulthood had broken Ray's heart.

She had married a man whose name was imprudent:
Mr Richard Longtrunk – a sociology student.
She lost her old name, but she didn't mind,
'Cos Dickie was handsome and decent and kind.

Tanya still loved the bikes, the shop and her dad,
But she'd taken a job from a newspaper ad.
It wasn't that great, but the pay was quite good;
She needed a real job, and Ray understood.

With a house and a fella she needed a wage,
But the man in the bike shop was feeling his age.
An old sixty-something with arthritic back;
Timeworn and threadbare, he was starting to slack.

For twenty-five years Ray tinkered and tailored,
He soldiered and spied and lumbered and laboured.
He was jovial still, but one cold Tuesday evening
He stood sad in the doorway, heavily breathing.

The years took their toll on Raymundo's old soul,
So to mull it all over he went for a stroll.
He still loved his shop after all of these years;
And as he circled the park he held back the tears.

You see Ray was retiring – a retired re-tyrer,
Though he needed a mimic, an apprentice, a Lyre.
A Lyre's a bird (from what I have heard):
"The superb Lyrebird," David Attenborough purred.

It's a copier bird; an impersonator.
(If you've not seen the clip, then YouTube it later).
Ray needed this mate to take over his shop,
But he couldn't afford for the standards to drop.

He was racking his brains for someone worthwhile,
A someone to run it in a similar style.
He thought and he thought, he thought more than he oughta.
"I know," thought Raymundo, "I'll employ my daughter."

To be continued...

#4. Introducing Detective Stranger McKrayne

Apples in the Summer

It was 1981, in the autumn of the year, when Stranger McKrayne stopped off for a beer and some bar snacks after his beat. Stranger had just turned thirty. He was a curly-haired bloke of average height and not yet a private detective, just a humble bobby on a North London patrol. After stripping from his rather natty uniform and throwing on some trendier garments worthy of the early eighties realm, Stranger McKrayne very uncharacteristically wandered through the heart of Islington and out into the night.

Stranger was a good policeman, deserving of his badge and helmet. He was a reticent guy – quiet, but without the social awkwardness. He was born and raised in the murky overspill of Northern London, the first and only son of his corned-beef-sarnie-loving parents, Shandon and Veronica. Shandon McKrayne had always been madly in love with his son. As an only child, Stranger was the victim of being spoilt, but the McKraynes were blameless parents nonetheless. Shandon was particularly fond of the movies, and growing up Stranger was treated by his cinephile father to a routine Thursday showing of any film, whether worth seeing or not, at the cinema at the top of their road. This was a tradition that they both dared not break, even through the years of long working days and adolescent distractions. The two of them raided the pic 'n' mix stand far more times than was dentally healthy and sat through more bad performances than the autocue guy at the Oscars. As an adult man, Stranger's deep-rooted love for the high-budgeted Tinseltown delights never diminished. When times were tough, he had his father, and when times were good, he had the charismatic distraction of the cinema, and his father.

On the night that Stranger went out for his beer and bar nuts, he had previously arranged, like most every week before, to catch a bedtime flick at the same cinema with the same old man. *True Confessions* had just been released in the UK and McKrayne and McKrayne both had a date with De Niro. However, the plan had changed somewhat after Stranger had returned to the station from his mundane Thursday patrol to some more-than-welcome news. Stranger's eleven years in the force had not gone unnoticed (though he hadn't noticed the people noticing), but the noticers had been watching his career with a keen but unclean eye. Much to the utter delight and surprise of Stranger, he re-entered the station that evening as a detective: DS Stranger McKrayne. DCS Annette King and DCI Carl Gregory were the acting officers who had dubbed the humble Stranger, and as such they felt obligated to drag him out and wet the big baby's head. So Stranger, upgraded and chuffed to bits, retreated prudently back to his locker-room locker and switched his going home getup for his going out getup.

"...Hello? It's Stranger – are you there? Dad? Look, don't panic, but I can't make the cinema tonight. It's good news, I'll pop over tomorrow and tell you about it. I'm sorry to do this to you again, I'll make it up to you next week, tickets and sweets on me! Mum, if you get this first, tell the old man would ya?! All right, I love you both, bye."

The three detectives left the station in a happy left-right-left and headed up to the Little Fish Bar on Pentonville Road. They passed by the old cinema Stranger was boycotting for drinky-poos on the way, walking around corners with their unfastened trench coats swooping behind them, almost in slow motion, in the light breeze. As they edged closer to their destination, the discord of a half-hearted sound check could be heard. The dull *boing* of a flat bass note tremored the pavement, and the rickety backfire of a warm-up snare drum rattled the windows of the high-street shops. Tonight was bands night and tonight's band was getting ready. Stranger, Annette and Carl arrived at the bar. There was a small crowd of drinkers and smokers standing outside the front, slightly blocking the way in, but not completely. Stranger, letting his two senior detectives slither inside first, had his eye caught by the chalkboard that was leant against the side wall – he could just about see it through the fidgeting crowd. He smiled widely. If there was one thing he loved as much as the movies, it was the harmonic sounds of eighties pop gods Daryl Hall and John Oates, and as luck would have it, the Little Fish Bar on Pentonville Road was hosting a night with none other than Philadelphia Crop, arguably the greatest ever Hall and Oates tribute band.

The frothy top of DCS Annette King's pint lapped the sticky sides of her glass as she led the way from the bar to the three-seater table near the side of the stage at the back of the room. The malty liquid threatened mutiny with every careless step she took, dodging past the sea of tiny tables dotted around the tacky barroom floor like a piss-head's armada. She took one sidestep too harshly, rushing to secure the table, and – *splat* – a big fat dollop of foamy lager was thrown overboard and landed with a wet slap onto a table of dressy couples who were waiting for the show to start. No bother – accidents happen – and after a few quick-fire apologies from DCS King and an offer from Stranger to get some napkins for the mess, all was forgiven and mostly forgotten.

Stranger filtered back through the crowd to the bar, where a pile of double-ply napkins were neatly spiralled and ready to be snatched. He made it over to them easily enough, but when he reached out to nab a handful, he instead latched onto another hand, also in quest of the papery stack. The hand was soft, moisturised and warm. It was delicately reassuring. Clearly, this wasn't a man's hand. Stranger looked up, and he saw her for the first time – his tormented love. For now, they were just two strangers, affectionately watching each other: one warm-handed and open-faced, the other hungry-eyed and love-struck. Stranger pulled his hand back and allowed the lady to take her serviettes first, but she was quick to retake his hand and turn it over, palm facing the damp, cracked ceiling.

"You're a Virgo," said the woman.

"That's very clever," said Stranger.

"I'm Elsie. You've good hands…" Elsie gestured at him with a curious look, coaxing his name from him.

"Stranger… McKrayne. Stranger McKrayne," answered the detective.

"Well, Stranger McKrayne Stranger McKrayne, are you gonna buy me a drink or do I have to play with your hands some more first?"

Stranger ordered Elsie a drink, a Cinzano and lemonade. It came with a star-shaped cube of ice and a little cocktail-stick umbrella, though neither of them really knew why. They talked, and they laughed, and then they drank some more. Elsie pulled Stranger's hands out from the inside of his sleeves; they were a little clammy, but in fairness to him, the room was very warm. She inspected them for the second time that evening, this time a little more thoroughly.

Elsie had a sort of gypsy vibe about her and she was into palm reading. There was a gentle sass to her, enough to stand out from the rest but not so much as to brand her a bitch. She had big brown eyes that sparkled like camera flashes at a pop concert. Tenderly, she ran her fingertips along the inside of Stranger's hands, her freshly decorated nails softly grazing his skin.

"So, Mr Virgo, you're some sort of guard, or watchman... If your eyes weren't so friendly I'd say you was into heavy security," said Elsie, looking up from his hands to his eyes.

Stranger furrowed his brow and twisted his neck slightly to the side. "Hmm, not quite, but that's close. Very close. Well, I suppose..." He was cut off.

"Funny. I'm never usually wrong." Elsie flipped his hands over, the stickiness of the bar temporarily pasting his palms to it. "Well, you're definitely not a builder. I think you're Old Bill. Jesus, you're not a traffic warden are ya?"

"No," said Stranger with a chuckle. "But I'm a pretty good dancer."

They danced the rest of the night away, pirouetting uncontrollably around the crowded barroom floor to the harmonious melodies of Philadelphia Crop. Together, they were victims of the night, of circumstance, of coincidence... everything was perfect at that moment, except for the lager spill on the table that never got cleared up. They fell madly, abandoning their parties and choosing to spend the evening in each other's arms. They stood and awed at the godly renditions of 'Rich Girl' and 'Kiss on My List', tapping their feet and jigging their hips uncontrollably. After a couple of quick drinks more they danced a little to 'I Can't Go for That', becoming trend setters of the dance movement for the evening; the crowd all followed once Stranger and Elsie hit the floor. Eventually, when the night calmed, they slow danced to 'Sara Smile', the closing song of the epic forty-five-minute-long set.

The dance floor was half empty, or half full depending on how optimistically you view your boogie space. Stranger twirled Elsie around and then flicked her out towards the table where DCS King and DCI Gregory were sitting, watching in amazement at the shy detective's apparent self-assurance. Elsie twisted back into his arms and then out again the other way. Her dress swished towards the table where her friends were sitting, watching in equal amazement, as the light gust of her gown fanned an empty packet of crisps on the table, lightly sprinkling them all with ready-salted dust.

The music transitioned from the band's fading final notes into the jukebox's scratchy tunes. Elsie was in the bathroom while Stranger was outside, using the payphone to call his father.

"Dad, it's me again, are you in?" Stranger waited on the line for an answer. There wasn't one.

Elsie appeared from the bar, standing in the doorway and looking for Stranger. She saw him, his back facing her from inside the phone booth. She headed over to him.

"You get hold of him?" Elsie asked through the glass

door.

Stranger shook his head and opened the door, his eyes painted with silent questions.

Veronica McKrayne was a humble housewife. Her house was never untidy and her oven was never empty. Rarely did she leave the house past six in the evening and certainly not on a Thursday. Shandon McKrayne worked in the print for the *London Evening Standard* down on Fleet Street. He was as hardworking a man as any before him, and more so than most after him. He spent most of his time with the boys from work but would be home every night for tea with his wife. Thursdays he kept free, however, as Thursdays were always movie night.

Stranger was disconcerted: *where were they?*

SLEAZY DOES IT

It was half past eleven when Stranger McKrayne glanced across at his bedside alarm clock. His eyes, slightly wonky from the last glass of wine he and Elsie had shared, adjusted to focus on the smallish face of his clock. He was suddenly hit with an idea. He turned his head away from the alarm clock to face the other side of the bed. The side where Elsie was lying.

The cinema on Upper Street, where Stranger and his father spent most of their Thursday evenings, had a tradition. On the opening day of a movie the schedule ran a back-to-back showcase of whatever film had been released that day. The first showing ran from 10:00 am, playing right through until the last at midnight. This little quirk in the cinema's listings was usually wasted on the McKraynes' customary routine, but since Stranger had dumped his dad and missed the seven o'clock showing of *True Confessions*, the thought of the midnight showing lit up his face with the hope of a back-row blowy.

"Elsie," he said, "would you like to come with me to see *True Confessions*?"

Stranger's face knotted as a burp made its way up from his booze-lined gut and fizzed through his teeth. Elsie giggled as he apologised. All of the embarrassment, all of the alcohol and all of the sex rushed to his cheeks with an explosion of rouge. Elsie, turning in bed to face Stranger, looked admiringly at her late-night lover.

"Yeah, I think I would. That'd be nice". She paused to see Stranger smile. "I'm free Saturday...?"

Stranger sat bolt upright in his rumpled double bed, his hair roughed up and his socks still on. Excitedly, his smile widened.

"Nah nah, now. It's playing now... at the Green on the Screen. The Green, Screen, the Scree... the picture house down the road. It's opening night, it starts in about half an hour!"

He took a breath. The hot bedroom air rendered still as Elsie grinned at his boyish excitement. There was a short moment of romantic peace in Stranger's stuffy bedroom.

"I'm sorry, we don't have to go, we shouldn't go. It's just that I go every week with my dad and now you're here, I have a new job and I'm not thinking all that straight..."

Stranger was interrupted. "You betta shut up and get ready if you want us to make it." Sure enough, Stranger stopped talking. "Let me get dressed, get my stuff and we can go," finished Elsie.

Elsie got out of bed, her slender frame caressing the covers as she swivelled free from their shelter. Stranger watched her in delight. She made her way to his en-suite bathroom, picking up her scattered clothes as she went. At the bathroom door, Elsie turned back to Stranger, still cooling down in bed. She was relaxed, but her eyes were heavy with mixed emotions.

"You know, it's a good thing you're handsome, 'cos otherwise you'd just be lovely, and that'd never work." Her comment was sincere, though her tone seemed repentant.

Stranger wasn't all that handsome, but he was lovely. Elsie seemed blinded by this and to her he was as handsome as he needed to be. Some might say that it was a sure sign of true love. Some.

The slurred tunes of distant drunkards sang their way down Upper Street as Stranger and Elsie walked with their hands tangled together inside Stranger's coat pocket. The weather had turned, and a chill now filled the spaces between them. As they walked, they spoke of all things new to one another. Each step they took drew them closer to the cinema, and to each other. A house on fire would've struggled to match the sparks that flicked between them. However, at the corner of the road where they stopped to let a fire engine turtle from its station like a bloody stool, Elsie seemed off, as if suddenly hit by a devastating blow of intolerable conscience. Ironically, there had been a house fire not far from the Little Fish Bar, and the shrill screams of the fire truck had broken the romance just long enough for Elsie to blurt out what was troubling her:

"Stranger, I'm a prostitute."

The romance zipped away with the swirling gust left by the fire truck. Half in bewilderment, and half because of the remaining wails of the siren, Stranger asked:

"Sorry, what was that?"

"I'm a prostitute," Elsie said once again. Stranger sniggered almost mirthlessly, but Elsie was dead serious.

"Oh for fuck's sake! Wha..." Stanger huffed. "Why?"

"What d'ya mean why?" snapped Elsie.

"I mean – why?" Stranger emphasised the *why* a little more compassionately this time.

"I don't know. I just... am." Elsie looked deep into his eyes. "I sleep with men, sometimes women. I make money from it... it pays my rent."

Stanger was stupefied, and his face showed it. "I never paid you. You're not expecting money are ya? This is... this is such a strange joke."

Elsie looked at him with such an expressionless face that he knew this was obviously not a joke.

"I just don't understand, El."

"That's— not my name," interjected Elsie.

"All right. Elsie. I think my shortening of your name is the smallest of concerns at the moment!" Stranger forgot he was a bit drunk and regained full awareness of the situation.

"No, my name's not Elsie. That's my work name – it's safer to use. My real name—" she looked down at the floor before looking back up again at Stranger— "my real name is Sindy. Sindy Spreadum."

"What?!"

Elsie laughed. Then she stopped.

"It's just a joke. Well, the last bit was. The rest is true. My name's Sara, and I'm sorry."

Sara looked surprisingly calm for a woman who had just confessed to her date that she was, in fact, a prostitute. Stanger did not look so calm.

"Elsie, Sara, or whatever it is your name is... I can't be

sleeping with call girls, Jesus. I'm a newly promoted DS now as well! Not now, not in my position, not in any position, would this ever be okay!"

"There were a few positions you seemed okay with half an hour ago..."

"Why are you so jovial about this? You just conned a policeman into sex! I knew something was off – no normal girl has ever enjoyed herself as much as you did."

"Normal girl?!" Sara's smile faltered. "What's a DS?"

"It means Detective Sergeant."

Stranger paused to ponder briefly the potential complications of his actions, staring out into the night. "Oh God," he muttered, still with his gaze unbroken, "I can just see it now, at the city's annual fundraiser... 'Introducing DS Stranger McKrayne, the boner-boy bobby with this month's hussy.'"

"Oi!" Sara lost her cool, her finger held rigid and pointed at Stranger. "There's just as many with a dislike of you little piggies, you know! So enough with the insults." Sara dropped her condemnatory finger, as well as the other ones, back down to her side.

Stranger rubbed his eyes as he stood trying to process what had just happened. He was suddenly very aware of where they were and what was being said. Their public display of aversion was in full show of the Thursday night Upper Streeters. This was his neighbourhood. *This,* he thought to himself, *could be bad*.

"I've told you this as a precaution, even to help you, not so that you can have a dig, all right?" Sara continued despite the detective being slightly absent minded. "I really like you, Stranger, honestly I do..." In the wake of the news, Sara's promiscuousness became more identifiable, but her words seemed to ring true enough. "I've not tried to hurt you. I am as I am and all I wanna do is to finish the night with you, at the cinema, just as you asked me to."

"Oh, and I suppose you want me to pay?" remarked Stranger.

"Only for the popcorn, I can cover the rest."

Stranger turned to face the other way with a scratch of his head; the bright neon shop front of the off license across the road burned his weary eyes as it caught his look.

"I liked Elsie, it's a good name. It suits you, well, the you I've spent the night with so far. It's not illegal what you do, Sara, it's just highly unsanitary." He checked his words and he suddenly remembered something odd that Sara had said. "What did you mean when you said, 'as a precaution'? What're you helping me with?" said Stranger, spinning his head around to address Sara, his body still facing the street.

"Oh come on Stranger, you're a big boy, you know what sort of risks come with mixing with my kind."

"Are you talking about my job? Because I thought I'd already made it clear that I can't take... *this*, any further."

"No, I'm not talking about your job, I'm talking about my job. My job and my boss."

"Your boss?" Stranger's body now turned to match the way he was facing.

"Yes, my boss. My agent – my pimp!"

"You have a pimp?" Stranger's tone switched from defensive to inquisitive.

"Yes, I have a pimp – prostitutes have pimps. Not all of them, but a lot of them. Keep up, McKrayne, I'm trying to play ball here!"

"Prostitution may not be illegal, sweetheart, but pimping definitely is. They're nasty work. What are you doing knocking about with those fellas?!" Stranger was battling to forget the attractive woman he had met at the bar, but every time she caught his eye, he was reminded of her charm.

"Someone's always watching me, do you understand?! I'm surrounded by the people I'm trying to escape. Always. I fell in a long time ago and now I'm trying to drag myself back out. There's no P45 in my line of work, you're either in or you're out. Then you're done and finished either way..."

"Much like the men who pay for you then..." joked Stranger this time, though again in an untimely fashion.

"What the fuck is wrong with you?!"

"Me? What the fuck is wrong with you?! Stop trying to victimise yourself, you're the one who preyed upon me. I was supposed to be at the fucking cinema with Dad, God knows where he is. I didn't even wanna go for a drink, I just got pushed out the door and bundled into the bar regardless!"

"See. Not so easy when it's not you that's making your own decisions, is it?" Sara quipped.

"Ohhh... Go away. I don't need this, I don't need you."

"Well I need you."

"What does that mean? You've only just met me! This is all too much, you're acting as if we've been together for years!"

"Well, so are you!"

The street fell into silence. Fewer and fewer people dotted the pavement as Thursday night neared Friday morning. Midnight was creeping and neither Stranger nor Sara was budging an inch. It was as though both were searching for an impossible resolution, an answer to their own agenda. If it was an unsuspecting man Sara wanted, then there were more than enough scattered drunkenly throughout the chilly streets of London – ones that were more forgiving and less caring than Detective Stranger McKrayne. She was after him and only him. Similarly, Stranger was well within his rights and in an easy enough position to walk briskly away and shake loose the demons of the night. But he hadn't. He cared. Stranger had smelt, beneath the floral perfume, the vulnerability of Sara, and he couldn't bring himself to up and leave a desperate woman. Plus, there was a story here, and the detective in him wanted to press for more.

"Please Stranger, just one date, one normal night and I promise I won't bother you." Up until now Sara had been so good at making him believe in his own control of the night and of its outcomes.

"Why me, eh? Why out of everyone in the bar did you latch onto my hand?" Stranger's eyes narrowed with realisation. "You knew me. You knew who I was before you met me tonight, didn't you? That bullshit palm-reading crap, that was just a ruse to give me the horn, wasn't it?! Who are you?"

Sara was caught between a rock and a hard-on. Playing innocent would only lead to Stranger's eventual dismissal, and owning up would open up a whole new can of worms. Worms aside, she spilt the beans.

Sara had heard her pimp talking about a new policeman on his radar, some old hat who was honest, young and had come up through the ranks to be a newly promoted DS. It was in any pimp's interest, as well as his girls', to take note of their area's law enforcement officers and any new developments in their safety and wellbeing.

Sara, belonging to a less than eager ilk of call girls, rarely paid attention to the word on the street. Truthfully, sometimes she wanted to be caught, to be out of her dirtied shackles. But it was the only life she knew, the only home she had.

However, one night, whilst taking a moment in the rest area of her pimp's brothel, she overheard an almost routine conversation. The talk was between her pimp, 'The Captain' (as the sign read on his door at the back of the rest area), and a bent North London copper. Sara's ears pricked as the squalid police chief sat chatting to The Captain, explaining to him that he was about to promote a keen young policeman to a DS rank. Stranger McKrayne – the subject of the conversation, a good man with a dozen years of experience already in his locker.

The police chief and The Captain sat talking for a while about how to treat this news. Naturally, Stranger had to be promoted sometime soon otherwise some questions would've been asked and some unflattering queries would've threatened the illegalities of the police station. The problem lay in Stranger's honesty: an unbent policeman with every intention of remaining that way. But then again, as The Captain himself remarked, they always were.

The two men agreed that in time Stranger would most likely succumb to the deviant ways of The Captain and his bent police chief puppet – they had ways of making a man abandon his moral stance. The usual cocktail of sex, money and power eventually got the better of all the top brass. The Captain and his associates were indeed the puppet masters and they could make things happen and unhappen, appear and disappear, if they so wished. Ashamedly,

Stranger, innocent as he may have been, would've also involuntarily fallen under the underworld's wicked spell. Although what the two villains did not expect was that one of their own would be slumped in a sweaty heap of self-loathing outside of the office door, awaiting the chance to save herself from an eternity of misery, and to save another from the coaxing finger of evil.

"I came here tonight to save you. To drag you away from that bar and tell you all this," Sara proclaimed.

Stranger was in total shock. "So, you're telling me that you work for some almighty pimp that parades around half of London, doing what he pleases, and using the police force to get away with it all?"

"It's true, I promise you it's all true. They'll make you one of 'em, Stranger, truly they will, they're all corrupt, every last one. He was there, The Captain, he was at The Little Fish Bar tonight. He... he sent me to you."

Stranger looked back at Sara in motionless amazement. His words were far from him now; the night was lost to total despair. Sara was to do the talking from now until the resolution, if indeed there was one.

"After I heard them talking in his office, I knew I either had to hide, or abide. 'Who shall we send first then?' he said, your bastard chief of police. I could almost hear The Captain shrug – it was a pointless question, he doesn't care. He's never cared. He's won over almost everyone he's ever come into conversation with, but I know what he really is, there's no hiding behind that crooked smile... He'll do almost anything to get what he wants, to win. He's a powerful man, but he's a scared man, too."

Sara stopped herself for a second before continuing.

"I made an excuse to see him. I knocked on the door,

said that I was thinking of going away for the weekend. He wasn't listening, I knew he wasn't listening, I just had to be the first one they saw. I was. So they asked me the 'favour' that I was after, but of course, they had no idea. He's a clever man though, Stranger; nothing much goes over his head. He's never trusted me fully – he knows I'm not happy. That's why he came, that's why he sent the other girls down with me, in case I didn't do it."

"So, what now?" Stranger's voice was flat and monotone. "You've saved me as much as you can, right? The jig is up, I'll keep an ear to the ground and an eye on my colleagues. If this goes as deep as you say it does then I'm hardly going to bust it wide open, am I? At least not right now."

"Well what about me, huh?" Sara said with a tear in her eye. It was clear now that Sara was fragile, she was afraid.

"What about you?"

"Now you save me." She nearly trembled as she spoke now. "I knew you were a good man, Stranger, but I didn't expect to like you as much as I do. I came tonight for me, but now I wanna help us both." Sara meant every word she said. Tears spilled down her cheeks. "Keep me close, Stranger. As long as I'm nearby, they'll think we're both innocent... nobody else has to get hurt."

"Who..."

The detective stopped his sentence as if his voice were sliced with a blade. His head lifted and his vision tunnelled; fixed on a point beyond Sara's frame. He felt a cold shudder of dread tingle from his head to his toes.

"Mum and Dad." Stranger whispered his terrified words, but in the still night air they echoed hauntingly loud.

"What? No. They wouldn't, not just..." Sara's response was cut short by a happy, high-pitched voice behind her.

"Hello darling. What are you doing out here?" The voice addressed Stranger. Sara did not turn around to greet it.

"Mum, Jesus. What are you doing out here?"

"That's a new one. I've not been called Jesus before," said a male voice in response.

"Dad. What're you doing?" Stranger asked his father, who was arm in arm with his mother, Veronica.

"I believe your mother asked you first. Are you all right bud? You look like you've seen a ghost." Shandon McKrayne turned to look at Sara standing a few feet away from him. "Hello darling, I'm not sure I know you, I'm Stranger's father..."

"Oh God." Stranger was agitated.

"Well it's closer than Jesus, given that I made you," Shandon joked, "but it's still not right. And it certainly wasn't a virgin birth, was it, V?!" Shandon joked again as Stranger grimaced at his dad.

Sara introduced herself to Stranger's parents, though in another attempt to retain anonymity, she did so as Elsie. Before Stranger had the chance to conjure up a cover-up, Sara claimed herself to be his girlfriend.

"So this is what you've been up to the last couple of weeks, is it? Why so secretive Stranger? She's a lovely girl!"

"I know, Dad, it's not what you..."

"You know, I had to go and see *Chariots of Fire* all on my own last week. You missed a good one though bud, cracking film! Not sure about the music though, to be honest, thought it could've been catchier. Easily forgotten."

"Dad, I've been so busy with work the last couple of

weeks, they've really dumped everything on me."

"You should take it easy sweetheart, you have Elsie to think about now as well." Veronica McKrayne, as ever the caring mother. "Your father's dragging me along to this one tonight." She turned to Sara. "I'd never usually go out at this time, but I couldn't let him go out alone in the middle of the night. Plus, that de Niro is a handsome man, isn't he?"

Sara smiled and laughed politely.

"That's where you're going? To the Screen on the Green, for the midnight showing?" Stranger was puzzled by his parents' spontaneity.

"Well, I got your message and I thought I'd take your mother out for dinner. We ended up being at the restaurant far longer than we planned, didn't we V? We bumped into my old boss at the *Standard* and his wife, Indian fella, lovely, lovely man. We went down that new Italian place 'round the corner. Your mum had chicken and chips – chicken and chips! Can you believe that? Nicest Italian in Islington and she has chicken and chips!"

"Oh, I can't be doing with all them funny foods, it gives me gut ache it does! What was it your boss's wife had?"

"Carbonara," answered Shandon.

"Car-banera. Just the sound of it puts me off. There was bacon in it as well, I didn't think they could eat bacon..."

"No, it's beef they don't eat, it's sacred, and besides it looked lovely! I was nearly gonna order myself one to take home for tomorrow, but your mother's already made me corned beef sarnies. 'Ere, it's a good job Mr Raschid's not at the *Standard* anymore, ain't it? They're some pretty sacred sandwiches you've made me V."

"Oh no," Veronica laughed, "you don't think they could smell it on me, do you? I never had time to shower before we came out. I mean, I washed my hands after I made them, but they might've been able to smell it on me still, mightn't they?"

"Mum!" Stranger was getting embarrassed.

"'Ere, did I ever tell you about when I went to their daughter's wedding and one of the bridesmaids slipped me a mickey?"

Stranger shook his head. Sara looked confused; she didn't quite understand.

"You know, a Mickey Finn... she drugged me Elsie, can you believe that?!"

Veronica, once again addressing Sara, continued her husband's story. "Yeeaah. Oh, you should've seen it Els, I've never seen him in such a state. He was on the toilet for hours, I thought we had a leaky pipe! I still think it was all that dodgy stuff you ate at the reception."

"It was a curry Veronica, me and the boys go out for one every Tuesday! It was the bridesmaid, she slipped me a mickey, I'm telling ya!"

Stranger rubbed his face irritably; in his life so far he was yet to feel such levels of discomfort. Sara was laughing. Stranger finally interrupted them.

"You're gonna miss your film, ain't ya? It's getting on for midnight," he said.

"Oh God, yeah, look at the time, V? We better go. Anyway, what are you two up to? We saw you from away back there, looked like you was having a barney."

Sara took this as her time to strike. "Well, funnily enough, we were just talking about going to the cinema too. I want to go but Stranger doesn't, he's not feeling up to it all of a sudden."

They all looked at the detective collectively, though each had a different expression on their face. Shandon McKrayne had a look of dulled shock. He'd never known his son to turn down a cinema invitation, least of all on a Thursday night. Veronica McKrayne had a maternal look on her face, one that showed unconditional love and understanding, her presumption being that her son must've been too weary for the excursion.

"He's tired," she said, "he's been working too hard, that's what it is. How about I buy you a nice cup of coffee from that little stall inside the cinema, yeah? That'll do the trick, won't it? You can sit next to me sweetheart."

"Why would he want to sit next to you when he has this beautiful young lady with him?!" Shandon and Veronica seemed to have an answer for everything the other one said.

Sara had a familiar look of sass etched all over her face – a look Stranger recognised from their talks at the bar earlier that night. Sara was going to get her way at last, and they both knew it.

"Anyway, he's tired? Too tired?! What a load of old—" Shandon was stopped by his wife.

"Ah! You watch your language in front of this young lady Shandon McKrayne. Come on, my love, you come walk with me. We'll let the boys talk on the way to the picture house."

Stranger knew that between the three of them, he was not going to break free from the night's inevitability, so instead he surrendered. He gave in to the untimeliness of it all and walked with his dad, like almost every Thursday night he could remember, down Upper Street to the picture house at the top of their road. Shandon enthusiastically prompted the usual movie talk they always shared on their journey, though this time Stranger was far less engaged than usual. Veronica was walking with Sara a few steps behind them, asking her own questions, harmoniously unaware of how greatly their lifestyles differed.

"So, Elsie," began Stranger's mother, "what is it you do for a living?"

#5. Duck Off Howard: Trailers

Boogie Shoes

Click, click, flash! The herd of press opened fire with their fixed-focal-length-lensed cameras. Click, click, flash! The small rows of indie reporters were caged behind a worn-out crimson rope, boxed in by shiny metal poles outside the Raggabone Picture House on the Bournemouth seafront. The night was the 26th of September in the second millennium year. It was a warm Thursday evening. A leather-jacketed couple were walking excitedly along the gently curving road, their arms intertwined and their steps rhythmically patting the pavement. They stopped briefly at the split in the road so that the lady could light her cigarette; the gentleman shielded the coastal breeze from her with the span of his jacket as she caressed the spark wheel of the lighter. With an orange glow twinkling in her palm, she rose up from the shelter of the jacket with her lit cigarette, and as the smoke curled and cleared from her first puff, the soft fluorescent lights from the picture house headlined above them: A Declaration of War: The Uncut Story of Lars Månglehünd.

Fatality Productions were celebrating the release of their first full-length feature film and were subsequently enjoying the fancy shenanigans of their first world premiere. The night played host to a happy occasion. Janet Cartwright, an attractively petite woman with reddish-brown hair, a pale complexion and big, pouting lips, was at the forefront of the production company. Janet was a producer and a director: self-made and established by two unsuccessful short films, a writing stint at a failing network and a fresh set of bed linen set aside for the moneymen at the British Film Institute. Janet was horrendously gifted at making bad content. She honed it as a talent and literally butt-fucked the lottery fund for a feature in the millennium roster. The fact that Janet enjoyed sleeping around quite obviously boosted her campaign – her seductiveness won her the funding from both the BFI and a couple of slick-haired private executives for her avant-garde movie. The men behind the money were pigs and she knew exactly how to bring home the bacon.

DEALIO

A Declaration of War: The Uncut Story of Lars Månglehünd was a ninety-eight-minute feature based on the life and times of Lars Månglehünd, the ambidextrous Thumb War World Champion of 1998. Lars was half Danish and half German but had lived in the UK since the age of seven, when his parents had flown over to open a handful of bakeries in the south west of England, bringing with them their signature pretzels and pastries. Little Lars was born with an extraordinary disfigurement. He was gifted with not only a full set of eight long and strong fingers, but also with four flexing thumbs to compliment his already massive hands. Two thumbs on each hand, one sprouting from the other like Hydras heads. As you can imagine, life was unkind to Lars as a child. But one day in his later teenage years, he found a new hobby, a hobby that he was nigh on unbeatable at – the art of the Thumb War.

Lars had stumbled across the miniature sport accidentally whilst reading an unrelated book in the afterschool book club, held every Wednesday in the Upper School Library. A few brief passages about the playground game had been scribbled by the book's author, serendipitously, but what seemed to Lars almost intentionally. Overcome with curiosity, Lars read and re-read the words over and over, using his quartet of thumbs to flick effortlessly back and forth between the correlating pages. In his lowest moments as a confused and ridiculed teenage ne'er-do-well, Lars Månglehünd, the Thumb War Champion of the World, was born.

Lars trained every day after school with his yellow-striped hand grips his father had bought him as a stocking filler the previous Christmas. He sat in his room, strengthening his many fingers and thumbs so that they were not only great in length and number, but in girth and endurance also. He started visiting the library on Mondays and Thursdays, as well as Wednesdays, so that he could research the art of Thumb War and get to know his new obsession. Before dinner was served each night, Lars challenged both his mother and father to a Thumb War. Their hands were strong and well used from the constant kneading and folding of the foods in their bakery. They were a strong and worthy test of his abilities. The kids at Lars' school were unforgiving of his disfigurement. Their malicious slurs and constant digs slapped into him the introverted and reclusive traits he became so well known for in school.

Lars' situation soon worsened, though, as the rumours spread of his interest in the pussy sport of thumb wrestling. One dark day, Lars was tricked into a thumb war he had no chance of winning. That was the day Murph Connors and his boyfriend unfairly coaxed him into the alleyway behind the Lower School Gym, where they would sit and smoke between classes. As Murph and his crinkle-faced boyfriend peeled themselves away from the shadowy indents of the high gym walls, the promise of a just thumb war betrayed Lars, just as his parents' genetic coding had done when they cursed him with a foursome of thumbs, fifteen years prior.

Murph and Scott were not nice people. They were, however, very much in love with each other. To defend themselves from the inevitable onslaught of abuse the kids at school would give them, they chose to become the bullies; they were big boys and they knew how to fight. The kids at school kept their distance and let them be, mostly, but poor Lars had been in the wrong place at the wrong time when Murph decided to pounce. Lars was not such a big boy, and he only knew how to fight with thumbs.

The boys gave Lars his thumb war. They matched his four thumbs with theirs, but they cared not for the formalities of bowing and kissing, they went straight for the knuckles and used their index fingers to hook onto both of his right-handed thumbs – a highly illegal manoeuvre. The bones in Lars' strong thumbs snapped, but whilst he screamed through the duct tape that had been scratched across his mouth, the boys went to work on his left hand. A minute or so later, Lars was left alone and face down in the dirty alleyway with four broken thumbs and a cigarette burn in the centre of each of his palms. The duct tape had already been peeled from his fair-haired upper lip, but he lay agonisingly silent with his teary eyes closed and his shattered hands clutching the air out in front of him in desperation. But Lars was damned if he was going to let Murph Connors ruin his dreams. So, as he mustered the courage and might to pull himself up from the lightly littered walkway, he vowed to work twice as hard, once his wounds had healed, so that one day after his successes, he could track down Murph and Scott to bash their heads in repeatedly and unsympathetically with his shiny gold trophy.

Something, besides the obvious, happened in that alleyway. Lars had been left in the dirt with horrendous physical injuries, and some irreparable, undesirable mental injuries, too.

Lars left school at eighteen, and as most young adults his age were enjoying their last summer before being evacuated to university, he instead bounded gleefully into London town for the summer registration at the International Thumb Sports and Associated Recreational Society of Extremities. At that time his ambitions and his motivations were cut heartbreakingly short. Lars was informed that he would not be eligible for competition because of his additional thumbs. But even this unkindly news wasn't enough to shatter the world-beating illusions of Lars Månglehünd. After a short series of long hearings on the controversial matter, Lars was confirmed victorious in his appeals, and his rights as an able-handed athlete were confirmed as he was begrudgingly invited into the niche society. The rest was easy. Lars went on to compete in multiple tournaments around the country, expanding his terrain to Europe, and eventually cracking America and claiming the prestigious Thumb War World Championship Trophy (TWWC) for his own in both 1998 and 1999. By the year 2000, Lars had become a table-topping sporting icon – a hero and a near overnight success in the rather underground world of C-listed sports. Yes, it appeared that everyone wanted a little slice of Månglehünd Pie...

Lars - not his parents' infamous Månglehünd Pie, although everyone wanted a slice of that too... It was delicious.

...He was suddenly inundated with sponsorship from lesser-known brands. He had his face slapped on the second or third pages of near enough every free sporting handout – and all because Lars, the half Danish/half German twenty-two-year-old from Bathampton, was about to make and break history as the only soul, living or dead, to win the coveted TWWC award three years running. This was the turning point, the real trigger in Lars' self-assurance. Lars had come from the bottom to the top, but whatever integrity and decency he'd had had been left in that alleyway next to his old school gym.

FATALITY PRODUCTIONS

Janet Cartwright became interested in the Lars Månglehünd story back in September 1999. One morning, as she and the other commuters jiggled with the bumps of the busy rush-hour train, her wandering eye caught his name at the back of the local paper the man in front of her was skimming through. A lightbulb flickered in Janet's head. It was dusty and came on slowly, but a lightbulb nonetheless. Janet believed she had finally found her story, by chance, as she made her way to the office for a tense 10:00 am budget conference.

Janet was meeting with a member of the BFI and Lottery Film Fund regarding her grant application she had personally handed in a few months ago. The initial meeting (held pants-free) in the senior suite of the Eden Palace Hotel had gone well enough for Janet to be taken semi-seriously in her cinematic quest. Despite not actually having a script, or even a premise to run with, Janet was given the time of day one final time to pitch a project for funding. This time, though, she planned to do it with her clothes on. The Lars Månglehünd story was Janet's saving grace. He had unknowingly saved her from an embarrassing presentation of some of the most horrendous ideas doodled in the back of her ring-binder notepad. Mr Hannelly, the clean-shaven moneyman who had come to revisit Janet, was somehow won over by the slapdash pitch she had jotted down just before he arrived.

"Janet, I think this could be your best film yet... Congratulations, your funding has been approved. You may begin the preproduction of your movie with our full confidence and backing. Do you have a working title?"

"Thank you, Sir," Janet replied. "Although this is my first film, it will undoubtedly be my best. And no, as yet we do not have a working title."

Mr Hannelly rose up from his seat and buttoned up his double-breasted jacket. He held out his hand for Janet to shake, but as she clasped his greasy hand to seal the dubious deal, he snaked his other one around her backside and squeezed her bottom. Janet rolled her eyes. The embrace was unprofessional but not entirely inappropriate, a truth she so routinely had to accept given how she secured herself these call-backs in the first place. Mr Hannelly eventually let both his hands go and headed out of her office with a twisted grin on his face. Janet paused for thought. Her brow furrowed and her big red lips tightened in concentration as he reached the doorway and twisted the handle open...

"Given the nature of everything, perhaps we'll call it *Thumbing Up a Softie...*" She winked at Mr Hannelly. He turned to face her with an uneasy expression. "I'll be in touch," she said, blowing him a kiss as the wind blew the office door shut.

Janet and her modest team at Fatality Productions went on to produce the questionable biopic of Lars Månglehünd successfully. Lars was incredibly enthusiastic about the project, which was a saving grace as Janet had obtained the funding without ever once asking him for permission to tell his story. Lars was continually growing in confidence in the spotlight, therefore his eagerness for his own biopic was paramount in securing the vital go-ahead. Janet began to develop the idea in September 1999, and by September 2000 she had a full-length feature film premiering at the prestigious Raggabone Picture House. Although Janet's movie was given the green light by the British Film Institute, the allocated budget was still undeniably low, naturally, so meetings were met and talks were talked over the cutting of costs to make the movie all the more makeable. Some obscure rumours had spread from a galaxy far far away about a ghastly new method of filmmaking that came at a better price than the everyday 35 mm film stock – a new devilry, one that had the potential to make or break the industry noobs. With an open ear, an open heart and a pair of open legs, Janet was ready to listen to whatever the big boys had to say. And so, *A Declaration of War: The Uncut Story of Lars Månglehünd* was shot, in its entirety, using digital cinematography. This was a pretty damn ballsy move at the turn of the millennium, what with all those pesky bugs.

Her Night in Burning Armour

"Lars, Lars! What do you think of the film so far, you know... from the footage you've seen?"
"Lars, Lars! How soon after the premiere do you leave for the States?"
"Lars, Lars! How did you feel about Klint Buttafuoco landing the role of yourself in the movie?"
"Lars, Lars... LARS! Give us a big thumbs-up for the camera mate!"

The popcorn in the machine behind the second-floor counter was jammed and had taken away the attention of three of the servers, so quite the queue had formed at the crowded confectionary counter. Doug Granite, the manager of the Raggabone Picture House, was standing with his arms folded behind his back at the grand entrance to his cinema, the long red carpet landing at his feet from its dog-legged path around the outside of the building. Most of the critics, actors, crew and family members were already inside and dirtying up the Pic 'n' Mix cabinet, but Janet Cartwright, Klint Buttafuoco and his partner Garrias were yet to grace the scarlet track.

Klint Buttafuoco was a twenty-seven-year-old English stage actor from Glastonbury. Klint Buttafuoco, of course, was just his chosen stage name – his real name was *Clint* Buttafuoco, with a C. Klint had been plucked, like an ingrowing pube, from his experimental one-man show by Janet Cartwright while on tour. Janet had been given some free tickets to see Klint's organic farming awareness-raising show, "Braising the Steaks", by one of her many friends in the theatre, and after witnessing a performance dubbed "average at best; a backwards step in an already unpromising career"*, she waited outside the stage door and coaxed him into recreating Lars Månglehünd for the big screen.

"Lars, Lars! How confident are you in becoming the first person in history to win the TWWC three years running?"
"Lars, Lars! How do you feel about an openly gay actor playing you in your own biopic?"
"Lars, Lars! Are you concerned over the stigma your own sexuality may suffer as a result of this decision?"
"Lars, Lars... LARS! Do you have a favourite thumb, and if so, which one?"

Up in the projection room of the Raggabone Picture House, Lonny, the part-time schoolboy projectionist, was busy moving some old film reels from the 'Golden Age Week' the picture house had run a week prior to the screening. Below Lonny in the auditorium, a trio of grey-shirted ushers swept the aisles and thumped the dust from the backs of the mauve seats. Familiar Hollywood scores echoed tunefully around the screening room and the lobby as the countdown for the big premiere continued. Williams, Zimmer, Elfman, Morricone: each of them transitioned smoothly into one another's masterpiece. Then, as John Barry and The Royal Philharmonic Orchestra's turbulent sounds of the Zulu nation roared through the surround sound, Janet Cartwright finally pulled up to the pavement end of the red carpet. Janet was wearing a backless, blood-red satin dress that fell effortlessly from her collarbone to

---

* **D.H Greenfold** – *Sideline Theatrics Publication: Millennium Christmas Edition.*

the matching red carpet below her feet. Janet had arrived in a pair of black high heels but had decided to take them off and carry them as she strolled merrily to the cinema. On her barefoot journey towards Doug at the end of the carpet, she passed Lars and his date still jabbering away to the indiscreet press. He spun to acknowledge Janet as she slowed to greet him, then the two of them embraced in a wide-armed hug before the fidgety journalists.

"You're looking good Mr Månglehünd. A damn sight dressier than the day I met you."

"You're too kind, Janet. But I'm almost sure I was wearing a suit the first time I met you. In fact, I think it might've even been the same one. Don't tell that lot, though." Lars gestured at the press behind them.

"Well there's definitely something different about you. You've shaved maybe... Or perhaps you're standing a few inches taller than you were last year?"

"Perhaps. But you're not. Where are your shoes, Jan?"

"Oh, they don't fit me anymore..." said Janet with a wink. "Enjoy the night Lars."

Janet walked on as Lars swivelled back around to face the reporters; he was enjoying talking shamelessly highly of himself. Lars was wearing a black three-piece with a floral red tie, dotted with yellow and navy splodges. On his feet were a pair of shiny black loafers, initialled 'LM' on the heel, and on his hands were a tailor-made pair of grey hybrid nylon-silk gloves (handmade in Italy with an extra thumb-hold on each). The gloves were a new addition to Lars' expanding wardrobe and were his absolute favourite item of clothing. The nylon provided durability and moisture resistance, and the silk just felt good.

Doug Granite was waiting at the entrance of his

cinema to welcome in Janet and the other stragglers out on the carpet. He shook Janet's hand as she arrived, smiling. Doug was in two minds over the evening's proceedings. His face showed it, too – his chubby cheeks were etched with discontent. The Raggabone Picture House was no stranger to hosting semi-low-key film premieres. It had been an attraction to many indie filmmakers since it opened its doors to the world sometime in the seventies. The studios, or mostly the production companies, paid a pretty price to have their film screen at the pretty little cinema on the English coast; but not Janet. Janet approached Doug with an over-budget movie, an empty bank account and a new shade of red lipstick. Like the rest of 'em, Doug fell for Janet's charms when she kinkily promised the fifty-seven-year-old divorcee a night or two with her bad self. Janet also promised him that because of the PR she and her team at Fatality were pumping in and out of the movie, he could rest assured that his wee little cinema would be jumping on the big night. Regrettably, Doug shook on the deal. On the one hand – the one free from Janet's tender grasp – he cringed knowing that the confectionary bill Janet's guests would rack up on the night would not cover the hire costs. On the other – the one that was sweaty in the excitement of a feminine touch – he had been divorced for three years and was hornier than a rhino at a safari park orgy. Janet's word was as good as his, and a filthy pact had been made between the two of them. Doug would have his way, before Janet got hers.

The time was about 19:15 pm. The audience were being shepherded into Screening Room Three and the house lights were dimmed to about halfway down. The music was still trickling in through the speakers around the cinema, *The Great Escape*'s patriotic brass now setting the scene as the ushers' torches scanned the big room for seats like the searchlights of a WWII prisoner-of-war camp. Finally, Klint Buttafuoco arrived outside with his partner Garrias, both arm in arm and both dressed in matching black tuxedos. Garrias was a handsome Greek man. He was quite short and had the most brilliantly quaffed hair. He could wear a tux better than most anyone who tried. He and Klint quickstepped along the roped-off pathway, briefly stopping every few steps for a photo from the press (and the occasional local with a £5 disposable). The handful of reporters still pestering Lars soon noticed that the real star of the movie, Klint, was making his way towards them and so the questions halted as their gaze shifted to the gays approaching the picture house. Lars and his lady love also turned to see Klint, now sporting a slick hairdo and neat moustache, as opposed to the scruffier look he had adopted for the role of Lars. He awaited Klint with his arms outstretched.

Klint swooped in for a big hug. Garrias and Lars' blonde-haired escort also embraced and introduced themselves to one another. The couples then swapped partners and did it all again, though as most male strangers do, Garrias pushed his hand out towards Lars for a handshake but was met without a limb in return. Lars stared at the wavering hand pointed at his diaphragm for a moment, pulled his lips into his teeth, closed his left eye and his face leant to the right.

"Ooooh... hands are a no-no, I can't, I'm sorry. It's just, with the world championships being in a few days I just can't risk it, you know?! I can hug you though, if you want one? I seem to be giving them away these days."

"I reckon the moment's passed now, hasn't it, really?" replied Garrias. "Besides, you wouldn't want to be seen hugging TWO poofs on your own red carpet now, would you? Not after what I heard you saying to those reporters a little while ago."

Lars' faced throbbed with a shade of red not too different to the carpet they were all standing upon. "Sorry? I'm not sure what you're talking about, that's a damn dirty accusation you've just spat at me! We're all good friends here, what's your problem?"

"Give it up Lars, this event's been slapped all over the local news network. I saw your interviews on six different screens in the Dixons window on the walk up here."

"What's Dixons doing open this late on a Thursday?"

"I suppose it's late night shopping, or they just leave them on a timer... but that isn't the point, you fucking homophobe!" Garrias leant in closer to Lars. "I think you need to pull all four of your thumbs from out of your fudgehole and come back down to earth. You're a thumb war champion, Lars... what the fuck does that even mean?!"

"It means your boyfriend can afford to buy you some pretty little things now, doesn't it?! It means... Well, it means that my movie is about to start. Enjoy the night."

Lars pulled his silky nylon gloves taut, not unlike a Nazi officer, and took his leave. His plus-one, who had been in full conversation with the charming Klint Buttafuoco the entire time, said her goodbyes and chased her man down the crimson track. Klint and Garrias relinked their arms and posed for a few more photos before Doug summoned them in for the start of the movie.

Everyone in Screening Room Three was sitting

comfortably in the slightly inclining rows of slightly reclining seats. A soft cloud of muttering filled the room as they all waited patiently for Janet Cartwright to begin her pre-movie speech. Janet was standing in the walkway of the screening room, looking over a couple of cue cards, shielded from the crowd by the wall leading out to the double doors. As she quickly skimmed through her anecdotes and thankyous, Doug popped his head through the doors behind her, just in time, and asked for a quick word upstairs. With a huff, Janet complied. She tucked the cue cards into her bra and followed Doug out of the room, up the stairs and into a small, dead-end corridor, out of which sprouted the projection room and a small staff room. Janet hovered, mildly concerned, in the corridor whilst Doug ducked inside the projection room. A short moment later he re-emerged, with his arm lent heavily across the shoulders of Lonny, the part-time projectionist. The two of them were laughing.

Doug patted him on the back and said, "Thanks Lon, we won't be a minute. Get yourself a tea. Janet..."

Doug held the heavy door open and motioned for her to step inside, so she did. The door closed slowly as Doug shifted his weight and stepped inside after her.

Janet peeked through the window of the projection room into the auditorium below. She could see that her guests were becoming restless. She was supposed to be in front of them starting her speech and not stood above them in a silly and untimely meeting.

"So what's this about now Doug?" Janet twirled around to address Doug Granite, who was stood about four feet away from her with his suit trousers snuggled closely around his ankles. "Oh for f... What are you doing Doug?

Jesus, pull your strides up."

"Janet, you and I had a deal, remember? I let you use my picture house, free of charge, and you show me a good time... Well, the original agreement was that I be credited as an exec as well, wasn't it? But something funny happened this afternoon when Lonny and I sat down to test the roll – do you know whose name appeared to be missing from the credits list?"

"I'm sorry Doug, I just, I can't take you seriously with your trousers down."

"DO NOT INTERRUPT ME JANET CARTWRIGHT!"

"Well, you asked me a question so..."

"Listen to me, Janet. If you want your snazzy little evening to continue as planned, then I suggest you shut up and do as I say, because I am not starting your film until you honour our agreement."

Janet rolled her eyes disbelievingly and let out a troubled guttural sound. She flicked her look once more to the packed room below them, and then back to face Doug again.

"I'm not being funny Dougie, but why are you doing this now, huh? I was supposed to start my speech three minutes ago; do you want a good reaction from tonight or what?!"

"Oh, I really wouldn't worry about the time. I've been divorced for a while now, and pretty girls don't exactly flock to a balding fifty-something who spends most of his time in the back office of a seaside cinema... I'll make it quick."

Knowing full well that Doug meant what he said and would not start the movie unless she submitted, she submitted. With a second roll of her big brown eyes she waved him forwards; she slinked back onto the desk beside the film projector as Doug shuffled forwards a few feet like a randy little penguin.

The noise from the screening room below them was steadily growing louder, luckily enough, as it was masking the farmyard grunts Doug blew out every second thrust. Despite the undeniable humour in Janet's situation, the crowd really were getting agitated with the delay. Janet could hear the rowdiness through the projector window as she had her cheek pressed uncomfortably against the wall that encased it. Front cheek, that is. Although she did have her back cheeks pressed against it at first but in an attempt to better his angle, Doug had twisted her around like a pisshead waltzing a kebab leg.

Janet had had enough. Doug had had his moment and now as far as Janet was concerned, it was over. Well to be fair, as far as she was concerned, it was over before it had even started. With a screwed-up face and with her sweaty palms pressed firmly against the wall for resistance, Janet launched herself backwards and threw Doug off her. Caught unawares in the sudden thrash, Doug, in all his heaviness, tripped on the trousers that were still nestled around his feet. He tried to regain his footing after the slip, but he had become tangled in a loose extension lead that ripped, harshly, from the wall socket, as he fell back onto a flimsy wooden table that folded down the middle. Doug flattened one half of the table as he fell – the empty half closest to him, not the other half lining the back wall. Not the half with a small stack of 'Golden Age' filmstock.

Something miraculously catastrophic happened as big Doug tripped and fell from the backside of Janet Cartwright and onto the small table of film. When the old and weathered extension lead ripped from the wall socket it sparked, as dodgy connections sometimes do, but as it spat out its little blue and white sparks, one of them caught the dangling end of an old celluloid reel on the flimsy wooden table Doug was about to fall through. That shit is flammable. So when Doug fell back through the table, the flaming reel of film was catapulted up into the air. It ignited more and more as it pierced the muggy air of the projection room, arching as it headed to the opposite wall and, coincidently, towards the window that opened out into Screening Room Three. This all happened very quickly, but, backed by a tense and hollow soundtrack from downstairs' latest score, Zimmer's slow drums and gradual build-up of strings in Gladiator, it seemed to play out in front of Janet Cartwright in a slow-motion pace of about two hundred frames per second.

Needless to say, the burning film reel guided itself out of the projector widow with pinpoint accuracy and fell into the rowdy crowd of half-cut cast and crew. It fell all the way down, gathering heat and ferocity as it cut through the air, until it eventually landed in Seat 19, Row W, and into the lap of none other than Mr Lars Mångelehünd. The heat was on. The fire in his lap was already bad enough to leave a permanent mark, but the ball of burning film didn't just land in the lap of any man or woman unfortunate enough to be sat in its fiery path. Oh no, no, no. It had landed in the lap of the multi-thumbed world champion who was wearing his grey tailor-made hybrid nylon-silk gloves, ironically as a slight precaution against any small cuts or injuries one may sustain at any given time.

Oh how he shone that night; a dream fulfilled. Lars was one great big burning star.

Not only did his silk-based gloves erupt with flame,

but because of the nylon integrated into the fabric, they began to melt, like red-hot tar. It was a graphic scene. The blaze lasted no longer than thirty seconds before the quick-thinking ushers rushed in from three different angles; one with a foam-based extinguisher, one with a water-based one, and the other with the ice cream cart they used in intermissions.

The screams echoed out through the soundproof room. Most of the audience were either clinging to the outer walls of the room or had fled entirely. Klint Buttafuoco was on the phone to the emergency services while Garrias stood silently next to him. Lars, still screaming in terrible fits of hysteria and pain, was bent over the well-stocked refreshment cart with his massive hands buried in a cage of diddy, overpriced Cornish ice cream tubs. Doug Granite, trouserless and out of puff, hurled himself through the back doors of the auditorium to reveal himself to the carnage. Janet Cartwright, still with her knickers down in the projection room, watched the entire scene unfold in front of her from the projector window, like a low-budget high-angle shot.

Before Janet could even bring herself to move, the ambulance men arrived and began their distressing removal of Lars from the cinema and into the back of their van. The final image burnt into her memory was the poor man's smoky hands held stiff above him as he was stretchered off through Row W. The night was inevitably cancelled, the cinema closed and the film put on hiatus. For all involved it was a horrible night, but for Janet Cartwright of Fatality Productions, it was really fucking dreadful.

<u>THE RELEVANT IRRELEVANCE OF IT ALL</u>

In the hellish aftermath of the film premiere, Fatality Productions suffered a rather hefty blow, both financial and reputational. Lars Månglehünd's injuries proved to be even worse than were first assumed. He had suffered not first, not second, but third-degree burns to his bizarrely talented hands, as well as a pretty upsetting emotional relapse. Consequently, Lars was unable to compete in the Thumb War World Championships that were set to occur three days after his biographical film premiered. As such, he lost out on the chance to become the back-to-back-to-back winner of his beloved trophy.

The Raggabone Picture House was closed, temporarily, after a scrutinising health and safety check had flagged up an unhealthy number of hazards in the workplace. However, during its brief closure, Doug Granite suffered a massive heart attack and sadly died. It didn't take long for the cinema to come crashing down after Doug did. The Bournemouth seafront lost a monument and British cinema lost an icon. The Månglehünd case was dismissed as accidental, not an act of God, but more an act of Doug. Although sexual interaction was deemed illegal on site, there was no evidence of what had happened in the projection room on the night of September 26th, and Janet Cartwright was cleared of any charges. Doug Granite was, of course, dead.

The film, *A Declaration of War: The Uncut Story of Lars Månglehünd*, was met with great hostility after that night. The niche the film had created was already very small, and despite the initial reviews being reasonable, the rest of the industry turned its back on Janet's story. The nasty outcome of the premiere likely reminded everyone of the subject's stupidity. Cinemas and festivals were reluctant to house the movie, too. In a brash and illogical conclusion, the movie was branded 'cursed', and after a couple of cinemas washed their hands of it, the bandwagon rolled through Tinseltown and all the crazy cinephiles jumped on board. The consensus was that the movie and its big night had been reprimanded because of the way it had been digitally induced. A ridiculous notion, but a few too many had been reading into the Y2K Bug a little too much for their own good and were just awaiting a trigger to throw up the protest signage. Nevertheless, the film flopped.

Janet Cartwright and Fatality Productions were left penniless and shamed. For the next two years Fatality Productions stayed operational with a skeleton crew of just Janet, and nobody else. Janet was getting by, freelancing for other jobs – commercials and promos mostly – and invoicing under the company name. Klint Buttafuoco returned to the stage, touring with a small experimental theatre company in which he was cast as an environmentalist turnip in a pesticide-ridden turnip patch, in a play titled 'Sweet Potato Cry'. Mr Hannelly continued his role at the British Film Institute but logged a sincere complaint over the Janet Cartwright case. Following the incident, he had an indefinite veto put on all BFI collaborations with her in the future.

Duck Off Howard

It was as Janet Cartwright sat at the back of a stuffy studio, collating the lunch vouchers for the day's shoot, that she realised something had to change. Sure, the past had been cruel and unforgiving, but she was a filmmaker, a storyteller, and so literally nothing would or could stop her from dusting down and trying again.

It was the summer of 2002. On a hot August night in the garden of a candlelit country pub, Janet sat with a half-pint of pale ale and a hard-backed notepad, plotting her cinematic comeback. The pub was busy, the garden even more so. Janet had a small round table to herself, sandwiched between two longer tables of Thursday-night drinkers. With every sip of her beer, Janet swam deeper into her mind, searching for the story that would turn her career around. She breaststroked through the expansive creative caverns of her slightly intoxicated brain and found: nothing. With the second half-pint she scanned the garden for characters, inspirational prompts that could be fabricated into a story worth telling, but all she saw were smart/casual couples and the usual rag and bone that collected outside the fire exit door by the smoking area. After drinking her third, fourth and fifth half-pints at the bar, she resumed her spot in the pub garden. She kicked off her shoes to embrace the warmth of the night and the cool of her sixth beverage. Janet forgot about the notepad and the ideas that had been kept from staining it. Her ears peeled away to join the several conversations being held nearby, and she joyously eavesdropped on the stories all around her. She smiled with the jokes, she winced with the risqué anecdotes and she nodded along with the many split opinions fired from across the tables.

About three fingers' worth of pale ale rested flat in Janet's glass. The night was almost done and Janet was bent over, beginning to slip her shoes back on, when all of a sudden, from the table directly behind her, a hushed voice began to tell a story about a man with a colourful past. It was a tale about a crook, a local villain with a story – a story that was being channelled through the woman sitting with her back to Janet. Janet's ears pricked up as she listened in on the unfolding gossip. The woman spoke about the man and his story as if he were her own husband, her voice moving up and down to match her animated hands as she relayed the information to her fellow drinkers. It turned out that the speaker's friend, who was unable to attend the night's little gathering, had been involved in a deal of sorts with an amateur bad boy. The two of them were very much a team, until she had found out who he was and what he was doing, before she made like a banana and slipped right outta there... or is it split? She made like a banana, and peeled off? All of this was unnecessary information to Janet of course, but what *was* necessary to her was the mystery man's backstory: who he was and what he had done.

Luckily enough, the tipsy woman that was sitting behind Janet and retelling the shifty fella's story was speaking just loud enough for Janet to understand fully. She was able to transcribe into her notepad with her back to the gossip. It was unbelievable. The story poured from this woman's mouth with all the eccentricities of the second draft of a half-decent screenplay. Janet was captivated. Her hand plotted uncontrollably on the page with every detail spilt from the conversation behind, her heart gathered pace with excitement. This was it, she thought, the comeback script to redeem herself, a fresh idea worth investing in. When the story finally ended, Janet took a breath. She closed her notepad and wrapped the elastic tie around it to seal in the unpatented genius. Janet finished the last of her beer, which had turned warm and flat in her absent-mindedness. She headed on out of the gate and up the road to her sweet little one-bedroom house.

That night, Janet was unable to contain her enthusiasm; she had to write this script. As soon as she arrived home from the pub, she fired up the percolator and the computer. The night's social attire was quickly traded in for a baggy t-shirt and a pair of old jogging shorts – an outfit built for comfort and one that would ease the sting of the long night ahead of her. With her favourite Sea World coffee cup, she sat down at her PC. Slightly pie-eyed, but behind designer specs, she began to type.

09:00 am. The postman's chapped hand creaked open the letterbox. Nine hours had passed through the night and the early morning since Janet had begun her mission. The letterbox smacked shut as the postman pulled his hand back, free of the letters and junk mail he had pushed through. *Smack!*

Janet woke up in a daze. She peeled her heavy head back from the keyboard she had been dribbling on, stretched and let out a big sigh. She had dozed off – only for a half hour or so – whilst thinking of a title for her screenplay. Janet tumbled out of the chair, stumbled over to the kitchen and poured herself a cup of coffee. She stared out of the small, netted window and pondered. The title needed to be short and punchy, unlike her last project. Then, without inspiration or subliminal unknowing, she had it: a working title. It came to her like a big bolt from out of the very blue, and she liked it. So Janet and her coffee cup sat back at the computer, opened the document and typed the final three words of the screenplay. There it was; a first draft. Something Janet had not seen nor completed in nearly three years. Though this time, unlike the last one, she was sincerely proud of her efforts. So sincerely proud that she called on an old friend from her sweaty salad days, with high-ish hopes that he hadn't been too scarred by the past.

The audience babbled softly from row to row. The soft-edged spotlights of the theatre swept the stage from left to right, and then right to left, to finally meet in the middle. A rectangular trick box placed centre stage had been made to look like a vegetable patch. It began to move. Klint Buttafuoco sprouted upwards from it, without applause and dressed as a turnip. Janet was sitting three rows from the front, trying her best not to be seen giggling into her bag of jellies. The play was atrocious, an experimental piece of amateur dramatics with all the entertainment value of a smelly sock. After enduring the show, Janet crept around to see Klint in his decaying dressing room, armed with a bottle of midrange shiraz and a ninety-eight-page script.

"What're you doing Janet? What do you expect me to say? You already cocked up my big screen debut and so what, that wasn't enough, you wanna embarrass me all over again, is that it?!" Klint spoke into the mirror as he wiped the purple and beige make-up from his face.

"This time's going to be different Klint, I promise, a lot different."

"Lars had third-degree burns on both of his hands Janet. He'll never be able to open a packet of crisps again, let alone go back to thumb fighting!"

"It's wrestling... Thumb wrestling."

"Well whatever it is, he ain't doing it no more." Klint's voice deepened with sincerity.

"Lars was a knobhead anyway, he was so hell-bent on

proving himself to everyone that he turned into a monster. He was always gonna get burned, it was just a matter of when. He wasn't so keen on you and yours either, as it turned out," said Janet.

Klint blew out a troubled breath and lowered his bruise-coloured cotton pad from his weary face. "I know... But it doesn't change the fact that our film died, horribly! Your name's worthless on a CV – so is mine, to be honest. Fatality Productions is laughed at throughout the industry... Garrias left me, it's all such bad news Jan..."

"I'm sorry Klint, I really am, none of it went to plan. Tell you the truth, I didn't even have a plan! Although, to be fair, Garrias left 'cos you was shagging two of the chorus carrots in your show. That has nothing to do with me... thankfully. Please, just trust me Klint, one more time. I need this. YOU need this. I mean, look at yourself man, you're dressed as a fucking root vegetable! This is worse than when I first found you."

Klint spun around in his chair to face Janet and took off his spikey green wig.

"I'll read the script," he said. "Come back tomorrow night, we can talk then."

"Oh, you can't really expect me to sit through that shit two nights in a row?!"

"Oh, I'm sorry Janet, am I putting you out?"

Janet smiled; she had missed her friend. She pulled her hair back from her face and into a bun. She kissed Klint on his purplish forehead and set the script down on the table next to him before she made her way out of the stuffy room. Klint rocked back in his chair with his hands tucked behind his heavy head and interlinked his fingers. He glanced over at the script on the table and exhaled a long, smooth breath as he read the title aloud in a soft voice:

"Duck Off Howard"

There was a knock on the door of the dressing room.

"What now?" shouted Klint, still facing the table with the script.

A voice from behind the door called to Klint: "What's long, hard and likes to be nibbled on...?"

Klint rolled his eyes before answering the question: "I don't know."

"A carrot," said the riddle setter as the door flung open to showcase the men standing behind it.

"Two carrots," added the second costumed man.

***

The metronome of Janet's heel clipping the wooden floor echoed the long walls of Captain Grubbe's hallway as she sat nervously shaking her leg, waiting in angst for her meeting with The Captain. Klint was by her side, clutching the master copy of Janet's script and every so often placing his free hand onto Janet's quaking leg to settle her down. The two of them were sitting outside The Captain's office awaiting his welcome inside. They were noiseless, but despite the nerves they both had what appeared to be a small grin drawn across their faces.

"The Captain is ready for you. Please, come inside." The voice came from a tall, slender blonde woman holding a Filofax. As she walked off another voice sounded:

"'Ello Janet."

This voice was a lot deeper and scratchier. The welcome came from behind a cloud of cigar smoke, dancing its way upwards, towards the high, white ceiling.

Janet was first drawn to his shoes – the dazzle of them. The way the waxy wooden floor complimented their rouge colouring. The tassels dangling from the front, shining and perfectly frayed. Klint found himself fixated on his braces – their perfect elasticity as they hoisted his pinstriped navy trousers up, over his belly and his big broad shoulders. The buckles, collecting the stretchy fabric just above his pectorals: one golden, the other silver. Janet and Klint both looked up. The smoke faded, and there, behind fading grey swirls, stood the illustrious Captain Grubbe. He was large in all senses of the word. A big presence with a round face. His sandy-coloured hair had grey flashes throughout. He was an intimidating figure.

The Captain showed them into his office, once they had shaken hands, and they all sat down simultaneously. The Captain's wife, without knocking, entered the room quietly with a tray of hot tea and cold custard creams. She set the tray down on the near side of The Captain's big desk and smiled, unconvincingly, at his guests.

"Janet," she tipped her large head downwards, "Janet's friend." She left the room, slamming the door obscurely loudly as she went.

"That's my darlin' wife, The Baron. She has an unattractively big head. My sincerest apologies, it, errr, never used to be that big. Help ya'self to the biscuits. Custard creams... they're the bee's bollocks, ain't they?!"

Klint leant over to secure an unbroken custard cream. Captain Grubbe looked at Janet, a genuine look of intrigue washed over his face, sealed with a smile.

"So... I understand you're makin' another movie, is that so?" Captain Grubbe knew it was so.

"Yes," replied Janet. "That is so."

"Great news! Well done for gettin' back on it Janet, that's really great news!"

"Thank you. I didn't know you were such a fan."

"I'm not, I just hear things, must be these big ears of mine..."

Klint glanced at his ears; they appeared to be of average size, though the big square-edged glasses made every feature of The Captain's look small in comparison.

"Did you know I produced a movie a little while back?" asked The Captain.

Janet lifted her eyebrows.

"That's a silly question – I assume you did, otherwise, well, otherwise you wouldn't be sat 'ere now, would ya? But I did, it was my first venture into the wondrous world you all call 'film'. All I did was write 'em a big fat cheque, a sum I was promised to see back, with a hefty return I might add, and they throw my name right there across the screen, before the movie even starts... Can you believe that? I was overjoyed. I mean, I'm a sixty-one-year-old man, my days of gettin' excited are long gone. But when I saw my name up there on that screen, bone white in big block capital letters, oh I tell ya, I felt like a kid at Christmas I did."

Janet and Klint smiled collectively, rocking their heads and making short nasal laughs to humour The Captain's story.

"An executive. Well, who doesn't like the sound of that, huh?! I didn't 'ave to lift a finger, 'cept to sign a few cheques, and I was cashin' in off other people's hard work."

"What was it called?" asked Klint.

"Capitalism, I s'pose..."

"No, the movie. What was the movie called?" Klint asked a second time.

"Oh, it was a little film called *Enema of the State*."

"*Enemy of the State*?! YOU produced *Enemy of the State*, with Lisa Bonet and Will Smith?" Klint's excited tone had lifted his bottom a few inches from his seat.

"No, enema, *Enema of the State*, with Lisa Boner and Willy Stiff… It's a porn movie, Klint. Sex. It's what I deal in, as well as some other things. But it's a seedy topic for business, y'know? Film though, film; now there's a star-spangled industry. It's like the English countryside; it's cleaner, it's better and there's more room for development."

Janet's face knotted – this wasn't an entirely true statement. Klint reached for a second custard cream. Captain Grubbe nudged the tray towards him a little, easing the stretch but picking up a tea and a biscuit for himself at the same time. Then his wide eyes met with Klint's.

"How's it been for you since the incident mate? Picked up much work?"

Klint retracted back into his seat holding his biscuit; he wanted to answer The Captain's question, but then again, he really didn't. He lifted his shoulders a bit and nodded affirmatively but without conviction.

"Terrible what 'appened last time weren't it, just terrible," said The Captain. "Nobody's fault I s'pose… Just one o' those freak accidents that swallow everyone up with it… Still, the past is the past, and looking back only hurts your neck, right?!"

Klint bit down hard into his biscuit as the room fell uncomfortably silent. The clink of Captain Grubbe's teaspoon, knocking against the flowery teacup as he stirred, rang like a bell at a boxing match. The clinks seemed to count down the seconds, until the moody calm was interrupted by a double tap of the same spoon as The Captain finished stirring his tea.

"So..." The Captain paused and sipped his tea. "Would I be right in sayin' that you're after some money to make this movie of yours?" He then snapped his fat fingers together quickly and loudly; the noise made Janet jump. "Don't answer that... I know I'm right. I'm gonna go ahead and guess that the Film Council wouldn't touch you with a barge pole nowadays, neither would the studios. So this is very much a job for the privates, the stinking rich with a big fat chequebook and a lot of free time..." The Captain slurped his tea once again. "It seems I'm your man." His lips stretched from his left ear to his right.

"Well, we all know where we stand then, don't we?" remarked Janet.

Klint Buttafuoco, biscuitless and in over his head, picked up the master copy of Janet's script from the floor beside him and flapped it forward towards The Captain. The Captain leant in and met Klint once again over the silver tray of snacks, but as he reached out to take the script from the shaky-handed actor, he stopped and reconsidered.

"I tell you what. You can keep 'old of that boy, I think you're gonna need it more than I am."

Captain Grubbe then slid back into his chair as Klint did the same, still overwhelmed by the scenario but trying not to show it.

"I ain't got the time to sit and read this through and then call you back in for another round of tea and biscuits. How 'bout you just fill me in on what this story of yours is about now, then I can either give you a nod or a shake of my head… yeah?"

Klint peeked across at Janet and then turned his look back to face The Captain.

"Sounds good to me. Janet?"

Janet, spotlighted and in the hot seat, drew in deep through her nose and out through her big, red, pursed lips. Her anxiousness and uncomfortableness seeped through her dampening T-Zone like the condensation on a steamy bathroom mirror. She was still befuddled and fearful over what was going to happen next. After all, Captain Grubbe was a powerful man. Janet cleared her throat with one squeaky cough.

"Howard Morgan is a bastard. He's a married man with two kids stashed away in a cute little country cottage…" Captain Grubbe showed no sign of interest. Janet continued nonetheless. "He has this priceless antique car, something he has inherited somehow…" Klint shuffled from his right bum cheek to his left as he watched Janet sell her story, smiling along with the plot. "There's a dodgy gambling system, sports games being the sinful catalyst, mostly. These three blokes run it out of a nightclub backroom…" Captain Grubbe's big ears pricked up as Janet's story unfolded. He brought his teacup up to his lips but forgot to sip it as he fell further into Janet Cartwright's gripping storytelling. "...but she hasn't been the only one lured in by Howard. And until he got busted, she most certainly wasn't going to be the last. He had been using them all, you see, using their names and accounts and so on, all to get ahead in the numbers game that was this little betting scheme he had going on. They were all willing at first, sure, but Howard failed to tell them the real risk in their activity. There were others higher up, and the men in charge, they knew nothing about this; it's mutiny, he's using their system to better himself!" Janet had The Captain hooked, all she had to do now was keep him there, right there, right on the edge of his silver-studded, red leather chair, as she drew her pitch to a close. "And, of course, his wife knows nothing about it, something is obviously off but she's too busy wrapped up at home with her own demons and two demonic kids. But Howard's getting out of control. He's leading himself down a blind alley. He's not just into the betting, he has other addictions and problems too, ones he owes money to. The thing that he doesn't know is that it's all part of a higher cause, you see. The men he has been cheating out of a majority sharehold in the scheme were working for somebody else. Somebody bigger and badder..."

The Captain sharply raised his hand, stopping Janet mid-sentence. "Stop."

Janet stopped. Although he was motionless, Klint also stopped. Sound muted and the world stopped.

"I don't wanna know how it ends. No spoilers."

The Captain then took a big gulp of his cooling tea, clinked cup to saucer and arose to his feet. His looming presence was more apparent now than ever – he dwarfed the desk he leant over and his shoulders seemed to span the width of the south-facing window he stood in front of. The autumn sun struck him from behind and his great big shadow painted Janet and Klint's faces half black.

"Your story seems familiar," The Captain remarked. "You sure this ain't someone I know? Howard Morgan..." He chuckled to himself for a second. "You've won me over Miss Cartwright, you really 'ave. I think any man who refused a part in this would be a tit, and I'm far from it. Congratulations Janet, you can 'ave my money, pennies 'n' all."

"Well fucking hell." Klint clapped his hands together and spurted out his overdue obscenities.

The three of them laughed. Captain Grubbe walked around to the front of his desk and shook Janet's hand as she got up from her chair. Klint held his hand out, eagerly awaiting The Captain's firm grip.

"Now as excited as I am about this collaboration, I must stress that I am still very much a novice in the industry. I'm trustin' you – and you too, Mr Buttaworth – to make this worth my while. I don't do failure and I certainly don't suffer fools gladly. As the old saying goes, 'Fool me once, shame on you. Fool me twice... and I'll hurt ya.'"

Klint's eager hand fell limp as The Captain moved across to shake it.

"But if your movie turns out to be half as good as your pitch was, then none of us should have anything to worry about, should we?"

"Not at all, Mr Grubbe," responded Janet in a sure voice.

"Captain. Captain Grubbe." He shot a stern look back at Janet. His correction pierced the thin air between them.

He eased his squeeze on Klint's hand. He reached down beside the chair and picked up the script. Slapping it down into Klint's freshly squeezed hands, The Captain joked, "You best start learnin' them lines then, eh boy?!"

He gave a friendly jab to Klint's shoulder; the fragile actor stumbled back a little. Klint's face retracted inwards and he nodded at The Captain – his nerve had finally gone. The Captain wrapped his meaty arm around Klint's other, un-punched shoulder as he walked him to the door and apologised for the brash ending of their meeting, but after all, Captain Grubbe was a busy man and there were other matters for him to tend to throughout his day.

As The Captain reached the door with Klint, still nestled in the fold of his forearm and upper arm, he paused just before he pulled on the handle to release his guests.

"Klint, d'ya mind if I just 'ave a quick word with Janet alone? It'll just be a minute. I can call Big Nut and get you some more custard creams if you want..."

Klint, who had been looking forward to leaving the office, obliged The Captain's request, though he rejected the offer of any further saturated fats. He opened the door and returned out to the seat in the hallway. The door curled shut in front of him, sealing in the two-headed beast.

Inside the office, neither Janet nor The Captain retook their seats. They were both stood, waiting for the other to speak first. The Captain pulled on his braces to loosen the gathered shirt that had crumpled beneath them. He then wiggled all ten of his chubby fingers and thumbs, before clenching his fists and then pointing to the velvety box perched on the edge of his desk.

"Cigar?" he offered her.

"Erm..." Janet hesitated.

"We can share," The Captain interrupted. "Mi casa... I forget the rest."

Janet crossed her arms and tried her best not to look directly at The Captain. Not for the first time that afternoon, Janet felt truly uncomfortable – belittled and on the back foot. The Captain turned his back to her, hunched a little to clip his cigar and lit the end. Then, just like an old-school mob boss, he straightened his back up as if it were being retracted by a magnet, took two big puffs of the cigar and blew out the smog. Janet had begun to regret her choice to stay and talk some more.

"I really do like this idea of yours Janet… It's a lot better than the one about that bloke who had five thumbs, that's for sure!"

He turned around to face Janet once again. He was met with an emotionless stare.

"It was four," Janet replied in a dull grunt.

"Well, it may as well've been six, eh, 'cos it certainly left you with both of yours stuck up your arse afterwards, didn't it?! As impressed as I am that you clambered back onto that horse, I must say I am somewhat surprised. It takes a lot less to ruin a career than that I tell ya."

Janet bit her lip tightly. "Well, things change… that was two years ago."

"So was my holiday in France, but I still remember I 'ad a shit time. Things never really change that much Janet – we like to pretend they do, but they don't. It takes a lot more than time to wipe clean that long list of fuck-ups."

The room had gathered a mist from the slow-burning cigar. Janet bit the bullet and asked what The Captain had clearly been waiting for her to ask.

"So what do you want from me, Grubbe?"

Captain Grubbe let out a noise a lot like the sound of a punctured tyre. "Only what any investor really wants… just a guarantee. A contingency plan."

Janet swallowed hard. She had no idea what The Captain was going to say next, and the longer he talked, the more uneasy she became.

"You messed up last time Jan, it's not exactly a secret,

is it? I can't be seen doin' bad business, losin' money; it's not me, it's not what I do, it really gives me the arsehole. And with my blood pressure the way it is, I can't do that." The Captain had become very handsy in his rambling. The tone in which he spoke to Janet, though reminiscent of a denigrating old cockney, was kind of compassionate too. Classic Grubbe. "I have friends in all sorts of places, high and low. I know your game, I've 'eard all about Janet Cartwright, only recently in my search I might add... Don't worry, your antics haven't rendered you infamous just yet."

Janet was sitting with her purse and her tail between her legs, quietly brewing with discomfort. She sensed an unfair ultimatum.

"Here's the rub – if this movie goes down the tubes like your last one did, then you'll be workin' off your debt with me, with me... Understand?"

Still. Silent and still as the stillest, most silent thing you can imagine. A pin dropped and a moth farted. Janet drew a short breath in and opened her mouth to speak, but The Captain again spoke first.

"It'll be dirty work Jan, and I don't mean washin' dishes. I deal in depravity. You'd be bound to me, and most probably a few bedposts..."

"But..."

"There're no buts Janet, unless they pay extra for it... These are my terms and they don't change. I'm a dirty, nasty old man and I need my investment secured, and the 'ard ways come easiest to me."

The conversation had gone the way Janet had assumed it would but far from the way she had hoped. The truth was, she was industry taboo, and her desperation perspired through her as she sat, shaky-legged, in front of the big, bad Captain.

Klint had fallen asleep out in the hallway. He had the script wedged between his arm and his torso, occasionally dribbling along on its edges, as he flitted between dreams and twitches. He woke with a crooked neck and a lick of his lips when the office door in front of him opened. His sleepy eyes adjusted to see Janet and Captain Grubbe shaking hands in the doorway. The Captain tipped his head towards Klint and winked before gliding back into his office in his shiny shoes. That was to be, for now, the last either of them saw of Captain Grubbe.

Janet walked mutely out of the hallway and through the porch. Klint followed her but was struggling to keep up with her increasing pace. Janet dashed towards the front door and threw it wide open; the sunlight exploded through the gap and hit Klint's face with a warm slap. He scurried out through the door and called to her, though it fell on deaf ears as Janet stormed across the driveway and over to her car, fumbling for the keys in the grimy depths of her handbag. Klint reached the car just as Janet pulled the keys from her bag.

"Janet... JANET!"

Janet turned to face Klint with a face full of nastiness, her crinkled lips held tight with rage, her shoulders raised so high they almost brushed her ears. The car keys pointed outwards, aimed at Klint's throat...

"If you fuck this up for me, if you dare fuck this up for me, then I swear, Klint – I swear I will finish you. There'll be no stage for you to run back to this time because I will make sure you never, ever work again." She shook like a maniac.

"I didn't fuck anything up last time Janet – you're the

one who's had me involved in all of this, twice! You're the only one who has fucked us out of work, no one else. With a past like yours, you wanna be careful what you shake on, history repeating and all that. So how about you unscrew your face, put down the keys and tell me what he said to you?"

There was a moment where Klint was unsure; was she going to go for the jugular, or was she going to snap out of it and lower the keys to her rusty blue VW Polo? Luckily it was the latter.

"It doesn't matter what he said. We got the money... so let's make a film." Janet opened her car door. "But it has to work, Klint, it has to."

After a big breath out, Klint said, "Well, all right then. Let's do this." Then he jumped onto the bonnet of Janet's car with his arms spread wide and his head held high. He turned away from Janet and bellowed theatrically; "Come one, come all and see Fatality Productions' comeback flick: Duck Off Howard. In this gritty tale, Janet Cartwright directs legendary screen actor..."

"KLINT BUTTAFUOCO GET THE FUCK OFF MY CAR!"

December

Pre-production of Janet's film, Duck Off Howard, had been smooth and successful, much to the delight and surprise of nearly everyone involved. The script had been tightened, a cast of talented names and faces had been secured and Captain Grubbe's money had been continual in its doses. Klint Buttafuoco was ready to rock; he knew the script and the character outside-in. Janet had her crew down, she had her locations permitted and she had her ideas buzzing around in her head, ready for when they could fly from behind her pretty eyes and onto the silver screen.

On Friday 13th December 2002, an expensive car was shipped in from the overtly patriotic folk across the pond for the duration of the production. It was a classic 1956 forest-green Ford Thunderbird, shining and gleaming in the winter sunshine. The Thunderbird was being given a piggyback from Plymouth to Dorchester (the county town of Dorset) where Fatality Productions had their office. The car was imperative to the story. Howard Morgan, Janet's lead man, drove a 1956 forest-green Ford Thunderbird – the likes of which were, and are, very rare in the windy West Country. Part of Howard's look, style and swagger came from the car. It was a beauty. It looked even better than it did on the page of the order catalogue. Janet was overjoyed at its prompt delivery, too, considering she had riskily ordered it to arrive the weekend before the first day of shooting. The film was going to be shot one week before Christmas, for the seasonal scenes, and then picked up again ten days after for the following six weeks – a tight seven-week schedule, most of it in the post-Christmas lull.

On the Friday afternoon the Thunderbird was delivered, Janet was out on a late lunch meeting with Chloe Trundle, the production manager for the movie. She had planned to be there for the signing of the car but the lorry carrying it had been held up in some traffic on its journey along the coast, delaying it by a couple of hours. Fatality Productions' small office was bustling with activity. The usually tranquil workplace had been transformed into a manic stock-exchange floor, though some seasonal relief was provided in the form of some tinsel that lined the workers' computer screens. All throughout the day the crew were coming in and out of the automatic doors of Fatality Productions, signing sheets and asking questions. Janet had left Klint Buttafuoco, the saviour of the screen, in charge of handling the car once it arrived. He had been made a co-producer of the movie as well as playing the lead role of Howard Morgan. Janet had granted Klint his production credit wish after he re-joined her, even after the Lars Månglehünd fiasco and the pre-production 'business'.

It was at three o'clock that the haulage lorry finally arrived with the car. As a passer-by passed by, the high-visibility-jacketed delivery driver backed carefully into the loading bay at the rear of the office unit, struggling to gauge the space between the high curb and the half-open security gate. A passing pedestrian was quickly called into action as the lorry driver, who had under-turned and was revving furiously to mount the pavement in order to correct his angle, needed help in making the gap. The pedestrian was a man named Phil, and Phil was ready to assist. The delivery driver halted his thrusts and the semi-trailer rolled back down from the curb. The driver lowered his window and Phil offered his backing-in services, free of charge. After some messy turns in and out, the two of them managed to put the vehicle straight, and while Phil wound his hand backwards, summoning the truck and making little half-steps back into the loading bay, the driver entered the space with ease. The driver rested as the lorry's hydraulics sighed and lowered him an inch or two closer to the ground. He gathered his clipboard, papers and a pen and then exited the vehicle, looking for an adult to sign his sheets. Phil had hung around to shake the man's hand and chuckle politely over his terrible driving; however as the driver walked around to the back of the trailer and opened up the heavy metal doors, Phil's eyes ignited with a forest-green hue.

Up in the office's small conference room, Klint Buttafuoco was locked in a meeting with Geoffrey Skye, another co-producer of the movie. They were disputing the catering choices for the studio week after Christmas. Their slightly raised voices, on top of the several phone conversations being held in the hub of the office next to them, had masked the volume of the lorry backing in downstairs.

The lorry driver clambered up into the back of the trailer and began loosening the ratchets and lassoes that held the car down. Phil, the spectator, was keeping him company and had begun to throw compliment after compliment about the classy car his way. The driver loosened the handbrake off the car inside his lorry and very carefully rolled it back towards the tail lift. Phil had resumed his role of overseeing the backing up process and was waving the driver back once again. The tail lift, at the touch of a button, unfolded into a ramp from the back of the lorry down to the cracked concrete floor.

The delivery driver had nearly done his job, nearly. He was pressed for time now as he was yet to make his other delivery to a dairy farm in Wiltshire and the traffic had really put him up against the clock. The tail lift had re-folded and had gone up, the rolling shutter was down. Phil waltzed around the car, peeking in at the interior through his doublehanded sunshield, which he pressed gently against the freshly wiped widows. The driver, set on completing his mission, gathered his clipboard and sheets and looked around for someone to sign on the dotted line.

<u>PHIL</u>

Phil was an honest enough man, for a while, until life tired him. In the autumn of 2001, the last of his youthfulness betrayed him and left in a suitcase, along with his wife. Phil turned thirty-nine a month after his wife left him. Forty was coming and he wasn't ready, so he started drinking... a lot. A year or so later, Phil had hit rock bottom. Jobless, loveless and soon to be homeless, he set out on Friday the 13th, determined and slightly crazed, with the intention of holding up the post office in town, the one next to the bank...

Ill, at will, with no intention to kill, Phil obtained a replica 9-mil. It was cheap, it looked funny, it cost the last of his money, but to pull off the stickup he needed this gunny.

...But the fault in the stars was simply that Phil, despite his recent downfall, was a nice guy at heart. As he walked from his house to town that day, with a painted toy gun in his pocket, his conscience had tapped away at his skull, begging him to listen. Karma (something that Phil had once read about in one of his wife's old books) had suddenly come back to pay his mind a visit. One good turn deserves another. Phil, however, had misread the famous concept the first time around and so when the notion twitched in his jittery brain for the second time, as he made his way to the post office, he paraphrased the theory entirely. Phil was holding back the nerves, but he was losing the battle between guilt and his own mind. That was, until he passed by the back of Fatality Productions' office unit, and the struggling lorry driver that was misjudging his turn in.

One good turn forgives another less good one. Phil was sure this was what Karma meant.

DECEMBER CONT'D

"I don't s'pose you know who…" the lorry driver paused and ran his finger across the title page in his clipboard, searching for the contact name, "…Janet Cartwright is, d'ya?" the lorry driver finished.

Of course Phil didn't know who Janet Cartwright was; his silence very nearly showed it.

"You do work 'ere, d'n't ya?" The driver asked his second question.

No, he didn't. He had a fake gun tucked into his pants and he was on his way to shank the Royal Mail. Though Fatality Productions had a dirty past, Phil was not exactly employee material. He couldn't hang there in silence any longer – he'd been chatting away for the last ten minutes and now the sudden hush seemed weird.

"…Yeah… I do."

"Oh, my apologies, I did write 'ere that Janet wouldn't be round to collect, got the call on the way o'er 'ere. You must be Klint, right?"

"Yeah, I am." Phil regained some confidence in his voice.

"Hellova last name you got there fella. How'd you say that: Butter-fow-koo… that right?"

"Exactly. So, where do I sign?"

The driver handed his clipboard over to Phil, who proceeded to squiggle what he thought the real Klint Buttafuoco's signature could be, and as if by voodoo, Phil was handed the keys to his new 1956 forest-green Ford

Thunderbird.

The two of them shook hands before Phil helped the driver get back out of the gates and onto the parallel street – it was the least he could do, he was still very much in his good-deed debt. After the lorry had vanished Phil was left alone, struck with amazement and with a face like a horny schoolboy. He ran at top speed back to the car and twisted the lock to open the driver-side door. Phil slinked down into the driver's seat, pulled firmly on the lever that adjusted it so that his legs fit snugly into the footwell, and started the engine. The car shuddered as the engine roared up on the first attempt. Phil removed his toy gun from his trousers and placed it into the polished glove compartment. As the engine ticked over, whirring sexily under the hood, Phil steadied his excitement and praised the Karma gods. One good turn deserves another. That's what it meant.

The handbrake slammed down. The clutch eased up. The gearstick was rattled into first and the grubby brown sole of Phil's Lonsdale trainer spanked the accelerator hard. Phil screeched out of the gates and threw the car left onto the side road; he swung left again and then right as he found the high street. Phil rushed along the road, leaving the shops either side of him trailing in a colourful concrete blur as he neared the end of the high street. The newsagents, the Indian takeaway, the butcher's, the baker's, the candle shop, were all left in Phil's dust. As he passed by the Post Office, the one next to the bank, he screamed emphatically at the very top of his voice and sped off even faster into the distance – and just like that, Phil and the car were gone.

The conference room door was pushed open in a panic; its

heaviness failed to demonstrate the urgency in which it had been shoved. Janet appeared behind it, standing with a doggy bag half full of Moroccan salad and a takeaway coffee in her grasp, pinging her eyes back and forth from Klint to Geoffrey. The two of them were still debating the catering options, among other things, and the bickering had elevated to a more personal level after Geoffrey brought up his doubts about Klint's competency as a producer. It was late afternoon and Janet was expecting to see a classic car out in the car park, waiting in the dark for her to drive home in, but to her immediate surprise and concern it was nowhere to be seen. Janet needn't have asked Klint, or Geoffrey, about the car's whereabouts, because as she set her coffee cup down on the long table they were sitting either side of, something on Klint's face seemed to say "Shit!" He jumped to his feet and began apologising repeatedly. Geoffrey started his rant first, proclaiming to Janet almost everything he had been saying to Klint over the past two hours, but Janet wasn't listening. Klint interjected and allowed himself the pleasure of pity, claiming his lapse in attention was the result of Geoffrey's petty nit-picking, but Janet wasn't listening. Then came Janet, itching and chomping at the bit like a breakthrough featuring artist on a hip-hop track, just awaiting her verse, ready to tear it up.

There was no mention of where the car was, or what had or hadn't happened, at least not for the first few minutes. Janet was chasing Klint around the table, faking sideways and getting nowhere in their slapstick routine. Geoffrey had thought himself safe from the wrath, but when Janet couldn't get to Klint she turned on the next man she could find, and suddenly there were three adults playing catch-me-if-you-can. Janet was screaming, hollering across the table as she jogged around it. Klint was petrified, ducking and bobbing away from the tiny bits of rice and red peppers Janet was launching at him from her leftovers.

"Where's the car Klint?!" Janet stopped on her fifth lap of the table, staring down her two co-producers as they huddled together on the opposite side of the table.

"I don't know Jan, I haven't heard anything all day, I swear. Ask Geoff, we've been in here all day!" Klint's voice pinched at the end of his words, his response wiggled nervously from his lips.

"Well, can one of you shit-for-brains explain to me WHY I have an email saying that a great, big, expensive forest-green FORD FUCKING THUNDERBIRD HAS ARRIVED AND IS WAITING FOR ME WITH CUNT BUTTAFUCKO IN THE LOADING BAY OUTSIDE OF MY OWN FUCKING OFFICE?!"

Klint was puzzled, but that mattered not. He called Janet's name again, this time softer, but it was once too many.

"Jan..." he said.

"Klint, I swear to you, if you don't get out there and call that delivery driver up by the time I finish my sentence, I will not let you leave this office without my ring imprinted into that big, empty head of yours... DO IT!"

Klint did as she said, with haste. He dove across the office and latched onto the cord of the reception telephone. He caught the phone and dialling pad as it slid towards him, and he punched in the number scribbled on the notepad behind the reception desk.

The confusion shrouding the missing car escalated further as Klint's phone conversation with the delivery driver confirmed the signing of the car, by none other than himself. Klint proclaimed his innocence and absence from the signing, but as confused as he was, the driver was more so. After a mostly choppy conversation, compiled of half questions and blunt, irresolute answers, the two of them finally got to the bottom of what had happened that afternoon, when Klint asked the driver to describe to him the man who signed for the Thunderbird.

"Oh God no. Oh fuck fuck fuck. You do know what this means, don't you?!" asked Klint down the line.

"I reckon your car's been nicked," answered the delivery driver.

"I do too, though I really don't want to believe it. Any idea where this guy would've gone, did you talk to him at all? Did he say anything about where he was going?"

"We 'ad a chat, but he d'ent mention where he was going, only that he had to pop to the post office, but I never thought there were anything funny 'bout 'im... You sure this bloke weren't with yer? He didn't seem the type to be robbin' up cars, he was, well... He were nice."

"Nice? FUCKING NICE?! Do you think that maybe he was being nice because you gave him a set of keys to my sixty-grand car?! And yes I'm sure he wasn't with us, because he wasn't me!" Klint dropped his head as if someone had yanked on his chin, and as he came back up he looked defeated. "Where are you now, do you think you could help me find him?"

"Not likely. I'm stuck on the A350, outside Wiltshire, there's been a big fire 'pparently, o'er in the fields. 'Alf the bloody road's shut. Besides, it's not exactly my fault is it? 'Ent my job to 'elp pick up the pieces, really."

"No, you're right. It's not as if you gave the car to the wrong person – a fucking thief – now is it? Hope the traffic's not too bad for you mate! Good luck keeping your job, you, you... SHITHOUSE!" Klint bashed the phone down into the dialling pad, several times.

He dropped his head in shame. As he brought it back up, hoping to spot the missing car from out the office window, he was instead met with Janet Cartwright's reddening face. She was puffing from her nose like an angry bull. They shared a stare for a second or two, neither blinking, then Janet parked her bum on the corner of the desk and said:

"Find my car, Klint, and I'll try to forget that you lost it in the first place. But if on Monday the car's not on my set, then you better not be either, because if you are on my set, then you'd do very well to avoid me, because I will murder you. I mean I really will kick the living shit out of you. To be honest, I'm doing well not to strangle you now, so you should go. Go, right fucking now." There was no irony, no repentance in her voice.

The entire office staff watched as Klint rose up from his chair and collected his winter coat from the rack by the door, his shoulders sagging as he flung his tartan blue scarf around his neck. He was fretting over the likelihood of recovering the missing car, and now, not only the safety of his job, but the safety of his life.

The door shut loudly with the wind as Klint left the office and headed out to search for the stolen Ford. He walked along the breezy exterior corridor of the offices and down the stairs into the car park where the Thunderbird should've been resting. He flicked the collar of his coat up to keep his scarf in place and further shield his neck from the growing chill in the sunless December evening.

#6. The Siege of Raymundo J. Oldman's Second-Hand Bike Exchange Part Two: The Sunrise

Maker and Creator of the Devil

In the run-up to Christmas, about twelve days or so,
The air down in Frome was expanding with snow.
It was cloudy but festive and most definitely nippy,
There was an iced-over puddle outside the chippy...

In the cold roamed the shoppers, all manic with cheer,
The days were receding and Christmas was near,
So the people were desperate in their seasonal dashes,
Zipping through shops in consumery flashes.

But while the winter cold was delightfully frightful,
The mood in the town was as sweet as a trifle –
Like 'The Hobb's Sherry Trifle' in the Hobb's Cake Shop window,
Layering up a diabetic crescendo.

The trifle turned heads, t'was a merry creation,
And so the eyes ogled on with a hungry elation.
Yet the layers of yum were to cause a slight muddle:
It sat next to the chippy, and the iced-over puddle...

On a wobbly bobbly street that was cobbly
Some knees in the distance knocked on rather knobbly.
A hurrying skip chased a panicky hop,
As Tanya Longtrunk made her way to her shop.

A late morning dash. A half-dressed Friday scramble.
Given the worth of the day she'd taken a gamble.
A first day in charge with a new occupation,
A very big deal and a special occasion.

She couldn't believe it, she'd set three alarms,
Even two on the watches she'd strapped to her arms!
But the deep bliss of dream had lapped over her morning,
The unconscious forewarning transitioned to yawning.

As she bolted upright and adjusted her eyes,
She saw the red on her clock and the blue of the skies.
With the time as it stood she was pushing her luck,
And with dread in her eyes she yelled out, "Oh...!"

Her old man Raymundo had passed on the business,
And the last thing she wanted was to beg for forgiveness.
Her tardiness, surely, would disrupt the anointment,
She'd be red-faced and left in her dad's disappointment.

So she marched through the streets and prayed that her dad
Had overslept too, how she hoped that he had!
He was bound to be cross but that wasn't the bother –
The worst thing would be his rethink of the offer.

She couldn't go back to her job that she'd quit –
The shop had to work out, at least for a bit,
And plus, he was right: she'd be more contented;
He'd been there and done that, this thought he resented.

To Ray it was clear, he'd gone through it already,
Rejecting the risk for a life that's more steady,
But he knew where it got him, he knew where it ended,
So this substitute route was what he'd recommended.

Tanya trusted her dad and she took his advice,
And it wasn't exactly a roll of the dice.
She'd helped out in the shop since she was about eight,
But that was back then, and right now she was late.

So now Tanya steamed on and neared her arrival,
She turned onto the street with 'The Hobb's Sherry Trifle'.
Fighting the urge, but failing to do so,
She swirled her head round and looked into the window.

Her blue eyes grew wide and her smile returned,
And for just a short moment she wasn't concerned,
And it would have been okay, it would have been nice,
If Tanya had stopped, and not slipped on the ice.

Up went her arms and crack went her back,
With a slippery dance she came down with a thwack!
Her brown studded handbag tore loose from her grip,
But her stuff all stayed in from the fix of the zip.

She twisted her ankle, in fact rather badly,
But time there was none, no time there was, sadly.
So she shook off the blues and collected her stuff,
She pulled herself up despite feeling quite rough.

A few people witnessed, but all were too busy
To help up poor Tanya who was feeling quite dizzy.
Limping in pain, she walked on half a mile,
But when she spotted her shop, she let out a smile.

The shutter was down; her dad hadn't noticed,
A success more than welcome, as he lived the closest!
She sighed a big sigh and wiped sleep from her eye,
Hobbled up to the doorway, and thus, so and thereby;

Her day started true, a chance to debut:
The Thirteenth of December 2002.
Her shop was familiar, a nostalgic reminder,
And as she opened the till up, her dad loomed behind her.

"I bought you some flowers… and a personalised torque wrench."
Tanya spun round to see her Dad by the workbench.
"That's sweet," Tanya whispered, moving in for a cuddle.
"You're limping," Ray said. "Yeah, I slipped on a puddle."

With the coffee he'd bought them, the two of them sat,
A final pep talk, an encouraging chat.
"I trust you," he murmured, concealing the tears.
He lifted his latte. "To the next 25 years!"

An emotional Tanya walked Ray to his car.
He was spending his Friday at a Bath House & Spa,
And as he drove off with a bittersweet grin
She declared the shop 'Open' as she staggered back in.

She had a quick sweep and she straightened the desk,
She fixed-up her make-up so she looked her best.
The heater was laggy, so she gave it a shunt,
She switched the radio on and put the bikes out the front.

A wreath on the door hung a little lopsided,
With holly and mistletoe draped just inside it.
There was a tree in the window in front of the bikes;
It had pinecones and ribbons and soft amber lights.

The novelty bikes had been dressed up in bows –
Some Choppers and trikes that were lined up in rows.
A garland was plaited through the posts on the stairs
With red decorations wound through it in pairs.

The shop looked inviting; it had done before,
But now it was peppered with festive décor.
In her cosy retreat for the cold Christmas shopper,
Tanya steadied her nerves, as now nothing could stop her.

So on the day ambled as an easy induction,
A silky transition without interruption.
The only faux pas was her fall in the lane;
She'd mostly recovered but her ankle was sprained.

As she sat at the workbench, fixing a tyre,
A thought struck her mind and the truth did transpire:
"So now maybe this is the job of my dreams."
But the peace in this story is not as it seems...

To be continued...

#7. Duck Off Howard: Feature

I'll be home with bells on

"Cashier number four please," a robotic voice called out through the crackly speakers of the Dorchester Post Office.

Cashier number four was barely free before Klint Buttafuoco whizzed over and spat his questions into the thin, curved microphone. "Was there a man here, about an hour and half ago? Chubby bloke, about forty, with a crew-cut hairdo and a puffer jacket?"

"This is the Post Office luv," replied the big-haired lady behind cash desk number four, "there's been a lot of chubby forty-year-olds with crew-cut hairdos and puffer jackets."

Klint shook his head. "He would've been angry, probably, nigh on threatening..."

"Again, this is the Post Office. You're gonna have to be more specific than that."

Klint assumed that his identity thief had not visited the Post Office as he had intended to. A man hell bent on stealing a car would've surely been a memorable character to serve in a slow-moving Post Office queue. Klint's face turned with frustration.

"You wanna cheer up luv, it might never happen!" the cashier said to Klint. He snarled back.

"Too late, 'luv', because it has already happened."

"You know it's Christmas next week, don't ya? You'll never make his nice list with a face like that!" The lady grinned at her own insult.

Klint was not impressed, but he was fresh out of words to come back at her with and so he took his leave. He walked unsurely past the rest of the busy cashiers and the last-minute parcel senders that clogged the narrow walkway; all of them anxiously weighing their snazzy wrapped gifts. He counted his heavy, sombre steps, brushing past the cheery customers: one, two, three and…

"Cashier number four please."

Klint exited the Post Office to the same monotone robotic voice, ignorant as to where he could go next.

The twinkle of the high-street Christmas decorations mapped the town like an airport runway. The shop windows, mostly filled with glowing trees and yellowish fairy lights, were reflected in the shine of the cars that drove slowly past them. Their engines were rickety and struggling to get warm, but jolly, as festive tunes played unashamedly loudly through their radios. Klint walked past them all, oblivious to their charm as he scanned every road, side road and alley, desperately looking for the missing car.

The steady chant of a church choir echoed around the gentle bend of the high street, getting louder and louder with every hesitant step Klint took. His path was drawing him towards the police station, at first unintentionally, but as his brain churned uncontrollably in his head seeking a solution to his problem, he settled on the law. The choir gained traction in Klint's movements, the eerie gospel chants playing as a soundtrack to his journey, gripping the soles of his shoes and tugging him along the frosty pavement closer and closer to them. The police station was just behind and to the left of the church. The two dishonoured and fractured institutions had both been placed strategically at the beginning of the high street, like

Old Kent Road and Whitechapel with a hotel on each, just waiting for you to pass go and pay for your sins.

'Once upon a Christmas' – that was the hymn the choir was singing. It was a track taken from the 1984 Kenny Rogers and Dolly Parton TV special of the same name. The hymn was haunting; the a cappella tune sprung loose from the church, rendering the close-by pedestrians soundless, Klint included. He was yet to notice the choir's efforts, still searching the streets, knowing that his efforts were surely in vain. Though, it was Christmas after all, and a miracle could happen.

Whilst busy in his search, glancing across the road and down into a small side street where the baker's deliveries were made, Klint accidentally bumped into a Christmas shopper. She had two small bags from the jewellers in her hands and a hot chocolate smear across her top lip. Neither Klint nor the shopper were looking where they were going, though it was mostly Klint's fault, but before he could apologise and offer the cocoa-moustachioed lady a tissue, he saw it. As he turned to the woman, there – parallel parked outside the entrance to Fronnigans Hotel on Bleach Street – was the 1956 forest-green Ford Thunderbird, gleaming under the light of the hotel Christmas tree out in the driveway. Three Hosannas sang out from the church choir, each lifting an octave higher than the last and holding high and tight on the final one. Why was it there? Who would steal a car from an office block around the corner only to drive it as far as the high street? A dozen and a half questions and rapid responses fired into Klint's bedazzled mind. His eyes lit, they near enough popped from out of his face. He was rigid but ready to pounce. He brushed the lady aside and walked oh-so-cautiously over to the car, trying his best to look uninterested.

It was the right car for sure. Klint had seen the photos of the Thunderbird coming over from the States, and as he circled it, he was positive that they were a match. Suddenly, Klint became aware that the thief must've been inside the hotel – maybe he was robbing that too – but he was most probably keeping a close watch on the car he had just jacked. The car thief was surely dangerous, and now Klint had put himself in a less-than-safe scenario. The street was quiet. It was a tiny road that feathered off the high street. Next to no one came down it unless they were staying at the hotel or visiting its fancy-pants cafeteria. Klint shot back against the hotel wall and pulled his mobile phone from his jacket pocket. He hit speed dial 2 for Janet Cartwright and impatiently awaited her answer.

"What?" Janet answered the call.

"Janet, it's me, it's Klint. I found the car, I've really found it, it's outside Fronnigans, I'm there now!"

"What? Are you sure it's ours? Why's it there?" Janet's temper eased off a little.

"Yes, definitely! How many classic Ford Thunderbirds do you know that are knocking about around Dorchester?!"

"Don't get wise Klint, you're still in no position to. And what the fuck are you doing on the phone to me about it? Just get it back here!"

"Well, that's the thing... How am I supposed to do that?"

"I don't know, do I?! How did you even lose it in the first place? Consider it a role of being a producer – it's called problem solving. Just hurry up and get the car back!"

Janet hung up the call. Klint, the spy, was alone. He thought over quickly what to do with the car he had no keys to, but the answer never came. Klint then remembered where he had been on his way to before he unexpectedly spotted the car outside the hotel. The police, of course! The car was there with him and there was nowhere to run to; the station was less than a five-minute walk away. Klint flipped the screen of his mobile phone up to reveal the tiny dialling pad once more, although he was unable to tap the nine, nine and nine because right then a woman galloped out of the hotel entrance and over to the Thunderbird, flashing her keys as she did so.

She was about to get into the car – the key was aimed at the lock and she was going to open the door. Klint had to move, faster than he had been planning to. He was dumbstruck over who this lady was and what she was doing with the car. As far as he knew, the car had been pinched by a podgy guy with a naff haircut. That, however, was beside the point, because she was about to nab the car from under Klint's nose for the second time. He swept over to her, displaying a move caught somewhere between a fast walk and a slow jog, and complimented the car.

"That's a fantastic set of wheels you have there, miss."

"Oh, well… ta. Not much compared to the car that's on top o' them though, are they?"

What next? What could he say to stall the lady and steal back the car from right in front of her? They both looked as concerned as each other, clearly mistrusting the other's intensions.

"Whose is it?" Klint blurted out, implying that the car clearly wasn't hers to be driving.

"Eh?" responded the woman.

"Whose car is it?" Klint repeated his question but added the word 'car' into it this time.

"What d'ya mean whose car is it, it's obviously mine ent it?!"

"But whose is it really, who did you take it from? I know it's not yours, so just tell me."

The woman eased her key from the door; her shoulders crept up in the heat of the conversation.

"This car was my dad's and then when he died, he gave it to me. So it's mine, understand? Not me husband's, not any of his filthy little friends', mine. And who're you anyway, where'd you come from? How'd you know I'd be 'ere?" The woman folded her arms, the anger in her voice contrasting with the quaking of her foot on the ground. "You 'ent one of them bastards from this mornin', you're too soft lookin'. They 'ere are they? Hidin' 'round the corner, waitin' to snatch me up, s'that it?"

Klint, despite becoming more and more perplexed by the situation, was duty-bound to retrieve the car. He abruptly swooped in to swipe the car keys from her. His head throbbed with an ache of the day, and he couldn't bring himself to shout.

"Gimme the keys! This is not your car," he spoke softly as he lunged.

The woman dodged his outstretched arm and threw her arm at him, keys out turned and aimed at Klint's collarbone. Klint caught her hand before the jagged edge of the key pierced his skin through his woollen jumper. Klint twisted the hand, and the arm attached to it, and shoved the woman down into the long bonnet of the car. *Donk*. A head hit the shiny metal frame and suddenly the struggle was over. A limp, unconscious woman was Klint's prize for the evening. He pulled her back up, twice as heavy in his cold trembling hands.

This really was above Klint's paygrade. He was again at the mercy of the film industry's dirty underbelly. Subjected to a vile, corrupt and baneful executive, a director and producer whose main talent was dropping her skirt and raising an eyebrow, a movie almost in ruins, an unconscious woman and a stolen car. Captain Grubbe had been so wrong, THIS was the film industry exemplified. Welcome to Hollywood Klint Buttafuoco, you're gonna love it kid.

The weighty body flopped backwards in Klint's arms, not dead, just KO'd. The quiet street was still quiet. Nobody had seen the scuffle outside the hotel and Klint was keen to keep it that way. He rested the woman down onto the floor beside the car and checked for any onlookers, but still there were none. The only thing he could do was remove the keys from the lady's flaccid fingertips. They jingled merrily as they passed from one cold hand to another. Klint's face was sturdy but his lip was beginning to tremble. He dropped the lifeless arm back down to the floor and opened the car door.

The Thunderbird fired up. The exhaust kicked out a rush of smoke into the crisp winter air and the car growled low, waiting to be driven off, but Klint just couldn't do it. He could see the woman in his wing mirror, bundled on the cold hard ground, and he couldn't bring himself to just drive off and leave her there for the foxes to find.

With the engine still rumbling, Klint swung the door back open. The whoosh of air as the door opened blew the lady's hair from her face to reveal a bloody great bruise on her forehead. Klint pulled her up onto his shoulder and walked her around to the boot of the car, where he decided to store her. Balancing the dead weight on his shoulder he popped the boot with his free hand, carefully placing her into the car's trunk and then gently lowering the door back down to seal her into the carpeted tomb. Klint ruffled his hair vigorously; he couldn't believe what had become of the day. He was just about ready to implode, explode and burst a few lymph nodes, but instead he drew in a deep and cold breath and then re-entered the car.

By the time Klint arrived back at Fatality Productions' office, Janet was already stood waiting outside in the parking bays, shivering and chain smoking the evening away. The headlights of the lost and found car browsed past Janet's emotionless face as Klint turned into the designated parking spot. He was apprehensive and not overjoyed at finding the car. Perhaps it would've just been better if the car was gone and Klint had run away. The keys jingled once more as Klint turned them sideways and killed the engine. The car park was dark and so he left the lights on, allowing Janet to navigate her way over to him. She mooched around the car in slow circles, running her finger along the frosty paintwork, leaving an unbroken trail as she went. Klint sat terrified in the driver's seat, praying that she would soon say something to break the chilling dead air and finish the day. Janet just kept on walking around him, inspecting the vehicle and toying with him like a bear playing with its prey. She peered into the back of the car through the passenger side window she stopped at – her expression was still unchanged, but she held a good look for a minute before walking on again. The shine from the headlights bounced back off the creamy-coloured wall in front and left the car illuminated in a soft, yellowish glow, enough to reveal its contents, including Klint, to Janet as she peeked through the windows. The tension was too hard to bear – it was an uncomfortable end to an uncomfortable ordeal. Klint was too far gone, he had to say something to her, and so he jumped out of the car and declared:

“Janet there’s an unconscious woman in the boot. I pushed her into the car, by her head, and now she’s not moving.”

“Well...” Janet began. “Of course there is. Why wouldn’t there be, that sounds about right.”

Janet put out her cigarette and laughed to herself. She took another from her twenty-pack. Sparking it up, she dragged a huge lungful of smoky air in through her mouth.

“We’re going to Grubbe’s. Tonight.” She exhaled through her nose a long waterfall of grey fog. “This car is being kept in the safest place I know until Monday morning, when you’re going to go and pick it up from The Captain’s house before the shoot.”

Janet walked around to Klint and took the keys from him. She shimmied back to the rear end of the car and opened the boot, and sure enough, there, curled up and sparko inside of it, was a lady.

“Oh Klint, what have you done now? This ain’t good. Is she dead?

“No, she’s not dead. She stole our car Jan, I had to get it back. I didn’t mean to hurt her... Just got a bit carried away, that’s all.” Klint’s vulnerability seeped out through his voice.

“Well... I don’t know.” Janet paused momentarily. “Let’s just get to Grubbe’s – I’m sure that dirty dick is used to handling these sorts of situations, he’ll know what to do.”

And so Janet Cartwright and Klint Buttafuoco,

tarnished and torn from the inside out, crawled back into the 1956 forest-green Ford Thunderbird. They sat muted, headed for Captain Grubbe's big house in the country, weary and overly presumptuous of a change in their luck.

#8. José Romario Cobos de la Bell

Latino Heat

It was a Friday, an extraordinarily glorious Friday given the wintery season it had fallen in. But as fine as Friday was, this wasn't 17 Cherry Tree Lane. The only thing etched on the pre-park pavement was the semi-dried remains of Thursday night's kebab-coated chunder, and nobody felt the need to jump feet first into that. Not even the affable tramp Cardboard Keith, and he was renowned for falling legless into all sorts of things!

The park that Keith occupied was a hot spot for half-hearted mini-breakers. The kind of people who refused the excursion pamphlets in their B&B's foyer and so found themselves sprawled out and full of finger sandwiches on a picnic blanket in the closest park available to them. However, aside from cheap tourism, the park did play host to the most splendid Indoor Outdoor Bath House™ the West Country had ever seen, and so the turnstiles would turn stylishly all year round at the hands of several Speedoed front-crawlers and their locker-room change.

The Indoor Outdoor Bath House™ was a middle-class institution. It was sculpted meticulously to perfection in the 1970s and had housed many pruning punters from day one, when a certain Mr. José Romario Cobos Senior cut the ribbon and introduced his posey paradise to the world.

BRIEF BACKSTORY

José Romario Cobos Sr. came from a wealthy background of Spaniards; real classy folk but tightly wound with naughty little Spanish secrets. Sometime in his early thirties Mr José Sr. had found himself in a bit of hot water, whilst bathing in a bit of hot water at the bath house near to his residence in the Catalonian Mountains. José Sr. had been caught doing the dirtiest of dirties with renowned socialite Helena Bandero. This was a feat that should've been welcomed with applause by his peers, given her status and cup size, though unfortunately for José Sr. he was caught by a herd of Spanish ramblers in a less than flattering position between two olive trees. It also just so happened that Helena's status was trophy wife to the very powerful and well-respected Spanish diplomat, Paco Bandero. Her impressive cup size was a result of his large disposable income.

Papa José was in deep with the Spanish VIPs. He had cut his fair share of heavy-handed deals in the private sector, but when the public sector came knocking, the olive trees were rocking.

When word got out about Helena and José Senior's fling, the Cobos name was shamed. Deals ran dry and it became increasingly risky for the Cobos clan to dwell in the plush surroundings of beautiful Catalonia. A lot of angry men came looking for many pesos and a slice of justice for their diplomatic brother, most of whom had their tongues so far up the bumhole of society they were pretty much fellating Paco's chorizo-coated colon. So, one day, just as José Romario Cobos Sr. squatted peacefully into his bath, a half-dozen bad blokes came trouncing distastefully into his bath and sauna room in his mountain home. They pried him from his bubbles and slapped him down, bare-arsed, onto a very hot, very wooden sauna bench. The men were business acquaintances of José, old work buddies that had been wounded by his sudden demise and had felt the sting of his back-hander to Spanish diplomacy.

They explained to José Sr. that everything was not hunky-dory. They could take the loss for now, but worse things were coming his way. He was soon to be the severed head of a failing, corrupted empire, and that did not bode well with the recent news. José Sr. lived an easy life in the shadow of his honourable father, but after his sudden death he was left reeling as he became the heir to a business for which he had no acumen. So José Sr. did what he could but turned to unlawful trading and illegal money moving in order to keep afloat and preserve his father's legacy. This worked for him until his betrayal of an ally. He had really put his foot in it and there was no going back.

After an intimidating yet compelling little chat, along with some watered-down scare tactics, they gave José the option of staying in Spain and being very poor, very vulnerable and very alone, or leaving his beloved Mediterranean and maybe, just maybe, using the little initiative and charisma he had inherited from his papa to start anew someplace else. José Sr. never did get to finish his bath. He left sunny Spain and headed for a much cooler climate: the South West of ol' Blighty. He packed up quickly and came over with nothing but one hundred grand in his sky rocket, four tailored suits, a face full of charm... and his two-year-old son, José Junior.

José Sr. was a single parent. His ex-wife was a drinker and after a drunken public meltdown she was deemed too dangerous to care for her child, and so little José was handed over to his father, to raise alone. In the year that José Sr. had his son to himself the two of them grew inseparable. He was madly in love with his baby boy and even though his bad decision making had landed them both in it, there was no way he was handing him back over to somebody else. So, there were two of them escaping Spain, José^2.

After a painstaking few weeks of pondering and plotting in the park, José Sr. had his eureka moment. He had been out of the bath this time, though his eureka moment was about a bath. A bath house. A modern-day British bath house, in Bath. An Indoor Outdoor Bath House™ that had all the pizazz of his darling Catalonia, only without the heat to match it; but that's exactly where the bath house would get its mojo. José Sr. was to case his bath house in a lavish see-through shell to let in all the light that the South West had to offer. Which wasn't actually that much, but the facilities were heated and regulated from the inside (almost like a greenhouse for the wet and wealthy).

Contrary to his silver-spoon privilege and fortune, José Sr. immersed himself completely in his innovative project. He spent many days and many nights perfecting his designs and ideas, until eventually, he hit the pub. José Sr. was fully aware of the ramifications of the bad business he'd drummed up back home and he knew that any worthwhile money lender would laugh off his request of a loan. So instead, he sought out a funny-faced fella down the pub who put him onto a naughty geezer, who in turn put him onto an even naughtier geezer they all called Dorsal Finney. Dorsal Finney, the Irish moneyman, a shark in a sheepskin coat. Dorsal Finney took José's one hundred thousand and miraculously turned it into five hundred, but it came at a price. Dorsal was not a generous man, neither was he one for supporting projects in the community. He was a Great

White Shark, and José Sr. was making snap decisions once again.

Along with the half-a-million, Dorsal gave José Sr. some unreasonable deadlines for the payback; but as luck would have it, something very queer happened on Dorsal's first site visit to the bath house. As he walked onto the construction site, through the back gateway next to the cement mixer, just on top of where the baths were to be placed, he slipped in the most fantastic fashion on a rogue porcelain panel and hit his head, hard, on the side of a half-filled skip. Unconscious and bloodied up, Dorsal Finney fell backwards into the hollowed-out pool and never came back up.

Construction stopped. The site was tense. The foreman farted and it drew out like a final note of a jazz trumpet solo. But as José Sr. stood, messiah-like atop his bathing hole looking down at his lifeless financier, it occurred to him that nobody law-abidingly troublesome – and hopefully nobody at all – would come looking for Dorsal any time soon. There was no paper trail other than his ledger that led to José Sr. There wasn't a feud between them or anyone else that would trigger suspicions. As far as he knew and could work out, Dorsal wasn't an upstanding citizen who paid his taxes and put savings into a pension fund. By the looks of his teeth, it was uncertain whether or not he had ever even been to see the dentist. It was almost as if he were invisible. He was a shark, with very few ties and a big fat ledger full of illegals, and it just so happened that that ledger was tucked into the back of his jeans as he lay face down in the dirt. José Sr. quickly did the maths. It was a risky move, a criminal move, a really fucking stupid move, but seeing as though the reason he was in this situation was because of a risky, criminal and stupid move, he thought to himself, *fuck it*.

As José Sr.'s workforce semi-circled around him and the pool pit, he turned to address them and the unlikely state of affairs they were all now very much a part of. He pointed out that Mr Finney's preventable death would not only close down the site, the construction company and the bath house project, but also that, because of the fact that a now dirtied-up Dorsal was the moneyman behind the venture, they were all a little bit guilty of some kind of monetary fraud. Obviously, this wasn't actually the case for the builders. But they were, how do you say… a few petals short of a potpourri dish. A few squares short of a tartan scarf. A couple of shakes short of a sticky hand… They were as thick as two short planks, and right now José was holding a bloody big saw. He convinced them all that it was in their best interest to bury the body, cement it over and have him encased in a greyed shell under the site forever more. He promised them all a little drink for keeping it quiet, and since technically he didn't owe any money to anyone anymore, he was now in a far better position to do this.

So construction resumed and carried on well past regulation working hours into the hazy summer nights. José Sr. had clambered down into the pit and retrieved the black book from Dorsal's waistline, just before the dumper truck laid a big fat tonne of earth on top of his dead body. Around nine o' clock the morning after the accident, José Sr. took a short walk over to Dorsal's place just outside of town, down a shabby little side street roped off from the outside world by a droopy metal chain pinned to the two adjacent walls. He had left José Jr. at home with the nanny, as he did most days since construction had started, while he snuck into Mr Finney's remarkably well-kept bedsit. José Sr. had found the address on a letter that was tucked into the back flap of the ledger, a letter that was sent to Dorsal by someone called Colonel Mann. He didn't bother reading the letter, but he did find that it also contained £500 in £50 notes, a stupidly careless amount to send via post. Once inside the empty home, he rummaged a bit and then left the little black book teetering on the arm of the three-seater sofa (a sofa that was far too big for the modest-sized flat), and then he left.

Everything seemed to be going unnaturally well (albeit chaotically so) for José Sr. and his bath house, although he was wrong about one thing... someone did come looking for Dorsal Finney. Colonel Mann, the Mann from the ledger letter. He was Dorsal's powerful friend and a real big bastard. He came knocking on Dorsal's door a couple of weeks after his sudden disappearance. The Colonel was thickset, bald and olive skinned. He was cleanshaven and had three piercings on his left ear. He had the appearance of being ex-military, and that's because he was, before he was dismissed for being mentally unfit. Colonel Mann was now one of the heads in a mob of villains that controlled a lot of dodgy West Country money, and Dorsal Finney was one of the mob's sharks. Every week or so the Colonel planned to pop over for a cup of tea and a catch-up on where his money was; but, surprise surprise, the unexpected hit him between his cold, dark eyes. A bare flat... A flat that José Sr. had cleared out on his brief visit two days before. José Sr., the clever dick, had emptied the place to make it look as though Dorsal had done a runner. The only noticeable thing still left in Dorsal Finney's vacant home was a shiny black journal, still balancing impressively on the arm of the settee. Colonel Mann edged towards it. He had a look on his face that was a lot like the one you pull when you catch a smell of something nasty and you're not quite sure if it's you or not, but the only foul odour here was one born of treachery.

The Colonel was puzzled. He snagged the book from the sofa and opened it up to the page separated from the rest by a leathery tassel. The page read like a party guestlist of rottenness: names and numbers scribbled down and crossed through, workings to the right and left of them, mini sums and such to fill the spaces. It sort of looked as though John Nash had taken acid and ran out of window space... But right at the very bottom of the page was the name José Romario Cobos Sr. and the numbers '£500,000', and the word 'CLEARED' next to the crossed-through name. The Spaniard had cleared his own debt from the black book, but more amusingly than that, he had written the name 'Colonel Mann' and '£500,000', next to it.

FRIDAY 2002

The air on this particular Friday, as refreshingly unseasonal as it was, was thick with metaphorical grease. The atmosphere around South-West England was basted in the stuff, just as the set-menu'ed turkey was in the Frog and Fan pub, which funnily enough is where we meet José Romario Cobos de la Bell, the wavy-haired, clean-cut son of a Spaniard. José was reclined in the cosiest of pub armchairs. He had his arms creased to match his suit and his legs were agape, forming a suggestive and inappropriate 'V' shape, which not only tested the stitching of his trousers but also distracted the waitress from noticing that he'd not left enough change to cover his breakfast and coffee combo.

José was a good guy. His alluringly green eyes and the gentle curve of his smile confirmed this. The bill situation at the Frog and Fan wasn't a character reflection but a sure sign that he had other things on his mind. The misogynistic angling of his legs, as it turned out, was due to his place in the pub being in front of the wood burner and he had developed quite the sweat between his thighs, and so he was 'fanning the frogs', so to speak.

José had journeyed to the pub to meet with a girl, someone whom he had met at the mulled wine stand at the Somerton annual Christmas market the weekend before. But she was a no-show. The mulled wine mistress had stood him up. As unbelievable as it sounds, this failure in companionship had become a little too regular and all too apparent for José. I mean, given his Spanish heritage, his father's massive inheritance and his gentlemanly ways, you'd think he'd be torn apart like a contraband Crunchie six weeks into fat camp. Alas, he was hopelessly single.

José soon forgot about the lady and went about his business as usual, and on the plus side he had an extra twenty quid in his pocket as he only had to pay for one breakfast. Not that it mattered to him that much; José was loaded, but he was a humble man and a man that spent his cash in a less-than-frivolous manner.

It was the final Friday before José shut down the Indoor Outdoor Bath House™ for the holidays and so he had some affairs to sort before he jetted off to somewhere really fucking cold to see in (and ski in) the New Year. José was hosting a small Christmas do at the bath house and so he had gone shopping for some festive bits and bobs to makeover his father's watery palace. Scribbled on Señor Bell's wintery list of goodies was:

- Hot chocolate
- Mince pies
- Sausage rolls
- Polvorones (almond cookies)
- Mantecados (crumble cakes)
- Cardenal Mendoza brandy (Cardenal Mendoza brandy)
- Horny leaves (mistletoe)
- Tinsel (?)

On top of all that, José had to do the banking, get his hair cut, pretend he wasn't upset about being stood up and then get back to the bath house to set up the party.

He got the goods, and got his barnet chopped. He sorted his money, he got a little sad when he remembered being stood up, but as he made his way back to the park around midday his humdrum expression dropped when he caught Cardboard Keith's eye. José edged over to him for a chat, squinting in the frosty sunshine gushing through the trees. Cardboard Keith smirked back at him with a look that seemed to display all the booze he'd consumed over his many years.

Cardboard Keith was named after his structurally unsound, creative yet soggy, albeit cosy cardboard home. He occupied the spot just to the left of the park gates, under the cover of a gloriously grand silver birch tree. He wasn't the scruffiest of vagabonds – he managed to keep his beard well-kept and his hair flake-free – but he was an old drunk and he was a smelly one at that. Keith's spot was adjacent to Eli, the park's security guard, and his underwhelming security booth. Eli was a chubby man to say the very least. His love for cinnamon swirls was as thick as his coronary arteries and as deep as his crumb-filled belly button; he had a popped popper-button on his worn-out security shirt which allowed the debris of said cinnamon swirls to gather in his navel. Eli did not like Keith, but Keith did not like Eli either. There was a time when the two of them were more accommodating to one another, but years of drunken slurs, runaway pennies and the smell of secret-recipe chicken grated against years of useless antiperspirant, trouser hoisting and the smell of second-hand cinnamon, and this caused a sort of stalemate between two stale mates.

As José neared Cardboard Keith, his smile was becoming more apparent, as was the Zinger Tower meal in the bag in his left hand. José cared for Keith's misfortune with frequent chats and takeaway chicken dinners. There was something in Keith that José found humbling. He always took the time out from the days when Keith sat cross-legged outside the park to shimmy over and make him feel like more than just a stagnant gatepost. Eli, watching with mixed emotions, soon perked up when José winked and flashed the bakery bag in his right hand towards the booth.

José handed the chicken to Cardboard Keith, wafted his double-vented suit tails away from his bottom and then sat himself down next to his half-cut homie.

"It's not like you to be here on a Friday CK. What happened?" José enquired as he pulled his knees up to his lapels.

"You're a good'n Mario, y'know that. Not like that fat prick o'er there! Shelter was busy; some charity Christmas dinner crap they're puttin' on. Nice day ent it? Beats sittin' in a sweaty room full'a old drunks talkin' shit. I just 'ad me turkey and left," slurred Keith, with a mouthful of KFC.

José closed one eye to shield it from the glare of the sun and turned his head towards Keith. His look moved from Keith and his greasy snack to the crate of St. Austell's Jolly Holly Ale.

"You know, for a down-and-out you don't half drink well. That stuff's expensive."

"They're givin' it out wi' dinner at the shelter. Letting us 'av 'alf a fuckin' pint each... 'alf a pint with a three-inch 'ead! Merry soddin' Christmas to 'em too! I took it, from out the back. Took it all." Cardboard Keith cackled at his own antics before swigging from his bottle.

The two of them continued to chat about anything that Keith could make sense of, and then when José ran out of things to say, he stood up and took his sugary sweet bag of treats across to Eli.

Eli emerged comically from his cabin window like a portly meerkat working at a drive-through. He took the bag of cinnamon swirls from José. He gave him a soft pat on his shoulder and then a loving nod before he retreated back into his booth to watch over his knackered CCTV monitors.

Time was getting on, and time had not been on José's side that day. He left his unconventional friends to their nibbles and made a quick dash for the bath house to continue his Friday. He power-walked gallantly along the twig-coated pathway with his limber hips flinging from side to side under the shade of the covering trees. He swung a satnav-like left turn into the camellia show gardens and took the trail through the pretty flowers until he reached the wee brook and the ivy-clad bridge that hung over it.

José's bath house sat just behind the brook, through a

veil of willow branches that hung like icy tentacles over the slippery bridge. The Indoor Outdoor Bath House™ shone like a middle-class mirage. It was a spectacle; a rose among the roses. It resembled the Palacio de Cristal in Madrid's Parque del Retiro, which is a clear sign of where José Sr. sought architectural inspiration. For those home-grown visualisers, think Kew Gardens' Palm House but with more glamour. A certain, intangible *je ne sais quoi*, but Spanish.

Busyness shrouded the bath house on this day. The regulars knew this was the last day they could get a swim and a soak in before the New Year, and they all flocked to get a piece of Señor Bell's Christmassy spread too. José entered the bath house through the side door into the stock room, which was severely understocked. He side-shuffled his way through the maze of half-empty boxes and into the kitchen, where he set down his things. It wasn't long before Ren, José's fair-haired right-hand man, crept in to lend a hand.

Ren's titling as José's 'right-hand man' was one of great irony. A couple of years back, Ren had lost his left hand at the festival of La Tomatina in Buñol, a town just west of Valencia, Spain. The chaos arose after Ren had been overjoyed at being the victor of the Palo Jabón, the traditionally greasy pole that crowds of eager festivalgoers clamber up to retrieve the big ham sat at the buttery top. As he made his way triumphantly back down the greased-up wooden pole with his prized ham in his hands, his success was betrayed by a small pile of smuggled-in, unregulated tomatoes underfoot. The ham flew high as Ren slipped on the red fruit below him. He landed awkwardly on his tomato-splattered hand, and, as if by cosmic accuracy, Ren's victory meat came hurtling back down into the street at speed and squashed his already butchered left hand. Another silly, ham-fisted attempt at the Palo Jabón that rendered poor Ren ironically ham-fisted. The damage was too severe to fix; he lost the hand to the festival. So, Ren was quite literally a right-hand man, but he was José's, and José's only.

***

As Ren hunted for some sturdy trestle tables to accommodate the festive yummies, José put up the rest of the Christmas decorations. He lugged the big beauty out of his office and set it down in the reception area. He stepped back and dusted off his needle-covered hands, then he put them on his hips and grinned, childlike.

Kiki, the young, friendly-faced receptionist, joined José in a smile and all at once a surge of Christmas cheer seemed to fill the bath house, lifting heads and spirits. It wasn't enough, however, to lift Old Man Ray (one of the pool's regular customers) from the pool downstairs as the portable pool hoist malfunctioned and poor old Ray came crashing back down into the deep end. As Old Man Ray floundered with unease, he thumped another swimmer, an elderly lady who had been breast-stroking, in the side of the head with his flailing limbs. The pool hoist then arose from the water once more, this time hooking Ray's swimming shorts on the way up and thus leaving him suspended about three feet above the water. Ray was swivelling on display for a now unsmiling José, who had seen the whole incident unfold through the grand bay windows of the reception overlooking the pool.

José quickly made a dash for the pool, but as he bolted for the stairwell, the light string cables from the tree wrapped around his shoes and he tumbled to the floor. The big tree came crashing down towards him, the star atop narrowly missing his crotch but grazing his trousers as it fell to the floor. Still in a panic, José quickly straightened himself out and then untangled the cables from his feet. The slight pull in his trousers evolved into a tear as he lunged towards the stairwell once again. He scurried down the stairs, through the male changing rooms, and then he reached the poolside, where he found his on-duty lifeguard Dec, Old Man Ray and the other injured veteran circled together and chuckling at the drama that had just passed. José let out a sigh. He stepped over to console the group and after another sigh, he slumped down beside them in a damp squat.

STAN GETZ IT

Calm had returned to the bath house swimming pool area. José and the near-death squad were sitting poolside, dangling their tootsies into the pool and chin-wagging, whilst Ren was working across the pool, wrestling with the legs of one of the trestle tables he'd found in the storage cupboard. José had, for now at least, forgotten about his decorative duties, but Ren was powering on through with the setting up of his makeshift bar. He was pulling in resources from the kitchen as well as José's morning shopping trip to really fill out his table with tipples and tasters. The fact that Ren had only the one hand made the arranging of tables a lot more challenging than it should have been. He was moving slowly, machine-like, but with a very human concentration. Ren soldiered on regardless, and by the time José had risen and made his way back around the sun loungers, wishing his customers a very merry Christmas, Ren's rockin' bar was set and ready to go.

After being locked in a few less than engaging conversations with the more senior customers, José was finally able to join Ren, and now Dec, at the boozy trestle table for a glass of Cardenal Mendoza and a slice of Spanish Crumble Cake. For a short while the three of them had the spot to themselves. They ate, drank and were merry in each other's eclectic company, along with the steadily decreasing decanter of brandy. Eventually, others joined them at the bar. Yvonne, the bath house chef who had just shut down her kitchen for the lunchtime service and for the Christmas break, backed her way into the pool area from the kitchen with a big tray of sausage rolls. The scent followed her mazy path around the pool and sun loungers and hung in the air behind her. As Yvonne approached the bar and filtered through the crowd, the stragglers followed suit and José's minibar was the toast of the tarn.*

They were only about half an hour into the festivities when the provisions ran low and Ren was sent out on a resupply mission. The polite small talk had now given way to a chitter chatter of a more genuine nature, and it was clear that the seasonal cheer was rubbing off on some of the snootier members of the bath house. Señor José was happy. He had a stool perched at the end of the table where he could wink and nod charmingly at his guests as well as watch over his aquatic arena. Kiki had taken it upon herself to resurrect the fallen tree in the foyer and it was

* *A tarn is technically a pool, just with a glacial ancestry.*

now twinkling gloriously in the centre of the bay windows above the pool, so José could admire that, too. It was as he was sitting there, looking at the tree on high, that he heard a faint squeak of an opening door from across the room, over by the kitchen entrance and female changing rooms. At first he thought it was Yvonne, backing in with the second round of sausage rolls. But as he made a very unsubtle double take, he realised that it wasn't. It was someone new. Someone he hadn't seen before. The someone was a she and she was a bikini-clad vision, half cloaked by a paisley sarong and topped with a navy fedora hat. She was tall and tan and young and lovely. I'm tempted to say she was from Ipanema but honestly, I'm not too sure if she was...

José fell hard. Not only did his jaw drop but his heart did, too. He was as floppy as the hat sitting upon her head and he was overcome with first-sighted love. He watched intensely as the stunning brunette meandered her way across the floor, eventually dropping her towel and belongings off at a sun lounger near the rear patio doors. José watched more intensely as the mystery woman kicked off her sandals (Ipanemas!), peeled off her hat and sarong and swayed so gently towards the water. As she reached the shallow-end steps, José stretched behind to the snack table for a mince pie to calm himself; he smiled but she didn't see. Old Man Ray had no shame in ogling at the water bound beauty, but in fairness to the gawking onlookers, she sank into the pool with such grace and transitioned into a front crawl with such elegancy that when she swam past, each one she passed went "Aaah..."

About ten lengths in and around the same time as Ren returned from his supermarket sweep with a sackful of treats, the lovely lady emerged from the pool. She was glistening, almost shimmering between the water's reflection and the low-lying winter sun breaking in through the glass tank around her. By now, José had given his heart gladly. He was starstruck. After she had towelled down, covered up and headed over to the freshly stocked table bar, though, José's look began to sadden. His lustful eyes dropped to the floor as she looked straight ahead, not at him. The lady approached the bar, somewhere near the middle, and awaited Ren's scatty service.

"Señorita, can I interest you in a glass of Andalusia's finest?" asked Ren, with a brownish stain on his shirt.

The lady declined as she straightened herself out on the stool. Ren took a half-step to his left and used his good arm to showcase the jug of sangria that sat next to the stack of wine glasses on the table behind him. The lady declined once more. She then crossed her right leg over her left and leant her arms forward onto the table. With a hypnotic smile she insisted that Ren make her up a White Russian cocktail, and before he had time to pivot and ponder over his liqueur collection, José sprang from his stall in a hurry, as if his legs had cramped underneath him.

"We have some Kahlúa in the store cupboard, if you'd care to join me?" José exclaimed with an eager-to-please look about him.

"To the store cupboard...?" she remarked, sneering playfully at a sheepish José.

José shrugged and grinned flirtatiously back, before leaving the bar and heading across to the kitchen and the storage cupboard.

As José departed, Ren introduced himself to the lady, and soon after Dec did the same, having slid his way along the table. The lady, though mostly approachable, was not interested in the slightest. Truth be told she had her eye on José but was doing that odd thing that most women do when they pretend they're not interested in you and shrug off your friendly demeanour dismissively and abruptly as if you were a meaningless tool. Then you get all confused because you think they're telling you to eff off, though in honesty, and through every second look, they're screaming for you to stay and try harder, but you don't have the competency or knowhow to figure that out and so you scurry away and swing from lonely night to lonely night to lonely night in a confidence-shattering spiral of rejection... (*clears throat*).

Dec said hello.

"Hello," said Dec.

The still-unidentified lady turned her head to acknowledge him. She said hello back. Her look moved from Dec's eyeline down to his name badge. It read, 'Declán de Haulles'; she smirked and then pushed her neck out as if to get a closer look. Dec peeked down to see what she was looking at but checked back up in confusion after noticing nothing out of the ordinary.

"De Haulles. Your name is Dec de Haulles...?" the lady joked.

Dec's father was a carpenter from Belgium; his mother was a seamstress from Belfast. Dec was subsequently left with his awkwardly seasonal name. His parents hadn't even considered the comedy in in it for a second. Dec chuckled and then confirmed the unfortunate information. The lady chuckled too, but in a more sarcastic manner. She then took a seductive sip from Ren's brandy glass, leaving her lip imprint smudged on the glass, and then left the bar, heading straight for the kitchen and the storage cupboard…

José was bent over two gas cylinders and a box of tumblers, reaching in desperation for the dusty Kahlúa bottle that was on the bottom shelf behind them. It was as he clasped the bottle neck between his index and middle finger that he heard a knock on the door behind him. The knock shocked him. He jumped up in a fright at the sudden break in the tense operation and in doing so hit his head on the middle shelf above him. The Kahlúa bottle slipped dramatically from his fingers and smashed onto the tiled floor of the storage cupboard in a coffee coloured mess. José stood up rubbing his head and turned towards the door; he tightened with frustration until he realised who it was that had disturbed him.

"WHAT…" he said, before exhaling and loosening back up, "…is your name?"

The lovely lady in the doorway laughed. José pushed out one of those strange nasal laughs in return. His head hurt so he wasn't ready to chuckle completely. The lady extended her hand towards him, and with a kindly look she introduced herself.

EVANGELINE

The freezer peeled open. An icy cloud rushed out and into the air as a tanned hand reached inside and pulled out a packet of garden peas. The horizontal door then lowered itself back down again and made that cool sucky sound that freezers make when they shut. Evangeline fetched a tea towel from the side and wrapped it around the bag of peas before resting it delicately on José's head and sitting down on the worktop next to him.

The room was starting to fill up with a damp coffee smell as the puddle of Kahlúa trickled slowly out of the storage cupboard. Neither one of the culprits could be bothered to clear it up as both were far more interested in perching their pretty little behinds on the tiled counter and flirting some more.

Evangeline enraptured José increasingly as the two of them became better acquainted. However, you needn't be too educated to work out that ol' lover boy was blinded by tits, teeth and tush and chose to ignore her somewhat wily influence over him. Evangeline would continuously glance sneakily at José's watch, as if to monitor the minute hand and its incessant ticking. It was a hard one for José to call – after all, she was acting equally very smitten. Evangeline had popped up uninvited and completely out of the blue, but then again so do all great loves. The good-looking pair sat talking for a little longer than either expected, but the conversation between them flowed even better than the coffee liqueur did from out of the storage cupboard. It appeared that José and Evangeline were a nigh on perfect match, if there is such a thing – an imperfectly perfect match of young adults that had been hit hard with the love bug.

Evangeline was in town with her father, a single parent, though his business had taken him elsewhere. She was pushing twenty-one and was from a place that was smokier and more congested than Bath. Her father had a mistrust of her and her youthful rebellion. He was a busy man and parenthood had been thrust upon him uninvitedly by a deceitful and unlawful woman who had disappeared soon after Evangeline's birth. The two of them rarely saw eye to eye. It was obvious to her father that Evangeline had her mother's insatiable taste for sin. She certainly didn't share in her father's love of the law.

Time was getting on now, and if you ask me it took almost too long for Ren to come looking for the pair of them, still nattering away in the kitchen. He bopped into the room in an unnecessary panic. José and Evangeline flicked their look to the kitchen's double doors simultaneously. Ren deflated with an exaggerated relief at his discovery of the two of them. He stood in the doorway, keeping the right door ajar with his left hand (or what was left of it), and unconvincingly lied about how he was struggling to keep up with the demand of the regulars and that he needed the boss back at base to share the load. José was well aware of the demographic of most of his customers. He also knew that Ren was stretching the truth, he could hear it in his inconsistent tones. He usually handled his somewhat overzealous minion with poise, but José seemed a little off this time. After the two of them had quickly dashed back to the pool area, José's suspicions were proven to be true – the atmosphere was as pleasant and as contained as when he had left the scene forty-five minutes ago. So José had to wonder, why was Ren lying? Or at the very least exaggerating? Most definitely overstressing.

Ren's usually impassive face displayed the ambiguity that clattered inside his mind. José awaited his explanation, but the lull between them drew out too long; the faded clip-clop of unfaded flip-flops from behind the two of them broke Ren's train of thought and José's attention. Chev Collins, head of the Devonshire County Council, was making her way out of the Indoor Outdoor Bath House™ and flashed José a wave and a silent adios. José waved back at Chev and then looked back at Ren, shaking his head. José turned to leave, but as he did so, Ren placed his nub of a left hand onto José's shoulder and whispered:

"*Esa mujer* is out to get you Mario. Chev saw her in the changing rooms, looking through bags. She's a crook, *mi amigo*. There's something not quite right about her, *si*?"

José pulled away and straightened his shirt out with purpose to rid himself of his appendagely challenged friend.

"Unbelievable," responded José. "Lies will get you into all sorts of trouble, '*mi amigo*', and so will jealousy..."

Ren called out to José in a last-ditch attempt to salvage the moment, but it was too little too late; José's stride was unbroken as he coolly headed back towards the kitchen. Ren took a deep but stuttered breath and shrunk back towards the bar, where he and Dec finished off the Cardenal Mendoza in a sombre turn of events. José's glass sat half empty beside them.

José headed back to the kitchen to rejoin Evangeline. Throughout his very short walk back to her he psyched himself up for the heroic re-entry. He imagined it to be a 'swing in, sway over and sweep her off her feet' sort of thing, but that all changed (as it so often does) when he nervously burst in to see Evangeline posing topless and cover-girl-like on top of the fan-assisted electric oven. She smiled teasingly as she threw her bikini top at him. As it twisted through the air one of the straps whipped forward and caught his eye, but that failed to break the mood as Evangeline played José with, "Let's have a bath together... Señor Bell."

José, having already bundled in and bumbled uncoolly, steadied himself and laid a big wet kiss on Evangeline. It became passionate; the two of them fidgeted uncontrollably as their mouths intertwined and their hands wandered naughtily around each other, although this caused Evangeline's buttocks to turn the knob on the front left burner to a medium-to-low heat, an ideal temperature for simmering a chicken & chorizo jambalaya.

The atmosphere was smoking, quite literally so, as Evangeline's sarong was starting to cook from underneath her gently warming buns. She soon realised that the warming sensation was neither lust nor excitement but that her arse was actually starting to burn. She jumped down in a hurry and rubbed her heated backside, then spun around to turn off the smoky burner. All the while, José was standing very close to her still, undeterred by the slapstick setbacks and smiling like an orangutan at a banana factory. Evangeline spun back around to face José again. The two of them smiled at one another in a manner that, to them, seemed most definitely romantic, though for anyone watching, it would have seemed rather cheesy/corny.* Evangeline took José's hand and led him out through the kitchen's other exit/entrance and in the direction of the so-far-ignored bath-house baths. Somehow Evangeline knew exactly where she was going, despite this being her first visit to the bath house. Perhaps she had picked up the scent of bath salts. José was ignorant of her directional skill and was overthrown entirely by the beating of his heart and bulging of his pantalones, as he knew that they were on their way to do unspeakable things to one another

---

* **Cheesy Corn** – *A good accompaniment for the above-mentioned 'chicken & chorizo jambalaya'.*

amongst the plush surroundings of the thermal baths.

The customer entrance to the baths was at the bottom of a narrowing staircase at the back of the pool room. It was marbled, yet perfectly safe when wet. From the pool area, the staircase spiralled downwards and disappeared underneath the grand bay windows of the reception area above. The walls of the staircase were indented with ledges for the ferns resting upon them. The arched doorway at the bottom was rendered perfectly smooth and the slanted ceiling that led down to it was colourfully tiled and looked as though Gaudi himself had chundered all over it. One particular segment was beautifully mosaicked, with jagged shiny tiles painting an obscure scene: two olive trees, each on a mountainside above the horizon and leaning in towards each other, whilst below, a shark's fin broke the water.

The thermal baths were styled much like the old Roman ones that were not too far away (geographically) from the Indoor Outdoor Bath House™. There were four stone columns that added structural support to the ceiling – one either side of the entrance doorway and two opposite, at the head of the Baño Grande. The most mesmeric feature of the thermal baths was the method by which the water was transported and regulated into the Baño Grande. There was a miniature aqueduct system that iced the walls of the bath-house bathroom and carried the water from the pool tank above to the baths below. The system was extreme, but its eccentricity gave the bath house its pizazz. The whole place was a work of art, an aesthetically unrivalled water palace.

José and Evangeline were just about done. They

emerged through the staff exit and into the kitchen once more, damp and rumple haired. The two of them plucked a white chocolate Magnum each from the freezer and headed back to the pool area, hand in hand. As they stepped from the shadows into the now dimly lit pool room, they were presented with an odd scenario. They stopped dead in their tracks. Two green-shirted paramedics were across the room. The swirling blue light of their van shone from beyond the glass ceilings and doors. Evangeline dropped her jaw; José dropped his ice cream. He quickly shook loose his sweetheart and bolted for the paramedics.

There was the smallest of crowds crowding around the fuss. Most of the guests from the day had already left or had now been sent home. Only Ren, Dec and the two uniformed medical men were standing, crouched and stooped over the patient – the patient that was lying unnervingly still by the side of the bar. With a worried haste José skidded across the pool room floor in his water-spotted brogues. He tiptoed around the paramedic treating the casualty, widened his eyes and swallowed hard as he saw an unconscious and unresponsive Old Man Ray, lying flat on his back.

Half an hour or so had already passed since Ray had fallen to his knackered knees, gasping for air that just wouldn't come, and it really wasn't looking good for the poor old soul. Everyone was strangely silent. Except for the puffs of the working paramedic, the room was bone-chillingly quiet. Even José was left without words; his day had gone from top to bottom in as long as it took for him to drop his ice cream. Finally, as the weary-faced St John's Ambulance man rose up to stand beside his partner, he pronounced Ray dead at four minutes to four in the afternoon of Friday 13th December 2002.

José began to cry. He shivered and clasped both of his hands together, hung them around his neck and solemnly draped his head between his forearms. For now, he couldn't even bring himself to ask what had happened to his old friend, all he could do was cry. The inquisition would come soon, of course, because as the second ambulance driver called in the unhappy news to the hospital, José was left with the unforgiving task of calling Raymundo's lady wife and confessing this terrible trauma. It turned out that Ray had died from a complication with his heart, though not quite a heart attack. It was presumed by the paramedics that it was an overdue reaction to the fiasco with the faulty pool hoist earlier in the day. Ray had sunk a couple of brandies, and then a couple more, and by the time he was finally at his most relaxed, his ticker ticked out. And so, the legendary Raymundo J. Oldman came crashing down once more, though this time there wasn't anything to hoist him back up again.

THE TIME MACHINE

The aging St John's Ambulance driver and his other unnamed associate carried Ray's hefty corpse off on a stretcher and out into their ambulance in the staff car park. José watched and winced as they did so, still so unsure of what had happened to his friend. He knew now that he had to make the call; there was nothing left to do on his behalf at this point, except that. He unsurely swept back his hair and began to dial.

"Hello Joanie... sorry, Tanya? Tanya, it's José, I run the bath house and spa that your father comes... well, he came to. I'm sorry, your father is a member at my bath house. Tanya, I have some awful, awful news and I… Tanya? Hello, are you okay, can you hear me? Sorry what, Joanie? No, Tanya, I called about your father, Ray. Raymundo Oldman is your dad, right?"

José's tears dried as his voice dropped from the call. He was listening – all was not right at the other end of the line either.

"Oh my God, what are you talking about… Have you called the police? Have you called an ambulance? Jesus, Tanya, I don't know what to tell you… I had your father here today and he… he's sadly, well, he's not here anymore."

José awaited the response of an obviously distraught Tanya, Ray's daughter. José had found, however, that she wasn't distraught. She was hysterical, a woman in ruins.

"They've taken him," José explained, "the ambulance men, they've got him now, but he hasn't made it, Tanya. It was his heart, it gave up… What's happened over there? What's going on? …Okay, okay, he's been taken to the Royal United… yeah, but you should call help over there, quickly! If you need me to do anything then call me on this number. I'm so sorry, for everything…"

The conversation was as bizarre as it was sad. Ray's family was having troubles of their own. The terrible news that José brought upon them was just another solemn jab that diseased their already shit day. Heartbreakingly, Ray was celebrating today as the first of his long-awaited retirement. He had handed over the keys to his small business and headed out to rejoice in the warm freedoms of later life. The day had been cruel to a life that had been kind, but the fates of the world had ended Ray's short time with a remarkably amorous and coincidental finish.

The confusion and the bewilderment left José with a hollow ringing in his ears and an upsetting nausea, churning and swelling in the pit of his stomach. In search of comfort, he pivoted back around to seek solace in Evangeline, but she was no longer there. She could've been in the bathroom, or she could've been getting changed. He could've gone looking for her in the many dark corners of his bath house, but as he ran his left hand back through his brown, wavy hair he noticed his wrist was a little less weighty than he remembered it being before. Evangeline had made off with José's watch. José's leather-strapped, handcrafted Swiss watch. She ran right outta there with it and didn't look back, not even for a second. He had been played, Ren was right; she was a thief. José was left broken-hearted, alone and without his father's priceless timepiece.

The watch that Evangeline had stolen from José was about to get herself, and a few others, into an argument they'd had no intention of joining. It could've been different, equally as chaotic but a lot different, if she hadn't pinched the watch and wasn't a terrible person. Now she had thrown a rusty spanner into her own dirty works. José had inherited his watch from his father, José Senior. José Sr. had stolen the watch from Colonel Mann, the gangster, at the same time as the Colonel's incarceration in 1978.

The watch was a precious piece of Central European machinery that Colonel Mann wore only on the occasions that he deemed appropriate. At all other times it was kept in a small cabinet in the alcove underneath his bedside table, in an expensive looking watch box, purple in colour with a dotted golden seam. The watch was a good-looking accessory and he wore it well, but when he came to visit José Sr. at the bath house building site, it was to be the last time he would ever wear it.

The Colonel came to talk to José Sr. about his money, the disappearance of Dorsal Finney and why his name was scribbled into the Irishman's black ledger he had found in the flat at the beginning of the story. The Spaniard still owed the Colonel half a million, with interest. The Colonel's first suspicions, after seeing José Sr.'s name crossed through in the ledger, was that the Irishman had done a runner with the loot and had conned him out of his majority share. When Dorsal (deceased) failed to return his calls, the Colonel's suspicions deepened. He paid José Sr. a visit to try and patch things up and get back on top of the situation, but Señor Sr. was smarter, more charming and more convincing than history had led his associates to believe. When the two of them sat down for a chat in the makeshift office José Sr. had put together in the shower room site, his story began. He told the Colonel that he had paid back his debts to Dorsal already, and that the Irishman had indeed run off with the loot, but the lie didn't end there. José Sr., cunningly so, led the Colonel to believe that Dorsal came to him with plans of working together to diddle him out of his money and into prison. José Sr. played the whole thing perfectly. He played the victim at first, until the Colonel became agitated and threatening, and then came the real show. It was clear that Colonel Mann was unsure of the truth in the story – after all, why would Dorsal side with their debtor over him? Where would be the sense or logic in them partnering up? Then José Sr. hit the Colonel with the bombshell. Still playing innocent, he confessed to Colonel Mann who he was back in his

Mediterranean homeland. He polished the tops and sanded the edges but pretty much told the Colonel that he came from money, money on hiatus (hence the loan) but money nonetheless. After all, how could he have paid his debt back to Dorsal so quickly and so fully? He couldn't, clearly. But the Colonel didn't know that and was still none the wiser. He was now beginning to believe the oh-so-convincing José Romario Cobos Sr. and according to him, Dorsal had written the Colonel's name in his ledger for a joke, a ruse to throw him off.

"It was a trick, Señor," he told the Colonel. "He is a tricksy *hombre*, you know, Señor Finney. But I tell you this to help you, eh? It's one more trouble I do not need. He say he leave for a while, with the money I pay to him already. He say he wants me to go with him; he say to me, 'vámonos José, vámonos!' But all I want is my bath house, you know. So I stay, and I work – I have my money from home now, eh, so why all the running?"

Unbeknownst to the Colonel, José Sr. had found out how he legitimised his illicit cash and was about to play it against him. He was a devious fella and quite spiteful really when it came down to his survival and success. José Sr. was in truth a nasty bastard who, more often than not, fell on his feet. The Colonel was into gambling, betting shops and casinos, because that was his way of cleaning his dirty money for the tellers at the bank and the police on the street. The Colonel placed multiple bets on outcomes across the board with few, or none, that posed a big risk with short odds. That way, he only stood to lose the bookies cut, and the betting slips he got in return proved his cash was just his lucky winnings. Strategically he spread his money, minimising his chances of a loss, be it sporting or nonsporting events; anything worthy of a safe bet to clean his money is what the Colonel did. Casinos were an easier affair as he swapped in his dirty cash for chips, played conservatively for a short while and then ducked out with a clean cheque or legitimate cash with a genuine receipt. José Sr. informed the Colonel of his knowledge of this and told him that Dorsal was planning on dobbing him in to the police because of it.

"Then he keep the money I already pay back, and then he say he want to 'rub shoulders with my rich amigos back in Catalonia'," José Sr. went on. "I do not know what this mean, 'rub shoulders', but he say he wants to do it. He even say he perhaps invest some of your money for himself back into the bath house and other things. Of course I say no. I say why would I want to do this, but he get mean and angry, saying I have no choice because of what I already did. He say things like 'you don't know who you're dealing with' and 'you must do this if you want things to be okay'. So, honestly, I'm happy you come here, maybe you can help me deal with Señor Finney and get him away from my business…"

The Colonel was a bit confused, but he understood what José Sr. was saying. It was all bullshit, but he believed in it. Dorsal was shifty and exactly the kind of person to do that sort of thing, and José Sr. was very believable. Little did he know that Dorsal was dead and buried underneath the site they were chatting upon. The Colonel did acknowledge his fraudulent activities and he knew that it could get him into trouble with the law if the two of them did decide to rat him out. He was provoked into talking about his tricks and that's really all José Sr. needed. Something slightly resembling trust was building between them, but little did the Colonel know that José Sr. had already gone to the police, and they were listening in on their conversation through the small recording device tucked discreetly into his inside jacket pocket.

José Sr. had gone to the police soon after Dorsal Finney's death and immediately after sussing out who Colonel Mann was and what he did. He was taking no chances after things took an unexpected turn for the worst. When he scoured through Dorsal's bedsit he found the evidence that showed he was working on behalf of some nastier, more powerful men. So, knowing how the past had stung him and robbed him of his home once before, he decided to act first. He found out who the Colonel was and shadowed him stealthily to better know the man and the corruption he was dealing with. It was relatively easy to avoid suspicion, evade detection and keep his nose clean, as before the Colonel came to see him, he had no idea what the Spaniard looked like.

After finding out the details of the Colonel's scam José Sr. contacted the police with a bargain. The lies he told the police were pretty much the same ones that he'd just told Colonel Mann, but he made his claims to the police sincerer, as they had to be on his side for his plan to work. Whether or not the Colonel was on his side was irrelevant to his capture; all he had to do was get him to acknowledge and admit that he was laundering money and the police would do the rest. It did help his overall claim if all parties were in agreement with his story, but he was always going to plead innocent no matter who bought it. José Sr. ran to the law with his new information and agreed to partake in the entrapment of their common enemy. He was given a live transmitter to trigger as and when Colonel Mann dropped by and gave up what they both wanted to hear. He hid the small recorder inconspicuously inside his tailored, two-piece charcoal grey suit.

It took the police around fifteen minutes to arrive at the construction site in Bath where José Sr. and Colonel Mann were going over their quandaries. The conversation had sounded the alarm to the man behind the headphones back at the station and once the trigger was triggered and the bombshell dropped, the fuzz were on their way. Four uniformed officers rushed onto the scene and crashed through the temporary partition wall joining what was to be the towel room and the shower room. There were two other officers back at the cars ready to be called into action if things got rough. With one ear on their radios they leant proudly on the bonnets of their respective vehicles. The ensnarement took the Colonel by total surprise, and although José Sr. knew the police would be storming in soon after he hit the switch on the transmitter, he was also caught off-guard by their brash introduction. The officers moved in to cuff Colonel Mann, who was bigger and scarier than the four of them put together, but it was as they did so that the smaller, warier officer at the back of the pack sussed this out, and he realised that it would take all six of their squadron to restrain this monster. The three leading policemen shouted the Colonel's rights at him whilst wagging their batons provokingly, goading him to lash out irrationally, and lash out irrationally he did. Full of pride and hatred for the common law, Colonel Mann chose not to run from them but to stand and fight. As José Sr. tucked himself out of the way, the Colonel rose from his fold-up chair and readied himself for war.

Running into danger, he speared the first officer to the

ground – a dump tackle through the pasting table that was being used as the makeshift desk and coffee-cup rest. *Crash*. They both fell through the limp and dusty table and onto the soggy site floor. The Colonel sprung back to his feet; the policeman did not. The two officers (behind the first) were waiting for him with their batons at the ready. The fourth officer was making the call to the other two for backup. The Colonel, now with a nasty cut decorating his tanned, bald head, turned around, only to be chopped with the long, black length of the law: one to the shoulder and one to the ribs, then one to the face – the policeman's face. The Colonel landed a knockout righthander to the nose of the second officer, whose head wobbled on his neck like a pinball between bumpers. He staggered a bit before falling into an unconscious slump against the already damaged partition wall.

There were now only two, lined up together, ready to take on the beast. They were nervous and rightly so, as before they could bring themselves to act, the Colonel launched himself up into the air and propelled himself towards them. Soaring, Thor-like, through the space between them, he came down with all his force and landed the most almighty thump onto the helmet of his third victim. His neck sunk, there was a sickening crunch and the force nearly rooted the policeman's feet into the ground. The third officer tumbled backwards and joined the other two on the dirty floor. The fourth, the smallest of the team, was trembling as he watched his squadron destroyed before him. Colonel Mann turned to him and looked even bigger than he had done before; his knuckles were stained red and his face was mad with rage. The unlucky policeman shut his eyes and instinctively swung his baton at the villain, but the villain caught it in his massive hands. His eyes reopened to see the wicked grin of Colonel Mann, clutching the baton in his left and winding up his right for another knockout punch. The policeman swallowed hard and tried to close his eyes once more, but he was caught in a menacing staring match with the Colonel. He looked deep into the eyes of crazy as crazy drew its big hand back, clenched tight in a bloody fist. He was counting down the moments in his head before seeing stars, but they were moving so slowly, time was lingering in the sinister silence of the stare-off.

Then a small creak, came from the corner of the room, from behind the policeman and out in front of Colonel Mann, who broke the stare. The copper had won. The Colonel unclenched his fist and eased his grip on the baton, for in the corner, creaking between the wooden slats of the site walkway, was José Sr. The reason they were all there, the man behind the chaos; the orchestrator of the faceoff. The liar, the cheater, the thief. The Colonel wanted him, and not for any more talking. He wanted to hurt José Sr. the way he had tried to hurt him. The Colonel let go of the quaking policeman and brushed him aside. He walked menacingly over to the cowering Spaniard. His pace quickened as he got closer to him. But finally, the two officers from outside burst in and, along with the other the Colonel had just spared, wrestled him to the ground. It was three on one. The Colonel couldn’t keep his footing on the wobbly wooden slats as he was facing the other way, hellbent on pummelling José Sr. He came crashing down with the policemen on top of him. The first officer managed to pull himself up from the pasting-table wreckage and join in the fight, though the Colonel was thrashing about and not cooperating in the slightest. He wriggled and fought, swinging limbs about and frantically trying to twist himself free. His arms wind-milled around him, his sleeves rising up his forearms to reveal the expensive watch on his left wrist. He struggled and thrashed some more, the police doing all they could to keep him pinned to the floor. Then, as he flung his arms one last time, his watch; his leather strapped, handcrafted Swiss watch, flew off his wrist and up into the air. In the midst of the mayhem nobody noticed it, but when it landed at José Sr.'s shiny shoes, how could he not notice? Slyly he bent down to pick up the loose trinket; the others were still wrestling close by, but he was still safe from the carnage. He hid the Colonel's watch in his jacket pocket. Quietly he smuggled the priceless timepiece away from the dogpile and into his possession. About the same time as he did so, the fight ended. The Colonel ceased resisting as the smallest officer finally managed to cuff him. It was all over.

Colonel Mann was taken by the police and sentenced soon after. His days of hustling were over, because the big, bad Colonel would never again see life outside of prison walls. José Sr. was questioned repeatedly by the police and investigated semi-extensively as to where his money had come from and where Dorsal Finney had run off to. He was fortunate enough to still have a couple of wealthy, powerful and squalid friends back in Spain that stepped up for him when the British law raised doubts. When the inquisition became too intrusive, he manged to twist the arm of a few senior-ranking officials with some cheap shares and expensive champagne. The police seemed less bothered about Dorsal as time moved on. He was no big loss to them, or society, and he wasn't worth the paperwork the enquiry would cause. The story of how he ran off with the money seemed to please them enough, as before José Sr. had introduced his name to them they were unaware that he even existed. José Sr. was given a slap on the wrist and a mark on his record for transporting such large sums of foreign money into the country and unknowingly partaking in illegal payday loaning. Ultimately though, he was let off scot-free and was, miraculously, in the clear, with a jazzy new watch to boot. He went on to build his Indoor Outdoor Bath House™ unobstructed by nothing and no one, raising his only son, José Jr. as he did so.

As for Colonel Mann's watch, José Sr. wore it as a trophy almost every day from when he pinched it to when he eventually handed it down to José Jr. He wore it with pride, and it was his chosen accessory for all his fine suits. When he passed on the watch to his son he made sure not to tell him of how he came to own the thing, but only to look after it as if it were a piece of his very soul. José Sr.'s soul had been fading with illness, and the watch was his one and only horcrux. The watch was the tainted charm of the bath house. It was José Sr.'s reminder of how and why he succeeded in his grotty mission to regain power and traction in his life.

So that watch, the very same watch that Evangeline had pinched from José Jr., was already a stolen heirloom. It originated from a much nastier man and it was about to betray her. Because just like José Sr., Colonel Mann, too, had a son. His son was a little older than José Jr. but grew up to be just as tainted as his old man. Trevor Mann, aka Mr. Mann, was just eleven years old when his father was grassed up and locked up, but the now thirty-five-year-old remembered a few important things about his old dad. He remembered what the Colonel had taught him about betting shops, casinos and manipulating the odds in his favour. He remembered how he used to talk, albeit very rarely but always in abrasively quiet tones between long pauses. He also remembered his dad's old watch. He could spot that thing a mile away.

#9. Afternoon Tea

Stark raving mad!

The trainee barista's turtle-shell glasses fogged up from the overspray of the coffee machine's steam wand as she heated the milk for her customer's flat white coffee. She was new and nervous but was doing well overall. The till was being manned chiefly by Gillian Hobbs, the owner of the shop. The trainee barista had been till trained but as yet she was just the coffee maker, as Gillian was at the helm, schmoosing her customers. It was a busy day for them in the shop as Christmas was only twelve days away and the Friday shoppers were ducking in and out to warm their souls with a cake and a cuppa.

Gum Drops

The Hobbs Cake Shop was located down an old cobbled street in the heart of Frome town centre. It was a cherished establishment at this time of year in particular, as people sought seasonal solace in its mawkish displays. The big gun in the cake shop's arsenal of alluring displays was the Hobb's Sherry Trifle in the front window. It was a masterpiece of sugary installation, the very sculpture of all that it means to be a pudding. It was David by Michelanjelly, or that Guitar by Pablo Picustard... It was huge; the biggest dessert in the South West by a good few layers. The glass bowl that encased the beastly pud was shaped like a sundae dish but on a nuclear scale. The trifle had the usual stack of cake, fruit, sherry, custard, jelly and cream, except that in its massive container the many layers continued on and on. The final layer was of course snowy white, thick and creamy, but the daring devils who made it had crafted its stiff peaks into more than just the usual cascading cream tops. The top curled upwards and inwards, tapering like a Christmas tree. It was smooth and white, but the characteristic shape remained. There were treats nestled inside the creamy curls: sweets, chocolates and fruits, they glistened like the decorations they imitated. There was also a tinsel trail of raspberry-and-sherry-flavoured sauce, drizzled intricately around the white coils. Without a doubt, the trifle was the crowning glory of the shop's Christmassy exhibition, but there were several other impressive treats inside.

There was a gingerbread house proudly on show in the centre of the cake cabinet next to the front counter, as big as your average-sized doll's house and decorated beyond beautifully. There was a Christmas cake on one of the low shelves in the tearoom at the back of the shop, wrapped in a red ribbon with a gold floral trim. There was also a chocolate Yule log that was three feet long and as thick as a Christmas tree trunk, a three-tiered eggnog and cranberry cheesecake with a toy train circling around it, and a panettone with no distinctive traits. They were all scattered precisely around the twee little shop and the customers loved it, especially the ones who stayed for coffee.

***

When the temporary fog finally cleared from the barista's glasses, she was ready to serve. She poured the full fat milk over the hot shot of coffee and attempted her flowery artwork as the milk flow came to its end. It looked okay; it wasn't her best, but the perfecting of the niche skill would surely come with her many attempts over the winter period. She turned with the completed beverage to present it to her customer. Her hands were steady but still the warm china of the cup and saucer rattled together as she made the short journey across the floor. As she set it down in front of the gentleman at the counter, she was at last able to look up and smile in a friendly, outgoing and professional manner that outlined her high level of interpersonal skill... at least that's what her CV read. The man she served was tall, well-built and suited. He had piercing green eyes with strong, triangular eyebrows. His hair was short and neat, and his skin was freckled across his nose. He was a striking presence and he had a definite majesty about him. He seemed cold and distant, but the mystery of his unchanging expression made him incredibly attractive. His name was Trevor Mann and he was mostly known as Mr Mann to his peers and his enemies. The son of an incarcerated ex-military man, Colonel Mann, he was the top dog in a powerful crime ring. Trevor Mann was visiting the shop on business – bad business – and he needed his drink to start proceedings. The young barista girl had the honour of caring for the big man, and after she handed over his coffee, she began working on the other drinks for his party.

"If you'd like to take a seat I'll bring your other drinks over to you," she said, trying to suppress the nerves and live up to the written description of herself.

"Thank you," Trevor Mann replied as he picked up his coffee. "Thank you, Gill," he said, flashing a look at Gillian

Hobbs, the shop's owner.

His voice was bizarrely friendly. His muddled accent was caught somewhere between farm boy and Del Boy.

He walked away and out to the back of the shop to where the tables and chairs were. It was a smallish room a few steps down from the front with a dozen or so oakwood tables dotted about. Each table had four or five high-backed handcrafted teak-stained oakwood chairs around it. The tables had red runners across the tops of them with silver seams meandering symmetrically along the edges in swirly shapes. In the middle of each was a Christmassy centrepiece, wreath-type pieces with cinnamon sticks, pinecones and dried orange halves intertwangled into their bushy greens. Regal red candles were sat in the centre of them, one for each piece and all of them alight with slow-dancing flame, swaying with the gentle festive melodies playing out through the shop's hidden speakers. The room was nearly full. It would've been packed out were it not for one table.

Trevor Mann's clan were gathered around the furthest table from the front counter, tucked behind a slightly protruding wall that was striped with shelves full of baking books. It was down another couple of small steps and off to the right; the toilets were off to the left. Trevor Mann carried his drink confidently without a single drop breaking free from the cup. Given the busyness of the shop and the steps he had to endure, that was pretty impressive work. When he reached the table he found his companions silent – they were waiting for the big man to return before the talks began. Very rarely did anything in the group kick off without Trevor Mann saying it could.

The other men at the table, from the left of Mr Mann

and around in an anticlockwise loop, were Trevor Chaim (known more commonly as Dr Chaim), Hank Howardson or 'Hank the Bastard' as he had become better known, and Trevor Rockson aka Madd Rockson. Dr Trevor Chaim, or just simply Dr Chaim, was, as his title suggested, a doctor. He had studied and practised lawful medicine for thirteen years before he was caught selling prescription drugs to prescription drug addicts out of the back of his Merc in the privately-owned car park a stone's throw away from his lovely big house. The bad doctor had been jailed for two short years before he was let loose to roam the sticky streets of the criminal underworld once again. He was picked up by Mr Trevor Mann a year or so after his release and was recruited into his wee gang to help with the running of things. He was a smart cookie and had influences that came in handy for Mr Mann. Dr Chaim was a tall but slight man. He had round spectacles with sunglass lenses attached to the top of them by tiny hinges that he flicked down when the sun spiked through the West Country clouds. His blond hair was wavy and remarkably shaped with folds and flicks, and he wore a mustard-coloured button-up shirt with navy corduroy trousers. Aside from the other two in his team, his own company was his favourite, as that of any other was unworthy of his refined genius.

Sat opposite Dr Trevor Chaim was mad Trevor Rockson (aka Madd Rockson), the third in the treacherous trio of Trevs. Madd Rockson was a bit mad. He called himself Madd as he wanted to be identified by a name other than his given one of Trevor, and quite surprisingly he settled on Madd, with two d's. He owned a sandwich bar on the Strawberry Way Roundabout off the A303, though he was rarely there. Madd was a stocky bloke and wasn't that tall. He wasn't that short either, but stuck between the other two Trevors he was made to look a lot shorter. His hair was nearly all gone so he kept the bits that were left very short. Like Trevor Mann, he also donned a suit, though his was considerably less flattering around his paunchy parts. Madd was an old friend of Mr Mann; they had known each other ever since they were kids in the same children's residential care home together. He had had a rough start to life and most of his problems stemmed from his absent parents. He was a few years younger than the other two, though his appearance failed to show it. The way he followed their lead, however, was certainly indicative of that fact. Madd Rockson was no stranger to violence, but he was working on becoming one. The physicality that came with the lifestyle the Trevors had chosen for themselves was a last resort for Mr Mann and Dr Chaim, and slowly it was rubbing off on Madd. Occasionally he lashed out, but the outbursts were becoming less frequent. His lunacy was now mostly concealed behind the crazy blue eyes embedded in his rubbery face.

Hank 'the Bastard' Howardson was sitting in front of Mr Mann. He was the silly Billy Bear sandwiched between the intimidating white slice of Dr Chaim and the unnerving granary slice of Madd Rockson. Hank was the reason the four of them were all there. He had done something bad and was receiving his punishment. Hank's right leg was trembling and his hands were cold. He had ordered a tea from the front, but he knew he wasn't going to drink it. He was a scruffy-looking man with pushed-back dark hair and uneven stubble. He wore an old sports sweatshirt and jeans – a bad outfit for a bad man on a bad day. Hank Howardson had upset the apple cart by being sneaky with the Trevors' trust. He used to be an acquaintance of theirs, in the loosest sense, but now that was all over.

STRASBOURG

"How's Leyla?" Mr Mann asked Hank.

Hank chose not to answer; instead he blew out through his nostrils, sneering at the ambiguity of the question. With a scrunch of his fierce eyebrows Mr Mann showed his discontent.

"She's ya wife Hank, don't ya know how ya wife is? Aren't ya worried about 'er? Aren't you a little bit concerned for 'er safety on a day like today?"

With Hank's full attention Mr Mann plopped a brown sugar cube into his coffee. He didn't stir it. "I like the end to be sweet," he said, looking deep into the eyes of his prey, "the rest can be as bitter as ya like."

Hank gulped but tried his best to hide it.

"I only ask 'cos we must've given the poor woman one hellova fright this mornin', and as involved in all this as she seems, I know that really it's all your doin', so as far as a jury would judge, she's innocent. But us three ent the jury, Hank, we don't see things the way the law and reason would intend us to. It's a complex scenario you 'ave us all tied up in, it really is. Not to mention ya family – Leyla aside, 'ave you not been thinkin' 'bout ya boys?"

Hank's leg stopped quaking, his lips tightened. He scratched his cheek so roughly that he broke the skin beneath his stubble. The muddled man in front of the mob was having his moment of clarity about ten years too late. Happiness was now a thing of hindsight.

Hank Howardson was a married man with two young sons. His wife, Leyla, was an unhappy woman. His sons, Jack and Burt, were troublemakers. They all lived in a lovely country cottage down a cul-de-sac in Bradford-on-Avon. Hank, in a way, was a family man, but that small part of him was constantly being exorcised by the powers of the temptations of the underworld, and his family suffered as a result of both his absence and his unlawfulness. Hank had become so wrapped up in his dirty pastimes that were it not for the fact he lived with them, he would've forgotten about his wife and children completely. Now, sat in front of his maker with a guilty conscience, it seemed easy to reflect on a life of neglect.

Gillian Hobbs approached the table holding a tray with the rest of the drinks on it. She stepped down the small stairs and addressed the table of stern men.

"Okay, I 'ave a pot o' tea for one?" Gillian looked around for a nod or a gesture to signal whose drink it was that she had. There was nothing, so she asked again. "A tea? One of ya's ordered a tea?" Hank, coming back to earth, realised that it was his drink and half-raised his hand in acknowledgement. Gillian set the pot, the cup and the milk down next to him. She poured out a cup of tea for him and then called out her next order: "And a cappuccino, extra chocolate on the top?" Madd Rockson nodded in response and made a space on the table for his coffee. "And I s'pose then that the water is yours?" Gillian said, looking at Dr Chaim. "What's up, you on a diet or summin' Trevor?" she joked at the tall skinny villain, setting his water down on the table.

Dr Chaim was not on a diet, he just didn't like the coffee that Gillian served, and he didn't drink tea, but to be kind he cracked a smile at her quip. Then Gillian left and the table resumed its tensions.

"When we turned up at ya place this mornin', you know I could'a sworn I saw ya inside. Strange that we found you at that garage in Castle Cary instead weren't it... What happened there then?" Mr. Mann already knew what had happened, he just enjoyed seeing Hank relive the shit day he had had so far.

"I can get ya the money Trevor, I can and I will. It weren't meant to 'appen like this but I can get ya the..." Hank was sounding ridiculous and so luckily Mr Mann stopped him.

"Firstly, it's Mr Mann, not Trevor. You don't have the right nor respect to call me Trevor. Secondly, we'll get to all that but for now that's not what I asked ya. I asked you what happened this mornin'?"

Hank fidgeted a little and knocked his knee into the table. Madd's cappuccino quaked and spilt a little into the saucer. Hank's look shot over at him, horrified, and before he could spit out an apology, Madd removed the teaspoon he had left in his coffee cup and slapped it against the neck of the bumbling idiot beside him. Hank's flesh sizzled as the red-hot spoon seared his neck and temporarily branded him with an egg-shaped burn. Hank tried to shout out in pain, but the quick-thinking Dr Chaim pre-empted the wail and his long arm reached over to seal shut Hank's mouth and muffle his cry. All the while, Mr Mann was sipping his coffee and watching as if nothing at all had changed at the table.

"Now answer the fuckin' question or I'll pour the rest of it down ya lap!" warned Madd, with a screwed-up face and menace in his eyes.

Madd released the spoon from his neck and put in into Hank's teacup, then Dr Chaim removed his hand from across Hank's mouth and wiped it clean on his trouser leg. Hank slapped his cold hand onto his hot neck and wished he had the fight in him to do something about it. He didn't, so he spoke.

"I got 'ome round mid-mornin' and Leyla and the kids weren't in. The boys must've been at school and I dunno where Leyla was."

"Where'd you been, Hank?" asked Mr Mann. Hank dropped his head with the question.

"I stayed out."

"With ya little missus on the side, was it?"

Hank didn't answer.

"Go on..."

"I went straight up to the loft to... to grab me case and then that's when I heard Leyla screamin'. I'm guessin' that's about the time you lot turned up."

Mr Mann then finished Hank's account.

"Then you ran, both of ya, ran. Away from us an' away from that nice little house and ya two little boys. I was the one that suggested we go through the back to save causin' a street-side scene and you, you sneaky little bastard, took that chance to run, eh? And in a speedy car like yours you would'a been hittin' the horizon way before we even broke down the back door. So then what 'appened Hank? D'ya know what 'appened?"

"I didn't run away from me boys this mornin'."

"No Hank, I know you didn't. You ran away from those boys years ago, this mornin' you just got caught doin' it."

"So what? Where're they now? Where's Leyla? I told ya I will sort all this out so ya don't need to..."

This time Dr Chaim reached over to grab the teaspoon. He whipped it back out from Hank's tea and scalded the other side of his neck. Madd Rockson lunged over to cover Hank's mouth in a role-reversing manoeuvre. Hank's yelp seeped out a little before Madd got to him, but the noise went unnoticed in the busy shop. Hank's eyes began to water as his neck scarred with another red blotch; he needed to learn to answer the questions. Mr Mann took another mouthful of his coffee and laughed a little at the mess laid out in front of him. The quiet hum of the shop's Christmas tunes juxtaposed the mood at the table.

"Hank my friend, you really are a bastard, do you know that? I wanna know – what 'appened after you and Leyla sped off from us this mornin'?"

The other Trevors released their hold on Hank and nestled back into their seats. Hank ignored his burns this time before speaking.

"We drove out for Poole to catch the ferry. Leyla didn't know much 'bout what was goin' on. I drove out and headed for me parents, was the first place I thought of... I stopped to get petrol and then it all went t' shit. It's all shit; always, but it got a lot shitter then." His head and shoulders wilted, they couldn't get any lower than they were now.

"Pick ya head up you great tit! It's no good feelin' sorry for y'self now, is it?"

Hank lifted his head to face Mr Mann and looked around to make sure nobody was reaching for the teaspoon. They weren't, and so he continued.

"Me own wife, my Leyla, leavin' me for dead in the middle'a nowhere. Drivin' off and not comin' back... how could she?"

The three Trevors' expressions matched each other's

completely as they all struggled to see the fault in what Leyla had done.

"Don't play the victim Hank, you would'a left all on your own if it weren't for Leyla catchin' you with the suitcase! And are you really that surprised she left you? After all you've done? And to be honest, she's turned out to be a bit of a wrongen too, ain't she? But that's all your doin' that is, you turned a good woman bad, Hank." Hank showed a little discomfort at that last remark. It was true, but it wasn't Mr Mann's truth to tell. "Your Leyla sold you up the river, I bet you didn't know that. We wouldn't a known where you'd got to, were it not for 'er. She put the call in Hank, she bargained her own freedom for your where'bouts. The love's well and truly gone my friend. Funny thing is though, that neither of you, for one second, stopped to think or worry or do anythin' 'bout little Jack and Burt… You disgust me. Madd and I know all about bad parents and I 'ave a special hate in my heart for ones like you two. Good luck to your boys in their bleak future, 's'all I can say."

Hank tightened his jaw; nerves were being struck, but then clever Trevor picked up his teaspoon and pointed it at him with purpose. Hank jumped back in his chair and shuddered at the threat.

"The fact is, you've run away from your problems for the last time. It's wrong what you've done t'ya family. It's wrong what you've done to your so-called friends; but for what you've done to us, to me, wrong's just not the word. There's a price to pay for cheating the wicked, Hank. Don't play the devil at his own game." Mr Mann lowered the teaspoon from Hank's face and dipped it into the pot. "I told you when you first came to us, didn't I? I told you there was more to it than ya needed to know and that you should just walk away, didn't I? Didn't I say it?! And I told you the first time you got yourself caught up in this same mess! Even after they kicked seven bells of shit outta ya I said, walk away, don't mess yourself up any more than ya already 'ave, didn't I? And didn't I tell you that if I ever caught you sniffing around my business again then there'd be a lot more than just a kicking coming ya way, didn't I? I did. But the thing is, Hank, you're as thick between the ears as you are short between the legs. And you don't listen. Nobody listens. Nobody ever listens until it's too late, and even then they don't listen, they just sit and sieve out the pieces they think are gonna fix it... Your tea's getting cold."

Then Dr Chaim's long arm shot out from his sleeve once more as his hand cupped Hank's mouth shut again. Madd Rockson quickly picked up the teapot and emptied it into Hank's lap. The pot was three quarters full and still very, very hot. Hank squealed in pain, but Dr Trevor Chaim caught it in his big hand like a bad cough. The guilty man thrashed a little as his crotch swelled beneath his faded jeans.

"Stop whinging and drink some tea." Mr Mann was unshakeable.

Hank finished struggling and the boys let him go. It was hard to tell whether or not his eyes were watering this time with the pain or if he had indeed been broken and brought to tears. He pulled his jeans slowly away from his crotch as his breath withered with defeat. Picking up his cup, Hank drank a mouthful of his tea, slurping loudly.

"Nothing's gonna fix this Hank. And you know that, don't you?"

Hank swallowed hard as Mr Mann leant back in his

chair and prepared himself for a story.

"I lost my dad when I was eleven, Hank. Like you, he was a bastard. But unlike you, he was a good father. He was into all sorts of naughty bits, but he cared for me. I was too young to understand completely what 'appened to him but long story short, he got into some bad business. He went out one day and never came back. The police turned up at the house next mornin' and told me that Dad had been taken away. The silly sod had got 'imself caught. After everythin' he used to tell me about not getting caught, he went and got 'imself caught. 'Be as bad and as bold as you like,' he used to say, 'but just make sure you don't get caught!' As it goes, I wasn't a particularly bad kid given the circumstances, but it's hard to stay that way when you're raised by a villain and then thrown into a care home for abandoned kids. Where're ya supposed to go from there?"

Mr Mann stopped to take a mouthful of his coffee. Dr Chaim sipped his water while the others stayed still and hushed, waiting for the rest of the story.

"I met your man Madd in that care 'ome; we were roommates, weren't we? He was me little brother. You wouldn't believe it now, but he was as cute as a button back then. Two little Trevors, both left behind by their parents to grow up in a dirty old care 'ome. It was like we were meant to be, weren't it?" Madd smiled a little, without showing too much humility. "I managed, though I hated it. I missed my dad and I missed my own space, though I was sure me old man shared the exact same sentiments, but as I say – he shouldn't've got caught. It was his own fault. I decided that was the first and last time I was gonna suffer 'cos of someone else's mistakes..."

The conversation paused slightly as a mother and her

young daughter made their way down the steps and over to the toilets. Mr Mann took this moment to check his watch – it had just turned five o'clock. He was planning to leave as soon as his coffee and his story were finished. There was a party he had to get to, his boss's annual Christmas do out in his manor in the Cotswolds. The three Trevors were all attending and now they had a special uninvited guest to accompany them.

"We were in there for a while, gettin' by," Mr Mann reprised, "and then one day, this lady came in from outta nowhere. She didn't speak like the others that came in and out, lookin' round and eyeing up what child they wanted. She was from London, not the West. She was beautiful; it's a shame what the years have done to her now. It turned out her and her husband had just moved from the city and bought a big ol' grand house in a right lovely part of the countryside. I reckon she felt the place was a bit empty for just the two of 'em 'cos she came in lookin' for a kiddie to take home with 'er. After a couple of short visits, she chose your man over there, Trevor Rockson. Like I said, he was a right little cutie."

Hank laughed through his nose involuntarily and instantly regretted it. He braced himself for a third spoon attack or another hot lap or something worse, but all he got was daggers from Madd. A cold look of disdain while he finished off his extra-sweet cappuccino.

"He wouldn't go without me, and I wouldn't be left behind without 'im. So, she took us both. She didn't want me, but she got me, and I was way past affection at that point. I just wanted out. We were taken back to her big new house and that's when I met him: Captain Grubbe."

Hank's brain scrambled to remember where and when

he had heard that name before. It was most definitely a familiar one, although he couldn't place it just yet. There was an aloofness to it, though – he knew that Captain Grubbe was not a name you wanted to hear when being read your own sentence.

Madd Rockson then got up and walked to the counter to order another cappuccino. He didn't explain his movements to the others as this was a routine occurrence whenever they stopped for coffee. Dr Chaim gently grabbed Madd's arm as he walked behind his chair.

"Get it to go. He's gonna want to leave soon. And get me one'a them cookies at the front, will ya? The Christmas tree ones."

Dr Chaim let go of his friend and turned back around to face the table. The highly intellectual man of few words had finally spoken, and it was to ask for a Christmas tree cookie.

"The Captain wasn't fazed or bothered that his wife brought home two kids instead of one. In his world, it was a small and insignificant change. From the moment I saw 'im, stood there in that great big house, dressed in his finest and chewing on a cigar the size of a rollin' pin, I knew I'd struck gold. He was sort of my Daddy Warbucks."

"And that makes Rockson little Annie then, does it?" replied Hank, with rapid response.

The Christmas tunes skipped as if the shop's speaker system was annotating the conversation. Hank could hardly believe that he had said it himself, but being as though Madd was away from the table, his subconscious took the chance to have a swipe at his harasser. Dr Chaim laughed a little, surprisingly, and Mr Mann just stared in amazement. There weren't many people who would interrupt him once he had started to speak.

With a smirk drawn across his long, pale face, Dr Chaim struck Hank with a boxer's swing. His big, bony fist spanked Hank's right cheek so hard that it toppled him from his chair. A few people in the tearoom turned their heads to see what was happening, but the table was well hidden at the back of the room. The Dr shook his fist out and then stood up to pull Hank back from the floor and into the chair. His mouth was bloodied, and he looked as though he was seeing stars as he was plonked back down at the table. Mr Mann wasted no time in addressing the issue, though he still looked mostly unshaken by the pantomime of violence played out in front of him.

"The thing is Hank, you really can't get yourself into any more trouble than you're already in, so in a way you're a free man, for now. I'll let that one slide, but just know, there're more ways than you know that a man can be 'urt and still live to feel the pain. Carry on like that and you'll be begging for Trevor to give you another right-'ander just to distract you from what I'll be doing. I'll really fuckin' hurt ya. Not to mention what Madd'll put you through. He enjoys it a lot more than I do Hank. You know, we were supposed to be at Madd's shop now, drinking coffee and tellin' you off just like in 'ere, but someone over there tried to do us over. That really put me in a shit mood. Not so much 'cos someone thought they could get the better of me, because as you've demonstrated more than once Hank, people'll try it. No, I was annoyed because I like my routine visits to Madd's Sandwich Bar on a Friday. The coffee's good and free, it puts a smile on Madd's face, and unlike this place, it don't smell like the inside of Father Christmas's arsehole. But we had to change it up. I haven't told Madd 'cos, well, I know he'd overreact, get too nasty too quick – it always 'appens. You know the upstairs to Madd's place, that shitpit of a nightclub? Can you believe that little fella who runs it was gonna try and pull a funny on us tonight?! Luckily enough there're some people round there that like me a lot more than they like 'im, otherwise we'd be in as much trouble as you are Hank! Rest assured though, he's got one hellova night ahead of 'im. I don't think he'll be much more of a problem when we catch up to what's left of him a bit later. I'm roundin' 'em up tonight I tell ya, oh we're gonna 'ave some fun!"

Hank knew exactly who Mr Mann was talking about. He was no stranger to the disco tavern above Madd's Sandwich Bar. It was more than just the smell of old booze that coaxed him away from home and into the private booths of the Mantis Bar and Nightclub.

"...So I won't tell Madd about that, 'cos I don't wanna have to explain to The Captain why we had to clean your insides up off the bathroom floor of a small cake shop in Frome. But you've been warned, understand?"

Hank blotted his bloody lip with a serviette and wagged his eyebrows in acknowledgement.

"That's the thing, it's not just me you ripped off. It's not just Trev 'n' Trevor either. My old man, the one who's been good enough not to get caught, he's the one standin' at the top of all this. The Captain is at the top of the food chain and right now you're at the bottom. I gave you a chance Hank. You asked me if you could get involved, not the other way 'round. I want you to remember that, it'll make all this seem even more senseless to ya. You did what you had to do for us and then you should've gone away. If you wanted to carry on I wouldn't've 'ad a problem but you got ideas above your station, didn't ya? I don't believe I'm the first one to be using this system and I know I certainly won't be the last; however there aren't many that do what I do to make sure I don't lose. You, Hank, you started to make me lose."

The system Mr Mann was talking about was his and the other Trevor's shrewd strategy on the fixed outcomes of sports betting. They had begun, a little while back, spread betting to secure a pay-out. There were a few steps to their process and Hank had volunteered himself for involvement as a worker bee; laying down the bets for the boys back at base.

"You took my cash cow and you nearly milked it dry. If you wanted to cash in on your own system then you should've chosen a different stomping ground. What's mine is mine and you knew that from the start. Everybody knows that. You put us at risk of losing more than just a few bad bets first time round my friend..."

"You and those other wasters you call your mates," Dr Chaim added coldly. "You weren't 'alf bad at the number stuff Hank, so I have no idea why you hired such a braindead bunch to work on your behalf!"

Hank was listening as best he could, not wanting to provoke another punch.

"There's a whole other side to what we do, and for everythin' to work," Mr Mann explained, "a few routines have to be honoured. You fucked up, and you got caught. Don't. Get. Caught. It really is that simple. Those friends you pulled in to do your dirty work, they didn't deserve what they got but I had to make an example of 'em. You though, you've deserved everything you've got so far. We managed to patch up what you ripped open when the bookies caught you running amok. If we hadn't, well I reckon you know what would've been if that was the case – a lot more than a hot lap, I tell ya!"

A sweat broke out on Hank's forehead as, for the first time since being caught, he truly contemplated his demise at the hands of the three Trevors. As if on cue, Madd Rockson returned to the table with his takeaway cappuccino and the bad doctor's cookie. Hank's sweaty head was on a swivel as Madd passed behind his chair. The evidence of his prior disobedience was still bubbling from his upper lip and he didn't trust Madd to ignore the obvious. To his credit, or discredit (depending whose side you're on), Madd did ignore the obvious. He had gotten himself a Christmas tree cookie and was more interested in that than he was Hank, for the time being.

"I know they're still holdin' you for the money you lost 'em Hank," said Mr Mann, "and I don't blame 'em. Whether they messed up or not, they wouldn't've known they were messin' up if it weren't for you and your — unruliness... Is that the word, unruliness?" Mr Mann looked to Dr Chaim for assurance.

Dr Chaim nodded. "Unruliness, disruptiveness..." he chipped in.

"Bullshit," added Madd Rockson, wrapping his hand that wasn't holding his cookie around the back of Hank's neck. "You and your bullshit, Hank!" he finished, slamming down Hank's already throbbing face to meet with the hard, flat wooden table.

There was an inevitable clap of bone on wood. The table shuddered with a lingering *boom* as the cutlery shimmied, jingling in the reverb of the empty crockery. Hank stayed down, deliriously slumped in the bloody mess of his own mistakes.

"Madd, that's enough, pack it in!" Mr Mann snapped at his friend. "Hank, pick yourself up, I'm not finished yet."

Hank slowly craned his head back up to face the group. His nose was busted and there was a bruise on his cheek erupting like a dying star with interstellar colours. He snatched a handful of serviettes to blot his face.

"Ouch," he said, looking terrible.

"I know you owe that sneaky little fuck Faisal some too. Who knew you'd 'ave to pay for all that powder you've been pushing up your nose and all those dances you couldn't afford?! You've racked up quite the debt, but ironically, those people are on credit with me, Hank, and so I'm sorry to say that you owe me a lot more than you think you do, and so far I 'aven't even gotten an apology..."

Hank removed the sodden red tissue from his mouth and carped like a stroppy teenager. "I'm sorry."

"No you're not. Feelin' sorry for and being sorry are two very different things. You feel sorry for yourself, and that's 'cos you're the only person you care about Hank. But I 'appen to also feel a little bit sorry for ya... How is it that a man with everythin' is willing to bet it all away, for nothin'? Did the idea of an honest job ever cross your mind? Have you never thought that maybe none of this crap is really worth the hassle you've put everyone through? You 'ad a good start in life Hank, that's a lot more than can be said 'bout me. You also got a family, that fantastic car and that lovely house to keep 'em all in, and it still wasn't enough for you, was it?! It's the greed of the modern man that's killed you off Hank, it's not knowing how to let the bad guys be bad and the good guys be good. Trust me, if I wasn't built the way I was then I'd be away from 'ere, away from the rough, away from the Hank Howardsons of the world. I 'ad no choice. When I looked up at the sky all I saw was my dad, the nasty Colonel Mann, clouding over me like a bad habit. And when that shadow passed there weren't any sun there to break through 'cos there was already a great big storm cloud choking out the brightness. There weren't an escape for me Hank, but for you, I bet when you looked up you saw the inspirin' blue of a summer day – a man with the world at his feet, and you booted it away. Fuck you Hank."

Mr Mann finished off his flat white coffee. The last mouthful was as sweet as he'd hoped it would be and he smiled with the sugary kick. The Hobb's Cake shop was mostly empty now as closing time was nearing. The trainee barista was wiping down the tops of the counters and restocking the fridges and cupboards behind them. Gillian was gliding around the shop to the gleeful chimes of the instrumental Christmas tracks, straightening tables and reshaping the decorations. The boys were just about done.

"Here's what happens to people who mess with things they don't understand, Hank. With people they wish they hadn't... I remember when The Captain and his wife first took me and Madd in, things were a bit weird in the house. Aside from the obvious changes, there was summin' off with the troupe that moved up from the city with 'em. I never really asked, and they never really told, but I was old enough by then to understand. In a big house the walls talk louder – if you keep quiet then you can hear all sorts of things you're not s'posed to. There was more than one reason why they moved out to the country, and one of 'em was because of a girl, and the North London copper she was bangin'. This girl 'ad worked for Captain Grubbe for a while and as far as I know she weren't exactly the most willin' or best behaved one he 'ad. She was a beauty though; not as pretty as his wife was back then but there was summin' 'bout 'er that sent the boys wild. It was probably the 'fuck off' attitude she 'ad towards all of us to be honest. I could tell straight away that she was different from the mess of the rest – I think in all honesty she was a good person and that's what scared 'em the most. Anyway, it turned out this girl 'ad been sent to work on a copper that The Captain needed on his side, but she had some ideas of her own. The first mistake she made, much like yourself Hank, is that she underestimated how much the people at the top know. Not much gets past me, Hank, but even less gets past The Captain. This girl was after a way out and she found it in the policeman. So instead of all the coaxin' and manipulatin' she was sent to do, she decided to spill the beans on The Captain and his dirty tricks. You see Hank, I told you didn't I, you get used to people takin' you for fools in this game, but as soon as you start losing, that's when punches have to be thrown..."

Hank flinched and ducked as he assumed this was a cue for one of the boys to throw a punch at him. It wasn't, and they didn't. Instead the three Trevors just looked at Hank, squirming in cowardice behind the shade of his sleeves, and smirked in arrogance at the beaten man. It was quiet for a minute as Hank recomposed himself and then Mr Mann spoke again.

"The Captain was wise to 'er tricks, he always was apparently, but he let 'er believe that she'd gotten away with it this time. If you sell your soul to a devil it can't be bought back on your terms, there's no mercy in evil, and I can't for the life of me work out why people still seem to think that there is! Anyway, she got close to this copper and made moves she weren't supposed to. Grubbe must've known that by then the policeman would never've willingly succumbed to his tricks, the girl had already said too much. To admit defeat at the 'ands of a good man and one of his own, though, that was summin' The Captain wasn't prepared to do. Whatever 'appened between the two of 'em had obviously kept the wolf from the door, 'cos The Captain was rattled for once by the decency of an honest man. He was a problem, and one not easily solved.

"For a while the girl carried on working for Grubbe, and for a while the policeman turned his back on 'er, but as luck and life would 'ave it, she turned out to be pregnant with the copper's kid. A policeman and a prostitute 'aving a baby together, that still makes me laugh even now. There's summin' in that 'ent there? Besides the ridiculousness... It's kind of— endearing I s'pose. At least it could've been.

"She left to raise her little girl along with the dumbstruck copper, but all the while The Captain was plannin' his revenge. She'd made a fool of him. She'd messed with the status quo. She'd cost him the loyalty of the policeman. The other little piggies, it seemed, had given in to his big bad ways, but with a renegade on the inside, that little piggy stayed at 'ome. Before this little drama, I think The Captain must've already been thinkin' about moving away to the countryside. He had piles and piles of filthy money and they were getting too big for the stink of the city. He needed somewhere else to stash it, somewhere where it was less likely to land him in trouble. There's investment to be made outside of the city, people seem to forget that... He didn't. Twenty years ago, near enough to the day I think, Captain Grubbe and his wife moved out 'ere, away from the muck of London. He had the money and he had the power and about then, he 'ad me. And Madd of course. That's where our story starts. I remember the first time I saw him Hank, I thought I'd seen it in me dad, but to The Captain my old man seemed, pffft well, a bit powerless really. He was too brutish, too ready to raise his fists before his voice. The Captain took me on as more than just an adopted son, he took me on as a sort of heir to the Grubbe estate. Mum always preferred Madd, as he was the one she actually wanted to bring 'ome. I was okay with that, I've never 'ad a mum and you can't grieve over what you've never 'ad. You can only mourn what you've lost, and I've seen mourning like you never 'ave, Hank. People torn apart from the ones they love, loss without death – a broken heart really can hurt the most."

The shop now, aside from the four boys, was entirely empty. Everything inside was pretty much packed down, but before Gillian had time to flick the wreath sign around from 'Open' to 'Closed', one last customer dashed in through the frosted glass door, out of the cold. A young lady, with beautiful long brown hair and soft tanned skin, was just in time to torment the trainee barista before she hung up her apron for the day. The ring of the bell above the door rang offensively in Gillian and the barista's ears. The machines were still running but neither of them was expecting the harsh reprise of the steam wand scream. Gillian was good at reading the customers that came into her shop, and unfortunately this lady had all the tell-tale traits of a dawdler. She pasted a smile onto her face nonetheless and welcomed the latecomer into the warm. Gillian was right about her, it seemed, and she flashed a quick look of disapproval to the barista as the customer idly browsed the drinks board.

Back at the table, Mr Mann was nearing the end of his story:

"The Captain decided to bring the girl causin' all the trouble over 'ere with him and the others. He pried her apart from her six-month-old daughter and the policeman she was, by then, engaged to. Apparently, the copper 'ad taken her and the kid in, obviously having a change of heart. The mean ol' Captain broke up the happy home just as he intended to. I won't go into the details too much now Hank, I've been talkin' for too long, but there was no way out for that poor girl once she turned her back on The Captain. It came down to her or the child and she knew what she had to do. She came against her will and with no time for goodbyes. She was ripped from the safety of her new life and thrown back into the familiar cesspit of her old one, 'cept this time it was out 'ere in the country, and you know as much as anyone, Hank, that there are some right fuckin' weirdos out 'ere. I met 'er then, at the big house – my new home. If she was unhappy with her life before she came 'ere then when I met 'er she must've been nigh on suicidal. She was vulnerable. Miserable. Distraught. She had been well and truly broken. I was a boy back then and I knew no better than to pity her because, like you, she had everything, then in one fell swoop it was all gone... It's all gone, Hank. You're not going back, you're at the mercy of The Captain now. And who knows, maybe Leyla and the boys'll be better off without you around, just like that policeman and his daughter might've been better off without Sara. You're gonna be worked. You're gonna be used and you're gonna be made an example of. I really wish you'd listened the first time you got caught, Hank, because now, you're fucked."

Mr Mann's expression changed. The calm and reasonable tone of his voice faded. His green eyes seemed to dim to a poisonous black.

"You finished your tea?" he asked.

Hank didn't answer. He had hardly touched his tea; the cup was full. This made the crunch of the teacup on his head even more uncomfortable.

Mr Mann swiped the teacup from the table before Hank had a chance to duck, and he larruped it across the side of his already sore head. It was a vicious and unforgiving move. The brittle china crashed, with the slap of Mr Mann's heavy hand, against poor hapless Hank. With cold tea left cascading down the purple and red of his face, he cried out in pain. Trevor Mann had at last shown his power, the fury in him still rumbling as he dried his tea-splattered hands on his napkin. Trevor Chaim and Trevor Rockson also reached for the napkins to dry the tea spray from their shirts. They were used to Mr Mann's sudden flashes of malevolence but still it shocked them how bloodthirsty he could become out of apparent serenity. Sobbing and bleeding, Hank finally bailed out and stumbled to the nearby toilets to clean up.

"Follow 'im," commanded Mr Mann, not specifying who he was addressing. His jaw was taut and his wide shoulders rigid. He looked as if he had just doubled in size. "And get that tidied up while I pay the bill. I want everyone in the car by the time I'm done. Bring it round the back, we really need to get goin'." He cracked his knuckles and then rose to his feet, brushing the creases out of his suit and fixing his tie. "That's as violent as it gets tonight, understand? From now until tomorrow we're to be as ordinary as ordinary. I'll see you in the car."

Tick Tock

The mess and the noise of the final assault was unmasked this time by the quiet of the shop. Gillian and her barista, already peeved at the late arrival of the last customer, groaned aloud as they heard the smash of porcelain at the back of the shop. Gillian was wrapping up the leftovers behind the front counter and the barista was fixing up the winter-spiced latte for the young lady waiting on the other side of it. She seemed unfriendly, the young lady, as she stood watching her coffee being made, po-faced and impatient. Her stare was almost hostile. She wasn't a local girl. From the back of the shop, through the hazy smoke of the blown-out table candles, Mr Mann appeared, looking composed as he neared the counter, ready to settle the bill. Upon seeing him approach, Gillian set her tray of leftover treats down and took off her plastic food hygiene gloves. As polite as ever to those with whom he had no quarrel, Mr Mann joined the back of the small queue behind the young lady. Her coffee was ready now and she was about to pay. Gillian, now at the till, went ahead and rang up the medium spiced latte, happy to be able to close the register down for the day.

"That'll be £1.95 please m'darlin'," said Gillian, somehow managing to still force a welcoming smile.

The lady reached into her shoulder bag for her purse. She rummaged, looking bothered by the experience.

"Please don't call me a darling. Trust me, I'm not," she snapped as she found her purse and pulled it from the bag.

Gillian's face dropped with shock; the atmosphere soured. "If you have to call me anything, call me Evangeline."

Evangeline's accent gave her away as a tourist. The frostiness of her North London vowels made the weather outside feel like summer in the Bahamas. Mr Mann raised his eyebrows from behind Evangeline. Gillian, perturbed by the sudden backlash, just waited for the money, her welcoming smile at last diminished. A knife could have slashed through the damp, rank sludge of the atmosphere, but as Evangeline opened her purse to pay for her drink, an unexpected and uninvited trinket fell from the leathery folds inside. It was Colonel Mann's watch.

Mr Mann froze as the leather-strapped timepiece fell carelessly to the hard floor of the cake shop. The short blond hairs latent on his neck spiked upwards so suddenly that the static charge between them and his shirt nearly set his head alight. He knew instantly whose watch it was that had escaped Evangeline's purse. The synapses in his brain fired harder than a nun's climax as his vision narrowed and his breath drew inwards, cold and heavy. The clink of the precious glass on the watch face as it knocked the floor pierced Mr Mann's ears; the quiet ticking that struck through the long, drawn-out seconds boomed inside his muddled mind like a war drum. How did this random, bad-mannered girl come to possess his late father's favourite watch?

Evangeline stooped to pick up the fallen watch. She set it down on the countertop and gave over a handful of loose change to Gillian, whose cracked smile was slipping as Evangeline's presence bothered her more and more. Without a word, Evangeline swiped the watch and her coffee from the counter and turned to leave, but she was faced with the big, beating chest of Trevor Mann. He was beguiled by the familiar watch but was trembling with perplexity as to how it had made its way back to its rightful heir. He was rigid, immoveable from his feet up to his thick neck, encaptivated by the nostalgic charm of the bling in Evangeline's possession. She hinted for the big man to move aside, her eyes unable to roll in their sockets any more than they were, but of course, the solid wall of Trevor Mann was going nowhere.

"Excuse me," Evangeline growled, unknowing of who it was she was sassing.

"No no, excuse me... that's a lovely watch you have there. A real fine piece," the Colonel's son responded, still not making eye contact but instead tracking his father's watch in Evangeline's hand. "How'd you come to 'ave that? An old family heirloom perhaps... or maybe you stole it?" he asked of Evangeline, now engaging in eye contact.

Her lip twitched. She took a big slurp of her coffee to mask the discomposure on her face. Mr Mann laughed gently, showing his pearly white teeth shining in the reflections of the low shop lights: the headlight to the rabbit.

"Excuse me?" Evangeline repeated, more nervously this time.

"You said that already. And I said, how did you come to have that watch?"

"It's a long story, one for another time maybe."

"I've got time, especially for this. Believe me."

Mr Mann could see the terror building in Evangeline's stare. The cocksure queen was cracking. Gillian and her trainee barista were tense behind the counter, watching the drama building between their two customers in frustration; they were wanting to go home.

"...But I can see that these ladies don't, so how 'bout you tell me all about it outside?"

A wash of horror coated the faces of all three women. Other than Mr Mann, none of them knew what to do.

"Ladies, thank you very much and Merry Christmas. Gillian, make sure she gets her fair share of that," joked Mr Mann, as he threw down a small roll of notes onto the countertop, nodding at the new barista. "You, let's go." He wrapped his big arm around Evangeline so tightly that the lid of her coffee nearly popped off.

She struggled a little, but he was just too big. She wanted to yelp, but it was as if all the words had left her mind and abandoned her mouth in sudden fright. He walked her down the steps and towards the back of the shop, muttering wrathfully under his breath all the way.

"Don't you worry, Gillian," Mr Mann called out as they approached the back door, "the boys 'ave cleaned up the mess back 'ere. And it turns out this one is headin' in the same direction as us anyway. I'll see ya soon. And say 'ello to Rob for me."

Evangeline was stiff with dread. Her coffee and the watch were frozen in her grip, her belly was knotted and her face was ghostly pale. She was guilty. There was a retribution happening, an instant punishment afoot, but she was as puzzled as her captor was about how this had all happened so quickly and so unannounced. Noiselessly she was shuffled out of the shop with her feet barely touching the ground. In Trevor's big arms she stayed clamped as he led her out of the fire exit door and into the dimly lit back street.

The car was waiting: a stealthy black BMW 5 series

with tinted windows and shiny black alloys. It was KITT from Knight Rider for the conservative man. Dr Chaim was in the driver's seat with Madd Rockson and Hank Howardson snuggled up in the back. They had been waiting furtively, with the engine rumbling low. Mr Mann walked around to the passenger seat and folded Evangeline into the car to join the rest.

"Who's she then?" asked Dr Chaim.

"She, like 'im in the back, is a dirty fuckin' thief. What's your name again?" asked Mr Mann.

"Ev..." Evangeline began to reply.

"Evangeline! That was it, weren't it, 'darlin'. Evangeline's comin' with us. She's gonna sit 'ere in the front and tell me all about that fancy watch she 'as. Get in the back with them Trevor, I'm drivin'. And there's no coffee in the car," Mr Mann explained, snatching Evangeline's spiced latte from her and dashing it away behind him. "That rule applies to everyone, you know that Madd."

Madd took a last sip of his cappuccino and threw the remains out of the window next to him.

Mr Mann closed the door and headed around to the driver's seat, passing Dr Chaim as they crossed in front of the car.

"Keep sharp. There's two of 'em now, I need 'em both kept close and quiet," Mr Mann informed his colleague before they both got into the car.

In unison the three Trevors clicked their seatbelts in place and settled down into their seats. Mr Mann seized the Colonel's old watch from Evangeline and popped it down into the change well under the spotless dashboard. He held a stare at her, unblinking and wicked, and then at

Hank in the back before cracking a nasty smile and turning back around. He turned the radio on – pre-set 2 – and the unavoidable chirp of the station's Christmas songs suddenly filled the steamy car.

"Boys and girls," he said, still smiling, "Let's go to a party!"

#10. The Siege of Tanya Longtrunk's Second-Hand Bike Exchange Part Three: The Payback

I don't know karate, but I know KA-RAZY

At the end of the week, in the heart of the day,
The soft peace of Frome was about to decay.
The fresh country air wasn't blown quite as freshly,
It tasted quite foul, well, on one street especially.

But for Tanya the air tasted merry and gay
From the lunch she was eating, for now anyway:
A homemade lasagne with a cheesy roux sauce,
And a Rice Krispie cake for her secondary course.

While enjoying the still of the afternoon calm,
The radio played out the three-thirty alarm.
But as she moved onto pudding her heart quickly dropped
When the traffic update snapped, crackled and popped!

There suddenly came a halt in transmission,
As the front door peeled open for the devil's admission...
The winds whistled in through the wavering door,
Then as a soft gust blew, it crept open more.

The tring of the bell on the door started tringing,
And a child was stood in the doorway and singing.
Tanya was caught in a daze at her desk,
With a Bolognese stain on the lap of her dress.

His song carried gently on top of the breeze,
The tune was familiar but in Japanese.
The snow-clouds had parted and let in the light,
Though all was not calm, despite all being bright.

A heavenly glow silhouetted the boy,
A Christmassy show for Tanya to enjoy,
But as he stepped forward and onto the tiles,
There was an odd crooked look on the face of the child.

The boy kept on walking, while Tanya was gawking
For the singing had ceased and the boy started squawking!
Then in rushed another, maybe his brother,
And then came another, another, another!

Tanya was frantic, at sixes and sevens
When the kids bundled in... in their sixes and sevens.
In Christmassy jumpers their mission was folly,
They pulled down the wreath, the tree and the holly!

The attack was an ambush, the kids were relentless,
And Tanya's bad ankle had left her defenceless!
They tore through the shop like a human tsunami,
Though a couple were searching for something more calmly.

A scruffy-faced boy and his tomboyish sister
Hurled a bike pump at Tanya that narrowly missed her.
The commotion inside made a noise like no other,
She couldn't escape, so she dropped down for cover.

'Neath a sturdy old oak frame, she panted and puffed,
She hid and she hoped for the siege to be snuffed.
She could see through the desk the two that were checking;
The two at the top of their order of pecking,

They were here for a reason, and not for a fight,
Though what they were seeking was well out of sight.
Watching them search, she began to remember,
The man with the trailer who'd come in September.

"There's a handful of bikes," she remembered Ray saying,
"Some Japanese customs I'm keen for displaying."
As the youngsters turned 'round, it gave validation:
The Tamura children, from Bradford-on-Avon.

In the blitz and the bedlam it became quite apparent,
Their motive was clear and the plot was transparent.
Their bikes had been taken and sold to her father,
In this once-quiet shop, his forgotten nirvana.

"I'm callin' the police!" Tanya suddenly shouted.
The room then fell quiet, her position was outed.
A small voice broke the stillness somewhere behind Tanya:
"Can you give us our bikes back... Can ya, miss? Can ya?"

The man in the autumn, she remembered him coming;
He came with a trailer, and a Ford Thunder-something.
She'd been visiting Ray that hot day in September
When she noticed the bikes and all of their splendour.

But the bikes with this bloke were as hot as the weather,
They were packed in his trailer, all bundled together.
They were streamlined and shiny, as light as a feather,
The framework was black and their saddles were leather.

So Ray and the salesman they bargained together,
Doing bad business but feeling quite clever.
They both saw a profit with this new endeavour;
But the children were now at the end of their tether.

They'd come for revenge, they'd come for their bikes back,
They'd tracked down Ray's shop like a starving wild dog pack.
Their numbers were great and for kids they were smart,
They'd chased down their prey and had torn it apart.

The chill in the shop wisped around and around,
Then the silence was broken with an echoing sound;
An unpolished conker had hit the floor hard,
It slipped out of a rucksack that was faded and charred.

It jaggedly rolled, and stopped under the desk;
A girl shrunk behind it and, well, you could've guessed.
Her brown eyes met Tanya's, and with uneasy promise
She simply declared, "I don't 'ave 'em, kid, honest.

"You and your brothers 'ave all made a cock-up,
Your bikes 'ave been stored in my old man's lockup.
And I don't 'ave the card, the address or the code,
I don't even know where the spare key is stowed...

"So I think you should leave, 'cos this won't go your way;
I can't deal with this all on my first fuckin' day!
If you'd come in much nicer and not pulled this stunt,
I perhaps would've helped you, you ungrateful kids...

But you've ruined my shop and for that you're a felon,
I'm keepin' your bikes and I'm goin' to sell 'em."
Her bottom lip quaked with a dash of heroics:
"And the police 'ave been called, in case you don't know it!"

The girl had her doubts, but they came to a stop
When a voice on the stairs croaked, "Get out of our shop!"
It was Tanya's mum Joanie, she looked riled and wild;
With a shotgun she pointed from child to child.

With no hesitation and all in a state,
The kids ran out screaming without much debate.
But the oldest one stopped and he stared back inside:
We'll be back to get 'em, his hard look implied.

Then he strutted away, and disappeared with the sun.
With a terrified look, Tanya turned to her mum.
In part, she gave thanks for her sudden arrival,
But had wary suspicions of the waxy brown rifle.

"Oh don't worry Tan, there's no cause for alarm;
This is just my old airgun from Grandpa's old farm."
She laughed, "Twenty-five years and not one bit of
trouble...
And now on your first day..." Her words fell to rubble.

With that she collapsed, Joanie tipped over backward.
She fell with a smile, but her heart had been shattered.
It seemed somewhat peaceful, or calmly chaotic,
As if predetermined and no one could stop it.

Her eyes flickered twice as her breath drifted outwards.
Tanya stood trembling, lost and without words.
Joanie slipped into the deepest of snoozes,
Gently she slept, unaware of her bruises.

With her wrinkled eyes closed she welcomed in death,
Tanya tried hard just to draw in her breath,
But the air wouldn't come, so she dropped to her knees,
Calling her mother with gut-wrenching pleas.

She searched in her pockets for her mobile phone;
She couldn't bring Joanie back all on her own.
But the fact was that Joanie was not coming back;
There was no second chance. There was no time to act.

Still, she needed to call the emergency line;
For all Tanya knew Joanie might still have some time.
But her heart was in pieces, each beat was a sting
And as she pulled out her mobile, it started to ring...

"Hello," answered Tanya, while crying and grieving.
"No, this is Tanya… my mother's not breathing!
I need you to help me, please, what do I do?!
Please help me, please help her, she has to come to!"

Her brain was in meltdown, she was losing her mind,
She had no idea who it was on the line,
"I'm sorry, I am… I don't know who you are…"
It was José; the man from the Bath House and Spa.

In a soggy wet mess in a heap on the floor,
Tanya picked up where she'd left off before:
"They ruined my shop, they've murdered my mum,
They're all fucking guilty, every last one!

They gave 'er a panic, they startled and shocked 'er…
I need to call help; my mum needs a doctor!"
But the voice on the opposite end of the phone
Was calling up bearing bad news of his own.

Tanya's face dropped with what he had to say,
Because José was calling her up about Ray.
It seemed he was in a poor state of his own,
And what happened to him, had happened to Joan.

Their hearts had been broken, completely in sync,
At the very same time they had broken the link,
And it couldn't be fixed, it couldn't be changed,
One followed the other, now isn't that strange?

Now isn't that love? Now isn't that fate?
Now isn't that proof of devotion so great?
The news was romantic but morbidly so,
The end came for one but they both had to go...

But Tanya had stayed and was facing a crisis,
Her heart had been torn out and cut into slices.
It was too much to handle, it was too much to bear,
A harsh indication that life wasn't fair.

All at one time this disaster unfurled,
Her first day had been the worst one in the world!
A total eclipse as her new life was dawning,
She should've known when she slipped over that morning...

So now what would she do? How would she recover?
She'd just lost the shop, and her dad and her mother!
It was fated and dated and death hadn't waited,
The remnants of life were to soon be cremated,

And for now Tanya's smile would char in the fire,
The shop would be closed, and her future be dire.
But she wasn't a Longtrunk; no, she was an Oldman,
The child of Raymundo, whose spirit was golden!

So as Joanie and Ray left this world hand in hand,
Leaving behind their small mark on this land,
They moved on from this life and stepped into the other,
While their poor daughter Tanya had to try to recover.

Without continuation.

#11. SPANK

Stick and Move

It is as I sit at the bar, on a wobbly stool, inside the Mantis Bar and Nightclub above Madd's Sandwich Bar on the Strawberry Way Roundabout off the A303, a thought occurs to me; I am not that good a dancer. I hadn't given it much thought before now to be perfectly honest. I've been out dancing, but not for a very long time. I remember the last time I went out dancing – it was over twenty years ago now. It had been an impromptu routine complimenting the terrific melodies of an eighties tribute band at a small bar in North London. I remember it well; it was the night I met Evie's mother, a tactless and selfish old whore she turned out to be. I only notice my rhythmic disabilities now that I watch Faisal, the owner of the club, strut his funky stuff to the challenging beats of the Godfather of Soul, Mr James Brown. He really is a fantastic mover. I've never actually seen someone shift their body the way that he is shifting his. I am impressed, if not completely jealous of his ability to dance so well. It's a quarter past six in the evening, and the date is Friday 13th December 2002; today is cold but here in the bar it is warm, too warm. I have taken off my jacket and stored it inside the cloakroom at the entrance of the club, though I am regretting that decision. I'm worried that in a hasty escape attempt I may now have to ditch the jacket and run. But, in an attempt to blend in with the club-going folk of England, I chose to pay the pound and hand over my jacket. Temporarily, of course; as long as I keep hold of the little ticket they gave me I'll get my jacket back.

Although, if worst did come to worst then I'm sure I could retrieve it from the friendly cloakroom assistant easily enough. Unless she were to go through my jacket pockets. What if she goes through my pockets? What if she sees my badge?

Nuts and Bolts

I am drawing attention to myself, I know I am. I'm tense. I should order another drink, my glass has been empty for too long. The rest of the crowd in here barely wait for their last drink to end before ordering the next one. It's clear to me that the kinds of people that come to these places at this sort of time don't really come here for the music or the company. To my left there's the dancefloor, one that's very much in the style of a seventies disco dancehall. The coloured LEDs are on a constant loop, flashing and patterning the room with reds, yellows, purples and blues. To my right, towards the back of the room, there are three silver poles; shining and reflecting the colours of the ever-changing dancefloor. Each pole has a dancing girl either attached to it or close by, circling their individual stages and swinging their long hair around to enrapture the onlookers.

Six I count – six boobs bouncing uncomfortably to the music of ol' Jim Brown, unsupported and glorious. Did I know this was a strip club before I came in? I don't think so, but then again, I am not in the least bit surprised, given why I'm here. Although, where are those dirty dogs? There's no sign of them anywhere at the moment. What does surprise me about this place, though, is that of the twenty or so men that are inside, none of them are watching the girls. The only spectator I see is a short-haired lady, sitting directly in front of the middle pole. I can't see her face as she's facing the other way, but I can tell from her posture that she is relaxed. This is not a sore experience for her. What's odder is that the three dancing girls are all in time with one another but are all out of time with the music playing. Understandably, the chaotic funk of Maceo & the Macks is no Def Leppard; the girls are moving to their own beat. Their movements, though obviously seductive, seem lax and unimportant, and given that their boss is about thirty feet away from them and keeping better rhythm, I am wondering.

I order another drink from the bearded barman. He has a nametag on the pocket of his shirt, but it has faded. It looks like it once said Gary, or Garrias, but the text has worn so much that I can't be sure.

"Another Bud please…"

My request ends obscurely: I wanted to call him Garrias, but I stopped at just the G and made a strange 'gga' sound. He must think I have a strange speech impediment. I'm going to have to keep that up the entire time now; regular folk do not call barmen by their name unless they know them.

Faisal is still spinning sensationally around the disco dancefloor, chopping through the hot barroom air with his maniacal moves. He is the only one out on the floor, everyone else is either sat here at the bar with me or at a table, slumped over their own train of empties or leant back against their chair, wide eyed and watching Faisal do his thing. The sound of my second beverage knocking at the varnished wooden bar startles me, and I turn back to see the barman looking at me, his eyes dark and unwelcoming.

"You his latest then, are ya?" the man grumbles at me

as he takes my money.

He's clearly in the know of something I'm not; what does he mean? I can't ask. This place has something queer about it, I've felt it since I first stepped inside. I've been here for half an hour now and have not seen anything like what I was expecting; I'm chasing the right lead, I must be, but maybe they know who I am. Maybe the woman on the phone was right, and not just being overdramatic. Anyway, I can't ask what he means. He's pressing me for information; it should be the other way around.

"No," I say, as he puts my order through the till with his back to me, "Not me...gga."

I figure staying elusive and mostly unresponsive will fare me better than being compliant and communicative, at least until I know exactly what I'm dealing with here. He looks at me strangely as he drops the change into my clammy hands, I look strangely back as we hold a stare for a moment. He breaks it with a shake of his head and a tut. I win, but I'm being careless. Need to rein in the awkwardness if I am to make any gains in this investigation.

'Body Heat'; that's the song that's playing now. It's different to the one that I entered to, but still James Brown. I hazard a guess that the genre doesn't vary much throughout the night. Faisal is quite obviously a Funk & Soul man. I sip my beer and scan the room. A few of the fellas in here are fidgeting; they're getting ready to leave. That's a surprise at only 18:25. The girls are all on their respective poles; the one in the centre is upside down with her legs agape, holding her position remarkably well. The two either side of her are the right way up, though again they are far from being in sync with the backing track, and this time they are not even in time with each other. They're warming up, I've concluded. They're not yet on the clock, they can't be. I think they must be waiting for something else to happen, but there are drinkers already in, so I don't know what they're waiting for exactly.

More people are getting up now, ready to leave. I spy one man who has his jacket with him; he's pulling it off his chair ready to put it on. I definitely could have brought mine inside with me. My mind has been drifting all day – I can't stop thinking about Evie. She is becoming uncontrollable; how am I meant to steer her right again? I was clutching at straws bringing her along on this trip, but I couldn't leave her alone after last week. She's probably running amok over this way now, embarrassing me across the counties! No, she'll be fine, I'm sure of it. She's a troubled girl really – not having a mother has been hard for her growing up, I know it has. I've done my best but now she's an adult we're running out of common ground. I can't be a father and a mother.

That's it now, they've all suddenly got up and shuffled over to the exit hallway. Some of the guys are moving slowly, drunken and reluctant in their steps towards the door, but they are moving nonetheless. What the fuck is happening here?! I wish I would stop breathing so heavily; my drinking pattern has quickened and my mouthfuls are bigger. I'm trying not to let my confusion show, but I fear I'm failing. The music is playing still and the lights from the floor are in their usual metronome at a pulse of about 120 bpm. The air is still hot and stuffy, and the short-haired woman is still sitting in front of the pole dancers. In fact, we two are the only ones besides the barman, the dancers and Faisal who are left in here now. All seven of us are still doing the exact same thing we were doing fifteen minutes ago when I first noted the goings-on of this strange place. The short-haired woman reeks of familiarity now that I see her more clearly in the empty room. I can still only spy the back of her, but her mannerisms are recognisable to me somehow. Should I approach her?

"Why are you still here?" a voice whispers next to me.

Then I feel the nauseating hot breath of a man blow into my ear. I flinch and tweak my gaze from the mystery woman to Faisal, who had crept up next to me unnoticed.

"This one's a bit weird, Face," says the bearded barman behind us both. He has a dishcloth in his hand and is leant intimidatingly on the St. Austell's Jolly Holly Ale draught pump.

"So are you, Garrias, so are you," Faisal jokes back at him. Garrias, I was right! I knew it was Garrias.

His voice is strange, an accent of mongrel standards. He obviously comes from Middle-Eastern decent; he has short silverish hair, dark brown skin and a very faint beard, little more than neat stubble. His English is clean although caught in a West-Country-come-South-London crossover. He sounds almost South African, that's my go-to if I cannot place a person's accent. I should say something; the mood is changing for the worse.

"You're a handsome man," Faisal tells me. It shocks me and my urge to talk subsides once again. "You're far too clean-cut and sober to be knocking about in here. I haven't seen you before, but you're a bit late now I'm afraid... so off you fuck!"

As he smiles sarcastically at me, I notice two things. Firstly, his eyes are huge. He has done lots of cocaine. To be honest, that does explain his copious amounts of energy on the dancefloor and the shakiness of his leg as he sits here in front of me. Secondly, he has a colourful badge on his lapel. It's a two-digit U.S route shield with the colours of the rainbow striped down it, and the words 'Route 69' written on it. The top of the six and the bottom of the nine have little penis tips on them. Did I know this was a gay bar before I came in? No, no I did not.

I leave with my tail between my legs; I have nothing to bargain with this man face to face. 'Face', that's obviously what he's better known as around these parts. I did plan on sitting discreetly at the bar and then mingling unobtrusively as the night wound on, eavesdropping and keeping an eye on what goes on at this place. I hadn't planned for the sudden exodus, pole dancers or, ironically, the homosexual undertones. Also, my bad guys are, as yet, nowhere to be seen. As well as all that, I am thinking too much about Evangeline – it's clouding my judgements. Perhaps I should've left her at home after all, perhaps I should've stayed at home with her for a few days. Shoplifting, possession of a class A... No man should have to hear that his daughter has been doing these things, it's troubling and it's frightening. What's more, I can't believe that less than a month after I left the station to go private I was back there collecting Evie, paying her fines and pleading her innocence. What must they all think?!

Time to collect my coat, earlier than planned, but where did I put the little ticket? I knew I'd lose it, I should've just put it straight into my wallet. I should've just kept hold of the coat and saved myself a pound. I'm too hung up on this coat business, but it's just so silly of me to be that careless, I'm in real shit if anyone finds out I'm...

"Detective Stranger McKrayne. Lost your ticket have you, sir?" The cloakroom girl, less innocent and more sinister than I remember her looking, reads my name and then my mind.

She found the badge.

"It's company policy, we check everyone's pockets who come into this place," she says to me, straight faced and sat on her stool.

I can't help but to think that it's a little intrusive on their part, but then again a search is a search. I understand the safety measures taken by clubs these days. Although, if anyone was to bring anything illegal to the club then they'd be beyond an idiot to leave it in their jacket at the cloakroom. Then again, I'm the tit who left his private detective's badge in his.

"So it would seem," I reply to her.

I'm stood facing her, but not looking at her. I'm about a third of the way down the entrance corridor, which is mirrored on both sides and has a hardwood floor. It's polished, expensive looking. There are some steps, four to be exact, that lead down into the bar at one end, the same steps I just came up to get here; the cloakroom is at the other end. There's a kiosk a few yards further down towards the door, it's where you pay to come in, but nobody is there. I have a second or two to compose myself before I look up to confront her – my identifier. I puff out my chest and straighten my glasses, I'm close enough to the door to make a dash. Fuck the coat, I can get a new one. I need to get out of here, sharpish.

Bang.

The noise sends a gnawing screech through each of my ears and my face gurns as my gums tingle irritably. They're running, all of them running. Running at me. I can do nothing but freeze, cower and pull funny faces at the crowd as they bash their way past me, down the steps and into the bar. There's perhaps twenty-five of them, could be closer to thirty, I'm not sure. I'm lost in a gust of bodies, blown in through the front door. I can't quite make out the faces as they pass but I'm sure they're not the same ones that left before me. And mixed. Men and women, probably with a 5:1 ratio in the men's favour. They're noisy and flatfooted as they all stomp their way past me and out into the bar where I can hear Faisal shouting, screaming at them to get a drink and take their positions. Based solely on tonight's journey so far, I have to question my professional abilities and competency, as I have no fucking clue what is going on.

They've all gone. The corridor is once again mine. I'm startled to say the least, but I recognise that the distraction has taken the edge off my unveiling as a snooping detective. I'm facing the cloakroom girl again. She has regained the smile I remember from when I first came in, so I smile back. We say nothing.

I walk over to her countertop and say, "Eight one eight… it's my ticket number," though I'm sure she knows what I mean.

She's still smiling but she's not moving. This is the stalemate I feared over getting my jacket back, it's passive aggressive; she's pressed the red button, I'm in the shit.

"I'm glad you came, we all are. Especially her. She'll be so happy you're here!"

I want to know what she means, so much. The time to pretend has gone; I simply ask her, "Who?"

She looks at me as if she's captivated by me, and then she hands me a gun.

"It's about to start. You might want to leave your

jacket here, Detective."

There's a switch on the wall next to her; her eyes flash at it. Before I can do or say anything, she presses it, and the shutter falls down onto the counter and she is gone. The gun she pulled out sits in front of me, on the wrong side of the heavy metal blind. I can't help but feel extraordinarily out of my depth. I'm less than a month into my career as a private and this is not what I was expecting to be eased in with. This is espionage all right; clearly I've joined the big leagues, but it's heading down a route it never did when I was on the force.

CALEDONIA

Five distinct strikes of bass, brass and drum echo down the entrance corridor. It's the five hits of the timeless James Brown soul record, 'It's a Man's Man's Man's World'. The intro ricochets down the mirrored walls, resembling an Ennio Morricone soundtrack, bold and bereaving. I know something is happening inside the hall, because as the music drops out before the lyrics come in, I hear three things: a gunshot, a scream and a crash. I see one thing and one thing only. I see Faisal stumble back into my sights at the end of the corridor, below the steps, and crash backwards through one of the glass tables. There is red everywhere. I can't catch my breath, I'm not even trying to, I know there's no good air left to breathe in.

This is a man's world! This is a man's world!
But it wouldn't be nothing… nothing, without a woman or a girl.

There's a screen above me, above the cloakroom shutter attached to the wall. I noticed it on my way in but paid no attention to it. It's a security camera surveillance screen. It is split into four quarters for each of the four cameras that it picks up. This is the distraction from the distraction. Faisal can wait, he's going nowhere. This is the point in which I stop to watch, because while the music plays and the irrational sounds of gunfire from inside fill my ears, I can see the massacre that is happening less than one hundred feet away from me. There are six, possibly seven girls at the front of the room on the pole dancing stages; they each have guns and are firing them into the crowd. The crowd are frantic, naturally, and are ducking and diving for cover. They're scattering, but the dancing girls with their guns are relentless. The footage is in black and white but even so, the red that explodes from the helpless bodies inside is as clear as clear. It's somewhat cinematic, choreographed to unplanned perfection with the soundtrack to support it. The screen lags; it's obviously slightly faulty because the footage shows in slow motion. It skips at times as well, which edits the CCTV footage together like hectic jump cuts between frames.

The noise is crazy. Screaming, gunshots, the sound of glasses smashing and tables bashing adds variation to the tenacious sounds that fill the club, but I can hear James Brown above it all. The top left quarter of the screen is the camera feed from behind the bar. People are leaping over to hide behind it while stray bullets smash the cabinets and shelves of liquor on the back wall. I cannot see Garrias, but I can assume he is one of the bodies that are on the floor, collected in a heap. The top right quarter shows the footage from the camera that is on stage, behind the poles.

That's where the girls are, without formation but spread across the three podiums and firing maniacally into the room in front of them. A couple of them appear to still be topless; they're the ones from the warm-up. The others — well they must have come from out the back. The bottom left of the screen shows an empty shot of the LED dancefloor. At the edges of the footage I can just about make out figures legging it for the toilets that are to the left and right of it, but it seems they are locked because they cannot get into them. In the bottom right corner of the screen is me. The camera that is above the steps at the end of the corridor is what plays on this quarter of the security screen. I can see myself watching myself and I feel suddenly disgusted. I am massively ill-equipped and outmanned for a genocide, but I cannot stand and watch this horror show any longer. Instinctively I pick up the gun and I walk back into hellfire – back along Route 69 and into the areola arena.

As I make my way along the walkway, the endless mirrors on either side almost distract me from the bloodied man slumped down in front of me, but I have eyes only for what's ahead... Without warning, the mirrors start to smash. I disappear with each crack that bursts from them, and no I'm not being metaphorical. One by one, the mirrors quite literally smash. The noise is piercing. There's more red, so much red sprayed up the walls and on the ceiling. I'm hit. I fall to the floor clutching my head into my chest and my knees up to join them as I pull myself into a terrified little ball.

Shots fired, from a semi-automatic rifle. I can hear them coming in a blitz from behind me; that's what smashed the mirrors, that's what hit me in the leg. My trousers are splattered with red, but the walls paint a different picture. A butchery. How is there so much of it everywhere? I can just about peek through the gap in my folded arms to see a shard of the mirror that once was, leant against the stained corridor wall and facing back towards the cloakroom. In the reflection I can see the cloakroom girl standing there, outside her booth holding the firearm, but she's empty; out of ammo. My leg really fucking hurts, I can't bring myself to touch it or even to look at it. I had dropped my gun during the fall. Without having to look I know it's a little out of my reach, but I have to make a go of it. I have to act now while she's not shooting. Come on McKrayne, pull yourself together. I go for it. I uncurl myself and reach out for the pistol. My hand slips along the wooden floorboards through the red blotches that now polka dot them. I have it! In one swift movement I pull the gun into my chest, swivel on my back and open my legs.

Bang bang. Bang!

Through the V of my legs and with my left eye closed I shoot. Two to the chest and one to the head. She topples, dropping her gun as she falls. My accuracy is perfect, my mind is scrambled. I sit still, frozen in my shooting pose. The music plays behind me, James Brown still belting his voice hauntingly through me, it's a man's world... and I just killed a woman.

I lower my legs and teddy bear roll around to face the club once more. I'm close, close enough to be fully aware of the chaos inside. The shots still fire, glass still breaks, people are still shouting. Faisal is still strewn over the base of the broken glass table; I'm looking at him with a gentle quake pulsing through me until I notice the red dripping down my gun. The streak runs, unbroken, down the barrel and drips onto the floor. As it splats, I notice something odd on the floor next to the fresh blotch of red. It's a shell of some sort – it looks like the casing of a huge marrowfat pea. As I pick it up, I recognise its texture. The rubbery feel it has jogs my memory a bit, but before I draw my conclusion the periphery of my vison is distracted by a figure entering the frame ahead. I straighten up my back and draw the gun out in front of me, my sights set on the figure who I now see as the short-haired woman from earlier in the night. She is stood over Faisal's limp body, watching him as if waiting for him to resurrect, to jump back up to his feet for her. She has a gun in her right hand, a big one. It's a lot bigger than mine. My left eye is once again closed; I'm poised with my finger on the trigger and waiting for her to act. Finally, what I've really been wanting her to do happens: she turns and she sees me.

Calm but disordered, that's how I see this woman. She is wearing a mauve nightgown; it's made of silk, and she is barefoot. It's an incredibly attractive look, especially as she stands facing me, right hip dropped and with her rifle held on the same side. Her hair is short, like Mia Farrow in the sixties, but she is quite a bit older, perhaps in her mid-forties. Her face is more welcoming than it is alluring but she has a sass, an all-too-familiar sass. She's looking at me with a mischievous smile and not raising her gun at me as I am at her, and that's because she knows me. She knows me, and I know her. My God, how I know her.

"Sara?"

"Hello Stranger."

...Bang!

The song has finished, my hand is shaking and the mirage of Sara is still at the bottom of the steps. I shot her. With the gun in my hands I shot the projection of Evie's mother. It's a projection, a hallucination of anxiety; the panic of this evening. She's not real... so why is she slumped down next to Faisal, the camp middle-eastern dance sensation who owns a gay titty bar not too far from Yeovil in South Somerset...? What the fuck is going on?

I am hyperventilating now. I've forgotten what it's like to breath naturally and be unobstructed by the thick pandemonium of this place. She's there, she's right fucking there in front of me. Evangeline's mother, Sara, the woman who I had a baby with; the woman who upped sticks and ran away from the two of us twenty years ago.

Up she gets. Up onto her feet she's rising – Sara, or what my mind sees as Sara, is clambering back up to her feet despite the bloody gunshot wound on her chest. She's covered in red. I shot her right between her breasts and just below the neckline; even the paranormal don't just get up from that and say nothing. Who is she, why is she here and haunting me now, right now when I am most out of my comfort zone?! She's fully erect now, looking down and wiping her wound so very nonchalantly. There's broken glass everywhere and she must have trodden in some by now. My presumptions are proven correct as she puts weight back onto her feet and the crunch of glass squashes beneath them. Now she raises her gun at me, and quite rightly so. I shot first and cannot bring myself to move or hide or duck or anything and so I just stand here, unreadily prepared for the retaliation.

Bang bang!

"AghhhhhARGH!" She's shot me, twice in my already

wounded leg.

It's really fucking painful. I can't bring myself to look down at it, but I don't have time to contemplate the matter because Sara shouts loudly into the room:

"Everyone out, now... Quickly! GO!"

Her two shots at me are the last to be fired, it seems, as the chaos appears to stop and transitions into a stampede. A mad dash for the exit, the one behind me, at the end of the corridor.

I'm on the floor, clutching my leg. I can hear bodies moving inside. Chairs crash and people shout out in distress as the small crowd descends upon me; cascading around the corner and up the stairs like a tidal wave. For the second time in what has been no longer than ten minutes, I am ambushed by this mob. They're running out, bashing into each other, not caring how they get out, just that they do. They are clogging up the space between me and my imagination. Hurriedly they're filing into my vision and passing me, rampageous and red. All of them look to me as if they've been hit, been shot somewhere or taken a splattering of someone else's hit. I curl back up to protect myself as I lose sight of Sara and Faisal. I'm almost sure that when the crowd clears again Faisal will still be there, but Sara will not, because she ran away from me twenty years ago and I haven't seen or heard from her since. How unlikely it seems for her to be here, once again puppeteering one of the most obscure and messy chapters of my life. She's a haunting reminder of all that's evil in this world, nothing more than a ghost of regret and contempt.

They are moving, herd-like, out past me now, down the narrow corridor. They trample me, unknowing and uncaring that I'm down here in a bloody puddle myself. A few trip over me, unavoidably stacking it into my limp corpse; I am pathetic. This whole thing has been a disaster and now I'm getting what I deserve, a good kick in.

I'm losing track of nearly all my thoughts. They leave me like the people do that pass me on their way out, until they clear, and the way is once again empty. Faisal is gone, and so is Sara. The front door shuts behind me and I'm all alone in the corridor, curled up in the red that drips down the mirrorless walls and onto the floor. I sit up and with a quick glance behind me I can see that the cloakroom girl I shot has vanished too, though the blood is still in patches where she was on the floor. I turn my head again. The glass table I saw Faisal fall through is still smashed into little pieces and again there is red on the floor where he was slain in a bloody heap. I feel a throb of discomfort come from my leg, and I'm building up the courage to check on the wound. I have to, I can't just ignore it and pretend like it never happened, I need to assess the damage. I look down and see red all over my nice new trousers, but it's the kind of red I wasn't expecting to see. There's a slight tear, a small and disappointing hole in the fabric, no great gash or anything particularly gory. As I run my hand over the affected area, tentatively, I discover a strange truth, arguably the strangest of my findings so far: I have been shot with a paintball gun.

Paintballs? I can draw no conclusion as to why paintball guns have been used, but frankly I am relieved, though a little embarrassed that my injuries show nothing more than heavy bruising and the sting of inevitable blistering. That was one hell of a powerful paintball gun though, that's for sure; it's been modified, I'm guessing they all have. The firepower they hold, they are completely illegal, though that comes as no surprise.

After far too long on the ground I get up to my feet. My left leg hurts but it's a manageable pain. I can't leave – I have to inspect this place further, even if the boys from the betting office don't show. She said, she said on the phone that this is where they meet, where they do business. Madd's Sandwich Bar is underneath it for Christ's sake! Something's going on, somebody knew I was coming, absolutely they did, or maybe I've been set up. It's easily done when you're away from familiar territory. I'm walking down the steps again, my airsoft paintball gun gripped tightly in my hands. A thought occurs to me: perhaps this is some elaborate prank by the guys at the station back in London. Maybe they're messing with me, a little joke to say 'up yours' for leaving. It's a game, a ploy, a ruse – a Christmas fox hunt.

Oh no wait, it's not. There he is, Faisal, up on the centre stage being bound to the pole by three of the women I saw on the screen. Faisal's not dead, just unconscious. Obviously, he was shot at very close range by a very powerful paintball gun; much like my leg he will have a nasty-looking bruise once the paint is wiped clean. I clear my throat quietly. I'm going to assert some authority into the situation at last. Nobody on stage has seen me or heard me, though I can't help but assume that they know I'm here. They must know – it's almost as if so far I have been, besides being shot three times, ignored. Helpless and insignificant, I am a ghost in a room of ghouls, but now I'm going to change all that. I have the gun I was given still at the ready, but I think that the entire shootout may have been a hoax, a decorative display of red paintball madness.

"Put your gun down Stranger, you don't need to shoot

anyone else here."

I freeze. She's real.

Castaway

"You're real. Aren't you?!" I ask of the voice at the bar. The voice I know.

I'm beguiled by her face as I look at it with immeasurable scepticism for the second time tonight. Sara's voice chills me to the core.

"I'm real, Stranger. I'm real and I'm alive."

"You... You..." My eyes well involuntarily. A tear is rolling down my cheek. "You need to explain yourself, fast... EXPLAIN YOURSELF!" My voice judders.

I'm trembling, literally shaking. More tears fall slowly from my eyes, coursing down my cheeks as my teeth clench tighter together. Sara looks at me without a smile. Without the sass and without the chance to give me an answer.

"YOU'RE HERE?!" I can't stop myself from shouting; I am outrageously emotional. "WHY ARE YOU HERE?! WHY... IS THIS WHERE YOU'VE BEEN? HERE? THE WHOLE TIME, THE WHOLE FUCKING TIME!"

I can feel my blood pressure racing, I can feel every part of me tingle. I can feel eyes burning the back of my head; the girls are still up on the stage with Faisal, watching me explode from the inside out.

"Girls, would you give us five minutes please?" Sara asks of them, quietly and reservedly but still with authority.

"Five minutes. That's how much of your time I'm worth, IS IT?!" I'm furious, and rightfully so.

Sara doesn't respond, at least not to me. I want to shoot her again.

"Take him downstairs and make sure that when he wakes up he can't make any noise. Use the tape in my room," she coolly tells the girls.

They do as she says. Two of them are standing next to Faisal on the stage and the other is by a control panel on the wall at the back of the room. I don't know where the others are, I can't see them. The girl at the back flicks a switch on the panel and with it, the poles detach from the ceiling and begin to lower down through the floor. The small, circular stages they are standing on are lowering down, too. The girl at the back who initiated the descent has stepped onto the stage closest to her and she's falling slowly down with her pole. The other topless girls are both on the centre stage, disappearing downwards, as well as an unconscious Faisal and the pole he's strapped to. It's the finale of a sadistic Paul Raymond show, or the start of an X-rated Houdini trick. At any other point in time I would've been distracted, maybe even allured by what was happening onstage, but even though I know what is going on, I am still utterly engulfed in the confusion that Sara is causing. The poles are completely gone, as are all three girls and Faisal. The room is mine and Sara's; for the first time in twenty years, I am alone with my ex-fiancé.

"Stranger, I can't begin to tell you how sorry I am. How ashamed I am. I, I don't really know what to say. I don't know what to tell you except for the truth… I was hoping you'd come, but, but I didn't really expect you to. I've been so upset over the years that I've never thought of what I would say to you, and, and now you're here I feel the same as when I left."

Sara is snivelling. How dare she make this about her, about how she feels?

"They told me you ran away. YOU left me a note saying you were leaving the whole bloody country, leaving for good! So that's not true, is it, because you're here. Now. In front of me. You say you want to tell me the truth, so why don't you, huh? TELL ME THE TRUTH!" I know I need to calm down, so I take a deep breath. "Sara, I'm really confused, what's going on? Where have you been? Why are you back?" I'm in tears; a total wreck. My voice pinches at the end of every word; I'm a mess of a man. "You left me with a child. A six-month-old baby, Sara, our daughter, our baby girl. You left us!"

"Stranger you don't understand, I know you hate me but you have to try and understand... I had to, he made me, they all did, it was me or her." Sara is joining in with my tears now. "I h-had to, it was the only way."

Well, where do you go from here? I suppose the comfort you draw from these situations is that, as they say, 'the only way is up'. My eyes are stinging, and so is my heart. I have to begin my line of questioning, but my professionalism is being forfeited on account of my emotions. I'm steadying them, at least I think I am.

"What are you talking about? What do you mean it was you or her?"

"Grubbe. Captain Grubbe, the boss, he wanted to take Evangeline from us Stranger, he wanted her for his own. He saw through the whole thing. He let us have our little girl and then when it suited him he turned on us, can't you see? Couldn't you see? He couldn't let me leave him for you, he wouldn't let me raise the daughter of a senior police officer! He always gets his way Stranger, I couldn't let him have her too!"

I look back at her, almost as if looking through her.

This woman has been the bane of my life since the night we met. Never has anyone bettered me, betrayed me or beaten me like Sara has. How can I trust these things she says to me now, how can I be sure that the wool isn't being pulled down sharply and desperately over my eyes?

"Stranger, do you remember what I told you twenty years ago? Do you remember everything that happened between us? It's true, it's always been true. I knew that I could never win but I wasn't going to stand by and lose either. I gave myself up for you, for Evangeline. Do you have any idea how hard it has been? Do you see what I have put myself through for you both?!"

She's crying. Really crying. These are the tears of an honest woman, they have to be, and I have to believe that they are. I can't solve all this in my head in its current state, I need her help. I need her answers.

"What you've been through, are you serious?! Why didn't you take us with you? Why didn't you really run away? We could've fixed it, we could've made it all right, but you never told me anything, you just vanished!"

"Would you have left? Would you have really run away with me and Evangeline?"

No. I wouldn't have, she's right.

"I could've taken her, I thought about taking her away and bringing her into a better life than ours, but I just couldn't. I felt enough disgust, enough hatred for myself already for running from you, and I couldn't steal your daughter Stranger. I've had a bad life but that doesn't make me a bad person!"

"So why didn't you tell me? Why didn't you let me help you, let me help all of us?"

"I couldn't tell you Stranger, it wouldn't have stopped

any of it and you would've come looking for me, walking into trouble that wasn't yours to walk into. He was getting fidgety, they all were – the girls, the police rats, the lot of them. It wouldn't have taken long before he came for me and Evangeline, and probably you too! I had to do what I thought was right. I was made to come here, he sent me down here, The Captain – he bundled me into a car and that's the first and last I knew of it. He's had me here ever since, working. I'm paid but I am watched. I work here now and not for The Captain, but it's all still the same. The Captain didn't want me on the frontline after my last birthday and I get it; a self-loathing and insubordinate middle-ager isn't exactly a bedroom pleaser." Her shoulders sink, as does her tone. "It was a clear betrayal of their entire system what I – what we – did, Stranger. They wanted me to distract you, not start a family with you!"

"So you didn't run, you're saying you had no choice, is that it? You were the compromise?"

She doesn't answer. She doesn't have to; I can see, more than I ever could before, the truth in her makeup-smudged eyes.

"And what about Evangeline? Was she really our mistake or was that all part of your plan as well? Charm a detective into bed, enrapture his friends and family, have his unplanned child and then fuck off and leave him in a heap on the floor!"

It's surprising, even to myself, how easily diplomacy and my own rational conclusions escape me when I remember what Sara has done to me. I have waited two decades to explode at this woman. I'm proud I haven't bopped her on the nose.

"You know she was down to both of us! I fell for you

as well, you know – I've done wrong, but I do not blame myself for what happened that night I met you Stranger McKrayne. Do you really think that I wanted to turn up on your doorstep three months later, begging in the cold for you to let me in?!"

That's an image I have never been able to shake from my memory. Sara, the prostitute, standing out in the freezing December cold on my doorstep in North London. She told me that she was three months pregnant; I didn't believe her, but it turned out to be true. The one-night stand that changed my life; the night that sabotaged my peace. I had rid myself of Sara that night, or at least I thought I had; she had tricked me, and I wanted nothing more to do with her. Ironically, I would share something with her forever more. I hated the news at first but as time moved on, I learnt to cope. There was nothing I could do, I had played my part and I had to step up to the unfortunate challenge of parenthood.

Six months after that Evie arrived, and she was terrifying. Beautiful, but terrifying. I remember the panic, the anguish of my worrying how I would fare raising the unplanned child. The reassurance in parenthood is that in most instances there are two of you to struggle through together and when Evangeline was born, something in Sara changed. We were suddenly parents and something not unlike love sparked between us. Sara was maternal, warm and open; there was a scent of romance that exuded from her and my own paternal anxieties settled slightly with the new aura that blanketed our relationship. I proposed to Sara soon after the birth as I foolishly believed it the honourable thing to do. Six months after that, she ran out on us.

"I know absolutely nothing about my daughter except that she is my daughter, and if she's anything like her father, then I know I'm proud of her. There hasn't been a day when I haven't thought of you and Evangeline, and I know it's hard for you to believe but everything I have done has been for the best for you two... I loved you Stranger, I loved you for everything you were and everything I thought you could do... the same way I loved Evangeline."

Funnily enough Evie is nothing like her father; to be honest, she's a bit of a shit. I have to hug the poor woman. God, I hate myself for how pathetic life has made me look, but I need consolation as much as she does. I can't stand by and let her sob like this, and anyway who knows, she might really be telling the whole truth. I move in, my arms awkwardly and unconvincingly spread for an embrace. She falls into me; heavily and desperately she lands in my arms. I almost topple backwards but I don't, I just stand there and hold her, not knowing whether to continue crying with her or puff out my chest and take control. I do neither, obviously. I just stand there and receive the hug, provide the shoulder and wait for her to speak again.

"What's she like, Stranger?" There's sincerity in her voice, the snivels and bumbling vowels prove it.

What do I tell her? Ironically, I can't tell her the truth. I can't say that our daughter is a miscreant, an out of control criminal. I have to lie, for now anyway.

"She's... great. She's great and she's... she's beautiful. Just beautiful."

I remember the shouting match Evie and I had in the car on the drive down from London and my back pangs with a cold and unpleasant pinch. I suddenly dread what she's been up to all day on her own. I pull away from Sara quickly.

"Why did he want her? What use would he have had for a baby? What sick man takes another's child? Even for a pimp that's low!" A valid question.

Sara is regaining her balance without me there to prop her up. She slumps back down onto the bar stool.

"It was his stamp of authority, he wanted to show that he wasn't to be beaten. I don't think he thought his threats through, I don't think he ever has, but I couldn't risk calling his bluff. And plus, 'she' couldn't have children. I don't think either of them could, The Captain or his wife." Sara pauses as she wipes her eyes. "Oh yeah, he has a wife, one of us she was! Dirty old wench, one of the worst, but one of the prettiest for sure. Not so much anymore, that pretentious old windbag finally got the big head she deserved. She was, however, the apple of his eye, only after I said no though..."

I'm back to listening. My red-hot ears are pricked.

"He was all over me, all of the time. I couldn't go anywhere without his eyes following me, his hands wanting to touch me. I was bait, I was his taboo amongst taboos. Eventually it all got too much for him to bear: my dismissals, my lack of interest and my repulsion for him. But you know, just like a man, he believed my disinterest to be a sure sign of unequivocal lust. Wanker."

I can't help but chuckle at that. A statement of total accuracy.

"We had, well, I don't enjoy telling you this, but yeah we did things once, but I was young, and I was stupid. Very stupid. He wanted me more and I said no. I always said no. He was a pig and I seemed to be the only one there in that dirty old house that knew it, or at least knew it and didn't give into it. I was there because I had nowhere else to be, nobody else to be with. I was doing it to make my money and keep to myself, everyone else was there for the benefits, to brown nose. To..."

"I know all of that Sara. You told me all this twenty years ago when you lived with me, remember? We've had this talk, we've done the arguing... Now I just want answers."

"I know that, but it's still true. I need you to believe me. He never liked nor trusted me after I rejected him, and it only added fuel to the fire when I fell pregnant with Evangeline. He knew that ultimately he had no say in whether or not I was going to have her, but when he found out that I was having her with you, Detective Stranger McKrayne of the North London Police Force, he was livid. He couldn't swallow that one."

"But this 'Captain Grubbe', the man you've slagged off so much for being a bully and a tyrant – if he was as evil and as twisted as you say, then why didn't he do something before Evangeline was born? Why did he not come after us sooner?"

"The man is immoral, Stranger, he's a crook and a thief, but he's not a murderer, if that's what you're saying! He was biding his time to corrupt you, like he had all your mates in the DS ranks, but with me at your side he cottoned on that I was ratting him out, keeping you in the loop. He doesn't believe in honest mistakes. Like I kept telling you when we were together, he's always in the know."

Sara puts her hand on my hip. She's still perched on the stool and I'm still stood rather close to her. Her gown has loosened at the bust and I can see her blood-red bra.

Something flutters inside of my stomach; it makes a soundless rumble.

"Let me grab you a beer."

It's a fantastic idea. I feel slightly more comfortable for the first time since coming here as Sara lets go of my hip and hops over the bar to the beer fridge where she pulls two cold bottles from it. This may be the most I have ever wanted a drink in my entire life. Sara hands me the beer, and the cool glass in my palm calms me a little more. The cool beer sliding down my throat does the same. Sara stays behind the bar; she's leaning against it and facing me.

"So now you're going to fix it, right?"

I almost choke on my last mouthful. Before I can ask what she means, Sara goes on:

"You couldn't have done anything in that sleazy little police station of yours back in London, but now! You're a free agent, a real Detective; you can mend all of this. You can expose all of it, you can bring down Captain Grubbe!"

THE VOICE. The fucking voice on the phone, I knew I recognised it! It was her, Sara was the anonymous tip, of course she was, that's why I'm here. I've been played... again. It's okay this time around though, isn't it?

"So it was you on the phone, you're the one who told me about them, the three guys running the gaff! Why? Why have you turned on them all of a sudden, and why are you even here, working for the bad guys again? Why is all of this coming to light now? Why haven't you come home?"

"Like I said, you never could have strayed far enough away from the force to crack this, they had eyes on everything you did! Now, now you're your own master, yes?"

"I suppose you're right, but..."

"And I couldn't have come home, I mean I could have over the last few years, but how could I Stranger? Unfortunate as it is, my life is here now. It's not a good life but a life nonetheless. And if turning up on your doorstep twenty years ago was hard then how could I have done it now? What would I have said, what would you have said?! No, Stranger, you had to come to me. When I heard that you had left the police I knew it was time. It was now or never."

My thoughts spiral and flounder in my head, but Sara further interrupts them with her incessant chat. I'd forgotten how much she could natter on.

"Tonight is celebratory. It's been 20 years since Captain Grubbe moved out to the country from the city. It's his and his whore of a wife's 20th Annual Christmas Party. It's the 20th annual Grubbe-Nut Christmas Do, Stranger..." She is speaking as if I understand, as if I comprehend these things she's saying. I don't. "It's the biggest event in the Cotswolds' calendar!"

It's also the 20th anniversary of when Sara ran out on me. I just can't let it go, not yet. I hate Christmas, I really do. It happens every year and every year I'm reminded of the Christmas back in 1982 when Sara disappeared. Now, after today, my loathing for the holidays can only grow. Perhaps I should tell her about Evie, would that make me feel better about myself? If I told her that our daughter is a mess of a girl because of what she did to her. I want to but I can't bring myself to say it.

"They're going all out, with a huge fireworks display and everything," Sara continues. "There's going to be a lot more people there this year. The Captain is one for traditions and extravagance. Things have been rocky of late, though – nobody really knows why but business is not as it once was for him. So I think he's trying twice as hard to keep up his rich-boy façade this year... but I want you to crash it. So yes, it was me who tipped you off, but you understand that I couldn't have told you who I was on the phone, right?"

She was right. I wouldn't have believed it for a second. I'm still struggling to believe it's really her now. It would've discredited her entire ploy if she had said she was Sara. It's becoming clearer why I'm here, but more is needed in my inquiry. This is still a highly tense and extraordinary situation. I am leaning against the bar, my elbows damp with the red paint splotches they are dipped in. My outfit is stained and torn. I have gone past caring. Sara and I are looking directly into one another's eyes but there's no romance here, just an investigation.

"So why am I here, in the Mantis Bar of all places? What does all of this have to do with Captain Grubbe? You said that there was something being run out of here, that Mr Mann and his boys would be here, doing bits, but they're not. They haven't been all night. What has happened is – well shit, you tell me what the fuck happened here because I haven't got a clue!"

"I needed you here to see. To see what was really happening down here, to see how mad it can get. The boys were supposed to be here – they are usually, routinely every Friday – but there was a change of plan tonight. They were going to be ambushed, trapped by Faisal and his merry band of extras. He was planning an attack of his own, Stranger, and I foiled it! Don't you see, I turned it around, well me and the girls did. He's nuts, completely barmy – off his head on Charlie most of the time and it's got to him – he's paranoid and he's erratic. Faisal has been getting annoyed at Mann, Chaim and Rockson's use of his club and the little thanks he's getting for it in return. He believes that they're planning a takeover of this place, he believes that his dancing girls are being targeted for use in other, even less wholesome avenues, by none other than Captain Grubbe."

"Why? I mean, are they? Why does he think that? Drugs or no drugs, there has to be some reason he thinks these things?"

"They are. He thinks 'these things' because these things are happening. The substance abuse just makes him harder to negotiate with and his inconsistencies are making it more difficult for the boys and Grubbe to move in. Faisal lets them use one of his rooms to run their scams out of and in return they provide a protection service as payment for the inconvenience. It was fine and dandy at the start when they struck up the deal, but Faisal has grown to dislike the arrangement. So tonight, he outed his regulars just before he thought the boys were turning up and he hired in that crowd of layabouts to come and help beat up Trev, Trev 'n' Trevor. He wanted to send a message of his own, he sees it as the only way to get through to them."

That's mental, but it does provide me with a story as to what happened with the switch-up earlier. The drunkards who left unexpectedly early and the mob who rushed in and then out again very oddly. They were here for a fight, supposedly. I presume they were being paid to do it. Faisal wouldn't have endangered his regulars and most of them were too sloppy to even stand, let alone fight. It didn't happen, though, because there was a mass gun fun that ruined their fun. A paintball gun fight. It was Garrias and Faisal working together, surely, as they were the only two, other than the girls, who didn't leave. They were going to use the rent-a-crowd to act as if everything was normal for the boys when they arrived at the club as usual, but then they were going to lock the doors and move in for the kill… or capture. Thirty to three, they would've had no chance, but Sara and the girls obviously found out about their plan and chose to side against them. That's an odd decision to make. Why did they side against their employer, I wonder? I guess they told Mann, Chaim and Rockson about Face's plan to overthrow them and they avoided the danger. My guess is that they also gave the girls the guns and the go-ahead to fight back on their behalf. Faisal was caught off guard in his own twisted plan. Obviously they all mistook the paintball guns for real ones, at first anyway, and by the end of the ordeal the crowd were probably just wanting to get out of there. Plus, those were not your standard stag-do paintball rifles, those fuckers were dangerous. Faisal was knocked unconscious by a close-range shot to the head and now he's tied up downstairs somewhere. Garrias must have made a run for it along with the crowd. I need my pen and pad, this is all too much to digest and remember. So, Sara works for Faisal. Faisal works with Mr. Mann, Dr Chaim and Madd Rockson, and they all work for Captain Grubbe. Faisal is crazy, Captain Grubbe is the power-hungry head of this pretty extensive underground empire and…

"Mr. Mann, Dr Chaim and Madd Rockson. The three of them, the three Trevors, they are all in part ownership of the dodgy betting ring I told you about on the phone!" Sara adds.

I almost forgot she was here. My brain has partially recovered. My professional thoughts are returning.

"They have a system for winning at the bookies, sports betting in its dirtiest form, Stranger. Arbitrage betting, spreading the bets across different bookies; manipulating the system and pulling in favours to guarantee a win."

"I've heard all about Trev, Trev 'n' Trevor, but their crimes are in the past, and arbitrage betting isn't illegal. The bookmakers don't like it but that's only because it leaves them mostly out of pocket. There's no definite crime in mathematical betting."

"I'll make you right, Detective, but what if I told you that they play both the bookmakers and the bettors... What if I was to tell you that the three of them offer the bookies a protection service to rid them of any arbitrage bettors, and then cash in on their protection fee and the clever betting system?"

Intriguing, but hard to comprehend. I pry.

"So what, they claim to catch the people doing the spread betting for the bookmakers but they are the people doing it...? Surely that's illogical and obvious to the bookies; why the need to bet in the first place if they get their fee anyway?"

"Well that's just it, isn't it? They don't bet, that's the very nature of arbitrage betting – they get someone else to do it for them. They watch the markets and hire some other pleb to go and lay down the dough for them. They play the game, but the boys run the show."

Maybe she is onto something after all.

"They work the bookmakers on commission, that's the deal they shook on with them all. As and when they bust a dodgy bet, that's when they get their money. Though, between busts, that's when they place the bets themselves. So it's a 'one for them, three for us' kind of thing they have going on. They profit from the system regardless. When a bet goes bad, or their bettor messes up, then they move in to strike. They take down the poor chap who laid the cash for them and collect the bounty from the bookies. When a bet goes well, and the money comes in, they keep it. Then they sweep it under the rug and the bookmakers are none the wiser."

"So are people getting hurt? Who's involved in all of this?" This is the part where I do my job.

"Naturally. And there's a whole string of people attached to this, Stranger – the buck doesn't just stop at those three! Every once in a while, somebody has to mess up. Somebody has to make a mistake unknowingly. The boys have to seem as though they're holding up their end of the deal with the bookmakers. So of course, every once in a while... somebody has to get hurt."

"Play the system, the bettors and the bookies against themselves. Clever."

This is one hell of a lead; who knows where this will end? This is a detective's wet dream!

"So it's a mafia. We're dealing with a mafia?"

"Of sorts, yes. But they rip off the people they're supposedly protecting, AND they endanger the people working on their behalf – they turn on their own!"

"Well mafias aren't exactly known for being the most stand-up guys, they're to be trusted as far as they can be thrown. It sounds like an exclusively three-way thing; anyone else is just an accessory, a means to an end. In a syndicate, anyone who isn't someone is disposable."

"And that's my point. That's why you're here, now, with me! That's why I called you. They're disposable; they're nickable!"

"But they're not here Sara! You said it yourself, they're not coming. And anyway, they might be 'nickable', but they're far from disposable if they're the top dogs. If Mann, Chaim and Rockson go down, this whole thing goes down... Except, they're not the top dogs, are they? Of course, it's Grubbe. He's the one who pulls every little string here, and not just here is it? It's everywhere; it's everything. This is one hell of a bust you're wanting me to perform. I'm alone out here Sara – what do you really expect me to do?"

"But you're not alone, not this time. I'm with you now, Stranger, we can win this."

"Oh great, well of course we're unstoppable now, aren't we? The old team is back together: Stranger and Sara, the match made in heaven, because that has worked so well for us in the past, hasn't it?! I need time, I need more information. I need strategy."

"You need there to be mistrust... and it's happening, right now. The plan has come into effect mostly of its own coincidental doing. We can't be sure how long they're going to be on the ropes for. We have to strike while the iron is hot, before the wounds have time to heal. Grubbe is preoccupied, he has too many interests to keep him completely focussed on the nitty gritty of all of them. He's overrun and business is not booming. Now's the time to get to him – he's as vulnerable now as he'll ever be."

"And the party is tonight?" I'm catching on.

"Yes, exactly. Everyone you could ever need for this to work – witnesses, baddies, goodies – they're all going to be in the same place at the same time, tonight. Faisal has betrayed the Trevors, the Trevors are in trouble with their own scam, and the girls have all but had enough. They listen to me, Stranger, they follow me. They've shown what they can do here tonight, and we can all step up again against the real villain at the heart of all this."

"So you're not on Mann, Chaim and Rockson's side... so why did you interfere with Face's plan to catch them? Why did you turn on Faisal at all? It would've been one less thing for you to do..."

"Faisal couldn't have done anything; he'd have tied up those three, and then what? He would've jeopardised the plan, and when that failed I would've been left jobless and without revenge. It was an act of loyalty. It had to end this way so that I could get you here to talk. They all have to be taken out in the end, it really doesn't matter in which order it happens. Plus, it was fun," Sara winks at me with a glimmer of her former sass.

She is goodhearted, I think, but she is foolish. Her emotions and her impatience may just have got the better of her. With no solid evidence and with the lead being so fresh, it's doubtful that any arrests will be made that quickly. Unfortunately enough for Sara, the only people I have encountered thus far that have broken the law are herself and the girls she seems to represent. Vigilante isn't a welcome term to law enforcers; we are the protectors, although we are not always on time. There is a dark side to the law, I have seen it, but I have to believe that on the whole we are the good guys.

"Sara, these investigations take time, and personnel, you must understand that. I can't just go into that party all guns blazing on just your word, it doesn't work like that, these are very complex situations..."

But they have to start somewhere I suppose, and tonight is as good a night as any to earn my badge.

What do I do about Evangeline though? I can't drag her all the way down here and then spend the entire day and night away from her. She'll do something silly, I know she will, although if she was going to act up, then in all honesty she's probably already done so by now. Maybe I should go. I do have a curiosity about all this now. My mind is made up.

"I suppose you have an invite to this thing tonight then?"

Sara looks back at me as if I have just set her free. There's so much happiness exuding from every feature of her face that I can hardly help mirroring her. Perhaps I should say that I brought her daughter along with me and that she is back in Frome in the guesthouse waiting for me. At least, I think she is. No, that's probably not a good idea. Best leave that news until later, it could only hinder things if Sara is distracted. I can't help but feel manipulated – is this really my decision? But what harm can this do really? I survived the Mantis Bar massacre – after what's happened here tonight, nothing more can surprise or intimidate me. I want to appear in control of my own fate, and after so long apart and with everything that's gone on between us, I want to look unshakeable to Sara. I want her to see me now as heroic; as a fearless and matured man, not as the feeble policeman she picked up two decades ago.

"I have the car outside, but if you think..."

"You best shut up and get ready if you want us to make it. Let me get dressed, get my things together and we can go."

I blush with déjà vu.

D4 Damager

Sara walks around to my side of the bar with her shoulders sagging (slightly lower than they were before). We are both relaxing into this bizarre scenario, though there are tensions still fizzing between us. I finish my drink as she walks away to get her things. I do well not to watch. Instead I find myself staring out through the empty beer bottle and wondering how my life has managed to entertain the emotional ruckus of the past two weeks – no, scratch that, the past twenty years.

I turn around as the nightclub's tediously brilliant music strikes back up. The DJ, of course! I didn't include him in my round-up; he must've been hiding behind his decks this whole time. Sara has stopped dead in her tracks. She's immobile as the song plays out its infamous intro. I watch through her as the three silver poles, once again to the right of me, rise back up from the floor. The song is 'Get Up (I Feel Like Being a) Sex Machine' by James Brown. It's instantly recognisable as the great funkmaster himself gets it going by conversing with his band over his desire to boogie. The funk is coming. He counts it off: one, two, three, four. I count them off, the poles: one, two, three. I count again: one, two, three... four, five, six. The six girls who joined in the shootout with Sara are tied up, in twos, to the poles. They're elevating upwards against their will, splattered with red and with silver tape across their mouths. It's becoming a familiar sight, but it hasn't yet lost its shock factor to me. Faisal is gone, sprung free from the trap three of those very girls set not fifteen minutes ago.

It's madness for a second time. My hollow mind judders with the echo of the count-off. Though I'm not startled this time, I'm alert. Something else is about to happen.

Like before, the distinct strikes of bass, brass and drum sound out through the many speakers of the disco hall. There are more strikes than the last record and in quicker succession. As they hammer out through the speakers, I see the locked door of the men's bathroom burst open with a hefty kick and crash to the floor out in front of it. From behind it, Garrias the barman tumbles out, alone and looking riled. He has a gun – a paintball gun I presume, but from our distance apart I cannot make that call and be totally certain. Sara is still frozen in the foreground. I watch all of this through the back of her silhouette, knowing that if I could see the front of her she would look as bedazzled as I did earlier. Garrias quickly dusts himself down before he starts to fire madly into the room at us. His aim is lousy, but his objective is obvious – he wants to hurt us. His shots prolong the song's introductory notes. He is static. Rooted to the spot from where he's firing. Faisal has the other angle covered.

Yes, the disco king returneth to his glitzy throne. From behind the girls tied to the middle pole, Faisal erupts with vigour to join the fight he was robbed of before. With two guns and a powdery white moustache, he typifies lunacy, but there is something magnificent in his ability to move. Sara is pegging it towards me now; we both grab our toy-ish weapons from the bar and then dive over it to evade the red water-based war. Sara is staying down as I peek up to see what's going on, and what is going on is more of the same, except as Garrias edges closer to the poles with his sights set on us, Faisal is flinging his liquid-like limbs across the room in a display of shoot-dance-shoot. It's incredible – this is the collapse of rationality and the regurgitated rise of insanity. It's the final push of a fragile man. Face has completely lost the plot, but can I blame him really? Garrias is clearly taking this more seriously than his partner is. Faisal looks as though he is just out there for the thrill of it, and judging by the pale smear across his brown upper lip, he doesn't have much of a hold on the reality of the situation. The DJ has a gun of his own, but I can tell that he is reluctant to fire it. Every so often he cracks a shot, but he seems uneasy; the bangs and the splatters are all coming from the other two.

I pick a spot just behind Garrias and I shoot. It narrowly misses his head and paints the wall behind him red. It's a warning. He knows I can fight now, and he leaps for safety into a booth off to the left. I do the same with Faisal, though he is moving a lot and, as ever, unconventionally. His routine has no routine; I can't quite aim past him. Instead I go for the DJ and his sound system. Two shots to each speaker and one to the front of his decks. Holy shit, these guns have some power to them! The song jumps with the final hit; it kinks Faisal's movement and he seems truly agitated for the first time. He fires quickly at the bar. His confidence in the attack prompts Garrias to do the same from where he is hidden, and I duck down for cover. This is thrilling – a gun fight where the possibility of death is minimal. Sure, these things hurt, I have the purple throb of my leg to remind me of that, and one to the head clearly does damage, but they couldn't kill me with a shot from the range they're at now and I clearly have the better aim. I can topple them. I will topple them.

The shots slow but from the sounds I can tell that they

are moving slightly closer to us. Sara is bundled up under the bar next to a half-empty keg of lager, clutching her pistol. There's the briefest of breaks in the shots and I seize the moment, popping up to let off a few rounds. A few at Garrias, a few more at Faisal. They are both together now and so I can pick them off more easily; but as yet we are all unscathed, well, from this bout at least. I pull the trigger a final time for this round, I'll break again afterwards, but as I do nothing happens. It's jammed. The damn thing is jammed. I am in trouble now and if they can see my face then they'll know so too. I squeeze and squeeze but to no avail – it has knackered out. I drop down quick and go for Sara's firearm, but she knows something is wrong and she acts first. We meet as I fall and she rises. The many colours of the battered bar smudge behind her as we cross in the short fall. I can see her soul and I feel warm. I hit the soggy deck and gaze upwards at my ex-fiancé, my Evangeline's mother – she is about to make it right. Sara lights it up; from the harsh rip in the record I detect that she has annihilated the DJ. There's a lot of sharp sounds reverberating throughout the hall but none any louder than the cry of pain. I see her pivot slightly and adjust her aim – she's going for the other two now. Another cry; she's got one. This time the noise is more sinister. It has anger and frustration ringing between its unforgiving tones. I can't lie here making presumptions, so I hop up to see. Sara caught Garrias, nowhere that serious but from the fresh red stain I can see it's a direct hit to the arm. As well as that, I can see that next to him, behind a broken glass table and chair barricade, Faisal has had enough. His theme tune has finished, his time has been wasted and his patience has eroded. The crazy man steps up and struts through the blockade towards us; he shoots and a bottle of Drambuie on the ledge behind us smashes. He shoots again and this time it hits me right on my shoulder. It really fucking hurts.

"AghhhhhARGH!" I shout out.

I fall back into the liquor shelf and more bottles smash, each one more pungent and more expensive than the Drambuie. Faisal keeps shooting, but Sara does me the honour of shooting back. Of all the quickfire rounds she pings off, just two make contact with the nutty target closing in. Two paintballs, travelling at a speed of around 600 feet per second, nail Faisal on his already-bruised forehead and send him flailing to the floor in a heap of pain. All shots stop; I think it's over. Garrias has emerged from his blockade and is running to collect his downed, weary partner. He has no weapon and so Sara holds fire to watch him make his next move. He sweeps up the injured man and drags him back towards the steps and the entrance corridor. Besides the few groans coming from Faisal the room is silent. It has gone far enough, and everyone knows it. I watch as Garrias heaves Faisal up the steps and away from the battleground. Before he continues reversing down the walkway he stops to look at us. I'm not completely sure of the expression he is displaying but I can hazard a guess that it's one of scorn. He holds the stare for a short while and then is gone, pulling the injured out with him. The DJ, from behind his booth, dashes for the exit. His flat-footed run slaps the slippery floor and after another few awkward moments he is gone. I can understand his hurry, but he has absolutely nothing to worry about – everyone is knackered. Sara finally lowers her gun and there is peace in the valley for me… and for her.

There's a stinging sensation whirling around in my

ears, my shoulder aches and my leg is throbbing. I feel like I've been sucked through the engine of a jet aeroplane and then beaten up by the baggage handlers on the other side. I stagger up straight and place my hand on Sara's shoulder – I'm ready to leave. I'll call the guesthouse to speak to Evangeline whilst Sara is collecting her things; if she doesn't want to talk then I'll just leave a message with the owner. My hand is still resting on Sara's shoulder, but I don't know what to say exactly, except maybe the question niggling at the back of my brain. It's the only thing I can think of...

"If this is a gay bar, then why the pole dancers?" I don't have to know, I just want to.

"It's not a gay bar," Sara answers between panted breaths. "Well, not exclusively. It is until Mann, Chaim and Rockson turn up, and then the atmosphere loses its femininity." She turns around to face me. "Until the boys show up the main attraction is Face; he dances, and they watch. They're mostly friends of his, it's the less seedy half of this place. The lads don't go in for that sort of thing of course, so to appease them he has us start a shift just before they arrive. No one's forced to go but the regulars tend to vanish when the tits come out, then the real filth slithers in. It's bawdy at first, but then the real drunks come in late."

I wipe some paint from Sara's face with my thumb; I'm not sure why but I just do. I can tell she is hopeful for love, but I cannot muster those feelings. There may well be a time again for affection between us, but it is not now. She will understand that.

"Well then, you should go, Stranger. I wouldn't leave it any later than now. You should make your way over to Grubbe's manor in the Cotswolds, but I'd clean yourself up on the way."

"You're not coming? But I thought this whole thing was to..."

"Oh, I'll be there, Detective, but I have to treat my girls first. Looks like they've had it rough."

I had forgotten that the other girls were still tied up on stage. They had become ornamental in the fight.

"I can't leave them now, but I will meet you there, later on. It may be better this way anyway – he'd blow his top if he sees us show up there together. You work on him, I'll come in when the time is right."

"Right, okay." I don't know why it's okay, but it is. I know I shouldn't be going along with any more of this, but I can't help myself from agreeing. It's odd. I chuckle quietly, "I think I'm enjoying myself."

"Well don't enjoy yourself too much, you have a job to do and I need you as good there as you were here – better even!"

I chuckle again, a little louder this time, and then I leave. Around the bar I walk and across the floor I trudge. Climbing the small steps I can hear Sara's voice begin to soothe her friends, tied up on the pole-dancing stage, and my chest expands with purpose. I'll call Evie on the way now and tell her everything – well, maybe not everything.

I'm walking down the dark corridor, gathering confidence with each step. I reach the end of it and I push open the heavy doors to set myself free from this unhallowed ground. The full beam of the streetlight directly opposite makes me squint. It takes my eyes a few seconds to adjust. Before I walk out into the night and let the doors behind me seal in the madness, I hear another voice call to me from inside, and so I turn to see.

"Won't you be needing your coat then?" says the cloakroom girl as she holds my light-brown trench coat in her paint-stained hands. She's smirking, as am I.

"Yes, I will. Thank you." She throws it to me and I catch it.

I slip it on and rejig the collar so that it sits right. I nod my head to her and then turn again to face the outside.

"Good luck, Detective Stranger McKrayne," she calls as the doors pull slowly shut. Their slow whir matches the outside breeze.

With a huge breath in I step out onto the frosty pavement. I have a party to go to.

The dormant beast sleeps, belly-up in the softly rolling tide. Serenely he bathes on the break of the blue, impervious; waiting to be upturned for the feed.

#12. The Libertine

G-Unit

Captain Grubbe was decorated superbly with glittery things and encrusted with nobility… sort of. He had the appearance of a dapper old boy at the races and the agreeable linguistics of a croaky old cockney. Captain Grubbe lived, far from modestly, in his large country manor along with his big-headed wife, Baroness Big Nut. The reasoning behind her self-assigned title was almost insultingly simple: she was an incredibly pompous woman. Proudly fuelled by her husband's current account, she set about titling herself Baroness – you know, just because. Her full and actual name was Clara Bignôt; a woman of distant French descent. The less attractive name of 'Big Nut' was gifted to her by the ignorantly witty souls of North London after failing to pronounce her surname correctly a few times. She also had a great big head. It was no secret that Captain Grubbe despised his wife. He tried to hide it a bit but there's only so far one can go in obscuring scorn. He couldn't and wouldn't leave her though, for fear of what she'd take with her, that being an absolute shit-tonne of his hard-earned money and the secret of how he hardly earnt it.

The great and majestic Captain Grubbe was a motherbumping P.I.M.P. He was as far from his respectable and honourable disguise as his wife was from his life insurance policy. He had pimped his way through thirty dirty years and was still going strong. In the pimp game, The Captain reigned supreme; you only had to look at the size of his house to cotton on. His title of 'Captain' came surprisingly from the filth around him. Most of his customers, employees and acquaintances all admired him in one strange way or another, mostly out of fear. He boldly went about his unholy business every third or fourth weekend – there was a time when he managed a more full-time position, but when his money came in The Captain bought himself an early retirement.

Baroness Big Nut had once been the apple of Captain Grubbe's seedy eye. She had been one of The Captain's working girls, and one of the more popular ones, too. In her youth The Baroness was very beautiful, and Captain Grubbe grew to be very, very jealous. So he proposed, and when your pimp proposes to you, there's usually only one answer you can go for. The Baroness said yes, but it wasn't a forced marriage by any means. You would think that for her it was predetermined against her will, but Cap'n G had charm, wit, intelligence and the stature of an honest hunk. She was in fact very much in love with him too. However, the other girls did not enjoy this new arrangement. It came to light that they were all aflutter with devotion for The Captain and when Clara Bignôt bagged him for herself, it all turned rather sour down shag street. With a shiny diamond strapped to her fickle finger, it wasn't long before The Baroness abandoned her post and began her own gross reinvention. The Captain had seen how her being a part of the roster had caused upset in the camp and affected the business, so he subtly encouraged her resignation.

Much to the disappointment of Captain Grubbe, the years were neither kind nor forgiving to The Baroness. She grew annoyingly wretched and belligerent and of course, that infamously big head matured at an unhealthy pace.

Captain Grubbe was never really faithful to his darling wife. It was an unsanitary truth she had to live with given the nature of who they were. In time the affection dwindled between them completely and there was nothing drawing either of them back to each other besides the postcode they shared. The spark was no longer sparking, love had become nostalgia. The Captain had grown weary of his wife's distaste for who she really was and despite his half-hearted efforts to relight the fire, she was now completely un-wooable. The Captain snubbed her decision to identify as a Baroness, so instead he began to call her 'The Baron', as he felt it better suited her. She didn't like that.

Once a year, every year, The Baroness and Captain Grubbe hosted their infamously swanky Grubbe-Nut Christmas Do. It was ostentatious and it certainly wasn't a family party. There were no novelty Christmas jumpers. No red-lipped grandads napping behind the veil of their green crepe-paper hats. There were no grandmas waving Wii remotes at the animated figures on the TV, shaking distressingly to The Black Eyed Peas. No, the annual party was always packed to the rafters with pesky punters and big-wigged bigwigs. It was an event set up mostly because The Baroness needed the attention, her way of peacocking in front of the pretenders she called chums. There was an unwritten mutual understanding between The Baroness and her associates. They all knew that deep down their friendships were constructed solely on advertising their accomplishments, or lack thereof, and that the Grubbe-Nut Christmas Do was the perfect place to show them off. This made for very bitter relationships indeed, but to their credit they all did a wonderful job of grinning and bearing it. Captain Grubbe had a number of acquaintances in high places, none of whom suspected The Captain's carnal crimes but all of whom were invited to the party. Aside from pimpin', Cap had his chubby grubby fingers in a few, more wholesome pies, and the bakers were part of a small clan of guests that The Captain actually wanted at his party.

The Baroness had an extraordinary talent for exaggeration and so The Captain let her do most of the initial talking at the event as she welcomed the guests into their lovely big home. The two of them had a flawless cover-up story for the fame and fortune and little Mrs Big Nut could uphold it through any weather. Cap'n G was less meticulous about the details of his alter ego than his wife was. He was still involved in the dirty works of his empire and so for it to continue working he had to admit to what he was, but only to those that needed to know. To the bloated aristocracy and old money of the British countryside, he was under the cover of his more noble doppelgänger. The Grubbes had decided a long time ago, shortly after their picture-perfect marriage and relocation out West, that the business was booming too loud to go unnoticed. And because of Cap's sodomised shame and The Baroness' petty pretension, neither wanted to sell the story of how their love and success actually came about.

The Baroness began to tell of how Captain Grubbe was a real captain in the Royal Navy, a decorated war hero turned government advisor turned affable aristocrat. She, of course, came from old money and had inherited a prestigious name and a bucket of cash. The Baron also was a devout charity worker and human rights activist, funded and sponsored to high heavens by the UN. It was almost too elaborate to question, and besides, they had the fortune to back up the claims and the influence to overthrow impeachment. The lies were so far-fetched that people naturally assumed their accuracy. As the years rolled by, though, their story became dangerously warped. It had become an alternate reality. Those who knew the truth also knew to keep their mouths shut. Those who knew nothing except the falsities just gawked at The Captain's apparent admirable success and toasted to their unknowing involvement in it. Baroness Big Nut had begun to believe her own lies. She repressed the memories of her former whoredom and paraded forward into her principled role in society. The Captain was kept fairly rational by his occasional weekend pimping but even he had kept up his better appearance for too long to be completely sane. That being said, their fake identities were altogether better for it – if they believed in it, then why shouldn't others?

How Could It Be?

The day of the big party had arrived, and this year's was extra special as it celebrated twenty years of West Country Grubbe. There were more people attending and so there were more bangs and whizzes arranged to dazzle the new guests. The Baroness was scurrying around tweaking and twerking (no, wait... she wasn't twerking. God no, oh Jesus, could you imagine?) and was whipping the party palace into shape whilst The Captain was out shooting all day. It was an old hobby of his, mostly aiming at clay pigeons but sometimes rabbits too – very rarely at people though.

The house was being dressed fabulously by the help, along with some brutal scrutiny by Baroness Big Nut. Streamers and novelty bunting were webbed around the grand hall of the house. A great big bushy Christmas tree glittering with expensive silvers and golds was being displayed at the foot of the main staircase. Garlands, wreaths and festive ornaments clung to the walls and shelves of the downstairs, and clusters of sweets were put out in little bowls for the guests to nibble on as they toured the manor. The outside was aglow with neat trimmings of fairy lights and the low temperature of the late afternoon promised the magical shine of a silver frost later on. Inside, the caterers were cooking up a great big mass of finger-sized delights. The theme was Christmas and so the recipes were all generously laced with the flavours of a diabetic nightmare. Salt and sugar. Butter and cheese. Pastries and cakes. Nuts and spices. Meats and sauces. The chefs were given the green light on taste and the outcomes were to be beyond delicious – although most of them were already far too pissed to be considered a professional outfit. The alcohol people hadn't arrived yet (the cooks had been sipping on their own-recipe wine), because The Baroness had gone for a cocktail theme this year and with it she had hired an entire troop of flirty bar boys to twist, mix and rim the night away. They were due to arrive soon so some of the help that had been hired in were busy rearranging the furniture in the grand hall to make room for their fancy mixology station. It was certainly all go at the prestigious Grubbe Manor; the long list of to-dos was being ticked off and thus far everything had been running smoother than a slut's undercarriage.

Around half-past two, The Captain returned from his shooting trip. He was riding on top of a muddy old Ducati 450 Scrambler, roaring it loudly as he raced down the long driveway of his country home. The bike was barely big enough for his great frame to be draped across but even so,

The Captain looked beyond cool as he cut through the curtain of chilly December fog. He was back an hour or so earlier than he had planned to be; an unexpected and unexplained forest fire had caused his early return. The blaze had erupted in one of the farmers' fields that backed onto the shooting grounds where The Captain fired his guns. He parked his bike up under the cover of his open-fronted garage and then waltzed triumphantly through the house, with his catch in a bag over his shoulder. He had hunted some game after the smoke from the fire had clogged the skies and the clay pigeons he was firing at had disappeared inside the grey. He bowled through the deep walkways of his house and into the kitchen where he plonked the sack onto the worktop and smirked.

"Cook. Cook these pesky wabbits... And leave some vino for the grub, ay fella."

The half-cut cook fumbled for the bag, pulling the three rabbits out by their ears and thinking how best to flavour the beasts. With a wry smile on his wind-chapped face, The Captain reached for the whiskey tucked behind the spice rack.

"So, what be there for a hungry man to nibble on now then, my boy? I want summin' that tastes as good as it smells in 'ere."

Captain Grubbe poured a small whiskey into the cap and slurped it out loudly before quickly pouring another.

"Try this, Boss. It's a boiled bacon and spiced apple canapé we're sending out later. The cracker is..." The cook paused to burp. "Sorry. The cracker is chilli-flaked and has been fried off, so it's even crispier." He wiggled the tray of canapés out in front of The Captain. "The bacon's just come out the pot, take one while they're warm."

The Captain knocked back his second capful of bourbon and took a handful of the fresh appetisers. He popped the whiskey bottle back behind the spice rack and made for the door.

"Sterlin' work my friends, sterlin' work. I shall bother you no longer."

He headed out of the kitchen, popping one of the snacks into his wide, shark-like mouth as he walked. But before he got to the door, he paused as the crunch of the chilli-flaked cracker echoed in his jaw. The apple-topped bacon fused with its spicy base and Captain Grubbe moaned in appreciation.

"Oh, you guys," he sang, spinning on the heel of his boots. "This...this is good. This is really good." Then he threw another into his mouth and left the kitchen for good.

The set-up for the party was almost done. The cocktail bar boys had arrived in tight white uniforms and were unpacking their many alcohols and glitzy tools onto the bar at the back of the big room. The band were tuning up in the opposite corner to the bar, twanging strings and blowing dud parps as they fiddled their instruments into shape. The men of the band were smartly dressed in bowties and white jackets. The ladies were sparkling in elegantly bright dresses. The help were shining up the glasses and the silverware, checking reflections and wiping clean the smudges. The caterers were laying the table for their exquisite feast, straightening the whites of the cloths and putting out the non-perishables in festive crockery.

Baroness Big Nut was upstairs tarting herself up for the evening. She had a new frock, new hair, new shoes and an all-new shade of skin, funnily enough. If she featured on a Dulux Colour Chart she'd be a **Mucky Brown** - *'like an* *unwell poo'*. The Baroness looked as though she'd had her big ol' head buried firmly up her own arsehole for the best part of a week (which metaphorically speaking was obviously very true). Her dress was mauve in colour and frilled at the edges. It was a classically styled piece and she believed that she looked lovely in it, so that's all that mattered. The Captain scrubbed up pretty good. He sported a burgundy tuxedo with black lapels and bowtie, an off-white shirt and cherry-red loafers. There was a pocket watch dangling decoratively from his left jacket pocket and his hair was short but swept back. Both of them suited their false titles and as they stood, resilient and loveless, side by side in front of their walk-in wardrobe mirror, they managed to crack a smile.

***

The grandfather clock downstairs, ornamented with a gold-spotted garland, chimed six times as its three hands aligned in the middle of the clock face. The first of the night's many guests had begun to arrive in their shiny cars. They were background fillers really, people who had just about made the long invite list. There were footmen waiting at the end of the long, lit-up driveway. They were suited but each had a red and white Santa hat on, shielding their ears from the bitter evening chill.

Baroness Big Nut liked to tick every party attendee off her calligraphy-splattered invite list as they arrived, checking them into her home. She was positioned inside the second porch, just before the first hallway and the grand curly-wurlying staircase. She was perched dangerously close to the edge of her stall, half hidden behind an overly formal welcome desk which was sprinkled lavishly with potpourri and teeny-tiny chocolates.

The Captain liked to hang elusively upstairs for about forty-five minutes, just until people began to ask after his whereabouts. Then, and only then, would he twirl impressively onto the landing in full sight of the crowd of crawly-bum-licks gathered there below and shimmer in the great chandelier light for a while. With a bourbon in his hand, he would scan the room below for the people he wanted to speak with before swaggering down the stairs and eventually joining the festivities.

The Christmas Do was in full swing. Polite mingles, piano jingles and barbeque Pringles were aplenty. The crowds had shifted from the hallways and the stairways into the grand hall where the food, the bar and the band were waiting. The party was an odd affair though. Most everyone in that house was corrupted to their very core, looking for an in at any opportunity to nab some more of The Captain's money. At first glance, it looked to be your average Gatsby gig, but like a desperate fool with his last Lotto scratch card all you had to do was key away the shiny silver stuff and you'd be left with a dull, empty sack of spuds, promising nothing but shame. There happened to be very little real class there. It was all one big balancing act between dollar and disguise; a manky masquerade of money-mad monkeys.

As The Baroness sat at the entrance of her house with her fountain pen and parchment, taking names, The Captain was doing the rounds and keeping up appearances amongst a selection of people he quite frankly didn't like. To most (including Captain Grubbe) the room was full of opportunities for business rather than lasting friendships, so he had to circulate to test the waters and see which of his wife's esteemed guests were worth talking to more later on. The Captain did have a few actual friends there however, as a handful of his working girls were in attendance – although instead of donning their usual leave-nothing-to-the-imagination costumes, they dazzled in more elegant attire, though a couple exhibited about as much talent for disguise as Chief Inspector Clouseau. There were still some guests who were yet to turn up; the night was young-ish (despite the average age of the guests so far). For now, the Grubbe-Nut Christmas Do was unseasonably dull and predictable, but the fate of a pimp and a prostitute can turn on a chocolate sixpence.

A blacked-out Beamer crept up the driveway slowly in second gear and parked up outside the house. It pulled sluggishly into its designated spot, the soft crunch of the gravel underneath it discreetly announcing the arrival of the group inside. The engine cut out, and out stepped Mr. Trevor Mann. He neatened his suit and then walked around to the passenger side door and opened it for the young lady inside. Evangeline was the young lady. She looked awful. Mr Mann linked her arm through his and then headed for the house. The two back doors of the car then opened to reveal Dr Trevor Chaim on the one side and Madd Trevor Rockson on the other. The cogs in the Captain's greasy machine had arrived. Dr Chaim shut his door, but on Madd's side another guest slithered out: Hank Howardson. The black-eyed bean looked even worse than Evangeline did as he waited to be marched into the house.

The five of them headed inside, three of their own accord and the other two less so. The Baroness' nose was put out of joint as the boys approached her sweet-smelling half-table, looking mostly unfit for the glossy occasion and parading a couple of maltreated gate crashers through her spectacularly sparkly home. Already they were causing quite a scene for the smokers out the front and the odd guests not inside the grand hall, as it was clear that the boys were, and had been, up to no good.

"Hello Mum," said Mr Mann as he brushed past The Baroness with Evangeline forcefully locked onto his arm.

"Baroness," Dr Chaim greeted her politely as he, too, brushed past her.

"Sorry, Mum," Madd Rockson finished, as he walked past her with Hank at his side, slouching in weariness.

Slack-jawed she watched them all float by, sure to tarnish her soirée. The Baroness then left her post for the first time that evening, as she scrambled after her two boys and their plus-ones in a flailing attempt to cool the situation.

"Trevor!" she called out in a sort of whisper-shout. All three of the Trevors turned around in the hallway.

"What the hell are you doing?! Are you deliberately trying to ruin the night? Who are these people, where have you all come from? And Trevor, where is your suit?" she asked the doctor impatiently.

"It's out the back, in our room. I was just goin' to put it on," Dr Chaim replied.

"Good, then take those two with you and find somewhere to keep them hidden. Lock them in there if you have to, just don't let them out into the party, yes?"

"Yes Mum. Calm down, it's all gonna be fine. Dad knows all 'bout it," Madd said to his adopted mother, calmly and out of character.

Madd loved The Baroness. She was terrifically hard to

love but she was still the woman who had plucked him from the children's home all those years ago, and the love he was shown by her as a child still warmed his cold heart.

"Oh I bet he does. That doesn't surprise me at all – your father has no idea how hard I've worked to organise tonight, all he cares about is the glass in his hand and the..."

"Mum! Enough, we're goin' out the back to get Trevor's suit and deal with these two. Please go and sit back down, the party looks great." Mr Mann, as per usual, had the final word on the matter.

Baroness Big Nut had little love for Trevor Mann. She struggled in treating him as her son the way she treated Madd; he was, after all, an unchosen extra and not the child she had wanted to bring home. With Madd she felt comfortable, maternal. He reminded her of the smidgen of good in her life, or at least he used to. These days she felt little more than disregard for anything that wasn't silk-lined or five-starred. As Mr Mann had grown, The Baroness had come to fear him slightly, in the same scornful and uncertain way she did her husband. They were two of the same person, moulded from the unforgiving evil of their surroundings. Captain Grubbe had shaped Trevor Mann into the Mini-Me he needed to make sure his objectionable legacy lived on beyond his own years. The Baroness had witnessed this first hand and had learnt to handle her unwanted adopted son the same way she handled her once-wanted husband: by mostly ignoring his existence. She did as he insisted, though, and dropped the drama, for she herself was beginning to arouse suspicion by nattering on argumentatively in the hallway. She retreated to her stool and desk at the front of the house and seethed quietly behind a hard stare.

Mr. Mann led the pack through the first and second hallways, past the grand curly-wurlying staircase and out towards the kitchen. The boys' private room was behind the big kitchen at the back of the house, facing out towards the vast green fields. It was vacant now, except for the stack of fireworks that was being held there, waiting to be set off outside at midnight along with the others being stored in the cellar. The room was solely for the boys' business use, although they used the Mantis Bar and Nightclub to do the majority of their dirty work in, because if there was ever a raid or ambush then the damage would be to Faisal's property and not The Captain's. It also gave them a chance to check up on the coked-up disco king and make sure he wasn't overstepping any marks – but of course he had recently overstepped a big, sticky red mark and now the boys were having to rethink their meeting point. A few heads turned as Hank and Evangeline were walked through the house by the Trevors, looking stern and moving fast. As they passed the doorway that led into the grand hall, a man inside caught a glimpse of the group hurrying along and hoping to avoid detection from the party inside. He was standing alone, close to the door, with a glass of bubbles in his hand and a dejected look on his face. He was wavy-haired, green-eyed and olive-skinned. He was quite well known in the wealthy circles of the West Country, despite being a little reticent and keeping mostly to himself. His name was José Romario Cobos de la Bell and he owned the Indoor Outdoor Bath House™ on the outskirts of Bath.

José was supposed to be having a lovely evening as this was the first time he had ever been invited to the infamous Grubbe-Nut Christmas Do, after Baroness Big Nut had spent a day at his bathhouse and spa in the autumn and really enjoyed herself. The sullen Spaniard would have asked a mystery love along to the party after she had unexpectedly rocked his world, but then she ran off with his watch and he had been once again left alone. So as he stood there, miserable, tipsy and unwilling to socialise, the last thing he expected to see was Evangeline, the woman who had stolen his heart and his watch, walk past the doorway in the company of four other men.

At first he thought it was a concoction of the fizz he'd been drinking and the pain he'd been feeling; surely she wasn't really there? It must be delusion. José was in minor shock. Whether Evangeline was really there or not, he was still surprised to see her image float by. He chugged back his champagne and ditched the glass on the table beside him. He had to check... He poked his head around the doorway and out into the main hall where the stairs were. He saw that Evangeline was really there, and that she was in fact being led reluctantly through the big house by a big man in a big suit. Peeking out of the doorway, José watched the thief and her master traipse their way down the hall and into the kitchen, followed by the three other men. One of them had his watch – he knew it, they were all up to no good. José never got around to inviting Evangeline to the party, so she couldn't have known that he would be there. Perhaps she was working on The Captain's behalf, he thought. Maybe that's how he got all his money – he was nothing more than a kingpin burglar. Clearly José was wrong; because Evangeline worked alone, and the only reason she was at the party was because of a clumsy, if not serendipitous, mistake in a cake and coffee shop in Frome.

O Holy Shite

Captain Grubbe was busy making small circles around himself. Audiences swirled around his big ego, half pretending to listen to the stories he told and half pretending to care. The only ones listening intently to The Captain were Mr and Mrs Tamura, his newest and most diverse associates. They were both Japanese and they were both nursing a couple of festive Lemon Sours – regular Lemon Sours, just with Christmas-tree-shaped ice cubes. The Tamuras were a lovely, kind and hardworking couple. They were thrilled to have been invited to The Captain's infamous party after only just moving into the area, and as such they were dressed in their Friday night best. Mr Tamura was looking sharp in a tailored black tuxedo with fancy buckled footwear, and Mrs Tamura wore a navy-blue midi dress with kimono sleeves and a glittery sliver wrap through the middle. The two of them were doing the decent thing and paying close attention to their host's stories, but in truth they were very drunk. The Tamuras were making good use of the free bar and the fact that they had the night off from looking after their many children, and their drunkenness was quickly becoming as obvious as a red disc on a white flag.

There was a rumble in Captain Grubbe's rotund belly that drew a conclusion to his final anecdote, and he excused himself from the crowd to consult the brilliance of the buffet table. It occupied near enough the entire back wall of the hall and was as bountiful and colourful as Christmas itself. The smells, though there were many, fused together and rippled through the warm air of the room like a mouth-watering fog over a famished wasteland. The

Captain could hardly contain his excitement. He was a little tipsy and fucking starving. He had been waiting for his chance to tackle the feast ever since the caterers had begun their preparations that afternoon. With his eyes wider than a meth-head in a retinopathy exam, he grabbed himself a plate. Hungrily, he reached for the first of many dishes: the humble potato salad. The chives were strewn across the top artistically, the potatoes underneath all silky in their mayonnaise coats, pepper-splattered and still warm. The gleaming metallic ladle was reclined inside the dish seductively, waiting to be held. The Captain nearly dribbled into the butter dish beneath him; this was surely to be the pinnacle of his merry night. He scooped up the ladle, caressing the starchy miracle inside, and brought it up to dump it down on his plate, when a whisper behind him called his name and broke the moment.

"Captain. Captain!" the quiet voice called.

The Captain screwed his face in frustration and lowered the ladle back into the bowl. His stomach roared in vexation and he turned around, trying to look unperturbed.

"Yes, hello," he said as he spun around. The frustration and discontent returned to his face quickly when he saw who it was.

"Captain... Hi. Errrm, can we talk?" asked Janet Cartwright, with a very frightened Klint Buttafuoco at her side. "Outside, preferably..." Janet finished.

"Well, I don't like where this is goin'. You two weren't invited, were ya? How'd you get past The Baron then? She's usually pretty good at keepin' out gatecrashers!"

"Well, she's obviously off her game tonight, isn't she? Grubbe, please. I've got a bit of a situation."

"And you thought now was the best time to bother

me with it, yeah? I'm a little busy, can't you tell?"

"It'll be quick. It's time to be a producer."

"I thought I just put the money up...?"

"Well, yeah, so did I. But I also thought that, contrary to popular belief, Klint wasn't a dickhead. So I suppose we were both wrong!"

Janet's tones were harsh, the panic in her voice masked completely by the urgency. Klint stood beside her, listening in on the conversation but gawping absentmindedly at the sausage-roll mountain on the table behind The Captain. They were bronzed and warm. He was pale and cold.

"Oh is it? You all right Klint? You look like you've seen the ghost of Christmas future. I'd ask what you've done but I've got a feelin' I'm gonna find out very soon for myself."

The Captain had been dealing with Janet and Klint for a while, and although they still had respect for him and he still held the smiting hand of fear above them, there was a certain informality between them all now. The awkward pleasantries of strangers were never much of a thing between them even at the start, and so by now they were like family – distant, dysfunctional family.

"Ain't the film s'posed to be startin' Monday...?" The Captain leaned in closer to Janet, "What's gone wrong this time Jan? Am I gonna lose my money?" His cold breath sent a shudder down her back.

"No, of course not. Like I said, I just need you to help me with something. Something outside."

"Okay then," he said, standing back up straight, "but this is on my time, and I was just about to eat, drink and be merry. So if this is gonna change that, well then I won't be 'appy. Are we all goin'? Shit-for-brains 'ere, as well?" The

Captain loved toying with Klint, who was still standing ashamedly beside Janet. “Fucking starvin’ I am!” said The Captain as he dropped his plate back down unhappily.

“Come on,” said Janet. “Bring your drink though, you might need it.”

As the three of them headed out into the driveway, they of course had to pass The Baroness, sitting restlessly on her podium. As they whizzed by, she instantly piped up, already agitated with her sons and ready to snap at her husband.

“Where are you going? What’s going on? You and the boys are ruining this evening, do you know that?! I knew there was trouble when I see you two pull up. I can’t believe you stormed in there looking like that, Janet, I thought you had a little more class than that!”

Janet paid no attention to her, neither did Klint, but The Captain laughed out loud. He turned back to face his rouge-tinted wife.

“Class? Janet Cartwright? There’s a lot of empty space in that swede on your shoulders my darlin’, ain’t there, ’cos there’s certainly no fuckin’ brains!” He stepped up to her podium, unlovingly staring at her. “They’re all ’ere ’cos of me. They’re all ’ere to see me. So tell me exactly what I’m ruinin’, huh?”

They both held their nerve against one another. To an outsider you would never have guessed that there had once been love between them. The Captain swiped a handful of the tiny chocolates from the table top and smiled sarcastically, then he turned his back on his wife and rejoined Janet and Klint.

Janet headed over to the car. It was parked up on the gravel, away from the other cars. The sparkle from the frost on the car's forest-green paint looked somewhat magical. The silver rims were shining in the low light of the driveway. Janet stopped at the back of the car, looking tense and choosing her words as carefully as she could before saying them out loud.

"There's... well, there's... there's somebody in the boot," she said eventually.

"There's somebody in the boot?" The Captain replied, checking that he had heard Janet correctly.

"There is somebody in the boot..." Janet repeated, presenting the scenario with clarity.

"I think she's dead," Klint said, talking for the first time since arriving at the house.

"You think she's dead?" The Captain replied, again checking that he was understanding what they were telling him.

"For fuck's sake Grubbe, there's a girl in the boot and we think she might be dead!" Janet chanted back.

"A girl? What d'ya mean a girl? A little girl?"

"No, she's a woman. *Was* a woman. I didn't mean to... you know, she just fell... on her head. Hard." Klint was paler then before, his voice was all over the place.

"You've killed someone? A woman? Jesus H. Christ, how the fuck did you do that? And why've you brought her 'ere, what the fuck am I s'posed to do with her?!"

The three of them were all gathered around the boot of the car, each as tense as the next and all wondering when it would be that someone was going to open the boot up to reveal the lady inside. None of them wanted to.

"Well go on then, open it up..." said Janet, looking at Klint.

"What?"

"I said open the fucking boot up Klint!"

"Why me?"

"What do you mean 'why you'? Why do you think 'why you'? Because you're the soppy sod who killed her and stuffed her in there in the first place, that's why you!"

Then before either of them had a chance to bicker anymore, Captain Grubbe barged through them and popped open the frosted boot. A cold breeze hit their faces as the door cut upwards through the air, revealing the horror inside. Sure enough, as Janet had promised, scrunched up inside the boot was an unconscious woman. Her mousy brown hair covered her face and she looked as cold as the night itself.

"Bloody 'ell! I didn't think you 'ad it in ya Klint!" gasped The Captain as he stood with his hands holding up the boot, his large frame conveniently blocking the view.

"Eh?!" said Klint.

Captain Grubbe let go of the car and turned around to face them. He had a look on his face that wasn't too much unlike enjoyment. On seeing the woman laid out in the boot of the car, he seemed almost excited by it. He had been away from scandal and atrocity for so long that seeing the corpse in the boot had reignited his lust for abomination. Suddenly, in amongst the bougie atmosphere of his own Christmas do, The Captain had some real villainy to grab hold of and relish.

"Well, I'm glad you're enjoying this!" said Janet Cartwright to The Captain. "You must've dealt with a few of these before, so what are we supposed to do with her?!"

"These? Dead birds in the back of stolen motors? No, this'd be a first for me. But I can't wait to hear all about how this 'appened, how about we go back inside and have a little chat..."

Then The Captain was cut off by the dull groan of the undead behind him. He froze, as did the others. Was it coming from the boot? Again, another groan from behind The Captain. That one was definitely from the boot. The girl inside was alive. Captain Grubbe's wicked smile was now bigger than ever. Janet was still frozen, unsure of how to react. Klint sprung back into life along with the woman in the boot. He was in a daze, but the murderous guilt had lifted instantly from his shoulders and he was able to communicate once again.

"Holy shit!" he blurted out.

"Ho-Ly-Shit!" The Captain copied, spinning around to face the woman once more.

She was awake and rubbing her bruised head, still lying down inside the boot. She groaned a third time, louder and more consciously than before. Then came the shouting.

"WHO THE FU-"

Captain Grubbe slammed the boot door down to silence the woman.

The thud was harsh; Klint squirmed and Janet twitched in distress. The Captain had to seal in the woman's cries so that his staff and guests were not alerted, but he was heavy-handed in his reactions. They all waited, fearing that the resurrected woman had been murdered for the second time that night. The muffled sounds of the party massaged the space behind them. The dream was inside with a glass of champagne; the reality was outside with frosty bollocks.

The party sounds continued, dramatising the scene, but then came the stifled sounds of a confused and injured woman. The back of the Thunderbird shook with her discomfort; she was still alive. They all took a breath and relaxed with the news that they were innocent of murder once again. The Captain laughed off the lunacy, his previous hunger having dwindled.

"So, you wanna tell me who she is now?" asked The Captain with his hand resting on the boot.

"She stole the car," answered Klint.

"And how did she steal the car?"

"Well to be honest, I don't really know..."

"Right," said Captain Grubbe, his questions still unanswered.

"It went missing, then I found it, and when I did, that woman was about to drive it away. We had a scuffle and, well, then I panicked and put her into the boot, and we drove here."

"A scuffle? Well, I hope it wasn't too rough." The Captain was toying with Klint again. "So you saw all this, did you, Janet?"

"Unfortunately not. Klint came back to me and I made the call to come here. Aside from dealing with whoever it is who's locked in there, I thought we could leave the car here until the shoot starts on Monday, to prevent any further accidents happening. I assumed you'd agree – after all, you paid for it."

Janet pulled her cigarettes from her coat pocket and lit one nervously. Captain Grubbe reached over and pulled one out for himself. Janet did him the courtesy of lighting it. Together they puffed, the smoke meeting in the air before dispersing. They all stood triangularly, reminiscent of the standoff in *The Good, the Bad and the Ugly*, though it was impossible to label who was who.

"I think that sounds like a good idea. I say we get the car round the back and see who's in the boot together, eh? We can sneak her in through the back and into the boys' office – best not take her past The Baron or that big head of hers might just explode. Janet, you can walk with me. Klint, you pull the car round the side there."

And so they both did as they were told. Klint started up the car and drove it slowly around to the back of the house, where he waited for the others to join him. All the while, the lady in the boot was banging and shouting for her life, her heart pounding harder than her head was. By the time The Captain and Janet caught up to Klint they had finished their smokes, although they both looked as though they could've done with another. Janet was struggling to find solutions to her problems, The Captain was scheming ways to make the problems work for him; and as they approached the car, Klint caught the end of their conversation.

"So then that's what we'll do; we'll move the production base 'ere. You can use my office, Klint can use the boys', and I can see what's goin' on at all times if I 'ave to. The car stays 'ere and so do you." Captain Grubbe then spoke to Klint through the window of the car. "Klint my boy, you're more than welcome to stay in one of the spare rooms, but I won't make ya."

The window was closed, so The Captain's invitation was a little muted. Klint shook his head behind the glass – wisely he chose to reject the invite. The Captain smiled back at him.

"Well, if you're sure. The bed's always made... Now get out the car Klint."

It was becoming hard to hear him over the cries

coming from the boot. It was time to move the woman inside.

Klint exited the car and straightened his clothes. It was getting colder outside and all Klint wanted was to be indoors in the warm with a glass of wine. Janet was cold and thirsty too, though she desired a bottle of something, not just the one glass. For now though, they both waited at the boot of the car and readied themselves for the emergence of the woman inside. Captain Grubbe, the clear leader of the pack in all his grandeur, approached the boot and popped the lock to open it again.

WORKING MY WAY BACK TO YOU, BABE

Hank Howardson was thrown down into one of the armchairs in the Trevors' office and as he landed on the leathered cushion, he sank so low into it that he almost fell through the bottom. Mr Mann pulled up another chair beside Hank for Evangeline to sit on and he popped her down onto it, a lot nicer than Madd Rockson had done with Hank. Dr Chaim closed the door behind them all. He locked it up, pocketing the key, and made his way across the room to join the other Trevors at the desk in front of Hank and Evangeline.

Hank was breathing heavily, and Evangeline was struggling to breath at all. They were both afraid of where they had ended up, but only Hank knew exactly where they were. The delightful smells of the kitchen nearby toyed with the tension in the room. The Trevors were all looking very serious, but the wonderful wafts unintentionally added some light to the dark. The room was a good size; there were three leather armchairs, two that were taken by

Hank and Evangeline and one that was tucked behind the desk, being the one that Mr Mann was sitting on. The desk was a natural oak colour and had a garland wrapped around the front with a small red bow in the middle. The desk was centred in front of the only window in the room. The light that came in through it in the late afternoon, on a clear day, would ignite the room with the beautiful warm colours of the sunset. Now, though, it was as black as black outside.

"Welcome to Grubbe Manor," Mr Mann introduced. "If you're wondrin' why it's so busy, it'd be because it's Mum and Dad's big Christmas do...so Merry Christmas."

Hank and Evangeline listened intently to Trevor Mann. They sat tight in their seats, keeping as still as possible and hoping there was still salvation left for them.

"Now, neither of you were s'posed to be 'ere, and so we can't expect The Captain to be in the best o' spirits when he has to break away from the party to come deal with you two. Hank, I think you know that you're not going anywhere anytime soon, so you can buckle down; you're stayin' the night. Evangeline, your beef is with me, so as far as I'm concerned – and I am concerned – The Captain don't need to know what you've been up to. In fact, he don't need to know about you at all. I've got my ol' dad's watch back now, so really, that's all that matters now, right?"

Evangeline was sitting so very still, afraid to move.

"Right?!" Mr Mann, however, wanted a response.

"Right..." said Evangeline, dormouse-like.

"Wrong," decided Mr Mann. Evangeline gulped. "What about my time? The inconvenience of it all? You say it was some Spaniard that gave it to you, but that don't quite wash with me. I mean, where would he've got it from? Could it be that you're just passing the buck?"

"No, I swear to you I got it from him. He's the one you should be after, he..."

"He owns a swimming pool in Bath and he has loads of money and blah blah FUCKING BLAH!" Trevor Mann exploded into instant rage. The walls shook with the fury behind his voice. "Then why, my love, would he give his priceless stolen antique away to you? Seems a bit senseless to me."

"And me," Dr Chaim added.

"And me," Madd Rockson added also.

"Me too," said Hank, forgetting where he was temporarily.

Mr Mann slammed his hand down on the desk. The room shuddered again. In the confines of his own office he could be as loud and as intimidating as he wanted to be. Dr Chaim was perched on the corner of the desk but decided to stand up and remove himself from the conflict. He took himself into the adjoining room where he changed into his suit for the evening. Until the appropriate decisions were made over what to do with the perpetrators, there really wasn't much he could do except provide a looming protection. However, Hank and Evangeline posed about as much threat as a cotton bud in a cutlery drawer.

"No, I think you're more guilty than that," continued Mr Mann. "I'm not denyin' the existence of this Spaniard, but I need to understand how you, or him, or anyone other than myself came to inherit that watch. My dad'd be turnin' in his grave if he knew his old watch ended up on anyone's wrist other than mine. So you can understand my upset when I hear you talkin' bout you and some wanky Spanish bloke, lobbing it around between ya, can't ya?! No, we'll have a good ol' chat when The Captain comes and takes Hank away – just me and you – then we'll see if your story sticks! Till then, you're my date for the evening, understand? Smile, and be polite."

Evangeline was on the verge of tears. She could see no way out. There was nowhere to run, and hiding seemed just as impossible. Hank was scanning the room for anything he could use to escape himself. Any props to use as weapons, any other way out beside the locked door or the other one that led into the room where Dr Chaim was. There was the big window behind the desk, but that was behind the desk. The window was a large, canted bay window that was paned and double-glazed. It was clear glass but was frosted with the cold of the night. In the daytime the view from it was spectacular. It looked out over the vast country landscape with the dips and mounds and trees and grass that made it imperfectly perfect. The maple and beech trees plotted a colourful route for the eyes to follow; in and out of the fields and up and over the hilltops behind. Their reds and oranges bled through the pretty greens to make for a scene of unimaginable beauty, but presently there was a beast in the forefront.

The security light at the back of the house snapped on – there was movement outside. From the moonlit sky suddenly came an amber face-light. Act Two was starting. The illuminated patio was narrow and ran the width of the house. Below it, opposite the bay window of the room, were some steps down to the gravel track that also spanned the width of the big house. The patio slabs were newly jet washed, so the shine from the security light bounced right off them and the movement that had triggered it was revealed. There was a car parked up at the bottom of the steps: a 1956 forest-green Ford Thunderbird. A man was sitting inside the car in the driver's seat, his identity obscured by the shadows cast upon him. Back inside the room, Hank bolted upright from his previously slouched position, his heart banging hard in his chest as the curtain of darkness outside was drawn.

"That's my car," he declared. He jumped up to his feet. "That's my car!" he repeated, more animated than before and clearly distressed. "Leyla! Why's she 'ere, how'd you get her 'ere?!" Hank was bewildered. "Who brought her in? Let her leave. LET HER LEAVE!"

Mr Mann stood to meet Hank with a stern, ugly look on his face. "'S'cuse me? Sit the fuck down. Now," Mr Mann said calmly.

"That's me car, that's me fuckin' car!" Hank was getting mad. "Where're the boys? You didn't bring 'em in too?!"

"SIT DOWN HANK!" Mr Mann boomed.

Then he threw a stapler at his head. It hit, and Hank fell back into the armchair again. A small slice appeared on his forehead, and a dot of blood wiggled from it and down his nose.

"Madd, what's 'appenin', who's out there?" Mr Mann asked as he stayed facing his prisoners.

"It's Dad," Madd responded, his face pressed against the window.

"Well what's he doin'? Why's he out there?"

"I dunno, he's with a woman..."

"Leyla," Hank whispered to himself, guilty and panicked.

"...'ang on, there's someone else, another fella just got out the car..." Hank clenched his jaw as Madd described the scene.

"Who are they?"

"I dunno. She's got long red hair, looks a pretty girl from 'ere. He's tall... and dressed nice." Hank unclenched his jaw; it wasn't Leyla outside with The Captain.

"'Ere! It's them two from Dad's film; the actor and director woman. That's who it is." Madd turned around to face the group again. "'Leyla! Leyla!'" he called, mocking Hank. "You knob'ead!"

"Right. You all finished? Good. Now, The Captain's gonna be in soon, so Hank, I suggest you sit up and shut up. Evangeline, you're comin' out with me, we're gonna get a drink and come back when no one's around to distract us..."

Then suddenly there came a scream. A distressed, aggravated and throat-gargling scream. It came from outside the room, outside the house. They all stopped to hear it. Dr Chaim opened the door he was changing behind, his shirt only half buttoned up and his trousers open at the fly.

"What the bloody 'ell was that?!" he asked of the room. Nobody replied, as nobody knew.

The dust in the air was all that moved. The confrontation between them stopped, and so did the scream. It was cut off abruptly, as if with a chef's cleaver. Madd chose not to peek through the window again. He knew when to look and when not to. Instead they all waited in the quiet, heartbeats and snivels being the only sounds coming from them. However, there were noises coming from the group outside. The Trevors were mapping their movements post-scream, and they seemed to be nearing the room they were all in. Doors shutting, shoes squeaking, furniture bashing – all clues that The Captain and his guests were drawing closer and closer to their office. A heavy push of double doors – they were passing by the kitchen. The small applause of hard heels on the wooden floor – they were heading down the short corridor behind the room's connecting wall. The rattle of the door handle behind Hank and Evangeline – they were here. The handle fidgeted up and down unconfidently; whoever was controlling its movements was unaware that this door could be locked from the inside.

"It's locked," Mr Mann called out to them. The rattling stopped. Mr Mann turned to the half-dressed doctor. "Go open it, and do your shirt up... The Captain's outside."

Dr Chaim adhered to the request and went over to the door to unlock it. He buttoned up his shirt and trousers, then opened the door to reveal the noisy people behind. As surely as Madd had seen them through the window, there in front of the bad doctor were Janet Cartwright and Klint Buttafuoco. They were white-faced and tired, looking desperate for sanctuary. But this was no holy place they had stumbled upon; this was the devil's waiting room.

Janet and Klint entered without invitation, arms cutting through the tense dense air as they propelled their legs over the threshold. No introductions were made; apart from Hank and Evangeline they had all met before, though under less moody circumstances. There were no hellos or welcomes, no smiles or handshakes. Janet and Klint were there under orders and the others were playing guessing games as to why they had joined them. The confusion in the room didn't last long however, because soon after, the real shit hit the inoperative ceiling fan. The steamy brown bullet shot directly from the blood-red anus of Lucifer himself. It passed unscathed through the dormant blades of the heavenly glowing ceiling light and fan fixture and landed with a squelching *splat* into Hank Howardson's tea-stained lap.

Captain Grubbe appeared in the doorway with his gold-cluttered hand stuck on the face of the woman that was attached to his front. His face was semi-decorated with enjoyment and pride, the rest of it showing no more emotion than it usually did. Without the backstory to this one, The Captain's peculiar plus-ones were difficult to justify. But the room was already packed with peculiar plus-ones, so in a way they all cancelled each other out... (except that they didn't).

The Captain released the woman ahead of him, shoving her into the room so that he could close the door up behind him. She was the lady from the boot of the Ford Thunderbird, the phantom behind the screams. The boys in the room were quick to work that out, and they were all slightly surprised to see her alive and kicking. Captain Grubbe had hushed her moans with nothing more than the liver-spotted folds of his big right hand. Contrary to their prior concern, a life had been spared.

The lady stumbled ahead of herself before she turned back around to confront The Captain. She looked possessed. Her eyes were as dark as the atmosphere and her hand was raised and rigid; she was ready to slap, and indeed there was a slap; though it fell upon the very cheek of the woman who was poised to strike. The whip and crack of the skin-to-skin blow vibrated through the crowded room and was met with choral cringes before the lady dropped to the floor, wailing in pain. Captain Grubbe, the antichrist, shook out his hand and then readjusted the cuffs on his shirt. Everyone except Hank was watching him fearfully and hoping that they would not be the recipient of his next attack. Hank, though, had his eyes set on the woman who had been struck to the floor, as she landed next to the chair he was sat on. She dropped down heavily with the weight behind The Captain's dirty great swipe, but as she fell she landed not on her front, but on her back, face up and clutching her burning cheek.

"Leyla?" Hank said again.

"Oh shit, it is!" Madd laughed.

"LeyLey!" Hank got up off the chair and knelt next to his wife, his face as red and ruined as hers.

"Don't you fuckin' LeyLey me Hank!" she screeched as she brushed away his aid and sat up on the carpet.

"Why're you 'ere? WHY'S SHE 'ERE?!" Hank fired at the room.

"It's obvious, ain't it!" Leyla answered, as she struck her husband's cheek with the slap that was meant for The Captain. "I'm 'ere 'cos of YOU! You're a fuck-up, Hank! And you finally brought me down with ya!"

Hank didn't know whether to shout back or cry or both. Instead he did none of the above. He clambered up to his feet and strode over the short distance to Captain Grubbe; his fists were tight and his temper was blowing through his gritted teeth. He stood toe to toe with the big boss man and nobody could quite believe the action playing out in front of them. The room and all its components had finally gone completely mad. Hank did nothing as he reached The Captain, he just stood in his looming shadow and panted hot air, spitting onto The Captain's burgundy dinner jacket. The Trevors all smiled in the background – they knew what was coming. Leyla cared not to look at her husband; to her he was already dead. Only the unrelenting apparition remained to torment and disappoint her in person now. Klint and Janet didn't know where to look in a room full of unsavoury characters, so they just set their faces into silly unflattering positions and stood waiting to be addressed. Evangeline chose to watch the carpet and sob into her lap, unnoticed. She wanted nothing more than to be at home, reunited with her law-abiding father whom she had thus far shunned and taken for granted. She had dug too deep into the cavern of crime, and now she needed a rope to safety.

Hank was squinting at The Captain, his eyes sore with the pain of the day. His head was throbbing something nasty, but still he insisted on being Hank.

"What you doin' with my wife Grubbe? Why've you got her 'ere?" Hank asked Captain Grubbe, forgetting his manners.

The Captain looked through Hank's questions and saw that he was puffy-eyed and struggling. Calmly he removed his big square glasses from his face and, oddly enough, put them onto Hank's face in an apparent attempt to ease his visual difficulties. Captain Grubbe straightened the specs and then stepped back and nodded approvingly at Hank, who was baffled as to why he was being shown mercy and compassion.

"Better?" The Captain asked.

Hank nodded automatically, as if his head were on strings.

"Good," finished Captain Grubbe, just before he socked Hank right between the eyes.

Hank crumbled backwards with yet another hit to his face – the poor boy was reeling, but he was still on his feet.

Hank yelped – that one was by far the worst of the day. His nose was broken in an instant. The rest of the room flinched, half disturbed and half happy that Hank was the one who had received The Captain's next hit. Hank, still crying and clutching his bloodied misshapen face, steadied himself and clawed the broken remains of Captain Grubbe's glasses off his face. They fell to the floor in shards of glass and plastic.

"You broke my glasses," declared The Captain.

Hank could barely open his eyes, but he managed to force his right lid open just enough to see the next one coming. Captain Grubbe's big fist rapped across Hank's nose again, and this time Hank toppled. He fell next to his wife, Leyla, though as he wriggled in incredible pain she chose not to console or even acknowledge him. Captain Grubbe pulled another pair of glasses from his breast pocket and fitted them over his ears. They were an exact replica of the ones he had just broken on Hank's face.

"Evenin' everyone."

Nobody except Madd Rockson and Mr Mann were listening to Captain Grubbe – a situation that very rarely happened, especially on his own property.

"Don't worry, Hank's been a bit naughty, so he's being dealt with as such. Don't be a twat, don't get twatted, it's very simple. For the rest of you, though, I can see it's been a rough day, and you all deserve a drink…" he paused to look around the room at each person in it, "…but you're a bit rough round the edges to take in there with those mincers. Not a completely bad thing to be honest, but tonight I think you'll turn too many heads – break too many necks, I expect… nah, it's not worth it; none of ya are worth it, I'm sorry to say. But it is Christmas. Trevor, round 'em up and take 'em all downstairs."

"Downstairs?" Trevor Mann responded, unconvinced of The Captain's strategy.

"Yes, downstairs – I said downstairs, didn't I? So clearly I meant downstairs."

"Yes sir," Trevor Mann answered affirmatively, rising from his chair behind the desk in front of the rear window that was once again opaque. "You all 'eard The Captain. Get up, we're goin' downstairs."

And just like the wide-eyed Israelites on the mountainside that was definitely there and definitely happened, they obeyed his commands, and followed him into unnecessary turbulence.

Lo! days shall come, saith the Lord, and I shall make thee a new covenant with the house of Israel, and with the house of Judah, and with the House of Fraser Boxing Day Sales.

With that, Dr Chaim ducked back into the other room to throw on his tie and jacket. Madd scraped Hank and Leyla up off the floor and walked them both outside. He had one hand on the back of each of their necks as they sulked and whimpered like naughty schoolchildren caught in a scrap. Janet and Klint, after a shooing gesture from Captain Grubbe, left the room they had just entered and followed Madd out into the corridor. Then Mr Mann helped poor, sobbing Evangeline up from her chair and threaded her arm through his. She looked up at Captain Grubbe for the first time; her eyes were damp and dark, his were big and unkind.

"'Ello, and who might you be?"

"Eva..."

"She's my date, Dad. I brought her along for the night, I didn't mean for her to get caught up in all this."

"Well, fucking 'ell! And I thought you and the doctor had a thing going on. Don't you know it's rude to interrupt a young lady, Trevor? Unless it's your mother, of course."

Captain Grubbe looked at his adopted son and his mystery date. He sensed elephants in the room, but despite their enormity they were doing well to stay hidden. If there was one thing The Captain had learnt from life it was to take nothing at face value, but life had taught him so much more than that.

"You enjoy your night sweet'eart. Try and ignore all those idiots down there and have some fun... Evangeline? That what you were gonna say?"

Evangeline nodded sheepishly.

Dr Chaim stepped back in, fully suited and booted. He gestured at The Captain respectfully as he passed him on the way out of the room.

"Keep Madd in check for me tonight, won't you boy. I need a firm handle on things till everyone's gone. No mess," said The Captain to the doctor.

He agreed with another respectful nod and then left.

"I'll be down soon," The Captain then said to Mr Mann, "right after I fill m'belly. I'm starvin'! You seen that spread out there? Make sure you grab yourself summin' before you leave, my love. It's cold out there, 'specially for a bag o' bones like you. And help yourself to as much of the strong stuff as you like down there too, just leave a little whiskey for me eh?!"

Mr Mann and Evangeline left, voiceless and without romantic conviction. As they passed the big man in the doorway, Mr Mann's sleeve was tugged lightly but with meaning. The Captain leaned in and spoke softly into his adopted son's ear. The little humanity he had dropped from his face and voice like sunshine into dusk.

"Nobody leaves Love Town till I say they can. Just keep everyone together and I'll be down soon as I can," he said, pulling away as the charm returned with a smile. "See you in a bit then."

They left, through the office door and out into the short corridor, leaving The Captain behind. They walked the corridor together tensely. Then, as Mr Mann clutched the handle of the next door out and pulled it to, they were met by another sneaking stranger. He was standing in the centre of the doorway looking guilty, as if he'd had his ear pressed against the door when it was suddenly yanked open.

"José!" Evangeline gasped.

"Where's my watch, Evangeline?" José challenged.

"The Spaniard!" Mr Mann finished. "The Spaniard?!"

José and Evangeline couldn't hear him over the ringing in their ears. On an evening of fortuitous reunions, this one was fresh, fierce and foul.

"I need it back, Evangeline. So just hand it over and I'll leave you alone to swindle your new man." José was standing strong and sounding firm, concealing his indignation rather admirably.

"José, I... the watch, it's not..."

"José, yeah?" Mr Mann cut in. "I managed to get your watch off Evangeline," he shot a wrathful look at the girl on his arm, "I locked it away downstairs, to be safe... We're just headin' down there now, why don't you come get it with us? You know, make sure it's the right one 'n' all that, yeah? I'll get you a drink for your troubles, what you 'avin'?"

José looked unsure; Mr Mann's invitation was obviously loaded. He'd been blowing hot and cold all day, and now at the very end of it he was just about ready to burst with indecision. But what else could he do?

"Who are you then? And why did you take the watch from her? She been trying on with you as well, has she?"

"Sorry José, I've not got time for a chat, you either want the watch or not..."

"All right, all right. I'll come. I don't want anything else, no drink or nothing. Just get me my watch back, no funny stuff."

Mr Mann simpered. He then detached his arm from Evangeline's and wrapped it around José in his trademark display of dominance. As he did this, he jolted his hand forward and snapped his wrist backward, jerking his jacket and shirt sleeve back and revealing his wrist and the watch that was tied around it. The shine from it caught José's eye, and from his indecision and anger arose confusion and trepidation. Suddenly he realised the danger he was in.

"As if by magic," Mr Mann said.

He moved Evangeline on with his eyes. She walked ahead of them and down the small staircase on the left that he was motioning towards. She began her descent, knowing not where nor what she was walking down into, but surely whatever was at the bottom could only be as hair-raising as the man standing behind her at the top.

Mr Mann turned his wrist so that he could see the face of the watch. He looked past José and read the time, exaggerating his actions. José was frozen stiff in the poison of Trevor Mann's embrace; Shelob's prey, still caught in the surprise of it all he could do nothing except hope. Mr

Mann's eyes shifted from the watch to the man now in his arms.

"Time to party."

Then he made for the staircase, dragging the stiff Spaniard along with him. They reached the top and Mr Mann showed José the way, releasing him from his grip and insisting, "After you, señor."

Love Town

Captain Grubbe was once again at the buffet table, licking his lips and packing his plate. He was one of only a few people tickling their fancies at the big feast; the spread was nearly all his. He was in a world of his own, picking and mixing the fancy finger foods to arrange a mass of mess on his red-and-white china plate. But as he reached for the gammon slices, he noticed something peculiar in the peripheral margins of his vision. The ham was boiled and baked. It had been doused in a sloe gin glaze and cooked to perfection. It broke The Captain's heart to have to turn away from it, but there was something about the man at the far end of the table that stole his attention. The man was underdressed and double-dipping his tiger prawn into the piggy-pink well of Marie-Rose sauce. To Captain Grubbe he seemed out of place, even without looking directly at him.

The Captain shuffled carefully down the line, still crowding his plate with anything that would fit and nearing his anonymous guest with each handful. Then, just about the same time as he reached the pâté and crackers, the unidentified man pivoted to reveal himself to the room at last. He was tatty looking, but accidentally so. He looked tired but alert. It was none other than the ever-present Detective Stranger McKrayne.

"Ahh shit," said Captain Grubbe, as his plate dipped and off rolled a loose Arancini.

The Arancini ball hit the floor still intact, and without stopping it zig-zagged towards McKrayne. It meandered cruise-missile-like along the freshly waxed floor until it eventually kissed the detective's left shoe. McKrayne swung his head around to see The Captain gawking at him and his lost Sicilian snack. He smiled victoriously and headed over to say hello.

"Some tasty grub you've got here, Grubbe. Can I have a word...?"

"Stranger McKrayne, as I live and breathe," remarked The Captain.

"For now," Stranger quipped back.

Captain Grubbe laughed. "Is that a threat, detective? There's some people back at the station that wouldn't appreciate you talking like that."

Stranger laughed too, "Haven't you heard Grubbe, I'm not at the station any more... seems I can say whatever I want these days."

"Oh I 'eard – there's not much I don't 'ear about."

"Must be those big ears of yours, eh?!" McKrayne winked at The Captain. "So, can I have a word?"

Captain Grubbe was royally pissed off to see the detective there at his party, especially as he was once again about to eat. His face turned red. He threw down his plate, loudly, which caused a small scene amongst the rich, drunk socialites that were drinking champagne and listening to the band. The Captain calmed and the red mist cleared just in time to save face. He put his arm around Stranger.

"Let's go 'n' 'av a chat then, find out why you're 'ere."

Stranger shook The Captain's arm from his shoulder. He had been through enough today to not be intimidated by the cold clasp of evil.

"All right then; after you, detective." Then he whispered in Stranger's ear, "Go left. Down the stairs at the end."

McKrayne kept a poker face and then left the room, following Captain Grubbe's directions.

There was a secret room inside the manor, a place where The Captain could retire for a drink after a long day of being country Grubbe. It was hidden underneath the house in the basement, out of sight and mostly out of mind. The Captain had put a bar down there, a little dance area and some booths. It was a set-up reminiscent of the old bars and brothels he used to hang around back in London. Whenever The Captain would go down there he would either be alone or with handpicked company. Some of his girls were regulars down there as they provided the dirty old man with the explicit entertainment he needed to keep from tearing his cock off. The Trevors were down there sometimes; they visited only when The Captain needed them or when the occasion suited; like tonight. The Baroness had never been down there. She knew it was there underneath her floorboards, of course, but she had no desire to visit. To her, peeling back the sex-shop beads that sealed in the squalor of that place would be like opening Pandora's box. Captain Grubbe was as comfortable down there as he could ever be. This was the place that kept him rational, grounded as a pimp and nothing much more – the exact reason why his wife stayed as far away as possible, because it was a room representative of who she really was. The Captain called it Love Town, and that's where everyone was heading.

Unintentionally, The Captain had organised his own little soirée downstairs to coincide with the one actually on the official invite. If truth be told, he was planning on going down there anyway, but only when the Grubbe-Nut Christmas Do was over and the esteemed guests had left. Then and only then could he sink down into a filthy finish. However, due to the night's bizarre circumstances and the arrival of several unwelcome guests, he called the game early and headed downstairs.

At the bottom of the spiral staircase was the bejewelled entrance to The Captain's downstairs lair. It was raining down Christmas tunes behind the sweaty beads of the doorway, and through the gaps in them oozed the steam of a thousand sins. Detective Stranger McKrayne stood outside for a moment, collecting his thoughts and feelings, until Captain Grubbe nudged him forward into the warm haze of Love Town.

Inside the music was loud, but not too loud. The air was hot, but not too hot. The atmosphere was rough, almost too rough. The Captain anticipated that McKrayne would feel uncomfortable down there, but to his surprise the detective seemed more at ease than The Captain did himself. Stranger had nothing to hide and, thanks to what had happened at Faisal's bar earlier, he had nothing to be afraid of.

Behind the beaded veil of the subterranean chamber was a space far bigger than Stranger was expecting. It was a room big enough for a party for sure, though it was near enough empty inside. Either side of the entrance were two shiny black poles – vacant. There were two booths, one on either side of the room; they were large with round, brass-rimmed tables inside them. There were maroon leather seats circled around the tables, breaking every third cushion so that however crowded the table became, the guests could always escape.* The booths could be hidden behind the purple curtains that were on curved poles at the top of them, a feature that comes as standard but serves great purpose in scum-laden establishments. The entire floor was wooden and varnished, gleaming nicely in the soft lights overhead.

The detective and The Captain walked through the centre of the room, past the dancing poles and booths (one of which was full of people, but we'll get to that) and straight towards the bar at the back that was lit up in shades of green, standing like a potions cabinet in a witch's hideaway. The crystal shelves were filled with spirits, liqueurs and other naughty things that spiced one's palate. The bar top was copper but had flares of green where the spotlights above shone emerald spheres onto it. The two men stopped in the middle of the bar and were greeted by the welcoming smile of the open-shirted alchemist behind it.

"'Allo Bill," said The Captain to the barman.

Barman Bill – real name Bill Barman. Bill was The Captain's personal Barman and Bill fitted the bill better than any other barman, bar none.

"Make us summin' good, and strong, will ya?!"

The Captain was after something easier to swallow than the fizzy mess that was being flung around upstairs,

* Be excused (not escape).

and so Bill knocked up a couple of whiskey sours for him and the detective. The music was playing just about loud enough to hear in the background and that filled the silence between them as they waited for their drinks. Neither of them wanted to address the other without first being prompted; it was a cocktail of pride and apprehension that kept them from doing so. Soon though, the ice had to be broken, and it was Captain Grubbe that stood wielding the ice pick to do so.

"So, detective... To what do I owe the pleasure?"

"There's a lot to be answered for, Grubbe. I've been through hell and back just to get here tonight, and I've had very little pleasure in doing so. You might say otherwise, but I reckon I have you rumbled."

Both men were facing forward, refusing to look at one another as they sputtered meaningless words back and forth.

"Easy Stranger, I'd save the celebrations if I were you. You're swimming past the safety net boy, and there's all sorts of nasty stuff behind it." The Captain turned to face Stranger. "Whatever you think you know, detective, you'd do well to un-know it. Quickly, before anything else gets taken from you..."

Stranger's blood ran cold. He was making references to Sara, making indirect threats. He turned to face The Captain, nose to nose in the green luminosity of the spotlight above them.

"I have enough dirt on you to lock you up for the next thirty years. I could call in a squad now and have you dragged out through your own house like a rabid dog. In front of all those ponces upstairs. In front of all your sorry friends." Stranger lowered his voice to a whisper. "I know everything you're guilty of, Grubbe. Every–thing. Whatever's past that safety net is being hunted, and I'm..."

"Dad?" a snivelling, desperate voice called out.

Stranger almost choked on his words. A cold, fierce scratch scored his spine from bottom to top and he shivered with unfortunate certainty, staring out through the green. Captain Grubbe, who'd been reeling at the newfound confidence of his opponent, was now beaming at the apparent discovery of his daughter, right there in the basement of his house.

"Dad?!" the voice called again.

Stranger turned around to address the girl calling out to him. "Evie," his eyes welled uncontrollably, "it's okay...it's okay."

"'Dad'? You mean to tell me, by some strange and beautiful coincidence, your little girl has ended up down 'ere with us?"

Stranger didn't answer. He couldn't answer; he just stood looking at Evangeline wondering how and why.

"Oh well this is too good. This is too, too good."

Captain Grubbe moved around Stranger and over to Evangeline, who was sitting in the booth to the right of the bar with the rest of the gang from upstairs, all sitting sheepishly around the table inside.

"'Ello sweet'eart, enjoyin' your night? Stranger your dad then is he?"

Evangeline, like her father, couldn't answer.

"That means you're Sara's daughter then, dunnit?!"

The ringing in her ears came back. She heard only this.

The Captain beamed with excitement and nastiness. He got Evangeline up and out of the booth, away from Mr Mann, who had been sat guarding the felonious group until now. The Captain walked her over to McKrayne, his arm wrapped delicately around her. Reunited they all were – three quarters of a twenty-year controversy.

Stranger slapped The Captain's arm from his daughter's shoulder and yanked her over to his side of the battlefield.

"Don't you touch her! Evie, what the bloody hell are you doing here?" His arms grasped her shoulders now instead.

"Yeah, what are you doin' 'ere, 'Evie'?" The Captain asked, still smiling in success.

Evangeline couldn't get the explanation out in time, she was just too overwhelmed.

"She's been stealin'!" shouted Mr Mann from inside the booth. He was watching out of the corner of his eye.

"Stealing? Again? What've you stolen this time?" asked the detective, shaking her for answers.

"Watches," shouted José, also from inside the booth.

"Watches? What watches, how many watches?" Stranger was confused and concerned.

"Just one; a special one," answered Mr Mann.

"What have you been up to now, girl? I only left you at the B&B a few hours ago! I only brought you along 'cos I didn't trust you at home on your own, and you've done it again, you've embarrassed me again, haven't ya?!" Stranger was at the end of his tether.

"Taking things that don't belong to ya," said The Captain. "Disobeying the ones who care for ya. Meddlin' where you shouldn't be meddlin'; that apple ain't fallen far from the tree, has it McKrayne?" The Captain was really starting to enjoy himself again.

"Dad... I'm sorry, I didn't mean to – I didn't know what

I was doing. I don't know who these people are, and I'm scared. They got the watch back. I haven't got anything else, I promise."

Evangeline was truthful, for the first time in a while. She lifted her head up from the floor as her father eased his grip from her heavy shoulders.

"I try and I try with you, Evangeline I really do. And every time I think I'm getting through, you throw it back at me. What else am I supposed to do, huh? You've really got in with some people this time, girl, you know that? I dunno what you've done but it ain't good. I've got enough going on to have to sort your shit out every other day. When are you gonna grow up? When are you gonna start to appreciate everything I've done for you?"

"Quite the family drama we got goin' on 'ere, eh? Maybe I should call Sara down, get your mother involved as well!" Captain Grubbe was stirring the pot.

"THAT'S ENOUGH GRUBBE! You keep out of it!" snapped Stranger, still mad and getting madder.

"Dad, what's he talking about? Who's Sara?"

"Nobody. He's winding us up."

The Captain laughed, "Oh, she doesn't know. She doesn't know!"

"Know what? Dad?"

Evangeline looked at her father, her face and her soul in bits. His was, too; he stared back without an answer, without a viable solution to the mess they were in.

"I want to go. Dad, please, let's just go."

Stranger's anger softened; he came to realise that his daughter may be a criminal, but she was still his daughter, and this was no place for her to be. "You're right. You shouldn't be here... go."

Mr Mann shot up from his seat inside the booth, unsupportive of this decision. Captain Grubbe also showed discouragement for the detective's demands.

"Woah woah woah! Go? Go where? You can't go now, you'll miss all the fun. No no, you gotta stay. We've a lot to catch up on."

Stranger stepped in front of Evangeline, shielding her. "Grubbe, if I say she's going, she's going. She has no reason for being here, what's done is done and you know it. You wanna chat? You wanna catch up? Well so do I, so let's do it."

"What's done is done? What's done, detective? Done... no, she stays. You stay; we all stay. So sit your arse down in that booth, both of you, before I lose my temper."

Stranger looked deep into The Captain's eyes, matching him in every way; composed now and as irritated as the man stood before him. He clutched the mobile phone inside his jacket pocket and deepened his stare.

"Go ahead and lose your temper, it really won't help when the two dozen armed officers at the other end of my phone rush in here and wipe the floor with your forehead. One push, speed dial 1, and your reputation goes down quicker than your wife used to!"

"Pack it in McKrayne! How fuckin' stupid do you think I am?!"

Stranger whipped the phone from his pocket like a cowboy un-holstering his pistol. Trevor Mann jumped forward to The Captain's side. From inside the booth, Dr Chaim and Madd Rockson stood up suddenly to get a look at what was happening at the bar. The rest of the group in the booth were nail-bitingly quiet. The Captain held out his arm to stop Trevor Mann from advancing any further; he was looking slightly skittish, but The Captain was not so intimidated by Stranger's threats.

"Bullshit. You're bluffin', there's no one on the end of that phone other than your mother."

"Yeah? Why don't you chance it then... let Evangeline go and I'll give you the phone. I came here to talk, not fight, so I'd sooner end the night without the paperwork. But you understand I had to have a Plan B."

Captain Grubbe was unsure of what to believe. He knew what he thought he knew and that was clear, but there was still a chance that Stranger could be telling the truth. After all, it was surprising to see him here, underdressed and outnumbered, after all those years away from each other. Would he turn up unannounced and without a plan? Yes, he would, but The Captain didn't know that for sure. McKrayne was still holding the phone out in front of him, doing his very best to act dangerous.

"All I have to do is press the call button, Grubbe... all you have to do is let my daughter leave."

"Two dozen you say?" asked The Captain.

"All armed and ready," replied McKrayne to a noiseless void.

The Captain thought for a second. No one dared to move or make a noise.

"All right detective, I'll buy it; she can go."

"Dad!" Trevor Mann exclaimed.

"Wind your neck in boy! Wanna take responsibility for it all, do ya? Wanna be top dog? No, so go sit back down." Captain Grubbe's mood changed. Stranger had one-upped him.

"Quite the family drama we got going on... Best not call your mother down though, eh Trevor?" quipped

Stranger.

"Touché detective." The Captain appreciated good timing.

Evangeline stepped out from behind her father, bashful and disgraced. Still holding the phone out in front of him, Stranger moved her away with his free hand. He was delicately balancing the father and detective sides of him – one false move now and everything would come crashing down. All eyes were on him; even Barman Bill had fixed his look upon the stone-faced detective.

"Well...? Go," uttered Stranger.

"Where?" said Evangeline, muddled inside.

"Anywhere. Any place away from here, just go."

"Dad, I..."

"Evie, I'm not going to tell you again, just leave!"

And she did. Without an aim or a direction she ran out of the basement. Trevor Mann watched her leave, unimpressed that he never got to interrogate her further. José watched too, his eyes brooding, for Evangeline had once again escaped without a worthy reprimand and he, somehow, was in deep doo-doo.

Barman Bill cleared his throat and finally presented the drinks: two whiskey sours. Stranger retracted his phone and placed it back in his pocket. The Captain picked up the cocktails and handed one to his adversary. He held out his glass to toast the evening, leaving it hanging for Stranger to cheers.

"There's no one on the end of that phone, is there?" he asked as Stranger brought his glass up to meet his in a bitter clink.

"Just my mum."

Upside Down

It was as Evangeline ran from the basement that another woman arrived at the party and confronted The Baroness at her entrance table. The female guest was uninvited, but as the story has proven thus far, it really didn't matter. Dressed in a black-and-white striped playsuit and with short messy hair, she looked quite striking and a little out of place, but as the story has proven thus far, it really didn't matter.

"Oh no no no no no! No!" scrambled The Baroness as the lady approached.

"Where are they? The boys, where are they?" the lady asked the brutish baroness.

"No – you turn around and you go back to wherever it is you appeared from. I mean it."

The lady pulled herself in close to Baroness Big Nut. "Listen, you big fathead. Either you show me in, or I'll put you through this table." She meant what she said, and The Baroness knew it.

The lady pushed past and entered the party.

"When my boys find you they'll give to you exactly what you deserve! You little tramp! You'll be thrown out of here quicker than you came in." The Baroness was seething, nearly foaming at the mouth with outrage. It was clear she hated this woman.

"Aww, your boys..." said the woman as she stopped and turned to face the big-headed bouncer. "I've already had 'em," she said as she blew The Baroness a kiss, leaving her simmering with revulsion at the podium.

The lady floated through the hallway, peering into every alcove she passed, looking for Captain Grubbe and his troupe. She poked her head into the grand hall and quickly scanned for the men she wanted. Alas, they were not in there. Where to look next? Where else would The Captain be on his big night if not mingling around the buffet table? She left the room in vain and waited out in the hallway for a sign. Then, a small bang and a tiny crash came from the corridor to the left of the grand staircase. Evangeline came running out of the doors that led to the back of the house. She was on her way out, escaping Grubbe Manor, when the universe spat out a miracle and pushed her into the path of the woman searching for the company Evangeline had just parted from. The lady was no stranger to the house; she had seen many women before Evangeline running to safety from the direction that she had come from. It was dirty déjà vu. The lady grabbed Evangeline before she could fly by her – this was the best lead she had.

"Where've you just come from?"

Evangeline wriggled and writhed; tired of being manhandled, she pleaded for her to let go.

"Please, just let go. I don't know anything, I don't know anyone. I just have to go; I just have to leave."

"I'm not gonna hurt you sweetie, I just wanna know where you came from? Downstairs, yeah? Was Grubbe down there?"

The lady eased her hold on Evangeline as she was suddenly overcome with a divine paralysis. A warm tingle brushed over her head and trickled down her body, molasses-like, to her toes. As Evangeline gaped back with salty tears in her eyes, stinging the wounds of the day, the lady looked upon her with a tranquil mystification.

"Who are you? Do I know you?" the lady asked, but all

she got was a frightened, quivering shake of the head. "What's your name?"

But Evangeline shook loose; she was done with all the questioning. "I have to go," Evangeline said again as she ran out for good this time, leaving behind the short-haired lady, watching her run away as she stood inexplicably numb.

"Sara? What you doin' here?" called one of Captain Grubbe's working girls from across the floor. She was elegantly dressed in expensive fabrics. "Sara?"

She ignored the calls, watching as Evangeline disappeared out of sight, unknowing of who she really was: her daughter. Sara, the mother who ran out on her family twenty years ago, had felt something as she held Evangeline, but the two grown women were as complete strangers would be, looking into the unfamiliar eyes of one another and hoping for reassurance. Evangeline ran out on her mother just as her mother had ran out on her, and like ships that pass in the night they simply floated by on the choppy tide, each headed for their own unavoidable icebergs.

In the booth down in Love Town, things had really gotten cosy. Captain Grubbe headed the table whilst his trio of Trevors sat at three, six and nine o'clock in front of him. The rest of the group, which Detective Stranger McKrayne was now a part of, were all snuggled up between the butch bollards. Everyone there had their own story, their own confession, and Captain Grubbe was playing the leader of the mass intervention, sipping his whiskey and sieving through the perpetual bullshit.

"Right, so you're saying Leyla, Hank's wife and that lady right there, stole the car you just turned up in?"

"Yes," said Klint.

"No," said Leyla.

"The one that got dropped at the office today, in Dorchester?" The Captain continued.

"Yes."

"The car's mine you lyin' little shit!" Leyla snapped at Klint.

"What's 'appened to the car?" asked Hank.

"Shhh! So, Klint, the car Leyla was locked in the boot in... she nicked, from you, then drove a few hundred yards up the road and parked it outside a hotel."

"Yes. Fronnigans Hotel," answered Klint again.

"Why were you at Fronnigans?" Hank asked his wife.

"Well, Hank, after I left you at the garage I thought to m'self, 'Hmmm, do I go 'ome and get hit over the head by them lot, or do I run away from all the shite you dropped me in? Maybe have a life away from ya, maybe start enjoyin' m'self.'"

"But why Fronnigans?" Hank asked again.

"I were gonna stay the night, get the first ferry out t'morra."

"Bold move," said The Captain.

"I were checkin' they 'ad space, then I stepped out and, ironically, it were King Twat over there that hit me over the head. Next thing I know, I wake up 'ere."

"Shouldn't've stolen the car then, should ya?!" said Janet, tired of listening.

"Leyla didn't steal your car, Janet. I'm sorry to tell ya, but Klint lost it. Somehow, I don't know. But I can tell you now that Hank and Leyla Howardson own their own Thunderbird. The car outside is theirs." Captain Grubbe believed he had solved one issue, or at least partly solved it.

Hank Howardson: that name rang bells in Janet's mind. It rattled around her brain, probing in the darkest corners and trying to match a memory to it. Then it struck.

"Hank Howardson," said Janet, accidentally aloud. The group all looked at her.

"Duck Off Howard?" Klint gasped, coming to the same realisation as Janet. "Fuck off! That's Howard? You're Howard?"

"Who's Howard?" asked Hank, confused and hurting.

Janet elbowed Klint from under the table. "No one. Just someone that looks like you."

"Well, he must be someone. Your man 'ere just nearly pissed 'imself!" Hank probed.

"Howard Morgan?" interjected The Captain "'Course! That's why it sounded familiar – it's Hank!"

"Who's Hank? Well, other than me..."

"We're makin' a movie 'bout ya; you're famous, Hank. Dunno how, but somehow you've made it to the big screen. Klint 'ere is playing ya."

"What?" Hank's confusion was at a bewildering high. He was a little punch-drunk, but even so, the sudden revelations were incomprehensible enough for anyone to stagger over. "The fuck you talkin' 'bout?!"

"Take a breath Hank, it'll all start to make sense soon... I think. So, Leyla didn't nick the car, that means somebody else did. Boys, first thing tomorrow mornin' I need you to start huntin' down a 1956 forest-green Ford Thunderbird. If you need to know what it looks like, there's one parked outside your office. Little tip for ya – it's not that one. Okay, so here's what we got so far. Janet and Klint, you beat up Leyla thinking she nicked the car from the film that's now about Hank, Leyla's husband. Hank, you ran away this mornin', with Leyla, after the boys turned up at your place. Leyla, you drove off and left Hank at some garage in...

"Castle Cary," Leyla finished.

"...Castle Cary, right. Hank got you into all the mess he's got himself into with me, so you decided to do a runner, headin' for anywhere away from him, and us, and here... how'd that go for ya?" The Captain laughed to himself before he continued his diagnosis. "Trevor...s, you found Hank all sad and alone at the petrol station in..."

"Castle Cary," Dr Chaim finished.

"...Castle Cary, and took him to Gillian's place for a coffee and a talkin' to where you bumped into the detective's daughter, that right?"

"As rain," confirmed Trevor Mann.

"So, the bit I'm fuzzy over, aside from why you're 'ere detective, is why your little bundle of joy was at a tea shop in Frome with a stolen watch?"

Stranger had taken the place of his daughter and was nestled up next to Mr Mann, sitting quietly and ingesting the abnormality of the group discussion. His drink had barely been touched; he was trying his best to keep up and the cocktail would only encumber the investigation.

"So she really is your daughter then. The thief's dad... is a policeman," said José, still wondering how he had ended up where he was.

"And just who're you mate? What's your reason for being 'ere?" Captain Grubbe had not made José's acquaintance yet.

"Evangeline stole my watch. Right off my wrist. She came to the bath house and she, we..." he looked at

Stranger hesitantly, "well, it doesn't matter because she lied to me and then ran off with my dad's watch."

"Your dad's watch?" asked Trevor Mann, knowing the watch was in fact his own father's.

"Oh, you're José, The Baron's been bangin' on about you and your little spa for months… says I should go, might make me less of a cunt if I learn to relax and unwind – her words, not mine." The Captain turned his attention to Trevor Mann. "So what's got you so wound up?"

"The watch is mine," he grunted back.

"Claimed it already 'av ya? And how does José feel 'bout that?"

"Not thrilled to be honest. That watch, the one on your arm, belongs to me. It was taken from me this afternoon and I want it back. If she stole yours too then I'm sorry, but that's mine. It was my father's and I will have it back." José was showing gumption in a booth full of bullies. But he was wrong, and Mr Mann was right.

"And how did your old man come to own that watch? 'Cos my dad had one very similar to it, and I ent seen it for, pfffft, nearly twenty-five years, as tryin' as I 'ave been to find it… how old are ya?" Mr Mann pressured José, but the Spaniard dithered.

"I'd answer if I were you," Hank chirped, glad to be out of the spotlight.

"Twenty-five…" José said in the end.

"Startin' to see summin' 'ere, are you? Think your old man mighta pinched that watch from mine, which means he probably 'ad summin' to do with him gettin' put away."

José didn't believe the accusation. He only ever knew José Sr. to be a good man. He was completely unaware of the skeletons in his late father's closet, but they were in there, and they hummed.

"Impressive, but a bit uncertain don't you think?"

"No. I don't. Tell ya what else I think – I think you, the detective and his daughter were all in this together and the soppy little tart was just stupid enough to get caught!"

"Oi, you watch your mouth!" barked Stranger. "Now I don't know what happened earlier, but I can assure you that...."

"All right McKrayne, be quiet," sassed Captain Grubbe.

"I've sat here listening to everyone's bullshit and now suddenly you've a problem with me defending me and my own, is it?" said Stranger.

"Yes. So shut up. The problem I see here..." he went on to address the entire booth, "...is complacency and negligence."

"Big words," muttered Stranger.

"Well I'm a big man," continued The Captain. "Trevor, I'm sorry 'bout whatever's actually 'appened, but your old man; the real one, got complacent and negligent and that's why he got put away, and probably why he lost his watch. Same goes for you Giuseppe; had you been lookin' after the watch properly, little miss piggy pinch wouldn't've got it from ya, would she? I'm sure you two'll have more to talk about, but not on my time. So where to next, oh yeah – my two favourites, Mr and Mrs Fuckup. You two could write the book on it, eh? Klint, you lost the car by being complacent and negligent. Leyla's not got it, it's gone. But, luckily enough, Leyla's got one we can borra'. Janet, I'd say you keep me entertained, which you do, but there comes a time when you 'ave to think it's just not for ya, this film business, is it? I've laid out a plan for you two, so for now you're off the hook. So then there's the ones who're in trouble with me. The world's worst parents, Hank and Leyla Howardson. Complacent, negligent, ignorant, cocksure and disrespectful. Runnin' away from your kids, how 'bout we start with that..."

Hank and Leyla were sat with their tails between their legs. Hank had gotten Leyla into the trouble they were facing now, but they had both been guilty of abandoning their two boys. They weren't the best-behaved children, to put it quite moderately, but their mischievousness was a by-product of atrocious parenting. Leyla knew she was partly guilty but had to defend herself against the allegations.

"You've no idea what them kids are like. They're evil. They're worse than their dad, they're worse than you Hank! You don't see it, you don't care, they're always at me they are. Always up to summin'! D'ya know what they did this mornin', before this lot turned up? They was out settin' fire to the farmers' fields. Burnin' down the woods for fun, and fightin' with the Japanese lot over the road," Leyla panted upsettingly.

Hank felt less guilt than his wife, but he had recently come to realise the bad father he was and he, for the first time in years, felt bad about himself.

"Not the Tamuras? Little bastards!" Captain Grubbe liked the Tamuras.

"Truth is, if Hank 'adn't dragged me out and made me run I would've gone anyway. No good'll come of us all stayin' in that place together. I ran for m'self, but whether you think so or not I ran for them too. I could see what we'd done to 'em, poor bastards, and there were no goin' back. I 'ave to get out or else I'll end up hurtin' one of 'em, and as bad a mother as I been I ent never want to hurt 'em.

So fuck off with ya assumin' 'cos none of yas have had to put up with the shite I 'ave for as long as I 'ave. Wherever Jack and Burt are now, they'll be far better off than in a house with me and you, Hank, that's for sure!" Leyla was right, but she too underestimated the power of the universe and its unlikely ways.

Upstairs in the grand hall, Mr and Mrs Tamura had finally realised their own drunkenness. They decided it was high time they stopped bothering the bar boys with their Lemon Sour repeat prescriptions and headed home to their children. They had a quick look around for The Captain, but he was nowhere to be seen. They collected their coats from the cloakroom, double-kissed The Baroness goodbye and headed out of the big door of the big house. The car that was going to take them home was being pulled around to the front door from its parking space out on the driveway; it was part of a complimentary 'ride home' service put on by The Captain and The Baroness.

Mr and Mrs Tamura waited patiently for the car to reverse up to them. However, through the gaps in the frosted vehicles a cold wind blew in a foul odour that wisped around them in a sinister stink. When the wind dropped, the ill-boding rattle and whizz of a junior bike chain drew closer and closer. The Tamuras looked around for the source but found nothing, only the stark trees that blew in the night sky. The noise came closer again, consistent and familiar. Mr Tamura had a horrible, wrenching feeling in his gut as he sheltered his wife from the cold, scanning the driveway for movement.

From behind the bank that separated the driveway from the fields and gardens came flying over Jack and Burt

Howardson, out of the dark and up into the cool air. They were both atop the same bike; Jack was on the pedals and Burt was hitching a ride behind his brother with his feet planted firmly on the trick nuts. They hit the grassy knoll with impressive speed and were completely invisible, hidden by the mound until they breached it and came soaring across the driveway in dramatic fashion. Mr and Mrs Tamura were stuck in place, immovable from the cold and the Lemon Sours. The bike cut through the air, slow-motioned and brilliant. Burt looked cold although smug. Jack looked forwards, concentrating on the landing. Jack and Burt's stolen bike came down onto the gravel and they were level now with the bike's rightful owners, who, however, were far too drunk to recognise a bike they had bought for their children six months ago. Mr and Mrs Tamura waved politely at the fiendish children as, unknown to them, Burt snuck his slingshot out of his back pocket, ready to do something terrible. Jack pushed his brother's hand down and stopped the attack before Burt had a chance to launch it. Burt obeyed his brother's peaceful wishes.

As the Tamuras' car pulled around to them, Baroness Big Nut noticed the Howardson children out on the driveway and abruptly left her post to shoo away the intruders. The attempt was half-hearted but fully intended, but before she made it down to the driveway Jack rode away quickly, still with Burt clinging onto his back.

Jack cycled around the back of the house and into the garden. He followed the stony driveway around the property all the way until he reached the rear patio. The boys, now in the dark of the night, decided that they wanted off. It was cold outside, and the glow of the party lights indoors were too inviting to ignore any longer. They decided to bail out, ditch the bike and find a way into the house to get warm and find some food. The front was blocked off by The Baroness so they had to find another way in, but the dark December night made it hard to locate another entrance.

Jack gave one final push of the pedals. He called out to his brother behind him.

"Jump off Burt! On three, ready? One, two, three!"

They leapt up from the bike, ghostying it out in front, uncaring of how their hooky gift would soon land in the mud and stones. The bike rushed away from them, but as it zoomed along the stones adjacent to the patio, the security light snapped on and they were illuminated like prison runaways.

Crash. The bike clattered into the car that was parked up on the gravel – their mum and dad's 1956 forest-green Ford Thunderbird. The bonnet dented in and then the bike flipped up into the windscreen. *Smash*. The glass burst completely. Jack and Burt said nothing; they just looked on at the new mess they had made. Neither of them could quite believe just how out of hand the day had gotten, but it was too late to feel guilty now. Now they just wanted to get inside, get food and get warm. Unfortunately, now they had to do this whilst avoiding Hank and Leyla.

There was a small concrete staircase leading down under the house on the far side of the patio. It had its own security light connected to the same circuit as the patio ones, but the light was a harsher, more fluorescent white than the amber patio lights. The stairs were easy to spot when the lights came on, and that's where Jack and Burt decided it was best to sneak in. They ran past their parents' ruined car and over to the luminous steps like moths to a flame.

The stairs led down to a thick wooden door. It was dark and plain and sealed shut. Burt was ahead of Jack, only by a step or two, but he was the one who pushed the door in the hope of a way in. The big door opened up before him, into a dull-looking stock room that was barely lit. They were in.

***

"Oh, well there she is! It's a full house now – come and join us Sara, I was wonderin' when you'd show up. Tonight's just been one o' them nights innit. Half expectin' m' mum to turn up... that'd really throw me off, she died fifteen years ago! Come and sit down, sweet'eart."

Captain Grubbe was still mediating in the booth of baddies. Sara had just entered the basement bar, shocked to see so many people crowding around the one table. She spotted Stranger, sat facing away from her; she assumed he was not doing as well as he'd hoped from the way things looked.

"Had yourselves a little pre-party meet, did ya detective?" asked Captain Grubbe, sneeringly. "That must've been somethin' after all these years, eh? Bet that was one hell of a reunion! Have a good ol' catch up, you two?"

The Captain was acting his usual intimidating self, but he seemed less convincing than usual. A sweat had broken from his temples – he was, believe it or not, a little bit scared.

Sara joined the booth and squeezed in between Dr

Chaim and Stranger. All eyes were on her as she broke the unbearable tension with her entrance. Stranger could hardly bring himself to look at her. He had thus far failed in his whistleblowing operation; should he tell Sara that their daughter was there just a moment before she arrived? Surely Captain Grubbe would not hesitate in making it known if Stranger didn't himself.

"Your girl was just 'ere. Evangeline. Sat right where you are now. Surprised you didn't bump into each other outside – but I s'pose you 'aven't got a fucking scooby what she looks like, 'ave ya?!"

Sara's face drained to white and then flashed to red. She sprang up from her seat and attempted to leap from the booth. Mr Mann caught her in his big hands and tossed her back inside. Her eyes were as filled with tears as her heart was with anguish.

"YOU..." she started, before panting and sobbing. "YOU BASTARD!"

"Sara, don't!" Stranger prompted. "I'll take you to her. I promise. Just calm down!"

"I knew it Stranger, I knew it was her! I saw her – I spoke to her, but she ran away... I scared her, Stranger, I scared her and she ran away." Sara's mascara streamed down her cheeks in blackened tears.

"That apple really doesn't fall too far from the tree, does it?" quipped The Captain.

"SHUT UP. Just shut up fat boy! I hate you... I really, really fucking hate you. Why's she with you Stranger? Why'd you lie to me?" Sara's broken voice was the tone of the evening.

"'Fat boy'?" asked The Captain. "Right, well I think everyone could do with a drink, eh? Gettin' a bit much down 'ere, innit? Fat Boy…" he chuckled while the rest of the group sat quietly and watched.

Then, between the chuckling and the arguing, came a loud smashing sound from back behind the bar.

"Everythin' all right Bill?" The Captain called to his barman.

"Wasn't me Cap… think there's someone in the cellar…"

Trevor Mann rose up instinctively, ready to check out the noise.

"Ey! Siddown. I can go," said Captain Grubbe as he too arose. Trevor Mann sat back down.

The Captain squeezed past the rest of the gang and made for the cellar behind the bar. He was confident in his stride but wary in his thoughts. Barman Bill stood up straight as The Captain walked by, approaching the cellar door. He knocked on the door – a warning sign to those inside. The movement behind the door halted following the hollow thud. The intruders had been rumbled. Captain Grubbe threw open the door; the air whistled past him from the sheer force. His face softened as he saw the noisemakers in the dull cellar light. He was also relieved that, from what he could smell, the smash was only that of a vodka bottle – his whiskey was safe. He stood in the doorway, scheming and grinning his familiar, tyrannical grin. His mouth then levelled, and he addressed the trespassers in a stern voice.

"Up 'ere. Quick."

The Captain stepped back from the doorway as the guilty stepped out. Jack and Burt Howardson emerged from the cellar, sheepish and ragged. The Captain clutched the back of both their shirts, and they were suddenly elevated a few inches off the ground, hanging like fairground prizes.

"Leave the mess," The Captain said to Barman Bill as he headed back past him, "these two can do it later." Bill nodded.

The guests back in the booth were waiting with varied emotions to be set free or given answers. None had dared to move beyond the blockade of Trevors. The Captain arrived back at the table with his catch still hanging from his fists.

"Just what this party was missin', eh? The innocence of children. Hank, Leyla, these used to belong to you I believe."

They froze. Hank and Leyla were speechless, motionless and emotionless. For more than just the obvious reasons, they really didn't want to see their children there at the party in the arms of Satan.

"Save your questions, I'll tell you what 'appened," began The Captain. "Well, we all know what was goin' on over at the Howardson house this mornin' now, don't we? Well I wasn't all that shocked, I must admit, when I got a call from Trevor – that Trevor," he nodded his head towards Trevor Mann, "saying that not long after you two..." he swung his head around to address Hank and Leyla once again, "did a runner, these two..." he lifted Jack and Burt higher off the ground, showcasing them to the others, "turned up at 'ome, lookin' like they'd been up to no good."

The whole group looked on, scared for the children rather than themselves for the first time since arriving at the party. The Captain drew in a deep breath through his nose.

"I'll cut a long story short; I brought the boys 'ere

when I realised you two 'ad left 'em, or rather I arranged for 'em to be brought 'ere. My boys called and explained it all from your own phone, Hank. These two've been 'ere all day, playin' in the grounds. They were s'posed to be out in the barn, where I left 'em for the evening, but whaddya know; they've managed to sneak in. Couple of troublemakers they may be, but I can see a future for 'em 'ere, with me. Last time I took in a couple of unwanted littluns it worked out very well indeed, for everyone, but that was years ago, and I love 'avin' kids around. So if you're not gonna 'av 'em, then I will… 'av you anythin' to say for yourselves?!"

The world's worst parents sat gobsmacked and humiliated; the Howardsons were a disgruntled family in ruins.

"Unbelievable," The Captain declared, "simply unbelievable." His words were still aimed at Hank and Leyla.

Captain Grubbe was tired of talking, and tired of holding up the boys. He dropped them down. Jack, being taller, landed on his feet and regained control of his own movements. Burt was shorter, and so when dropped he wobbled and fell onto his backside.

As Burt toppled over, a couple of things fell out of his pockets. The slingshot was one, and the other was Hank's empty cigarette packet that he and Jack had stolen from the house that morning. The packet was empty, except for a few matches still in the bottom. Captain Grubbe hadn't noticed the loose items; he was facing the other way as he shamed the boys' parents. Leyla, however, did notice the things that fell from her son's pockets – she had seen them in action that morning as she watched Burt use them as homicidal tools. Leyla glared, still emotionless, at her boys as they glared back at her, petrified. Burt gathered the loose objects and quickly repocketed them before The Captain noticed, got back up to his feet and stood next to his brother quietly.

"You see all them fireworks back there, did ya?" Captain Grubbe asked as he turned to face the boys. "If you're lucky, and if you're good, you might get to see 'em go off later… and trust me boys, you wanna see 'em go off, 's gonna be like the Gulf War out there!" Jack and Burt looked on, unsure of what to say or do. "Now before you two interrupted me, I was in the middle of sortin' some drinks for everyone – see, we've 'ad quite the night down 'ere and we are all very, very thirsty." The boys were unsure of where The Captain was going with his story. "So 'ere's a job for ya… back in that cellar, on a shelf just above the fireworks, is a bottle of whiskey I want ya to get for me. It's brown glass, quite big and very special. I saved that bottle for a very special night, and I think this might be it." Captain Grubbe dropped down to Jack and Burt's level, squatting courageously in a tight-fitted suit. "If you do that for me, then I might even let you 'ave a drop…"

Jack screwed up his face as he remembered how much he had disliked the taste of his father's whiskey earlier on that morning – the last thing he wanted now was more. The Captain noticed his reaction.

"Right then, you're out. You stay 'ere with me," he snapped at Jack. "So, youngen, you up to it?" he then asked Burt.

Burt looked confused, but he understood exactly what was going on and what was being asked of him. He nodded his head.

"Good boy. Now you be careful, yeah? That's my best bottle you're gettin', I don't wanna single drop spilt, understood? Break that bottle and I will... well, best not to break the bottle. And watch out for them fireworks too, they cost me a small fortune and if any of 'em are soggy then I shall be lighting the rest of 'em with your brother's head, okay?"

The Captain had succeeded in intimidating the boys, or at least he thought he had. Burt looked over at his mother. She was still staring over without blinking. The last time she had seen Burt he was trapped between enemies, holding an empty bottle of whiskey as the forests behind her house burned in the fire he had started. Now she was trapped. They stared on through each other, knowing of the other's thoughts and both equally as rumbled as the other, but through the stillness and the staring, a plan was formed – formed through apocalyptic familiarity.

"Well then?" said The Captain. "Off you go... wait, what's that?"

Burt swallowed hard as Captain Grubbe pointed at his pocket. Burt pulled out his grandfather's slingshot.

"No, no. The other one. What's that?"

Burt swallowed harder; it was the cigarette box with the matches inside. Jack looked a little puzzled as to why his brother was resisting showing or telling, but Leyla was as nervous as Burt. She suddenly showed emotion in her stare, panic, and The Captain became suspicious. He looked at Leyla who was looking at Burt, then he looked at Burt who was looking at Leyla, then he repeated:

"What's in your pocket son?"

Slice. The beaded entrance to Love Town whipped open. The rattle echoed through the basement bar and filled the short space between the song change. There were two men standing in front of the swaying bead strings; they were still but agitated. Captain Grubbe forgot Burt and forgot his question as one of the men shouted out to him:

"Grubbe! You wanker!"

The Trevors all jumped out of their seats. They moved quickly to The Captain's side. Stranger caught a whiff of familiarity in the caller's tone, as did Sara. They too stood up to peek out of the booth.

"It's Face," said The Captain. "Fuck me, it's Face. That you Faisal?" he called out.

"You know it is, Cap. What, 's too far to come over 'ere and see for yourself? Bit too much of a walk for ya, eh?" This time the taunts came from the other man at the door.

Klint Buttafuoco's ears pinged to attention from inside the booth. He and Janet had become lost in a world of, apparently, unassociated drama. But he recognised the other man's voice for sure as he called out to The Captain.

"Garrias," he whispered to himself. A rush of wistfulness pulsated between his ears.

The crowd waited in the tense, dense atmosphere. The new song was building, and much to the men at the doorway's delight it was a funky, soulful little number. Everyone waited for orders while the jingle of the piano through the speakers tantalised the funk in the room. The Trevors were stern and ready to pounce, whilst Captain Grubbe was softer in his expressions, unwilling to make the first move.

Thud. Thuds between ivory tinkles; each one gave Stranger and Sara an uncontrollable twitch. The groove was building.

The funk dropped at the right time. James Brown sang as Faisal danced his way into the room, accompanied this time by his own barman, Garrias. Faisal bopped and turned and jumped and cut as if on strings; he couldn't help the beat pulsing through him. Garrias moved too, almost in unison, only better. He complimented Faisal's chaotic, sensational moves with grace and counter-moves. They were routined, edging into the underground dancehall, beating the stuffy air away with loose hips and quick kicks. They were brilliant. It was like a show of dominance, not with fists but with funk. The Captain, The Trevors, Stranger, Sara and now Klint were all watching in awe. For a moment everyone forgot why the room was so hostile, everyone was dumbfounded and distracted – everyone except Leyla and Burt.

Leyla made eyes at her son. Big, scary eyes. She got his attention and mimed to him what he needed to do.

Get the whiskey. Use the matches. Run!

She mimed it twice, wide-mouthed and desperate. Burt understood, and he understood the urgency. He sloped off back to the cellar to complete his mission while the madness and silliness of the adults in the room played out like a cabaret before him.

Faisal and Garrias were still dancing, giving it their all as if auditioning for a part in The Captain's imaginary dance ensemble. They were unprepared, but when James Brown struck, Faisal was helpless; his unconscious mind ran with the excitement in the music. Klint was shocked to see his old flame Garrias, especially in the way he was seeing him now.

"I never knew he could dance like that," Klint said aloud. Nobody listened – they only watched.

Barman Bill was in a trance, too. He had stopped tidying the bar and was fixated, like everyone else, on the impromptu dance act. This helped Burt sneak back past him and into the cellar.

Click – he found the light switch. The boozy room was illuminated with the reflections of a thousand multicoloured glass bottles. The floor was grey and unfinished. It was covered mostly by fireworks. Boxes and bags and more boxes piled up in big stacks. Some had cosmic designs on their packaging, some had friendly technicolour splodges, and some had what could only be described as satanic imaginings pasted on the boxes. It was an expensive, extensive and offensive collection sure to be a phantasmagorical exhibition of explosives.

It didn't take Burt long to spot the whiskey. It was in pride of place, on a shelf directly opposite the doorway, glinting with brown refractions. It was easily reachable. All Burt had to do was get a boost up from the fireworks boxes below it – a makeshift stairway to the devil's beverage. He had come this far, he had seen what he needed to see, and all that was left to do was to conquer. Burt climbed atop the first box; it was small and decorated with jagged-edged spirals and comets. 'Galaxy Burst' was the name on the front. From it, Burt climbed to the second box. This one was darker and had small silver streaks across the packaging with orange tails fading off the back – 'Meteor Shower'. The final box was large, like the-last-present-on-Christmas-day large. It was hellfire red with blackened patches making out patterns and shapes. There was a face in the painted flames, a chilling design that was headed 'Lord of the Dead'. Burt was not afraid, he was focussed. He climbed onto it and grabbed the whiskey bottle with both hands.

Faisal and Garrias were close to the gang now, still dancing, but the novelty and the surprise were wearing off. Anger was returning to the faces of the damned and the diabolical. Faisal dropped down low and popped back up quickly with a spin. It was the final move of his routine, and as he sprung up from the floor in front of Captain Grubbe and the three Trevors he did something very, very silly. *Whoosh* – Faisal threw a punch, a good punch, at The Captain. It was heartfelt and true, a clean swipe with a strong fist. On any other day and thrown at any other person it could have been a knockout blow, but it wasn't. Captain Grubbe caught the flying fist and twisted it around effortlessly. Faisal screeched, James Brown-like, and fell to his knees. Garrias rushed over but Madd Rockson bopped him on the nose. Klint gasped.

"Don't you touch him! Don't you touch him!" he cried out at the boys.

"EVERYONE SIT THE FUCK DOWN NOW, I MEAN IT. NO MORE FUCKING GAMES!" The Captain almost burst into pieces he shouted so loud.

The foundations of the house shuddered around them. The glasses and bottles on the bar shelves rattled in fear. The group did as they were told and scurried back into the booth and retook their seats. Madd Rockson pulled Garrias up from his knees and led him into the booth. Captain Grubbe had mutated into a much scarier, much nastier and much less diplomatic version of himself, and given that the original wasn't all that pleasant, that meant he had become outright terrifying. He dragged Faisal by the wrist over to the booth and slung him in between two of the sofa chairs. He straightened his back out tall, just to hear the crunch of bones.

"So then..." he started, but failed to finish.

He felt a tap on his back. It was Burt with the whiskey bottle.

Gloucestershire Burning

The Captain turned around and looked down at me with a predator's stare. I handed him the brown glass bottle. He took it from me without a smile, without a word. He coughed as he faced the group inside the booth again.

"Does anyone know what it says on this label? Huh? Anyone wanna take a guess as to what this very special brew's called? No? Named it myself... it's called Astaroth – devil's juice." He moved his hand to show the group the label that did in fact say 'Astaroth' in thick red pen. "I've waited twenty-two years to drink this, and I can't think of any better company, than all of you, to drink it in. Cheers."

He grabbed his empty glass and poured. Nothing came out of the bottle, not one drop. His face, if I could've seen it, would have been a picture.

Fizz. The noise made The Captain nervous. He turned around to face me, but the match I had lit was already burning bright. We both looked down at the damp, sticky floor.

I dropped the fire. The ember tumbled slowly down to the flammable trail I had laid all the way from the cellar to my feet. I was an arsonist twice in one day. The Captain swiped at me but was too late in his reactions. Jack lunged at me, though not to stop me but to save me.

Whhhmmphh! The floor was alight with oranges and blues. Faisal had lit up the floor before but not like this; this was terrific. Jack whipped me away quickly and we both sprinted for the beaded door. The adults were slow and surprised, they all lingered in turmoil too long to be safe. The burning trail erupted down into the cellar, all the way over to the large pile of fireworks.

Jack and I legged it across the floor, flung wide the beads and sprung up the small winding staircase. There was pandemonium behind us now as the grown-ups were shifting. We reached the top of the winding stairs and threw ourselves out the door. We landed inside a corridor in the big house, the screams and the panic still behind us. I jumped up and threw myself back at the door, swinging it shut without really thinking what I was doing; I had that buzz again and I was hardly in control of my own actions. Jack jumped up too. There was a smokiness rising now – any minute the banging and whizzing would surely start. I slid the bolt across the door; this was bad.

"BURT! What're you doin'?!" Jack shouted; I didn't respond. "Mum and dad..." he said with compassion. I didn't respond.

We looked deep into each other, right into the very thoughts, the feelings. There were people on the stairs, and from the sound of it there were people fighting down in the bar still. I eased my hard look to a guilty gaze.

"Come on!" I said.

Jack shook his head. But we ran. Down the corridor, through the house, past the lady with the massive head standing at the front door and out into the cold night again. Running, so much running. We ran down the long, gravelled driveway until we heard them: the bangs. We skidded to a halt in the dark; the small stones crunched and scraped underfoot.

The sky suddenly illuminated like a treacherous

rainbow. A murderous hallucination. A scathing aurora. The noise was consistent with quickfire scuds and metronomic thuds. The display had started, and within seconds it ramped up its intensity. The back of the house exploded with blues and greens; streams of molten gunpowder flew up into the sky, painting shapes into the passing clouds. *WHAM!* The side windows burst with a yellow glow, orange in the centre and whizzing like the sound of a thousand drunk mosquitos. Jack's face was aglow with the colours of the lightshow; I'm sure mine was too. The Captain was right – I would not have missed this for the world. Another plume of purples and pinks erupted from the house. The night was alive. The party was dead.

Then the earth roared. The sky turned a hellfire red, fractured with black patches in ominous shapes. The air cracked, hard, just before it boomed the loudest boom of all. The house disappeared behind red smoke; it had to be the finale piece; the big one, 'Lord of the Dead'. There was fire and frost, and the swift, unassailable retribution of a loosely hinged youth. A sharp zing shot through my ears and annihilated what was left of my conscience. I felt warm inside. I shut my eyes and reached for my brother's hand. Merry Christmas, I thought to myself.

Devil Child – that's what they used to call me.

21661780R00194

Printed in Great Britain
by Amazon